FIVE

Ursula P. Archer was born in Vienna in 1968, and worked as an editor at a publishing house. After the success of her first young adult novel, she now dedicates much of her time to writing fiction. She lives with her family in Vienna. *Five* is her first thriller for adults.

URSULA P. ARCHER

FIVE

TRANSLATED FROM THE GERMAN BY
Jamie Lee Searle

VINTAGE BOOKS
London

Published by Vintage 2014

2 4 6 8 10 9 7 5 3 1

First published with the title *Fünf* in 2012 by Wunderlich, Rowolt Verlag
GmbH, Reinbek

First published in Great Britain in 2014 by
Vintage
Random House
20 Vauxhall Bridge Road
London SW1V 2SA

www.rbooks.co.uk

Addresses for companies within The Random House Group Limited can
be found at: www.randomhouse.co.uk/offices.htm

The Random House Group Limited Reg. No. 954009

A CIP catalogue record for this book is
available from the British Library

ISBN 9780099583868

The Random House Group Limited supports the Forest Stewardship
Council® (FSC®), the leading international forest-certification
organisation. Our books carrying the FSC label are printed on FSC®-
certified paper. FSC is the only forest-certification scheme supported by
the leading environmental organisations, including Greenpeace. Our
paper procurement policy can be found at:
www.randomhouse.co.uk/environment

Typeset by SX Composing DTP, Rayleigh, Essex

Printed and bound in Great Britain by
CPI Group (UK) Ltd, Croydon, CR0 4YY

Prologue

The place where his left ear used to be was throbbing to the rhythm of his heartbeat. Fast and panicked. His breath came out in short, loud gasps. Nora was just a few steps away from him, leaning over the table where the pistol and knife lay. Her face was contorted, but she was no longer crying.

'Please,' he whispered, his voice hoarse. 'Please don't do it.'

Now she let out a dry, strangled sob. 'Be quiet.'

'Why won't you untie me? We still have a chance . . . please just untie me, okay? Okay?'

She didn't respond. Her right hand wavered shakily over the weapons, which gave off a dull gleam in the light of the naked bulb.

His whole body convulsed with fear. He writhed around on the chair, twisting as far as the ropes would let him. They cut into his flesh, burning him, as unyielding as steel bands.

But it's not my fault, it's not my fault, it's not my . . .

He screwed his eyes tightly shut, only to open them again. He had to see what was happening. Nora's hand was on the knife now.

'No!' he screamed, or at least he thought he did. 'Help me! Why won't anyone help me?' But now, when he most needed it, his voice had abandoned him. It was gone, and soon everything would be gone, for all eternity. His breath, his pulse, his thoughts. Everything.

Tears he was unable to wipe away blurred his sight of Nora, who was still standing there in front of the table. She gave a drawn-out wail, softer than a scream, louder than a groan. He blinked.

She had picked up the pistol, her right hand quivering like an old lady's. 'I'm sorry,' she said.

He wrenched his body backwards and forwards in desperation, almost tipping the chair over. Then he felt the cool metal against his cheek and froze.

'Close your eyes,' she said.

Her hand touched his head gently. He felt her fear, as great as his own. But she would carry on breathing, carry on talking, carry on living.

'No,' he whispered tonelessly, finding his voice again at last. He looked up at Nora, who was now standing right in front of him. He wished fervently that he had never heard her name.

N47° 46.605 E013° 21.718

The early morning mist enveloped her like a damp shroud. The dead woman was on her stomach, the grass beneath her soaked with dew and blood. The cows were taking care not to graze there, which was easy enough; the meadow was large, and the thing lying there in the shadow of the rock face unsettled them. A brown cow had ventured over shortly after sunrise, lowering her heavy head and licking the flaxen strands of hair with her rough tongue. But finding her discovery to be unpalatable, she had soon returned to the rest of the herd.

They kept their distance. Most of them just lay there, chewing the cud and staring out at the river. But even the ones that were still grazing avoided straying too close. The scent of death made them uneasy. They much preferred to stay where the first beams of sunlight were pushing through the mist, etching bright patterns onto the meadow.

The brown cow trotted across to drink from the trough. With every step, the clapper in her bell struck against the metal, producing a tinny sound. The rest of the herd didn't even swivel their ears. They just stared stoically at the water, their lower jaws grinding constantly, their tails swishing to swat away the first flies of the day.

A gentle gust of wind swept over the meadow, brushing the woman's hair aside and exposing her face. Her small,

3

upturned nose. The birthmark next to the right-hand corner of her mouth. Her lips, now far too pale. Only her forehead remained covered, where her hair and skin were matted with blood.

The morning mist slowly frayed out to form isolated veils. These eventually wafted away, clearing the view of the meadow, the cattle, and the unwanted gift which had been left there for them. The brown cow's muffled lowing greeted the new day.

As always, Beatrice took the stairs two at a time. She skidded along the corridor, racing past the second door on the left. Just seven steps to go. Six. Reaching her office, she saw that no one was there but Florin. Thank God for that.

'Has he been in yet?' she asked, slinging her rucksack onto the revolving chair and her folder onto the desk.

'Good morning to you too!'

How did Florin always manage to stay so upbeat? She hurled her jacket towards the coat rack, missed and swore loudly.

'Sit yourself down and catch your breath. I'll get that.' Florin stood, picked her jacket up from the floor and hung it carefully on one of the hooks.

'Thank you.' She turned her computer on and hurriedly emptied the contents of the folder onto her desk. 'I would have been on time, but Jakob's teacher caught me.'

Florin went over to the espresso machine and started pressing buttons. She saw him nod. 'What was it this time?'

'He had a temper tantrum, and the class mascot caught the brunt of it.'

4

'Oh. Was it a living thing, dare I ask?'

'No. A cuddly toy owl called Elvira. But you wouldn't believe what a huge drama it caused – at least ten children in the class were in floods of tears. I offered to send a crisis intervention team across, but the teacher wasn't amused. Anyway, now I need to arrange a substitute Elvira before Friday.'

'That sounds like quite a challenge.'

He frothed the milk, pressed the button for double espresso and then crowned his work with a little dusting of cocoa. Florin's calm demeanour was gradually starting to work its magic on Beatrice. As he put the steaming cup down in front of her, she realised she was smiling.

He sat down at the opposite side of their desk and surveyed her thoughtfully. 'You look as though you didn't get much sleep.'

You can say that again. 'Everything's fine,' she mumbled, staring intently at her coffee in the hope that Florin would be content with her brief response.

'No nocturnal calls?'

There certainly had been. One at half-past eleven, and another at three in the morning. The second had woken Mina, who hadn't gone back to sleep again for an hour afterwards.

Beatrice shrugged. 'He'll give up eventually.'

'You have to change your number, Bea, it's been going on long enough. Don't keep giving him the opportunity to wear you down. You *are* the police, for heaven's sake! There are steps you can take.'

The coffee was sublime. In the two years they had been

working together, Florin had gradually perfected the ideal blend of coffee beans, milk and sugar. Beatrice leant back and closed her eyes for a few seconds, longing for just one moment of relaxation. However brief it might be.

'If I change the number, he'll be on my doorstep before I can count to ten. And he is their father, after all; he has a right to contact his children.'

She heard Florin sigh. 'By the way,' he said, 'Hoffmann's already been in.'

Shit. 'Really? So why isn't my monitor covered in Post-its?'

'I appeased him by saying you'd phoned and were on an outside call. He pulled a sour face, but didn't say a word. The good news is that we'll have some peace from him today because he's in meetings.'

That was more than good news, it was fantastic. Beatrice put her cup down, tried to relax her tensed shoulder muscles, and started to sort through the files on her desk. She would finally get a chance to work on her report about the stabbing; Hoffmann had been nagging her to do it for ages. She glanced over at Florin, who was staring intently at his monitor with an expression of utter confusion. A strand of his dark hair fell forwards, almost into his eyes. *Clickclickclick*. Beatrice's gaze was drawn to his hand as it clasped the mouse. Strong, masculine hands: her old weakness.

'Problem?' she asked.

'Unsolvable.'

'Anything I can help with?'

A thoughtful crease formed between his eyebrows. 'I don't know. The selection of antipasti is a serious matter.'

She laughed. 'Ah, I see. So when does Anneke arrive?'

'In three days' time. I think I'll make *vitello tonnato*. Or maybe bruschetta? Damn it, I wish I knew whether she's eating carbs at the moment.'

Discussing menu planning wasn't a good idea; Beatrice's stomach immediately made itself heard. Quickly thinking back over what she had eaten so far today – an inventory which amounted to two biscuits – she decided she was perfectly entitled to feel hungry.

'I'd vote for *vitello tonnato*,' she said, 'and a quick trip downstairs to the café.'

'Already?' He caught her gaze and smiled. 'Okay then. I'll just print this out and then—'

The telephone rang, interrupting him. Once he answered the call, it was only a few seconds before his dark expression told Beatrice to forget about the tuna baguette she had been dreaming of.

'We'll be there right away.' He hung up the phone and looked at her. 'We've got a body, female, near Abtenau. It seems she fell from the rock face.'

'Oh, shit. Sounds like a climbing accident.'

Florin's eyebrows knitted together, forming a dark beam over his eyes. 'Hardly. Not unless she was climbing with her hands tied.'

The corpse was a bright stain against the green, flanked by two uniformed policemen. A tall man, bare-chested under his dungarees, looked at them curiously. He was standing in the adjacent field, holding a small herd of cows in check. He raised his hand, as if wanting to wave at Beatrice and Florin, but then lowered it again.

A rocky crag with an almost vertical twenty-metre drop towered over the meadow, jutting out in stark contrast to the idyllic landscape.

The forensic investigators, Drasche and Ebner, had clearly arrived just a few minutes before them. They were already clad in their protective suits, busying themselves with their instruments, and only nodded briefly in greeting.

A man was kneeling down right next to the pasture fence, filling out a form. He was using his doctor's case as a makeshift desk. 'Good morning,' he said, without even looking up. 'You're from the Landeskriminalamt, I take it?'

'Yes. I'm Florin Wenninger, and this is my colleague Beatrice Kaspary. Is there anything you can already tell us about the deceased?'

The doctor pushed the top back onto his pen with a sigh. 'Not much. Female, around thirty-five to forty years old. My guess would be that someone pushed her off the rock face last night. Cause of death probably head trauma or aortic rupture — the neck wasn't broken in any case. You'll need to ask the forensic pathologist for more detailed information.'

'Time of death?'

The doctor blew out his cheeks. 'Between two and four in the morning, I'd say. But don't hold me to that. All I'm supposed to do here is certify the death.'

Drasche trudged over, carrying his forensics kit. 'Did anyone here touch the body?'

One of the policemen spoke up hesitantly. 'The doctor. And me. But just to feel for a pulse. I looked for ID or a wallet too, but couldn't find anything. We didn't alter her position.'

'Okay.' Drasche beckoned to Ebner, who was poised with his camera at the ready. While the forensics team took photographs and collected samples, sealing them in small containers, Beatrice's gaze rested on the dead woman. She tried to fade out everything else around her: her colleagues, the traffic noise from the main road, the chiming of the cowbells. Only the woman mattered.

She was lying on her stomach, her head turned to the side. Her legs were bent out to the right, as though she had been paralysed mid-sprint. Her hands were behind her back, her wrists lashed together tightly with cable tie.

Eyes closed, mouth half open, as if death had caught up with her while she was still speaking.

Beatrice's mind instinctively filled with images. The woman being dragged along through the darkness. The precipice. She struggles, digs her heels into the ground, pleads for her life, but her murderer grips her tightly, pushes her towards the edge, waits until she can feel the depths of the abyss beneath her. Then, just a light push in the back.

'Everything okay?' Florin's hand touched her arm for a second.

'Sure.'

'I'm just going to talk to the others. I'm guessing you want to immerse yourself for a bit, right?'

That's what he called it. Immersing oneself. Beatrice nodded.

'Don't go too deep.'

He walked over to the two officers and engaged them in conversation. She took a deep breath. It didn't smell of death here, just cow dung and meadow flowers. She watched Drasche as he pulled a plastic bag around the woman's hands. Ideally, she would have liked to climb over the fence to have a closer look at the body, but forensics wouldn't take too kindly to that; Drasche in particular could get very touchy. Without taking her eyes off the dead woman, she walked in a small arc along the pasture fence, trying to find another vantage point. She focused her attention on the woman's clothing: a bright-red silk jacket over a floral-patterned blouse. Expensive jeans. No shoes; the soles of her feet were dirty and speckled with blood, as if she had walked a long way barefoot. Amidst the dirt, there were dark flecks on each foot. Small, black marks. Or perhaps something else . . .

Beatrice knelt down, squinting, but she couldn't see clearly from this distance. 'Hey, Gerd!'

Drasche didn't stop what he was doing for even the blink of an eye. 'What?'

'Could you take a look at the victim's feet for me?'

'Just a second.' He fastened the transparent bag with adhesive tape before moving down to look at the lower end of the corpse.

'What the hell?'

'There's something there, isn't there? Characters of some kind, am I right?'

Drasche gestured to Ebner, who snapped a series of close-ups of the feet.

'Tell me!' She lifted the barbed-wire fence and ducked underneath. 'What is it?'

'Looks like numbers. There's a series of numbers on each foot. Could you please stay where you are?'

Beatrice struggled against the temptation to go further forward. 'Can I see the photos?'

Drasche and Ebner exchanged a glance which betrayed both irritation and resignation.

'Show her,' said Drasche, clearly disgruntled. 'It's the only way she'll leave us in peace.'

Ebner put his camera onto viewing mode and held it out for Beatrice to see.

Numbers. But not exclusively – the first character on the left foot looked like an N. Written in an unsteady hand, the oblique line tailed off in the middle before starting again. It reminded her of Mina's handwriting back in kindergarten, the strokes leaning precariously against one another like the walls of a ramshackle old hut. The N was followed by a four, a seven and something that looked like either a zero or a lower-case o. Then another four, a six, another six, a zero and a five. Black, irregular strokes.

She zoomed in. 'Are they painted on? With a waterproof pen maybe?'

She looked at the other foot. Again a letter first, then a series of numbers. An E with crooked horizontal lines, followed by a zero, a one, a three. Then another of the little circles. A brief gap, then five more numbers. Two, one, seven, one, eight.

'No, they're not painted on.' Drasche's voice sounded hoarse. 'I'd say they were tattooed.'

'What?' She looked closer. Now that he'd said it, it suddenly seemed like the only plausible explanation. They were tattoos. But on such a sensitive part of the body, surely it was quite rare to have such a thing. So now the question was: did she already have them, or had they been inflicted on her by the killer?

She wrote the number combinations down in her notebook.

N47 o 46 605

E013 o 21 718

The pattern seemed familiar, but where from? It wasn't anything connected to computing, nor were they telephone numbers. 'I feel like I should know this,' she murmured, more to herself than her colleagues.

'You should indeed,' said Drasche through his face mask. 'And if you promise to leave me in peace, I'll enlighten you.'

'It's a deal.'

'Those aren't o's, they're degree symbols. Try putting the number combinations into your GPS. They're coordinates.'

She wanted to tell Florin the latest developments right away, but could see he was in the process of questioning the farmer.

'I came out at half-six to bring the cows in for milking, and that's when I saw her. I could tell right away that she had to be dead.'

'Were the cows in the meadow overnight?'

'Yes. I bring them out after the evening milking and back in again in the morning. My farm's only a few hundred metres away, so it's an easy job.'

So the animals had been stomping around in the meadow all night long. That meant forensics were unlikely to get any usable footprints from the perpetrator. If there had ever been any, that is. She positioned herself next to Florin and held her hand out to the farmer.

'Kaspary.'

'Pleased to meet you. Raininger.' He gripped her hand tightly, not letting it go. 'Are you with the police too?'

'Yes. Why?'

He gave a wry smile. 'Because you're much too pretty for nasty work like this. Don't you think?'

The last sentence was directed at Florin.

'I can assure you, Frau Kommissarin Kaspary is not only very pretty, but above all exceptionally intelligent. Which happens to be the deciding factor for our "nasty" work.' His tone had become just a fraction cooler, but Raininger didn't seem to notice. He carried on beaming at Beatrice, even after she had forcefully freed her hand from his grip.

'I'd like to continue, if you don't mind.' Florin's voice was like bourbon on ice: cold, crisp and as smooth as velvet. 'Did you notice anything out of the ordinary yesterday evening?'

'No. Everything was just the same as always.'

'I see. And did you happen to hear anything during the night? Any voices, screams?'

'No, nothing. So did the woman fall down from the crag? Or did someone attack her? There was an awful lot of blood on her head.' He sounded eager to know more. No wonder really; next time he met the other farmers for a beer they would be desperate to hear his story, so he had to know the details.

'We don't know yet. So is the crag accessible by road then?'

The farmer thought for a moment. 'Yes. It's easy to get to from the other side. There's a dirt track that goes almost right to the top.'

Beatrice saw Florin write in his notebook: *Tyre tracks*. All she had written in hers so far were the coordinates.

Underneath, she scribbled in shorthand the information Raininger had given them.

'Does the woman look familiar to you?' she asked. 'Have you see her here before at all?'

The farmer shook his head vehemently. 'Never. And I've got a good memory for faces. I'm sure I would have remembered hers. Especially with that beautiful blonde hair. Is it natural?' He grinned broadly, revealing a toothless gap in the top left-hand side of his mouth.

'If you don't mind,' said Beatrice in a gentle but firm tone, 'we're the ones asking the questions.'

But the farmer didn't have any useful information left to offer. He set off reluctantly back to the farm, his cows in tow, glancing back over his shoulder after every few steps. Beatrice waited until he was out of earshot.

'The victim's feet,' she said.

'What about them?'

'They were tattooed. On the soles.'

He caught on right away. 'So you think the murderer left her some kind of memento?'

'Possibly. But I think it might be a message.' She showed him the two sets of numbers.

'These were tattooed on her feet?'

'Yes. The northern coordinate on the left foot, and eastern on the right.'

Florin immediately strode off across the meadow back towards the crime scene, completely disregarding the potential damage an encounter with a cowpat could inflict on his bespoke shoes. He stopped at the pasture fence and stared over towards the body, his head cocked to the side.

Beatrice had almost caught up with him when her phone started to vibrate in her jacket pocket.

'Kaspary.'

'I'm not going to let you mess me around any more.' Every last word was dripping with contempt.

'Achim. Now's not the time.'

'Of course not. It's never a convenient time for you, is it?' He was on the brink of shouting. 'Even when it's about the children, or—'

'The children are fine, and I'm hanging up now.'

'Don't you dare, you—'

She ended the call and put her mobile back in her bag.

Take a deep breath, she told herself. Focus on the job at hand. But her hands were shaking, she couldn't think clearly like this. *Shit!* Crossing her arms and tucking her hands out of sight, she walked over to join Florin.

'I'd like to know where her shoes are,' he pondered. 'If she lost them in the fall then they should be around here somewhere.' He paused and looked at Beatrice. 'Are you going to tell me why you look so agitated?'

She didn't answer, and Florin lowered his head knowingly. 'Achim, right?'

She pulled her shoulders back and straightened up. 'You were saying something about her shoes?' She tried to pick up on his train of thought, keen to deflect the attention from herself. 'I'm sure forensics will cover the crag too. If she really did fall, then we might find the shoes up there.'

But he was still staring at her intently. 'I'm such an idiot!' he exclaimed.

'Why? We can't be sure about the shoes. Who knows whether we're going to find—'

'Not about that. You still haven't eaten anything, have you? You must be on the verge of fainting.'

'Oh.' Tuning into her body for a moment, she registered a searing sensation in her stomach – which might have been hunger – but not the slightest hint of an appetite. 'No, there's no rush. Crime scene work always turns my stomach anyway.'

She left it at that, not wanting to get drawn into a discussion. A light wind picked up, making the thin plastic bag around the dead woman's hands rustle as if she was kneading it from the inside.

The pathologist's vehicle bumped along the country lane towards them. After it had come to a standstill, a stretcher and body bag were lifted out. Drasche nodded, giving the green light for the woman to be taken away. They lifted her up and the wind caught her hair one last time. Beatrice turned away.

Before the vehicle set off on its way to the pathologist, Florin leant over to the passenger-side window. 'Tell Dr Vogt I'd like the preliminary results today if at all possible.'

Beatrice's mobile began to vibrate in her jacket pocket. It was sure to be Achim again. This time though, she wouldn't pick up. But she took the phone from her pocket just to check, then sighed loudly. The call was from the school.

'He emptied the entire contents of his milk carton into the pot plants! It's just not acceptable, do you understand? The plants belong to the whole class, and if they die you'll have to replace them.'

'Of course. Just let me know if that turns out to be necessary.'

'He's not an easy child, you know.' The teacher at the other end of the line sighed. 'Please speak to him again. It's high time he learnt that rules apply to everyone, including him!'

'Of course. Out of interest, did he say why he did it?'

The teacher snorted. 'Yes, he said that water is too thin and he wanted the flowers to have a proper drink.'

Oh, Jakob, my sweet little Jakob.

'I see. Well, then at least he didn't mean any harm.'

'I guess. But he's seven, for heaven's sake. At some point he simply has to learn to do what he's told.'

Beatrice suppressed the desire to shout down the phone at the woman.

'I understand. I'll speak to him.'

'Thank you. Let's hope it does some good.' The teacher hung up. Feeling overwhelmed with hopelessness, Beatrice tucked her phone back in her bag.

At Florin's insistence, they stopped off at Ginzkey's instead of driving straight back to the office. 'Vegetable curry helps to restore inner balance,' he informed her, ordering two portions. By now, Beatrice was starting to feel as if her stomach had been sewn shut. It was only once the aromatic plate of food was put down in front of her, and she had shovelled in the first mouthful, that her appetite finally kicked back in. She devoured the entire curry, then ordered some cake and hot chocolate.

'Sugar therapy,' she explained. 'It generates temporary feelings of happiness. By the time I feel sick I'll have

17

forgotten about everything else.' She was relieved to see Florin grinning.

'Will it spoil your appetite if we talk about the case?' he asked.

'Not in the slightest. Once we get back to the office we can go through the missing persons reports. Our investigations are just a stab in the dark until we know who the woman was.'

'Well, that's not strictly true. Thanks to your discovery.'

'Do you really think the coordinates are connected to her death? The tattoos could be old. We should wait for the pathologist's report first.'

'Definitely.' He drank his espresso down in one gulp. 'But I'm still going to put the numbers into my GPS all the same. You never know, we might find something useful.'

Outside, the skies were clouding over. They hurried back to the office, where they were greeted by a message from Hoffmann asking to be updated on the new case. While Florin went off to look for their boss, Beatrice turned her computer on and loaded the page with the missing persons announcements.

A fifty-five-year-old woman with short grey hair who had gone missing from the local psychiatric unit. No. An unemployed twenty-two-year-old who had made suicide threats. Another no.

The third entry unleashed that subtle but familiar tug inside her, like a divining rod quivering and latching onto its target.

Thirty-nine-year-old female, blonde, green eyes, 170 centimetres, slim. A dark brown birthmark above the right-hand corner of her mouth. Special features: none. So no tattoos then.

Name: Nora Papenberg
Place of residence: Salzburg, Nesselthaler Strasse.

The woman had been reported missing four days ago by her husband. Beatrice only turned her attention to the photograph after reading the statement through in full. It was a snapshot, and not really suitable as a missing persons photo, because the Nora Papenberg in the picture had been captured whilst laughing gleefully. Her eyes were half shut, and she was holding a champagne glass in her right hand.

Mouth open, eyes shut. Exactly the same as in the meadow, and yet so completely different.

Beatrice made a mental note of the corresponding features: the rounded chin, the snub nose and the birthmark at the corner of the mouth. Their corpse had a name.

She told Florin as soon as he came back from talking to Hoffmann. 'Nora Papenberg. I've already googled her. She was a copywriter in a small ad agency. There are some photos of her online, so we can be pretty certain it's her.' She passed a pile of printouts over to Florin's side of the desk.

'Right, let's get cracking then.' The vigour in his voice sounded false, and Beatrice knew why. Now came the hardest part of the job: informing the next of kin. Disbelief, tears, devastation. *That's not possible, it's not my husband, my wife, my child. There must be some mistake. There has to be.*

19

They got stuck in traffic even before they reached the Karolinen bridge. Stealing a glance at her watch, Beatrice realised she would never make it on time now. She pulled her phone from her bag and quickly dialled a number.

'Mama?'

'Bea! It's so lovely to hear from you. Are you already done for the day?'

'No, unfortunately that's why I'm calling. We've got a new murder case, and . . .'

Her mother's sigh echoed down the line. 'And you want me to pick the children up from the childminder?'

'Yes. Please. I'll be as quick as I can, and you won't need to cook anything, I'll see to it when I get back.'

'Frozen pizza, I know.'

Beatrice closed her eyes. As if her guilty conscience needed any more ammunition.

'No. In actual fact I was planning to make a broccoli bake. That's quick too.'

If broccoli bake didn't win her mother around then nothing would.

'Fine then. I'll pick them up, but it would be nice if you could give me more notice next time. I do have other things to do, you know.'

'Yes. I know. Thank you.'

They turned off into Aigner Strasse, where the traffic finally eased up. 'You don't have to tell him.' Florin stared fixedly at the Audi in front of them. 'I'll handle that, okay? You just make notes. Unless I overlook something important, then speak up.'

She could have hugged him. He was voluntarily drawing the losing card. The way she sometimes did with the children, just for the pleasure of seeing them hop around giggling, overjoyed to have beaten her.

Did Nora Papenberg have children? As Florin parked the car opposite the house, Beatrice scanned the garden for telltale signs. No sandpit, no children's bikes, no trampoline. Just one of those Japanese Zen gardens with patterns raked in the sand.

'We're too early. He won't even be home yet,' said Florin as he turned the engine off.

They got out and rang the bell anyway. Almost immediately, the door was opened by a man wearing jeans and a checked jacket over a dark green polo shirt.

'Are you Konrad Papenberg?'

'Yes.'

'We're from the police.'

Beatrice saw the man flinch, saw how he searched their faces in vain for the trace of a smile, for a sign of the all-clear. Then she saw the realisation dawn.

'My wife?'

'Yes. I'm afraid we have bad news, Herr Papenberg.'

'Come in, please.' He held the door open for them, turning his ashen face to the side. Most people looked away at that moment, when nothing of finality had yet been said. It was about maintaining that state for as long as possible, drawing out these last seconds of merciful ignorance. He gestured for them to sit down on the sofa, then jumped up again and brought them water from the kitchen, unbidden. The glasses shook so violently in his hands that he spilt half of their contents.

21

Florin waited until he had sat down and was looking at them. 'We have every reason to believe that we've found your wife. She was discovered this morning in a field near Abtenau.'

'What do you mean, every reason to believe?' His voice was surprisingly steady.

'It means that we've identified her based on the missing persons photo. She didn't have any ID with her.'

'But she always has it on her . . . in her handbag.' The man swallowed, kneading the fingers of his left hand.

Beatrice made a note: *Bag missing.*

'You will of course have the opportunity to identify her personally if you feel able to,' Florin continued gently. 'I'm very sorry.'

Papenberg didn't reply. He fixed his gaze on a spot on the coffee table, moving his lips wordlessly, shaking his head in brief, abrupt motions.

In ninety per cent of cases, the husbands are the murderers. That was Hoffmann's rule – and it was fairly accurate. But this man's reaction was so faint. He didn't yet believe it.

'What – I mean, how . . . how did she . . .'

'At the moment we have to assume that she was murdered.'

He breathed in shakily. 'No.' Tears filled the man's eyes and he covered his face with his hands. They paused to give him time. Beatrice handed him a tissue, which he noticed only after a few seconds and took hesitantly.

'You last saw your wife on Friday, is that right?' asked Florin.

Papenberg nodded. 'She went to a work dinner in the evening, by car. She arrived without any problems, but left early, at half-ten. I spoke to her colleagues; they said she told them she was coming home, that she had a headache.'

He glanced at Beatrice, looking strangely hopeful, as if she could create some equation from her notes, something that would give everything some sense. 'Her colleague Rosa said that she received a call shortly before she left.'

That was important. 'We'll certainly be speaking to your wife's colleagues,' said Beatrice. 'We didn't find a mobile on her though. Do you know which model she had?'

'A Nokia N8. I gave it to her . . . for her birthday.' His voice broke. His upper body doubled over, shaking with suppressed sobs.

They waited patiently for him to gather his composure.

'Could you please give me your wife's mobile number? We'll check to see who she spoke to.'

Konrad Papenberg nodded weakly and pulled his phone from his trouser pocket. He opened his contacts and let Beatrice write the number down. 'I phoned her at least thirty times that night.' His words were hard to make out, his voice bloated with grief. 'But she must have turned it off, it just kept going straight to answerphone.'

'When you reported your wife missing, you said she had her car with her. Is that correct?'

He nodded without looking up, scrunching the tissue in his hand.

'A red Honda Civic?'

'Yes.'

'There's one more thing we need to know, Herr Papenberg.'

'Yes?'

'Did – does your wife have any distinguishing features?'

He looked up. 'Like what?'

'Scars, any obvious birthmarks, tattoos?'

His trembling hand moved up to his face and pointed to the right-hand side, just above his mouth. 'She has a birthmark here. It's her beauty mark.'

'Okay.' Florin cleared his throat. 'Nothing else? No tattoos?'

'No. She always thought they were tasteless.' A spark of hope smouldered in his eyes. 'Maybe it isn't Nora after all?'

Beatrice and Florin exchanged a glance.

'I'm afraid there isn't any doubt,' said Beatrice softly. 'And not just because of the birthmark.'

That was enough for now. 'We won't disturb you any further. Can we call anyone for you so you're not alone? If you like we can arrange for someone from the counselling team to come and see you.'

'My brother.' Papenberg's voice sounded strangled. 'I'll ring my brother.'

While he went to make the call, they left the room and waited in the hallway. There were some framed photos on a dresser: Nora Papenberg immortalised in all manner of situations. In a summer dress on the beach, looking tanned. In hiking gear in front of a summit cross on a mountain. Building a snowman with a group of friends while clad in a quilted jacket and bobble hat. In every single one, she was laughing and full of life, but unmistakably the same woman whose corpse they had seen that very morning.

'There were five days between her disappearance and the presumed time of death,' Beatrice pondered out loud. 'That's a long time.'

'It certainly is. Which suggests she was held captive before her death. What are your thoughts on the husband? My hunch is that he's being genuine.'

'I agree.'

'But we'll still have to look into it.'

'Of course.'

The door to the living room opened. Papenberg came out, his eyes red and swollen. 'My brother will be here in twenty minutes. If you don't have any more questions . . .'

'Of course. We'll leave you alone now.' They were already by the door before Beatrice realised that she was still holding the snowman photo in her hand. She felt her cheeks go red, and was just about to put it back on the dresser when Papenberg took it from her hand.

'That was such a great day. Ice cold and clear. Nora said the snow was like icing sugar,' he whispered. 'She loves the snow so much, and nature, everything about it.'

'I'm sorry,' murmured Beatrice, simultaneously loathing herself for uttering the worn-out phrase. But the man wasn't even aware of their presence any more. He nodded absent-mindedly. His steadfast gaze was fixed on his wife's face as she stood there amidst the blinding white, laughing for all eternity.

'That's a bunny rabbit, see? And this is an angel, it just drilled a hole in the cloud and that's why it's raining.' Jakob held the drawing so close to the pan of broccoli that the paper started to buckle from the steam. Beatrice gently herded him over towards the fridge, where she pinned the picture up with two magnets. 'It's wonderful. Did you draw it at school?'

'Yes. Frau Sieber gave me a star for it,' he beamed. Beatrice squatted down to hug him. At least one of them had ended up having a good day. 'And Mama, look.' He wriggled out of her arms and poked two fingers into his mouth. A wobbly tooth.

'Great!' she marvelled, before hearing a hissing sound behind her. Boiling water was sloshing over onto the hob and from there down to the floor. Beatrice cursed inwardly, pulling the pan aside and turning down the heat.

'Go and play with Mina for a little while longer, okay? I'll call you when dinner's ready.'

'But Mina doesn't want to play with me,' moaned Jakob. 'She always says I'm a baby and that I don't know anything about anything.' Nonetheless, he trudged obediently back to the children's room, making loud engine noises as he went.

Beatrice wiped up the mess on the hob and floor, then diced the ham, peeled the potatoes and – once the bake was finally in the oven – sank down, exhausted, onto a kitchen chair. In front of her on the table lay a letter from Schubert and Kirchner, Achim's lawyers. She threw the letter unopened onto her hated 'To do' pile and pulled out her notebook.

Ad agency: Who was at the party? Did anyone else leave at the same time as Nora Papenberg?

Phone call. How soon after it did Papenberg leave? What exactly did she say? Is it possible that she went to meet someone?

Find out caller's number.

Where's her car?

Five days before the murder – why so long???

She flicked back through her notes to the ones she had made right after leaving the crime scene.

Killing method – Why would someone choose to push their victim from a rock face?

She read through the farmer's statement again – he hadn't heard anything, hadn't seen anything, the same as always. Above it, she had scribbled the coordinates. Beatrice closed her eyes and summoned the image again – the victim's feet lying sideways as if mid-stride, the digits lined up on the soles. The tattoos hadn't been done by a professional, that much was clear. They had been done by an amateur. By the killer. Or the victim? Hearing the timer start to peep, she opened her eyes again. Time for dinner.

'Are we going to Papa's again this weekend?' asked Mina, dissecting a broccoli floret into microscopic pieces.

'Yes, that's the plan. Why? Don't you want to go?'

'No, I do.' A tiny green fragment had clearly found favour, and was being transported into her mouth on the fork. 'He said he might be getting me a cat. If it lives with Papa, can I stay there more often?'

Beatrice almost choked. 'We'll discuss that when the time comes.' *A cat!*

'Me too, Mama, me too!' mumbled Jakob, his mouth full.

'Forget it, doofus, it's my cat.'

'Silly moo!'

Mina ignored him. 'If Papa calls again tonight, can I speak to him?'

'Me too!' yelped Jakob excitedly.

27

'No. We don't make phone calls at night-time. Papa will soon realise that.'

She got the children ready for bed and let the CD player read them the bedtime story she had no energy left for today. Then she sat down on the balcony with a glass of red wine and read back through her notes. Again and again, she kept coming back to the coordinates.

Letting the wine swill around in her mouth, she tried to taste the notes of blackcurrant and tobacco touted by the label on the bottle, but didn't succeed. So she drank the glass down in one long gulp instead. Tiredness pulled at her with its heavy hands.

She turned her mobile off and unplugged the landline from the wall. Achim would have to find another way of amusing himself tonight.

Three yellow Post-its, full of Hoffmann's indecipherable scrawl, were waiting for her the next morning on her computer monitor. A reminder about the reports. She rolled her eyes.

'We'll give Stefan the files, he needs practice anyway. Report writing is character building. Oh, and he's already checked out the list of Nora Papenberg's phone calls – and guess what!' Florin was standing at the espresso machine in a get-up that was very unusual for him – cargo pants, T-shirt and hiking shoes – and was just finishing off his cocoa-powder-dusted masterpiece for Beatrice. 'The call that we suspect lured her away from the party came from a telephone box on Maxglaner Hauptstrasse. I've sent forensics there, although I'm pretty sure they won't find anything.' He looked up. 'Speaking of telephone calls – how was last night? Did you manage to get any peace?'

'I did actually, but only because I unplugged or turned off anything that could possibly have rung. So I had seven outraged messages from him on the answerphone this morning, telling me he was out of his mind with worry about the kids because he couldn't get through.' She took a sip of coffee. It tasted wonderful.

'Well, the important thing is that you were able to get some sleep. Listen, the pathologist's report isn't in yet, so I suggest we concentrate on another aspect of the case first.'

'The coordinates?'

'Exactly.' He waved his mobile in the air. 'I've just installed some new navigation software. It looks like we're heading off into the sticks.' He spread out a map and pointed his finger at a section of forest near the Wolfgangsee lake.

'There? Are you sure?' Beatrice wasn't sure what she had been expecting from the location indicated by the coordinates. But certainly something more interesting than trees.

They took Florin's car. Beatrice lowered the passenger-side window. May had only just begun, but it was acting like a much balmier month. Argentine tango played on the stereo. For a moment, she daydreamed that they were setting off on an adventure, with a picnic basket on the back seat and all the time in the world stretching out ahead of them.

A thought occurred to her. 'What if the place we're driving to only has some private significance? Like the scene of an argument? Or quite the opposite – a first kiss, a promise, a sexual act, something that happened between people but left behind no visible trace? Then the location may well be the key to the case, but we'll never find the lock.'

Florin just smiled. 'That's very possible. But I don't think we should ignore the tattoos either, do you? I can't imagine that they'll be of no use to us whatsoever.'

He was right, of course. And, worst-case scenario, they'd be spending a sunny May morning in the countryside, far away from Hoffmann and his Post-its. Just that alone made it all worth it.

'What do you think we're going to find?' she asked, as the car wound its way along the serpentine road up the Heuberg mountain.

He shrugged. 'Let's see what jumps out at us. If I get something fixed in my mind I'm more likely to overlook the thing that really matters, just because it looks different to what I expected. By the way, you'll be pleased to hear I've finally made a decision.' Florin raised his eyebrows. That meant: *Ask me.*

'About what?'

'*Carpaccio di Manzo.*'

'Come again?'

'The antipasti problem, remember? Carpaccio's the ideal solution; the perfect start to a wonderful meal. Anneke will love it.'

The air rushing past carried the scent of fresh earth and lilacs into the car.

'I'm sure she will.'

They parked the car opposite a restaurant. The path in front of them led across a meadow, which was flanked by grand estates and a magnificently renovated old farmhouse on the right-hand side. Florin held his mobile out in front of him like a compass. 'Four hundred and thirty metres as the crow flies if we head north-west. But I suggest we follow the path at first rather than fighting our way through the undergrowth the whole way.'

Apart from an elderly couple kitted out in Nordic walking gear, there was no one else to be seen in the woods that morning. The path crossed an astonishingly clear stream and branched off to the right at a yellow trail sign marked '*Steinklüfte*', which showed the way to the stone chasm.

'Not much further.' Florin showed Beatrice his mobile, where the black–and–white destination flag had already come into view on the display. The path was becoming steeper now, winding upwards through high rocky crags, past fallen trees with toadstools growing out of their stumps. One tree trunk stretched out across the path, forming an archway.

'All we're going to find here is pretty scenery,' murmured Beatrice. 'How much further is it?'

'A hundred and twenty metres.'

She started to keep a lookout for something unusual, but it was difficult when she didn't have the slightest idea what this 'something' might be. There were rocks, numerous rocks of differing sizes. And another stream.

'Forty metres,' announced Florin.

All around them, huge stones propped one another up. Trees were even growing out of some of the steep, moss-covered formations.

'Fifteen metres.' Florin stopped in his tracks. 'We should be able to see something from here.' He set off again, but walking more slowly now, his eyes fixed on his mobile. Beatrice tried to ignore the tug of disappointment in the pit of her stomach. Okay, so there was nothing here, but that was only at first glance. It didn't necessarily mean the coordinates were useless. They would have to take their time, be thorough. Assume that there was more behind the tattoos than a murderer with an unusual fetish for feet and numbers.

'Here.' Florin stopped again. 'Somewhere within a three-metre radius of this spot; unfortunately the mobile won't be any more precise than that.'

Dry leaves crackled under their feet as they slowly paced around. This spot didn't look any different from all the others in the surrounding area: trees, rock formations, dead wood.

Beatrice pulled her camera out of her rucksack and started to take photos. She tried to capture everything; it was entirely possible that the pictures would reveal more to them later than they were taking in right now.

'Over there is something called the "Devil's Ravine",' commented Florin. 'The name sounds appropriate, but they're the wrong coordinates.'

'Let's take a look at it anyway.' Beatrice sat down on one of the knee-high rocks and looked around. 'So this is roughly the right spot?'

'Yes, pretty much. It's supposed to be eight metres to the east of where you're sitting now – whatever *it* may be.'

She took a deep breath of exquisite sun-warmed air. It was filled with aromas. Resin, leaves, earth.

Eight metres.

She looked more closely at the terrain around her. No, there was nothing unusual. Just rocks.

But maybe they had to look further up? At the trees perhaps?

Shielding her eyes with her hand, Beatrice squinted in the sunlight, gazing up at the treetops and upper branches. But all she could see was forest.

No clues, no sign of any kind.

Florin's expression betrayed the same dissatisfaction she herself was feeling, but his voice still sounded upbeat. 'It seems you were right again, Bea. Who knows what significance this place has for our tattoo artist? What he may have experienced, seen or heard here, perhaps even years ago.'

'Indeed.' She took the water bottle he handed to her and drank three long gulps. But something felt wrong.

There is something, but we're not seeing it. We're doing something wrong.

We're not seeing it. The thought stuck in her mind. We're not seeing it because we're not supposed to see it? Or because we need to try harder?

Her gaze settled on one of the taller rocks, which had a stone leaning against it. Colour-wise the stone hardly stood out, being just slightly paler, but unlike the rock behind it, it wasn't covered in moss.

'Or because it's hidden,' she said decidedly.

'Sorry?'

Beatrice stood up and paced the short distance over towards the rock. She had to climb a little in order to get to the spot that had caught her attention. Holding onto a tree that had wound its roots around a lower piece of the rock, she pushed against the moss-free stone with her other hand. As she had suspected, it was just propped up against the rock.

33

Behind it was a cavity, a small dark hollow. She took a close-up photograph, struggling to keep her balance in the process. For a split second, the flash from her camera illuminated something pale inside the hollow.

'Look.'

Florin was clambering over to her, tugging a torch out of his rucksack. Its beam illuminated some earth and a few brown leaves, from beneath which a spider hurriedly scuttled away in search of new shelter. The light stretched back through the hole and picked up something white. Plastic.

Silently, they both took out their gloves and pulled them on. Florin reached his arm into the space and pulled out a box with a white-and-blue lid. An airtight food container. 'It looks new,' commented Beatrice.

'It feels heavy. Full. Have you taken all the photos you need?'

She nodded.

'Good, then let's climb back down.'

They knelt next to one another on the soft forest floor. Florin unfastened the container on all four sides, then lifted the lid off carefully.

Something large, wrapped in kitchen towel. On top of it was a neatly folded note, not handwritten, but word-processed. Florin unfolded it, and Beatrice moved closer to him to be able to see properly.

Congratulations – you've found it!

This container is part of a game, a kind of modern treasure hunt using GPS. If you've stumbled upon this by accident, then this hunt has now come to an end for you. Close it again immediately and put it back where you found it. It's in your own best interests, trust me.

*If you **were** looking for it, I'm sure the contents of my 'treasure chest' will be of interest to you. In contrast to the way this is normally done, you don't need to put the container back in the same spot. Take it with you and search it for fingerprints. In one sense at least, you definitely won't find any.*

TFTH

'It sounds like it was hidden here especially for us,' said Florin slowly. He folded the note up and slipped it into a plastic evidence bag. They both stared at the container and the thing that was awaiting them inside it, wrapped up in the kitchen towel. Then, although some irrational part of Beatrice was still hoping he wouldn't, Florin reached for it. The paper towel slipped to the side.

Her first thought was that it had to be a fake. A Halloween prop, still in its original packaging. But her stomach responded more quickly than her mind, delivering a wave of nausea before she had even registered all the details.

'Shit,' whispered Florin.

'Is it real?'

He took a deep breath and swallowed. 'Yes. Do you see the frayed edges? I'm no expert, but . . . to me those look like the marks of a saw.'

Employing a painstakingly trained reflex, Beatrice suppressed the images hurtling into her mind and forced herself to look at it without emotion.

A hand. A male hand. Severed just below the wrist. Shrink-wrapped in a thick layer of plastic film, like vacuum-packed meat. The skin of the hand was white, with blueish discolouration on the tips of the fingers and around the nails.

She looked more closely at the amputation wound. She could see bone, and an artery that was protruding a little.

'So this means we have a second body.' Florin's subdued voice sounded as if it was coming from far away.

'Either that or a victim with only one hand.'

He nodded. 'Or maybe someone just helped themselves to hospital waste. I'll call Drasche.'

Beatrice hastily put the camera between herself and their find, taking a number of shots. Then she inhaled sharply and put the camera aside. 'Florin! There's something else in the box. Under the hand.' She gingerly pulled out another piece of paper and unfolded it carefully. Florin put his mobile back in his pocket and came over to her side to read.

Unlike the first message, the words on this note were handwritten in ink, with broad arcs and loops.

Stage Two
You're looking for a singer, a man by the name of Christoph, who has blue eyes and a birthmark on the back of his left hand. Some time ago – it may be five years or even six – he was a member of a Salzburg choir, in which he very proudly sang Schubert's Mass in A flat. The last two numbers of his birth year are A. Now square A, add 37 and add the resulting sum to your northern coordinates.

Take the sum of A and multiply by 10, then multiply A with this number. Subtract 229 and then subtract the resulting sum from your eastern coordinates. Welcome to Stage Two. We'll see each other there.

For a long moment, the birdsong around them was the only sound to be heard. Beatrice read the text a second and a third time. A man called Christoph? Schubert's Mass in A flat?

No, don't think just yet. Just register first impressions. A woman's handwriting. She herself wrote very similarly – more evenly and a little less elaborately, but with a comparable flourish. She turned around to face Florin.

'Do you understand any of this?'

'Not even a little.' He shook his head without taking his eyes off the note for a second. 'The box was at the spot corresponding to the coordinates on the corpse.' He squinted, as though any beam of light would distract him from making sense of it all. 'We find a clue, with which we can then draw up some new coordinates. And we also find an amputated hand. But why? What's the point of this? Why is he so brazenly shoving his victims right under our noses instead of hiding them?'

'Because he thinks we're stupid. That's what he wrote, after all. Or she.'

'But why? Does he *want* to get caught? Or does he think he's so superior that there's no chance of that?'

Beatrice placed the lens cap carefully back onto her camera. 'Who knows? Maybe he wants to send us off on the wrong track.'

'With body parts?'

She looked at the dead hand. It was a left hand. There was an indentation on the ring finger, about three millimetres wide.

'Well, by using body parts,' she said slowly, 'he can be sure that we really will follow the trail.'

Drasche appeared within the hour, wearing the same sour expression he always had when someone else had been the first to get their hands on a piece of evidence.

'We were careful,' Beatrice assured him. 'Is there any news on Nora Papenberg?'

'There was no sign of rape, nor any foreign tissue under her fingernails. We found some tyre tracks near the scene and on the way to the crag, but the results aren't back yet. No footprints that could belong to the perpetrator, unfortunately. We'll keep you posted. Where exactly did you find the container?'

Beatrice showed him the hollow in the rock. 'We took photos while we were there.'

'That's better than nothing, I suppose,' grumbled Drasche, pulling his gloves on. 'At least he did me the favour of vacuum-packing the amputated body part. Conserved evidence – you don't get that very often.'

Back at the office, Beatrice connected the camera to her computer. A few moments later, the pictures appeared on the screen, one after the other. The severed hand in its airtight container. While Beatrice clicked through the photos, Florin called Stefan Gerlach.

'Even Hoffmann will have to realise that you don't have time to type up reports right now,' he explained, rolling his chair over to her side of the desk.

'The box is a well-known brand, and mass produced.' Beatrice pointed her pen at the website she had just called up. 'This one here must be the same model as the one we found. The lid with the blue edge, you see? And the double lock on the longer sides. One hundred per cent air- and watertight, it says in the description. "Can easily transport liquids and store intense-smelling foods like fish or cheese without any unwelcome smells."'

'Perfect for body parts then. But our perpetrator took it one step further and vacuum-packed the hand just to be on the safe side.'

Beatrice looked back at the photos of the opened plastic container. 'He didn't want anyone to find it by accident,' she pondered. 'Not even a dog. And given that he doesn't seem to rate the intelligence of the police very highly, he assumed it would take us a while.'

There was a knock at the door. Stefan poked his head in. 'I hear there's some boring typing work for me? Bring it on!'

'You're a star.' Beatrice gathered the files up into a more or less orderly pile to hand over to her younger colleague, but his attention was now entirely absorbed by the photos on the screen.

'Oh. That looks nasty. What is it?'

'That's what we'd like to know.'

'A hand? Was it just lying around like that, packed up like it came from the freezer cabinet? Bizarre.'

Bizarre pretty much hit the nail on the head. 'No, it was in a plastic container. There on the right in the photo, you see?' Beatrice gave him a friendly nudge with her elbow. 'And now scoot, my dear. This isn't your problem. Be thankful for that.'

But Stefan couldn't tear his gaze away from the screen.

'That seems incredibly strange. Doesn't it remind you of something?'

'No. Should it?'

Stefan leant over and pointed his finger at the rock hollow in which they had found the box. 'Was it in there?'

'Correct.'

He took a sharp intake of breath. 'Then that's the most perverse trade I've ever seen.'

'The most perverse what?'

'A trade. You take something out of the box and put something else back in. That's how it works.'

Beatrice saw from Florin's confused expression that he had understood just as little of Stefan's observation as she had.

'Oh. Sorry. You've never been geocaching, I guess?'

'What's that?'

Stefan looked from her to Florin and pulled up a chair. 'It's a kind of treasure hunt. Someone hides something, and others try to find it. The thing that's hidden is called a cache, and this plastic container in the photo looks like a typical cache container. May I?'

Beatrice surrendered the mouse to him and shifted to the side so he could position his chair between her and Florin.

'What did you call it again — a cash?'

'Yes, that's right. C-a-c-h-e, pronounced cash. People put all kinds of things in them.'

'A treasure hunt,' she declared. 'Sounds promising. Do people use GPS for it?'

'Oh, so you already know what I'm talking about then!' said Stefan, disappointed.

'No, not in the least. It was just a good guess. Carry on.'

'Okay. So, first you sign up to the internet site, it's called Geocaching.com. All the caches all over the world are recorded on it.'

'Well I never,' said Florin. 'And lots of people do this?'

'Absolutely,' explained Stefan enthusiastically. 'Millions of people, particularly in the US, but it's getting more and more popular here in Austria. So, you register, under a nick-name – mine is "Undercover Cookie", for example.'

Beatrice couldn't help grinning. 'Lovely. I'm afraid that name might stick from now on.'

But Stefan wouldn't be distracted. 'Then you select a cache in the area you want to go to, save the coordinates in a specially designed GPS device and set off. Usually the destination will reveal a tin or a box, something watertight, and in it will be a logbook so you can make an entry. The bigger caches often contain objects that you can take with you if you replace them with something else. And that, ladies and gentlemen, is what you call a "trade".'

Coordinates and watertight containers. It all seemed to fit. Beatrice clicked on the photo of the first message and zoomed in so they could read the text. 'Are messages like this the norm too?'

'Yes. That's a cache note.' He beamed first at Beatrice, then Florin, clearly proud of himself. 'You find an explanation like this in practically every cache. It's intended for people who haven't yet heard of geocaching and stumble on a hiding place by chance. See, the owner mentions that here.'

'Stop – use layman's terms. The owner is the person who hides it?'

'Exactly.' Stefan gave Beatrice an apologetic look.

'Abbreviations and specialist terminology are used quite frequently in geocaching.' The mouse icon hovered over the photo of the cache note. 'So, when he says this about the fingerprints – *in one sense at least, you definitely won't find any* – he means the only ones will be those on the hand itself, right?' he speculated.

'It seems so.' Beatrice had reached automatically for her notepad and was starting to jot down Stefan's explanations. 'He or she clearly has a sense of humour that takes some getting used to.'

'You can say that again.' Stefan pointed a pencil at the four letters the note was signed off with: *TFTH*.

'What does that stand for? Are they elaborate initials of some kind?' asked Florin. 'Theodor Friedrich Thomas Heinrich? No, wait, I get it, it must be another puzzle.'

'Not this time, it's just the usual abbreviation. He's thanking you. "TFTH" stands for "Thanks for the hunt". You're right, he does have an odd sense of humour.'

'Or she.' Beatrice clicked on one of the other photos: the note, written in what seemed to be a woman's handwriting, sending them off on another hunt. 'Does that mean anything to you? Stage two – what does that mean? The second level?'

'It's the next stage of the treasure hunt.' Stefan reached for the mouse and enlarged the picture. 'What we have here seems to be a multi-cache. That means there are several stages. You find Stage One, which gives you the clues for Stage Two, which in turn provides the clues for Stage Three, and so on and so forth, until you get to the final destination. Normally you find the container only at the very end.'

'We can probably say goodbye to any concept of "normal" in this case,' remarked Florin. 'Is there anything else we should know?'

'It's not just a multi-cache,' said Stefan, after thinking for a moment. 'For that you would only need to count something – steps, trees, gravestones – in order to get the next coordinates. But here you have to solve a puzzle too. That makes it a mystery cache.'

Beatrice made a note: *Mystery cache*. 'Thank you, Stefan. You've helped us a great deal. TFTH. Thanks for the help.'

But Stefan didn't want to go just yet. 'Can you tell me more about the case? How did you find the container? Oh, hang on, it's connected with the woman from yesterday, right? The corpse in the cattle pasture?' He gave Beatrice and Florin an earnest look. 'Couldn't you make use of an extra pair of hands for the investigation?'

'I'll speak with Hoffmann. If he agrees to give us more people, you'll certainly be our first choice.'

Stefan seemed content with that. He set off back to his office, the pile of papers tucked under his arm.

Beatrice snapped the lid off a neon yellow highlighter and began to structure her notes.

'Stop me if I'm talking nonsense, but wouldn't it be a good idea to look for someone from the caching scene? It's quite obvious that our man – or woman – knows their stuff here. Or would it be better to solve the coordinates for Stage Two first? If Stefan is right, it sounds like – after Stage Eight or Thirty-three or Ninety-two – it'll eventually lead us to what we're looking for.'

'The murderer, you mean?' Florin scratched himself behind

the ear. 'Do you really think he'll offer himself up as the prize for us so enthusiastically and eagerly solving the puzzle?'

Beatrice looked at the photo of the hand again. 'It's probably just wishful thinking,' she said. 'But the way he's been acting so far, it doesn't seem so far-fetched an idea.'

The forensic test results from their find came back the next morning, even before Nora Papenberg's autopsy report.

'Say goodbye to any hopes about the amputation having been done in a hospital,' said Florin, his expression grim as he scanned through the report. 'The hand was cut off with a wood saw, post-mortem thankfully, and must have been shrink-wrapped straight afterwards. Traces of wood shavings were found in the wound.' He put the report down and rubbed his eyes. 'This is pretty messed up, don't you think? Particularly considering no mutilated corpse has turned up anywhere.'

Not yet. But it soon would, and then they'd have not one murder case to contend with, but two. Unless the perpetrator had hacked up someone who had met their end through natural causes.

The perpetrator. The *Owner.*

'Let's start the search for the next stage then,' she said.

Two copies of the photographed handwritten note were just gliding out of the printer when Hoffmann came storming into the office − without knocking, as usual.

'Kaspary, what an unfamiliar sight. You're actually at your desk during office hours!'

'Good morning,' said Beatrice. 'I missed you too, sir.'

'So what's happening with those reports? I've been told

you offloaded them onto young Gerlach without discussing it with me.'

'I did indeed. You weren't around to consult, unfortunately. Stefan very helpfully offered to take on the typing for me.'

The corners of Hoffmann's mouth, which were droopy even at the best of times, sank even further down his face. 'Well, you always were good at delegating unwanted tasks, weren't you, Kaspary?'

Beatrice decided not to dignify that with an answer. Instead, she stood up and fetched the pages from the printer. The photo quality wasn't great on normal printer paper, but it would have to do for now.

'The press are breathing down my neck about the murder, as I'm sure you can imagine. So I hope you're going to have some results for me soon. I'm relying on you, Florian!' He ran his hand through his thinning, dirty-yellow hair and trudged out of the room.

'Just wait, soon you'll be on first-name terms,' said Beatrice with a smirk. 'He seems to have a real soft spot for you.'

'I can't believe he called me Florian!'

'Well, the boss is too busy for minor details like that. It's only an extra "a". Don't be such a girl, Wenninger!'

Don't be such a girl was one of Hoffmann's favourite catchphrases. Beatrice secretly suspected that his aversion to her was based on precisely that: that she was a girl, and what's more – making it even worse – one who spoke her mind.

She handed Florin one of the printouts. On her copy, she underlined *Christoph, birthmark, Salzburg choir* and *Mass in A flat* with her yellow marker.

'That's all we have to go on, right?'

45

'Well, it's something at least. Although practically every choir sings Schubert's Mass in A flat.' A few clicks of the mouse, and he was on YouTube. Operatic tones resounded out from the computer's tinny-sounding loudspeakers.

'Good grief. Yep, that's clearly a hit,' sighed Beatrice.

Half an hour later, Florin slumped back in his chair and sighed. 'From the looks of it, pretty much every Salzburg resident is in a choir,' he said. 'There are more choirs than there are churches. I reckon we'll easily find fifteen Christophs, and for every one of those we'll need to inspect the back of his left hand and check his year of birth.' He pressed a tablet out of the blister pack that lay next to his desk lamp, swallowing it down with a gulp of orange juice. 'These are the kind of things that make being a policeman so much fun.'

'Headache?'

'A little. It must have been Hoffmann's voice – I can't cope with the frequency.'

'Either that or you've been hunched over your desk again.' She stood up, went over to him and started to massage his neck muscles. She felt his surprise as he tensed up for a few seconds, but then he relaxed.

'We'll have to speak to the choirmasters, one after the other,' she murmured. 'By phone.'

'The Owner wrote that this Christoph guy was in the choir more than five years ago. I would take that to mean he isn't there any more. A bit to the left, please – yes, right there, that's perfect. Thanks.' He sighed.

Smiling, Beatrice pressed the balls of her thumbs into the

knots between his neck and shoulders. 'So we'll ask them about former Christophs, too. And about a Schubert Mass that was rehearsed over five years ago.'

It was taking for ever. After two hours on the phone, Beatrice had got through just half of her part of the list, and had already found six Christophs — four active choir members, two inactive. Florin had five, including one where the choirmaster couldn't really remember whether he might in fact have been a Christian instead.

He was just noting down the details from his last call when the telephone rang.

'Yes? Oh, hi. Is there any news?'

Beatrice saw him raise his eyebrows. As he listened, he silently mouthed the word 'pathologist'.

'Yes, I'd definitely like to know the details. Can you tell me anything about the tattoo yet?' He nodded, jotted something down, then took a deep breath. 'Okay. And the other thing?'

He started to write again, but then stopped short and looked up, visibly perplexed.

'What is it?' whispered Beatrice, but Florin just shook his head.

'And there's no chance you could be mistaken? No? Okay. Yes. Thanks, I'll try to make some sense of it. Send us the full report as soon as it's ready. Yes, you have a good day too.' He hung up.

'What is it?' pressed Beatrice. 'What did they find out from the autopsy?'

Deep in thought, Florin stared at his notes. 'We were

right about the tattoos being recent,' he said, speaking slowly. 'They were done while she was still alive, about eight to nine hours before she died.'

Beatrice's toes curled up involuntarily inside her shoes. 'Oh, shit.'

'Yes. That's one thing. The other is that traces of blood were found on her clothes, and it wasn't hers.' He smoothed his notes out flat, as if that would somehow help the words make more sense. 'But . . .' he continued hesitantly, 'it did match the samples from the amputated hand.'

'What?'

He nodded, almost apologetically. 'The blood was found on her jacket, blouse and trousers, and there were some small traces on her hands too.'

The image that Beatrice had created of Nora Papenberg's last hours in her mind suddenly started to crack. Lonely, frightened, tied up somewhere in the dark – perhaps it hadn't been like that after all. She had someone else's blood on her, the blood of a dead man. 'Were there any scratches, any skin cells under her fingernails?'

Florin shook his head. 'Nothing of the sort. She had some grazes, of course, but they probably came from the fall off the rock face.' He rubbed both hands over his face. 'You're thinking there might have been a struggle, right? The man attacks Nora Papenberg, she defends herself, making him bleed in the process – but what then? She kills him and saws him up into pieces? Hides his hand away in a plastic box? And then commits suicide? It all sounds pretty unlikely to me.'

But the message they had found with the dismembered hand had been written by a woman, Beatrice was sure of it. 'Well, we should ask the husband for a sample of Nora Papenberg's handwriting anyway,' she murmured, looking at her copy of the note. The script was very rounded. Quite girly, even. No man wrote like that. At certain points in the text, you could see that the writer's hand must have been trembling.

Beatrice traced the letters with her finger: *it may be five years or even six*.

Why were the clues so vague? Did the Owner want to make it extra hard for them so more time elapsed before they found the next coordinates?

The Owner, a man. Or maybe it was a woman. Maybe it was a woman who was already dead, who had left behind a strikingly unusual legacy.

Beatrice leant over the photo and propped her forehead in both hands. It was time to come up with some scenarios.

Let's assume that the man whose hand they had found really had been killed by Nora Papenberg. That she had mutilated him, written the note, hidden the cache. Had the victim given her the tattoo first? If so, then there might be traces of her blood on the sawn-off hand. Beatrice made a note.

New scenario.

Let's assume that the dead man hadn't been the one who tattooed her – could Nora have done it herself? Beatrice's common sense cried out in protest. Why would someone tattoo themselves on such a sensitive place as the soles of the feet?

Self-punishment was one possibility. A form of penance, perhaps for killing and dismembering the man. And then

. . . Papenberg had fastened her hands behind her back with cable tie and jumped off the cliff face.

Absolute nonsense.

'Florin, is it theoretically possible to tie your own hands up with cable tie?'

Florin looked up from his notes. 'Of course. You'd just need to use your teeth to do it at the front. But behind the back – I imagine that'd be pretty difficult. Impossible, in fact. Unless you're flexible enough to climb through your own tied-up hands, if you see what I mean. Or . . . if you had a vice to clamp the ends of the cable tie together, then you could tighten the noose while your hands are in it.' He frowned. 'But then you wouldn't be able to get the clamped end out.' He pushed his notes aside. 'Are you wondering whether Nora Papenberg staged the whole thing herself, including her own death?'

'I just want to be certain we can rule it out, that's all. The way things stand, she seems a plausible perpetrator in some ways: the blood of a murder victim on her clothes and possibly even her handwriting on the note in the cache box.'

'Which we still need to check out.' He rotated his pencil between his fingers, lost in thought. 'So far, Papenberg's record seems completely clean, not so much as a parking ticket. If she did kill the man, then it was probably in the heat of the moment. Or self-defence.'

'Let's look at the facts. The unidentified man whose hand we found died before Nora, do we agree on that? Good. So logic would suggest that there's a third person involved.' With the tip of her finger, she fished a few specks of wood from her mouth which had ended up there as a result of all the pencil-chewing. 'After all, Nora did get a phone call from someone during her work dinner. Maybe it was a lover? So she fakes a headache and rushes off to meet the guy. But they get caught in the act, the wife tattoos the coordinates onto Nora, kills her husband, saws him up into pieces and hides one of his hands in the forest. Then she pushes Nora off the rock face to her death.'

Even before she had finished the last sentence, Beatrice was already shaking her head. 'No, women don't act like that. A dismembered body suggests a male killer.'

'There are exceptions.'

'True. We shouldn't rule out the possibility, but still . . .' Beatrice reached for her notepad. 'The ad agency. We need to question every single person who was there that evening. We'll pester the pathologist's office to give us the report on the sawn-off hand as soon as possible. And we'll follow the Owner's clues.' She looked at Florin, hoping for his agreement, but he was gazing beyond her into the distance.

'Those five days,' he said. 'So much time between her disappearance and her death. If we only knew what happened in that time span . . .'

Without breaking eye contact, Beatrice pinned the enlarged printed photo of the letter on the board above their desk. 'You're right,' she said. 'In five days, a person can change completely if you push them hard enough. We should keep that in mind with everything we find out about her.'

The thought stayed with her for the next few hours. *Five days*. She completed the list of choral Christophs and unearthed contact details for former choirmasters, but those five days kept circling relentlessly in her mind.

'Good afternoon, this is Beatrice Kaspary from Salzburg Landeskriminalamt. Am I speaking to Gustav Richter?'

'Erm, yes. What's—'

'Don't worry, nothing's happened. I just need some information from you. You lead the Arcadia chamber choir, if I've been correctly informed?'

A relieved sigh. 'Yes.'

'I have two rather unusual questions. Do you have a choir member called Christoph? Or a former member? The time period in question would be the last five to six years.'

'Why do you want to know that?'

'It's connected to a current investigation. Unfortunately I can't be any more specific than that.'

'Aha. Yes, we do have a Christoph. Two, for that matter – Christoph Harrer and Christoph Leonhart – and they both still sing with us.' A brief pause. 'Are they in some kind of trouble?'

'No, absolutely not. Did your choir perform Schubert's Mass in A flat around six years ago?'

This time, his answer came more quickly. 'Yes, that sounds about right. Let me think for a moment – yes. It must be almost six years ago now.'

Beatrice highlighted the two names.

'You've been a great help, thank you.' Her hand continued to hover over the notepad; one final question was burning on her tongue.

She took a deep breath.

'Is that all, Frau Kommissarin?'

'Yes. No, sorry, just a moment – there's one more thing, and it might sound strange, but I'll ask anyway. Do either of the two men have a birthmark on their hand? Something big, quite noticeable?'

'What? Why do you ask?'

Beatrice sighed inwardly; it was an understandable reaction. 'It could be an important detail in the case.'

'A birthmark?' He sounded slightly irritated, as if she was trying to make a fool of him. 'I've no idea why that might be of interest to you, but I'm afraid I can't help you there. I tend to concentrate more on my singers' voices, as it happens.'

Three further telephone enquiries revealed yet another Christoph. After that, the only choirs left on the list were the very small ones, and the ones whose choirmasters she had been unable to reach. 'That's already fourteen we have to check out in person.' Beatrice flung her pencil down on the desk in exasperation. 'With my luck the last one will end up being the one we're looking for. None of the choirmasters so far knew anything about a birthmark.'

'Same here.' Florin's outstretched arm fished for Beatrice's notes. 'I'll just type everything up, then get Stefan to hunt out the addresses.'

'Okay. I really need to grab a bite to eat. Can I bring you anything?'

Florin shook his head silently, already populating the table on his screen with names. The glum twist of his mouth reflected her own mood: yet another weekend without any time off.

One steak sandwich later, Beatrice ran into Stefan on her way back to her office. He was eagerly waving a sheet of paper at her.

'I've got a few addresses for you, and also the rehearsal times for four of the choirs. Interested?'

'You bet. Thanks!' She quickly scanned through the information. One of the choirs was rehearsing tonight at seven in the Mozarteum. She could just make it if she picked the kids up first, cooked them dinner and then asked Katrin to watch them for an hour. The neighbour's daughter's piggy bank must be almost bursting by now.

'Perfect.' Florin nodded as she explained her plan to him. 'I'll pick you up at a quarter to seven.'

By seven, after laminating schoolbooks, putting a load of washing on, cooking carbonara and taking a quick shower, Beatrice was sitting in the passenger seat next to Florin, hoping she didn't still smell of garlic.

'Christoph Gorbach and Christoph Meyer. Blue eyes and a birthmark. It shouldn't take long.'

'No,' replied Florin gruffly.

Beatrice resisted the impulse to give him a friendly nudge – after all, he was concentrating on the road. 'You're annoyed because of this weekend, right? Have you already told Anneke about the new case?'

Florin shrugged. 'I'm wondering whether I should cancel. I mean, there's no point her coming all this way if I have to work.' He turned off into Paris-Lodron-Strasse.

'Why cancel just yet? We'll bring Stefan onto the team – he's really fired up by the case and practically working on it already anyway.' She looked at Florin's profile. 'He and I will make sure that we find the right Christoph, then . . .'

Florin braked abruptly and manoeuvred into a space that had just become free at the side of the road. 'Have you considered the possibility,' he said, his gaze fixed on the rear-view mirror, 'that this whole puzzle nonsense could just be a red herring? The sick little mind games of a killer who wants to throw us off his scent by sending us on this ridiculous birthmark hunt?'

The idea had indeed occurred to Beatrice, earlier that evening when she was in the shower. They certainly couldn't rule out the possibility that they were allowing themselves to be led down the garden path, giving the killer enough time to erase his or her tracks.

'We'll see. If it turns out there's no man who meets the Owner's description, then all we'll have lost is a little time.'

'Yes, but we'll have lost it to him,' Florin objected.

The plastic container pushed its way back into Beatrice's mind. The dead hand.

'We don't have any other choice but to play the game, Florin. I don't like it any more than you do.'

They parked up and got out. Florin took her arm as they crossed the road, making their way towards the steel-and-glass cube that housed the Salzburg Mozarteum. 'The thing that makes me most angry,' he said, 'is the feeling that he's really enjoying all of this.'

'Pia mater, fons amoris'

Male voices singing in unison. A slow descent into inconsolable grief.

Beatrice paused in front of the door to the rehearsal room and lifted her hand to turn the door handle. But she couldn't bring herself to push it down. From all the songs they could have been rehearsing, it would have to be this piece.

'Pia mater, fons amoris
Me sentire vim doloris'

The female voices had tuned in now, soaring and full of hope.

'Fac, ut tecum lugeam.
Fac, ut ardeat cor meum
In amando Christum Deum,
ut sibi complaceam.'

Beatrice hadn't heard it since that day, but every note was familiar to her, every detail burnt into her memory. The smell of incense and flowers and grief, but above all the bitter metallic taste on her tongue that had stayed with her for months on end. Guilt was something that had to be suffered slowly.

'Beautiful,' whispered Florin at her side. 'I don't know what it is though . . . Puccini?'

'No. Joseph Rheinberger, the Stabat Mater.' She could feel that something inside her, something that had to remain hard at all costs, was starting to be softened by the music.

'I'm impressed. Where do you know it from?'

'It's often sung at funerals.' She pressed the door handle down brusquely. 'Right then, it's time to play. Our move.'

While Florin asked the two Christophs to step out of the rehearsal room so they could speak with each of them in turn, Beatrice pushed the unwelcome memory back into the hidden recesses of her mind, the place where it usually stayed, and tried to concentrate on the matter at hand.

It soon became apparent that they hadn't hit the bull's eye first time. Christoph Gorbach had only been in the choir for just under two years. The backs of his hands were very hairy, making it hard to tell at first, but on closer inspection there was no birthmark. Christoph Meyer, in turn, was a little hesitant to show his hands to Beatrice initially, but that was more down to his chewed fingernails than any conspicuous changes in skin pigmentation.

'Well, it was always unlikely we were going to find him right away,' said Florin with a faint smile as they left the rehearsal room and walked back out to the car. 'Anneke's flight is landing in Munich at half-two tomorrow, and I was hoping to pick her up,' he added. Feeling his sideways glance, Beatrice nodded.

'Let's work flat out in the morning, then you head off whenever you need to. I can carry on with Stefan and come in at the weekend.'

'Are you sure?'

'Yes. Achim will have the kids.' *He said he might be getting me a cat.* She turned her head to the side, gazing out of the car window.

They were almost there now. As Florin double-parked in

front of her building, she nodded to him, opened the door and got out.

'Wait, I almost forgot!' He turned around and reached for something which, in the dark, just looked like a shapeless lump. 'Make sure you tell Jakob they're an endangered species.'

Grey-brown fur. Huge yellow plastic eyes. 'Elvira the Second,' murmured Beatrice. 'Thank you. You've really helped me out there, I'd forgotten all about the massacred owl.'

'Don't mention it.' His eyes were tired, but he was smiling broadly. 'Sleep well.'

Her laptop was whirring so loudly that Beatrice worried it would wake the children, who had reluctantly crawled into bed only half an hour before. Jakob had immediately grabbed the new Elvira, stubbornly refusing to give it back. He gave in eventually, but not without a great deal of tears, for which Mina had called him a 'stupid crybaby'.

No, the laptop wasn't running very well at all. Beatrice gave it a smack, which instead of muting the noise just made it more noticeable. Presumably something had made its way into the ventilation slot and was now rattling around in the cooling system. Another quick smack and the rattling became a hum, considerably quieter now. Good, that had clearly done the trick.

Beatrice checked her emails, making sure there was nothing that needed an immediate response, then opened her browser.

She typed *www.geocaching.com* into the address bar. The site appeared on the screen; the colour logo and, a little further down on the right, an icon in the form of a little television with the prompt: *WATCH! Geocaching in 2 Minutes.*

The link led her to an animation which depicted, more or less, exactly the same things Stefan had explained to them the day before. Watching the little white cartoon figures search for orange boxes amidst a colourful animated landscape, Beatrice thought about the Owner. It was very likely that he had watched the film at some point too. Had he intended to fill his caches with such macabre contents back then?

'*He*'. *Why is the killer always a he in my head?* Her fingers drummed on the touchpad, making the mouse icon dart across the screen in abrupt jolts. On the right-hand side there was an option to select caches in your neighbourhood, but the coordinates could only be shown once you had registered and logged on.

A Basic Membership on Geocaching.com is free, the site announced cheerfully. Beatrice clicked on the grey button and was redirected to the registration form.

A username. Reminded of Stefan's – 'Undercover Cookie' – she couldn't help but grin.

Lost in thought, she stroked her fingertips across the keyboard. Something inconspicuous, innocuous. The cuddly owl caught her attention. Elvira. Excellent – but unfortunately the nickname was already taken. 'We won't let that deter us though, will we?' she murmured, typing *Elvira the Second* into the text field.

The registration process was uncomplicated enough, and soon the coordinates of the hiding places lay before her; it was even possible to look at each individual one on a geocaching Google map.

The maps were a great deal more helpful than the coordinates. Without hesitating for long, Beatrice searched for Lammertal, the region near Abtenau where Nora Papenberg's body had been found.

No, there was no cache listed there. There were a few in the surrounding area, clearly marked by little white box icons with green or orange lids. On the other side of the river, a blue question mark denoted a – what had Stefan called it again? – a 'mystery cache', that was it. But none of the hiding places were within 500 metres of the crime scene. Without taking her eyes off the map, Beatrice leant back and dragged the mouse down eastwards. She lost her orientation and accidentally expanded the scale so much she could see half of Salzburg. *Your search has exceeded 500 caches*, the program complained.

'Okay, calm down, hang on.' She zoomed back in. The stone chasm had to be somewhere around here. Searching the map, Beatrice noticed that there was a regular cache very close to the place where she and Florin had found the box with the dismembered hand. She read through the profile of the corresponding owner, then the comments of the successful treasure hunters. The container was hidden in a hole under a rock. But the most gruesome object in it was apparently a cross-eyed plastic pig.

Shaking her head, Beatrice leant back in her chair. What had she been expecting? That the killer would leave clues on the Internet for them?

On the off chance, she clicked through the profiles of the users who had commented on the stone chasm cache. Most of them would be easy to track down through the details they had given, and some had even included a photo – often depicting them out in the countryside, smiling, with a muddy plastic container in their hands. The picture of Nora Papenberg building a snowman would have fitted in perfectly here.

Beatrice read the entries and profile descriptions until her eyes were so tired they began to sting. Stefan had already spent the previous evening looking in the forums for leads, for any conspicuous members from the local area. It was a Sisyphean task. But if the perpetrator was from the geocaching community, it wasn't entirely impossible that he might betray himself through a post. They couldn't rule it out, at least.

Beatrice altered the map on the screen again and clicked on the second-nearest blue question mark she could find. It revealed a Sudoku, the solution of which was supposed to give the correct coordinates. Was that the standard kind of puzzle? Another blue question mark, however, revealed a load of numbers with no apparent system. It was a complete mystery.

She tried to suppress a yawn. 'Pretty complicated, huh, Elvira?' The cuddly owl's yellow plastic eyes stared unseeingly into nothingness.

Beatrice carried on searching, stumbling upon an online dictionary devoted exclusively to geocaching. One of the first links led her to a list of abbreviations. 'TFTH' was there, the one with which the Owner had so sarcastically signed off his message. Perfect. She decided she would read on for a little bit longer, then go to sleep. With the end of her working day finally in sight, Beatrice fetched a glass of wine and shunted her notepaper to the side. No more revelations would be presenting themselves today, no flashes of inspiration which ran the risk of being washed away into the depths of claret red forgetfulness.

She took a sip from her glass. The abbreviation 'BYOP' meant 'Bring Your Own Pen', and was usually found in caches that were too small to contain writing utensils of their own. 'HCC' was 'Hard Core Caching'; 'JAFT' stood for 'Just Another Fucking Tree' and denoted a *Tree Cache with Rope Technique*, whatever that was supposed to mean. Beatrice squinted, trying to ignore the headache that was threatening to take hold. She would have to go deeper into this material to make any sense of it, much deeper.

It was 10.35 p.m. She yawned again and caught herself wishing she could just snuggle up against the furry owl and go to sleep.

The shrill tone of the telephone was like a sudden punch to the chest. Beatrice jumped up from her chair, ran across the lounge and practically ripped the handset from the unit. Had the children woken up? Hopefully not. A telephone call this late could only mean something had happened. Another dead body, or another body part . . .

She braced herself for anything; anything, that was, except Achim's nightly onslaughts.

The stupid asshole.

'How lovely to actually get through for once.' As always, his voice was dripping with contempt. 'Make sure they're ready tomorrow, half-one on the dot. And this time remember to pack a jacket for the kids, and by that I mean one each. Mina almost froze to death last time.'

Don't let him get to you. 'Of course. Tomorrow at half-one,' she said curtly. 'And stop calling at this time of night – the children don't just need their jackets, they need their sleep too.'

'I don't need parental advice from you—!'

Acting on reflex, Beatrice hung up. Another thing he could use against her. The cosy sleepiness from a few moments ago had vanished; her heart was beating so hard it felt as if she'd just come back from a long run. But at least the children didn't seem to have stirred. She bookmarked the cache dictionary and shut down the laptop, unplugged the telephone, turned her mobile off and went to brush her teeth. As she brushed, she realised she was humming something, but couldn't place the sombre melody at first. Then she realised: it was the Stabat Mater.

'Herr Papenberg? I'm sorry to disturb you, but we need your assistance with something.' Beatrice strove to inject the right balance of sympathy and efficiency into her voice. 'Would you be able to provide us with a sample of your wife's hand-writing? A letter, a diary – or something along those lines?'

'For what?' He sounded exhausted.

'We have a note that may possibly have been written by your wife. We need to have the handwriting compared by a graphologist.'

She could hear him struggling to keep his voice steady. 'A note? Can I see it?'

'No, I'm afraid not. There's some information that we can't even make available to the next of kin. Not yet, in any case.'

'I understand,' he said wearily. 'Okay then. I need to run a few errands and I'll be in the area anyway, so I'll drop off a sample of her handwriting for you.'

'That would be great, thank you very much.'

That morning, Hoffmann had appointed Florin leader of 'Project Geocache', a name that had amused Beatrice for several minutes even though she couldn't have explained why. He now came through the door with Stefan in tow, who was beaming across his unshaven cheeks. 'I'm officially on board. Give me some work to do!'

'You'll live to regret it,' said Beatrice in mock earnest, pressing the list of choir rehearsals into his hands. 'We're still missing the rehearsal times for some of these. It would also be helpful to find out the private addresses of the singers we need to speak with. It's possible that some of the choirs are performing this Sunday, so I'd like us to check those out together.'

Stefan gave an exaggeratedly snappy salute, already on his way back to his office.

It's good that he's motivated, thought Beatrice with a glance at the clock. It was only half-nine, but she felt as if she already had an entire working day behind her. She had slept badly last night, dreaming intermittently of Achim and sawn-off limbs. Then she had just lain awake in the darkness, trying to make some sense of the case.

'We need to question the people from Nora Papenberg's work as soon as possible.' Florin pushed a piece of paper over the desk towards her, a printout of the contact details on the agency's home page.

'I know, and preferably today. We can do it as soon as I've spoken to Konrad Papenberg. He's bringing a sample of her handwriting across, and I really need to ask him something.' She wiped her eyes, too roughly; a few eyelashes were now clinging to the back of her hand.

'Should we send one of the others? Stefan could do it, or Sibylle, she—'

'No.' Hearing the hardness in her voice, she tried to soften it with a smile. 'I want to speak to them myself, otherwise I'll lose my sense of the case. It already has too many components as it is. The body, the coordinates. Then the puzzle, dismembered parts of a second body, and blood traces from that body on the clothing of the first. All of these things are connected, but I can't figure out in what way.' She inhaled deeply. 'Not yet, anyway.' *And I don't want anyone to beat me to it.* She didn't say it out loud, knowing that Florin was a great believer in teamwork and collaborative brainstorming. That was a good thing, of course — for him. But Beatrice found it hard to think clearly as part of a team. She had to do her thinking alone, or with one other person at the most. Any more than that and she just found it disruptive.

The shiny silver ballpoint pen which Florin was rotating between his fingers cast elongated reflections on the wall. 'Well, I still think it's possible that one of these threads is designed as a distraction for us, so we confirm the Owner's belief that the police are incompetent.'

Without saying anything in response, Beatrice began to sort out the files strewn all over her desk. The photo of the hand with its macerated skin, enclosed in plastic shrink-wrap. She placed it to the right of the photo of the stone chasm where they had found the box, and diagonally opposite the photo of the handwritten puzzle. She paused to take it all in. Then she changed the order around, waiting for the pictures to tell her a story. But they kept their silence.

'I'll tell Stefan to go with you to the agency,' she heard Florin say.

'Perfect.' She glanced at the clock and wished she could pick the kids up from school and drop them off at Achim's right away. Then she would have crossed one thing off today's to-do list. 'By the way,' she added, more loudly this time, 'the new owl was a hit. The children love it.'

'Good, then at least one of my missions has been successful.' He pushed back his chair and stood up. 'Keep your fingers crossed for my next one; I have to go and discuss our plan of action with Hoffmann. See you later.'

Konrad Papenberg arrived shortly before ten that morning, looking as though he had lost ten pounds in the last two days. Beatrice led him into one of the consultation rooms. She apologised for the stuffy air and opened the window.

'Yesterday I went to . . . identify Nora.' After every word he spoke, Papenberg seemed to need to summon up new strength. 'It was her . . . and yet it wasn't. Not properly, do you know what I mean? She wasn't a person. Just – a thing.' A jolt passed through his body; he turned aside, took a tissue from his pocket and wiped his eyes.

Beatrice paused to give him a moment. 'Yes, I know what you mean.' It wasn't a lie. She had never subscribed to the belief that dead people just looked as if they were sleeping. They looked like a foreign species. Shockingly different, even if they had died peacefully.

Papenberg forced a smile. 'Thank you. I realise this is nothing new for you.'

'That wasn't what I meant.' Beatrice searched for words.

'It's not something you ever get used to, that's the thing. It's always hard, every single time.' She fell silent. Was she bothering him with her own sensitivities? 'I'm really very sorry for what you're going through, that was what I wanted to say.'

He nodded jerkily, abruptly, without looking at Beatrice. 'The handwriting sample,' he mumbled, lifting his bag onto the desk.

A notepad, full of scribbled writing. Nora Papenberg had filled a good forty pages with brainstormed ideas, trying out and discarding advertising slogans alongside comments like 'too lame', 'stale', 'dull' – or 'not bad', 'has potential', 'promising'.

Beatrice would have been willing to bet two months' wages that the handwriting here was the same as that in the message in the cache box, but it would be unprofessional to jump to conclusions. Before she had the graphology report in her hands, nothing could be regarded as a sure thing.

'Thank you.' She laid both hands on the notepad. 'I'll make sure you get it back once we no longer need it.'

The man standing opposite her was gazing into space. 'A colleague of yours questioned me yesterday. He wanted an alibi from me, for the night when . . .' He was kneading the fingers of his left hand. 'I don't have one.' Now he looked Beatrice straight in the eyes. 'Are there many people who have alibis for crimes committed between two and four in the morning?'

'No.'

'I didn't . . .'

'We have to ask. It's part of the routine investigation process.' Beatrice tried to add some warmth into her smile. 'There's something else I'd like to ask if possible – don't

67

worry, it's not connected to you.' She stroked her fingers across the notebook, feeling the swirling imprints left behind by the pressure of Nora Papenberg's pen. 'Your wife liked spending time in the great outdoors, is that right? Is it possible that geocaching was one of her hobbies?'

Konrad Papenberg's expression was one of confusion. 'Geo – what?'

Perhaps not, then. 'Geocaching,' repeated Beatrice, disheartened. 'It's a kind of treasure hunt. You use a GPS device, work with coordinates . . .' She kept her gaze trained on his face, but the last word didn't provoke any reaction from him.

'Oh, right, yes, I've heard about that somewhere,' said Papenberg flatly. 'And it . . . it sounds like something Nora would have enjoyed.' He swallowed and looked up at the ceiling to blink back the tears that were building up. 'But it's not something we ever did. There's . . . so much we never did.'

Beatrice handed him a tissue and waited.

'How long were you married?'

'Almost two years. We met three years ago. Next week is – would have been – our anniversary.'

'I really am very sorry.' She stood up and pushed the chair back. 'We'll do everything we can to find her killer.' She really meant it, but her words still sounded hollow. 'If something else comes to mind which you think might be helpful to us, do please get in touch, okay?'

Konrad Papenberg nodded absent-mindedly. He let Beatrice walk him to the door and went to shake her hand, only then noticing that he was still holding the crumpled-up tissue in his. As if this discovery made everything even worse, he leant back against the wall and closed his eyes. 'I just really need to know what happened,' he whispered. 'Do you understand?'

'I do, very much so,' answered Beatrice. 'We won't give up, I promise.'

She watched him as he went back outside to his car, a green Mazda that he had parked with one wheel up on the kerb. His posture didn't change, whereas the opposite was often the case when people left the police station and felt that they were no longer being watched.

Beatrice turned and went back to her office, the notepad clamped tightly under her arm. Florin must still be talking to Hoffmann. His mobile was on his desk, seemingly forgotten. The display lit up, indicating an incoming call or message.

No, she wouldn't look to see what it was.

What would even make her contemplate such a thing? It must be the lack of sleep.

She opened up her contact list on the computer and dialled the graphologist's phone number.

'Juliane Heilig.'

'Beatrice Kaspary here, Salzburg Landeskriminalamt. I need a graphology report, a handwriting comparison. Can I email the documents through to you?'

'Of course. What exactly would you like to know?'

'Whether the two pieces were composed by the same person.'

'No problem. How urgent is it?'

'The beginning of next week would be great. But if you

could give me your first impressions today – off the record, of course – then that would be a great help.'

A brief pause. 'I'll see what I can do.'

Beatrice stared at each of them in turn, the cheerful scribbles on the notepad and the copy of the handwritten cache letter. 'It's very probable that one of the samples was written under stress. In extreme circumstances.'

'That's useful to know, thank you.' Heilig gave her the email address, and Beatrice sent the documents through to her. She had barely sat back down at her desk before Stefan rushed in.

'I've got almost all the rehearsal times for the choirs now – it was quite a mission!' He looked at Beatrice expectantly, prompting her to nod in approval.

'Excellent work.'

'Thanks. Three choirs are singing on Sunday – two at Mass, one at a wedding. If we split them up between us we could check them all out.' He handed her a note detailing the names of the choirs in question, along with the times, churches and addresses.

'Good work, Stefan. I mean it, you're being a great help.'

He beamed. 'I'll go and make some more calls – it makes sense to get through the list today.'

On his way out, he almost crashed into Florin, who was storming in with a dark expression on his face.

'Bad news?' asked Beatrice.

'No. Just Hoffmann's usual persecution complex. The press are on his back, so he wants to give the journalists more information than we'd like.' Florin sank down into his revolving chair and darted a glance at the clock on the wall.

'He doesn't like the fact that we didn't inform him right away and give him the chance to check out the crime scene himself.'

That was nothing new. 'But we tried to.'

'Yes, I know, but he says we didn't try hard enough. Anyway, he's sulking and lashing out. He wants us to put pressure on the husband. Let's hope he cheers up over the weekend, otherwise he's going to be constantly sticking his oar in.'

Half-past ten. For the third time, Beatrice tried to reach Dr Vogt at the Institute for Forensic Medicine, but still without success. Then she tried his mobile. To her surprise, she got through.

'I'm busy,' said Vogt, without wasting time on a greeting.

'I'm sorry to hear that. But I'm still going to need some preliminary information if I can't get the report before the weekend.'

'The Papenberg report?'

'No, the one on the severed hand. In order to find out who it belonged to, I at least need some clues.'

The pathologist sighed. 'There's not much I can tell you. The hand belonged to a man, but with the best will in the world I can't tell you when he died. The decaying process was delayed by the plastic shrink-wrapping, so there was no maggot infestation or anything of the sort.'

'I see.'

'The victim's age is equally difficult to estimate. I'd say somewhere between thirty-five and fifty. The blood group is O positive.'

'Have you already taken fingerprints?'

Vogt cleared his throat. 'Of course. I'll do my best to get the report to you today. And there's one more thing – the man must have worn a ring for a long time, because there was an indentation on the fourth finger. I'm guessing it was a wedding ring. If I had to hazard a guess, I'd say that he had a rendezvous with a lover and took the ring off, or that he was recently divorced.'

Jealousy climbed back up on Beatrice's list of potential murder motives. 'Thank you. So the report . . .'

'Will be with you as soon as possible. Of course.'

Between thirty-five and fifty years old. Beatrice searched despondently through the information on male missing persons, expanding her search to the whole of Austria. Three of the notices had been filed in the last week, but the individuals in question were either older or significantly younger. So was no one missing the man whose hand they had found?

She scrolled through the remaining reports, one after the other, searching for possible connections to Nora Papenberg, for similar professions. When she next glanced at the clock, over two hours had passed. Damn it! She jumped up, wrenched her bag from the back of the chair and dashed towards the door. She'd be lucky to get there on time, yet again.

The traffic was heavy, as it always was on Fridays, and by the time Beatrice finally pulled up at the school she could see Mina and Jakob sitting on a bench in front of the entrance, waiting for her. Mina was gesticulating in front of Jakob's face, clearly giving him an important pedagogical speech.

'You're late,' said Mina accusingly as she got into the car. 'I know, I'm sorry. Did you guys have a good day?'

'We made an alphabet chain,' crowed Jakob cheerfully. 'Do you know what my favourite letter is?'

'Hmm. J?'

'No, X. Exxxxx!' He pronounced it, savouring the sound.

'And how was your day, Mina?'

'It was okay. Can we drive a bit quicker?'

Back at home, Mina rushed straight over to her bag, which was half-packed in the children's room, and stuffed two of her bathing suits in it. Beatrice put some fish fingers in a pan on the stove, checked Jakob's report book for any messages announcing impending disaster, then added jackets, rain trousers, pullovers and an additional pair of shoes to their bags.

'Has Papa already bought you toothbrushes?'

'Yes. Mine is green and has a car on it,' cried Jakob. 'Can I watch TV?'

'No, lunch is nearly ready.'

The frozen fish fingers were sizzling away nicely, but they only had fifteen minutes. She was sure to have forgotten something – *oh, God, their pyjamas.*

'No one go near the stove,' she ordered, running over to the cupboard to take out two pairs of pyjamas.

Her mobile vibrated on the worktop, playing the first few bars of 'Message in a Bottle', signalling the arrival of a text message.

If there was a guardian angel for single mothers, then it would be a text from Achim saying that he was stuck in traffic and running late. Beatrice stuffed the pyjamas in the bag and reached for the mobile, pulling a fork from the cutlery drawer with her other hand to check the fish fingers.

73

'Wash your hands, you two, dinner will be ready soon!' she called towards the children's bedroom, turning up the heat before wiping her fingers on a kitchen towel and pressing the menu button on the mobile. She opened the message.

It was from an unknown number, and it consisted of just one word.

Slow.

Her first thought was that it was a wrong number. What was it supposed to mean? Was someone asking her to slow down? She stared at the display, trying to make some sense of the message, then remembered the fish fingers. She pulled the pan off the hob.

'Come and sit down at the table!'

Slow. The word crept into her consciousness as if it were trying to illustrate its own meaning. Could it be . . . that the Owner was making contact with her? Was that possible?

All of a sudden, she felt hot, far hotter than standing over the stove had made her.

In his cache message, he had addressed the police directly. What if he was doing it again? Did he want to make contact personally? But — why with her? And where would he have got her number from?

'Mama, I want ketchup!' Jakob's voice forced its way into her mind as if from afar. She had to be patient for a moment longer. Soon Achim would be here, and then . . .

'I'll get it. Leave Mina's glass alone.'

'But she's got more juice!'

Beatrice decided she would call the number. That would be much better than spending her time guessing. But only once the children had gone.

When the doorbell rang, Jakob was just shoving the last bite of fish finger into his mouth. 'Papa!' He jumped up, knocking his chair over in the process, and ran out into the hallway.

Beatrice ran after him, but Jakob had already managed to reach the intercom system. 'Papa?' he mumbled with his mouth full.

She took the receiver from his hand. 'You know very well that you're not allowed to buzz anyone in!'

'But—'

'No buts. Go and wash your face. You're covered in ketchup.'

The irritated snort that came through the intercom was sufficient for her to be sure it was Achim at the door. Beatrice pressed to buzz him in, hearing his footsteps on the stairs seconds later. For a moment she wished she could run away and avoid seeing him, but by then his head, with its thinning blond hair, was already visible through the banisters.

'Hello,' she said, attempting a smile which was intended to signify a willingness to be civil. 'The children are almost ready.'

He glanced at her briefly and didn't even reply.

'Papa!' cheered Mina from behind her. 'Guess what? Today at school I was the only one who knew that Helsinki was the capital of Finland!'

'That's excellent, Mouse. You're the best.' Achim leant over to Mina and pressed her against him, prompting unexpected tears to well up in Beatrice's eyes. For heaven's sake, what was wrong with her? She turned away quickly and fetched the children's bags. Despite the fact that Achim still refused to look at her, she used all the energy she had to keep her smile going. In five minutes' time, the encounter would be over. At her side, Jakob was tugging at her trouser leg. 'Mama?'

'Yes?'

'Can't you come too?'

She knelt down next to him. 'No, unfortunately I can't. But you'll have a great time, and if you want you can call me in the evening. Okay?'

He nodded uncertainly. 'I packed Fleece,' he whispered. 'Do you think Papa will be mad at me?'

Fleece. Also known as the grubbiest toy rabbit in the world.

'No, Papa understands that you can't sleep without him.'

Achim had released Mina from their hug. 'Come on, kids. Let's get some fresh air, it smells awful in here!'

'I don't think so,' protested Jakob. 'It's fish finger air!'

'Exactly.' A disdainful shake of the head as he rolled his eyes. 'And let's make sure you get a proper dinner tonight too. Come on, we're off!'

Beatrice hugged her children. Mina was in a hurry, struggling to get loose. 'Are we buying the cat soon?' she asked as she ran down the steps. 'I've already thought of a name.'

'Remember, Sunday at half-six, on the dot,' said Achim to Beatrice, before taking Jakob by the hand and leaving. Instead of waiting until they were out of sight, Beatrice shut the door right away. Only now did she realise how hard she had been gritting her teeth; they were hurting.

She flung the window open, letting fresh air into the apartment. She could hear Jakob's cheerful jabbering coming from downstairs, and she felt her stomach clench painfully.

Then she remembered the message on her mobile. *Slow.*

The prefix was, if she wasn't mistaken, that of a prepaid provider which sold cards and top-up codes in supermarkets. Beatrice opened the message and pressed 'Call'.

A friendly female voice informed her that the connection was not available right now and that she should try again later.

Slow. It's an observation. Or an accusation. Directed at us because we haven't yet decoded the clues to the next stage?

If that was the case, then the Owner had exposed himself in a way that could prove to be his downfall. Slamming the window shut with a bang, Beatrice grabbed her car keys from the counter and set off back to the office.

The Department of Public Prosecutions took less than an hour to approve her request to have the mobile phone located. While Beatrice sat with the phone to her ear, waiting to be put through to the technical department of the mobile provider, her gaze fell on a new neon pink Post-it that Hoffmann had stuck to her monitor. *Meeting on Monday, 3 p.m., attendance compulsory.* Wonderful. That was sure to be the highlight of her day.

A young male voice spoke up at the other end of the line. 'What can I do for you?'

'Beatrice Kaspary, Landeskriminalamt. I need some information about the number 0691 243 57 33. I'd like to know whether it's contracted or a prepaid mobile.'

Silence. Then: 'You're from the LKA?'

'Yes, Beatrice Kaspary, Murder Investigation Department.'

The sound of paper rustling. The clatter of a keyboard. 'It's a prepaid card.'

Shit. 'So I presume you can't tell me who it belongs to?'

'No, I'm afraid not. People don't have to give any ID when—'

'I understand,' she interrupted. 'Okay, then in that case I need the mobile's identifier. A message was sent from the number at 13.17 to the following recipient.' Beatrice recited her own number. 'I'd also like to know which network the device was connected to at the time. How long will it take you to get that information?'

She must have sounded extremely bossy, as when the man at the other end answered, his voice sounded both intimidated and defiant at the same time. 'I'm not sure. It's the weekend, so I'll need to see if there's someone here who can—'

'If no one's there, then you'll have to get someone there!' She tried to rein herself in and adopt a more friendly tone, but her insides were vibrating like a plucked guitar string. 'It's important. It would be an immense help if you could get the information to me as soon as possible.'

'I'll see what I can do.'

Beatrice hung up and propped her face in her hands. *Slow?* If we are, then it's certainly not because of me.

She pulled the pathologist's report towards her and immersed herself in the details relating to the severed hand.

The sawdust which had been found in the wound came from bay and spruce trees – the most common in the local area, so not very helpful. Earth had been found under the fingernails, and there were also traces of soapy water on the skin – presumably the killer had washed the hand before shrink-wrapping it—

'Beatrice?'

She jumped. She hadn't heard Stefan come in.

'Yes?'

'I spoke to the agency earlier – they'll all be there if we go now.' He smiled, shy and excited, as if he had just asked to open a Christmas present two days early and was now waiting expectantly for her permission.

She couldn't help but smile back. 'Right. Thanks for taking care of that. I'll just get my things together. Can you grab the Dictaphone?'

The stale biscuits laid out in a bowl on the circular conference table seemed appropriate for the sombre occasion. Two men and three women were sitting around the table. When Beatrice and Stefan walked in, the taller of the men stood up and stretched out his hand. 'Max Winstatt. I'm the owner of the agency, and I want to offer whatever assistance I can to help you find out how Nora died.' His accent indicated that he wasn't from Salzburg; perhaps the Ruhr valley, thought Beatrice.

'I'm Kommissarin Beatrice Kaspary, and this is my colleague Stefan Gerlach.' She put her bag down on a vacant chair. 'Is there a room where we can talk without any interruptions? I'd like to speak with each of you alone.'

Winstatt nodded emphatically and led Beatrice into a neighbouring room, which was dominated by a large glass desk. 'You can use my office.' He paused at the door. 'Rosa, could you bring us some coffee, please?' he called out. 'You'll have a cup, won't you, Frau Kaspary? With milk and sugar? We're all so devastated by Nora's death, it's hard to believe she was . . .'

Beatrice waved Stefan over to put the Dictaphone on the desk. She took her notepad and pen out from her bag.

'We can start with you if that's okay, Herr Winstatt. Would you please close the door?'

He followed her command at once, then sat down in his chair and clasped his hands on the desk.

'Could you describe for me the evening of Nora's disappearance – from your perspective? Everything you can remember about the course of events, and of course everything that relates to Nora herself.'

He paused a moment before starting to speak. Good. Perhaps that meant there was more to his rhetoric than just smooth clichés.

'We reserved a table at the restaurant for 7 p.m., and Nora was one of the first to arrive. She was in a cheerful mood and seemed completely carefree, if you know what I mean.'

Beatrice nodded. 'What was she wearing?'

He only had to think for a moment. 'A red jacket. Trousers. I can't remember what was under the jacket, something nondescript. But Rosa took some photos that evening. Erich too, on his mobile, if I'm not mistaken.'

Beatrice and Stefan exchanged surprised looks. 'Excellent. Do you have the photos here?'

'I'm sure Erich has his phone on him, and Rosa might have her camera too. It's one of those compact ones, so they're really easy to carry around with—'

'Okay,' Beatrice interrupted. 'Let's come back to the photos in a moment. So, Nora was there early and in a good mood. What happened next?'

'We all had an aperitif, and then I made a short speech.

We had just managed to secure a budget which is amazing for a company the size of ours, you see – that's why we were celebrating. Then we ordered the food.'

'Was Nora sitting next to you?'

'No, she was next to Irene. Irene Grabner, she's a copywriter too. But I know what she ordered – fish soup to start, then sweetbreads in Madeira sauce. I had the same, that's why I remember . . .'

What an inappropriate moment to become aware of the emptiness of her own stomach. Beatrice thought with dull longing of the biscuits on the conference-room table.

'We all had wine too, in case that's important,' Winstatt continued.

There was a knock at the door, and one of the female employees came in balancing a tray with three coffee cups.

'Are you Rosa?' asked Beatrice.

'Yes,' said the woman, looking at her boss hesitantly. 'Rosa Drabcek.'

'Do you have your camera with you? The one with the pictures from the work dinner?'

'I . . . I think so. I'll go and see.'

'Then we'll speak to you next.' Beatrice took one of the cups with a grateful smile, then sipped the coffee. Black and strong. Her stomach contracted in protest, but she drank another sip regardless.

'So, you had wine.' She picked the topic of conversation back up. 'Did Nora drink a lot?'

Winstatt hesitated. 'No, I mean . . . one glass, or maybe two. Plus the Prosecco we had at the beginning of the evening. She certainly wasn't drunk, if that's what you mean.

Slightly tipsy at most.' He stared down at the table, embarrassed. 'Do you think she would have had a better chance against her murderer if she had been completely sober?'

'That's hard to say. Please continue.'

She could see from his face that he was trying to compose himself. 'We were halfway through the main course when her mobile rang. She took it out from her handbag and made some jokey comment about her husband. Then she said something like, "Oh, it's not him," and answered it. We carried on talking, of course, so I don't know what she was speaking to the caller about, but after a few seconds she got up and went off towards the toilets with her phone.'

'As if she didn't want anyone at the table to hear her conversation?' Beatrice interrupted.

'Yes. Or perhaps it was just too loud and she wanted to find somewhere quieter to talk. That was the impression I had, at least. But if I'm honest I wasn't really paying that much attention to Nora at the time.'

The telephone conversation. She glanced questioningly at Stefan. He understood at once and, in a barely perceptible movement, shook his head. That meant the list of Nora's phone conversations which they had requested from the provider hadn't arrived yet.

'She wasn't on the phone for that long,' continued Winstatt. 'Three, maybe four minutes. Then she came back to the table.'

'Did she carry on eating?'

Winstatt shrugged his shoulders apologetically. 'I'm not sure, sorry. Probably. But then she left about twenty minutes later. She said she was heading back home, that she had a headache.'

That corresponded to what Beatrice had found out from Konrad Papenberg.

'When she left the restaurant – was she alone, or did anyone else leave at the same time?'

This time, Winstatt shook his head decisively. 'She was definitely alone. It wasn't much later than half-nine, and we tried to convince her to stay, but she didn't want to. She looked pretty exhausted too, so I don't think she was feeling very well.'

'Okay. Thank you. Right, so I'd like to speak with . . .' She glanced at her notes. 'Rosa Drabcek next. And also see the pictures on her camera if I can.'

Rosa Drabcek wasn't a secretary but an executive assistant, as she emphasised right at the start of the conversation. Stefan, who had unwittingly stuck his foot in it by mentioning the word 'secretary' as they introduced themselves, nodded guiltily. Beatrice, on the other hand, only had eyes for the camera, the small, metallic blue device that was resting in Drabcek's hands.

'I haven't yet downloaded the pictures from the meal,' she said apologetically, 'but the display is quite big, so you should be able to see everything well enough.' She turned the camera on, activated the viewing mode and handed it to Beatrice. 'I took quite a lot of pictures, but I hope they can be of help in some way.'

Hohensalzburg Castle, illuminated at night, was captured in at least ten images. There was a wonderful view from the restaurant over to the mountain and castle, and it was clear that the executive assistant hadn't been able to get enough of it.

Next, the table, smartly set and still free of guests, plates and mess. Four photos. Winstatt, standing behind a chair with his head turned to the side. Then the castle again.

'The camera takes good pictures, don't you think?' commented Drabcek.

Sure, if you looked beyond the nondescript subject matter . . . Beatrice clicked on impatiently to the next photo, and the next – there was nothing she could use here. But they would still copy all the photos to a memory stick to be sure.

Beatrice looked up. 'Do you mind me asking why you took so many pictures? You must have hardly had time to eat.'

A shy smile. 'It's a new camera. I wanted to see what it can do. I really love photography, you know.'

Finally, some pictures of people. A young woman with an updo, wearing a short electric blue dress. A man with glasses and an expensive-looking suit – if Beatrice's memory served her correctly, he was sitting outside right now, waiting to be questioned.

Then, right at the end, Nora Papenberg. The clothes she was wearing in the picture were without a doubt the same as those she had been found in. The jeans, the red silk jacket, the blouse with the delicate flower pattern. High-heeled red shoes which matched the jacket. The shoes that hadn't yet turned up.

Nora was beaming into the camera, making a victory sign with the fingers on her right hand.

The next picture. Nora sitting next to the woman in the blue dress. 'Is that Irene . . .?'

'Irene Grabner,' Drabcek eagerly completed her sentence. 'Yes. She always dolls herself up like that.'

It suited her though, Beatrice reflected. She clicked further forwards. Nora and Irene with their arms around each other's shoulders, smiling. Then a picture of the young man in a suit, one of Winstatt and another woman, and numerous shots of the whole table; the group now seemed to be complete. Drabcek was taking the photographs, of course, although she was in a few of the last ones herself. 'Nora took those,' she said softly.

Nora. Beaming happily in every shot. Beatrice continued to scroll through the images. Aperitifs, the group clinking glasses. The meal being served. A few close-ups of sumptuously presented plates. The colleagues, eating. Conversations.

Then, suddenly, Nora's seat was empty. Beatrice squinted. Was she visible in the background at all? No, not in this photo. The next one had been taken from a wider angle, but the background was blurred. Another picture, a red splodge which looked like the colour of Nora's jacket.

Five photos later, she was back at her seat. Even on the small display, Beatrice could see that something must have happened, as Nora was no longer smiling. Her eyes were gazing past the lens. Into nothing. Or into herself. In one of the subsequent shots, she had pulled the candle across the table towards her and was staring into the little flame.

Then came a series of photos in which Nora was nowhere to be seen. They were all of her colleagues, laughing, toasting, gesticulating. A half-full and an empty bottle of wine stood on the table.

I can't let myself think too single-mindedly, Beatrice reminded herself. The call wasn't necessarily the catalyst. It's entirely possible that she really had just drunk too much alcohol and given herself a headache.

In the next photo, she was sitting there, both elbows propped on the table in front of her, holding her head. Then there were several of the desserts, followed by a group picture in which Nora's chair was empty again.

Nora didn't appear in any of the final photos. Beatrice passed the camera to Stefan. 'We'll copy the pictures to a memory stick and take them with us. I hope you don't mind.'

'Sure, no problem.'

While Stefan pulled a laptop and USB cable from his bag, Beatrice leant over the desk and looked at Rosa Drabcek silently for a few moments. Usually this made people begin to talk hurriedly, blurting out things that they might not otherwise say, but Drabcek clearly wasn't one of those people. She remained silent.

'Was there anything about Nora Papenberg's behaviour that stood out that evening? Even something seemingly minor?'

She shook her head. 'No. She was just her usual self – until the headache started, anyway, but even that wasn't out of the ordinary for her. She used to get migraines from time to time. She always had a packet of tablets on her desk.'

'Did Nora mention who she was speaking to on the phone?'

'No. But then I didn't ask.'

'Okay. I'd like you to tell me about the evening from your perspective.'

Her narrative differed only marginally from what Winstatt had told them. Once they had finished, Beatrice saw Rosa Drabcek to the door of the office and asked her to send Irene Grabner in.

Even without the electric blue dress, Grabner looked – how had Rosa put it? – dolled up, that was it. But she was clearly one of those women who could wrap themselves in a tablecloth and still look fantastic. Stefan was beaming at her, transfixed. Beatrice shot him a quick, chiding glance, upon which he toned down his smile to a more professionally acceptable level.

'You were sitting next to Nora Papenberg at the work dinner. Please tell me everything you can remember from the moment after Nora's phone rang.'

Grabner lowered her head and wiped a tear from the corner of her eye with her perfectly manicured hand. 'We were having so much fun at first,' she said. 'Nora was in a really good mood. I mean, it was mostly down to her that we had managed to secure the budget. It was really *her* evening. When her phone rang, she giggled, saying it was sure to be Konrad asking her to smuggle some of the dessert out in her handbag.' Irene Grabner broke off, looked away. 'We were really good friends, you know? I'm . . . I don't understand . . . how . . .'

Stefan nodded. 'Take your time.' Noticing that he had lowered his voice by an octave, Beatrice couldn't help but smile.

'So, her mobile rang, and Nora looked at the number on the display. "That's not Konrad," I remember her saying, but she answered it anyway, saying something a little cheeky like, "Anyone who's calling me in the middle of a party had better be male, young and gorgeous."' Grabner took a deep breath. 'Then she stopped smiling, stood up and went into a faraway corner of the restaurant. I didn't hear anything of the conversation – all I could see was her back.'

'Were there any other people over where she was talking?' Beatrice interjected. 'Who might have heard something?'

She shook her head. 'No. I think she intentionally sought out a quiet spot, so she wouldn't be disturbed.'

'And then what?'

'I asked her who it was, and she just said, 'Oh, no one you know.' And that it was nothing important. But from then on, her good mood had vanished. She left soon after, and I wish I'd gone with her. But I didn't know . . .'

Grabner's voice failed her. Beatrice felt the urge to give her a hug, to tell her how well she understood what she was going through. She wanted to tell her to exorcise the word 'if' from her mind.

If I had gone with her.

If I had taken her home.

If . . .

Beatrice dug her fingernails into the palm of her hand. Her own problems had nothing to do with this case. She smiled at the woman, giving her a moment to calm herself down.

'When Nora left,' she probed further, 'did she say she was going to drive home? Or was she going somewhere else?'

'Home. I'm sure of it. She had one of her headaches, and wanted to go to bed. I remember Herr Winstatt offering to get her a taxi – the company would have paid for it of course – but she said she was fine. The migraine hadn't kicked in fully, and she didn't want to leave her car there overnight. That was typical of her, and it would have been pointless trying to convince her otherwise.'

'Do you have any idea of how much Nora drank?'

Irene Grabner looked at her hands, which were clasped

on the table in front of her. 'Not exactly. But she wasn't drunk, if that's what you mean. She knew she would be driving, after all, so she didn't overdo it.'

No new information arose in their conversations with the rest of the agency colleagues. At the time, none of them had placed any great significance on Nora's early departure. They were shocked by her death, as could be expected, but there was nothing out of the ordinary in their testimonies. The photos which Erich, the account manager, had taken on his mobile didn't show anything that Rosa Drabcek's pictures hadn't already captured, but Stefan transferred them to his laptop nonetheless.

Before heading off, they had a look at Nora's desk.

Organised chaos. It was very similar to how Beatrice's desk looked when she was immersed in a case: the seemingly random distribution of documents on the desk forming an associative network that stretched out before her, all the component parts communicating, forming links, reaching their invisible tentacles out towards one another.

Maybe that's how Nora had worked, too, when she was dreaming up an advertising campaign. Another parallel jumped out at Beatrice: the yellow Post-its on the computer screen, except here they weren't from the boss but from Nora herself. That same handwriting again, now so familiar.

Pick up jacket from drycleaners, said one of the notes. The other two revealed telephone numbers, scribbled alongside the names they belonged to.

'Do you know who these people are?' Beatrice asked Max Winstatt, who was waiting behind her.

'Business contacts. A graphic designer and a client we're hoping to get a follow-up commission from.'

The desk drawers were much neater than the surface of the desk itself, containing stacks of writing paper, headache tablets, cough sweets and a half-eaten bar of chocolate, 70 per cent cocoa. Seeing it suddenly made Beatrice feel much sadder than any other detail of the case had. It would never have occurred to Nora Papenberg that she wouldn't be around to finish it.

She turned away hastily. 'That's all for today. Thank you for your help.'

Winstatt accompanied her and Stefan to the door. 'If you need anything else, please don't hesitate to call me.'

'Of course.'

The car was parked in the next street. Stefan laid the laptop gently on the back seat before getting behind the steering wheel. 'Oh, shit. This wasn't a short-stay parking zone, was it?'

Beatrice, who had only just opened the passenger door, leant over and reached for the piece of paper that was tucked under the windscreen wiper. 'No, it's just some advertisement, there's no—' She had been about to say, 'plastic sleeve around it', but the words stuck in her throat. She stared at the unfolded piece of paper shaking in her hand.

TFTH.

The Owner had sent them another message.

Drasche sniffed disdainfully as he took the little plastic bag Beatrice had put the message into. 'And I'm assuming you touched it without gloves, right?'

'Of course. I thought it was just a flyer.'

A grim nod. 'So you said.'

'If you had your way,' said Beatrice, 'we'd never be allowed to take our gloves off, because the whole world is made up of potential evidence, right?'

A trace of a smile crept across Drasche's face. 'Yes, that's pretty much it.'

Back in her office, Beatrice called the mobile provider to chase up the research on the text message. To her surprise, they were ready with the results.

'We were just about to call you,' said the young man at the other end of the phone. She heard him shuffle through his paperwork. 'The mobile the card is being used with isn't connected to a network cell right now. It was last connected when the text message was sent, the one you received. At 13.16 at a UMTS cell in Hallein.'

'What can you tell me about the phone's owner?'

The *owner*. She tried to rein herself in. *Don't jump to conclusions*.

'I can give you the IMEI and the IMSI; in other words, the mobile's device number and user identification. That's all, I'm afraid. I can also block the number for you if you like.'

'No, certainly not!' The words tumbled out. Every sign of life from the Owner – if it was him who had sent the message – was another chance that he might let his guard down.

Each of the two numbers was fifteen digits long. Beatrice

got him to read them out twice to eliminate any possibility of making a mistake. 'Thank you. I just have one more request – I need a complete list of the connections that were made by this mobile, if you could get that ready for me.' She gave the man her email address, thanked him again, hung up and leant back in her chair. With any luck, she would have a name soon. If the mobile hadn't made its way to its owner illegally, then he had blown his cover with that text message. But only if he was that stupid. She pushed the thought away and concentrated on the IMEI she had noted down. She remembered something Florin had told her a few weeks ago when he had turned up in the office with a new phone. Just to be sure, she checked the information online too.

The first eight digits of the IMEI formed the TAC, the Type Approval Code, in which the third to eighth numbers were the decisive ones – denoting device brands and types. If you knew how to read them, that was. Which she definitely didn't; she would need to consult an expert, or at least Stefan . . .

Following a flash of inspiration, she typed *TAC end device analysis* into Google and found a link promising to reveal the corresponding mobile model upon the code being entered. Beatrice typed in the first eight digits.

Bingo.

Manufacturer: Nokia Mobile Phones
Model: Nokia N8-00
TAC: 35698804

She felt her pulse start to race, but wasn't yet sure why.

The phone was a Nokia, which wasn't uncommon by any stretch of the imagination. But in this context . . .

Rummaging through her papers, she found the notes from her first conversation with Konrad Papenberg, the day they had informed him about his wife's murder.

There it was. Nokia N8.

I gave it to her for her birthday.

She stood up and turned the espresso machine on. But on remembering how much coffee she had drunk at the agency and how disgruntled her stomach had been, she turned it off again.

It could be a coincidence, but she doubted it. Gathering up her notes from the conversation with the provider, along with a printout of the online analysis page, she went off to Stefan's office. 'Could you find out who this mobile is registered to?'

He glanced at the papers, his finger wandering to the neatly circled IMSI code. 'Sure, no problem.'

'Thanks.'

At the door, she realised that her curt request had implied he had all the time in the world, but she left it at that. She was willing to bet anything that the name his research unearthed would be Nora Papenberg.

The evening sun painted stripes across the wooden floor of the balcony. Beatrice shunted the little round wooden table into the pink-tinged light and laid her Friday evening meal out on it: sushi from the Japanese restaurant two streets down. She opened the plastic container, inhaled the aroma of fresh fish and ginger and hoped that her appetite would finally kick in. But no such luck. The only dinner of interest to her was the agency one after which Nora had disappeared, running off into her murderer's arms. The Owner, the master of the cryptic messages.

The most recent note, meticulously examined by Drasche, hadn't offered up any new clues. 'Not one single fingerprint, apart from yours of course,' were his words. 'We're still investigating the ink type, but it seems to be from some bog-standard mass-produced biro.'

Drasche hadn't been interested in how the very existence of the note told them a great deal about the Owner. That wasn't his job.

When she had driven home that evening, Beatrice had parked her car a street further up from her apartment, looking around several times to check whether anyone was following her, or even just watching her. She hadn't noticed anyone, but had double-locked the door behind her just in case.

She sighed, looked at the sushi box on the table and found herself thinking about beef carpaccio and Anneke, even though she'd never met her. Dinner for two by candlelight. She wondered whether she should put a candle on her balcony table.

But she deposited her rattling laptop on it instead and had another look through the photos of the agency dinner, cursing when soya sauce dripped down onto her grey marl jogging bottoms.

She concentrated on the pictures taken around the time of Nora Papenberg's departure. The last one, which depicted a scene of carefree hilarity, was of Nora and Irene Grabner, their heads close together and tongues stuck out. Like a couple of schoolgirls. After that, Nora's chair was empty. A few clicks later, Beatrice found a photo in which Nora could be seen in the background, recognisable by her red jacket.

She enlarged the photo. The resolution was very good. The closer Beatrice zoomed in, the clearer the view of Nora Papenberg's face became – her eyes wide open. She was covering her nose and mouth with her left hand, as if she was shocked or about to throw up. In her other hand, she was holding the mobile to her ear.

The call had come from a telephone box, they knew that now, and it had definitely unleashed a reaction. She clicked through the remaining pictures. There wasn't even a hint of a smile on Nora's face, not in any of them.

Had she left to drive to the phone box? To meet the caller? Was he her murderer? Or the man whose blood was found on her clothes?

'Why didn't you tell anyone?' Beatrice asked a distant-looking Nora in the photos that followed. She was pictured with her gaze averted, her thoughts clearly elsewhere, an outsider amidst the laughing group.

According to the records, she hadn't contacted anyone after the ominous call, at least not from her mobile. Not even a brief message to her husband, letting him know she would be late.

Was it a rendezvous he wasn't supposed to have known about? Or had she actually left in order to get home as quickly as she could, to reach her safe haven? Had she been intercepted en route?

Beatrice had eaten all of her sushi without having tasted any of it. She went to throw the packaging into the kitchen bin and was just letting the lid drop back down when she heard her mobile. 'Message in a Bottle'. A text message.

Her pulse quickened. Stay calm. It might just be Florin; he texted from time to time.

She wiped her hands on her jogging bottoms and went back out to the balcony. It could just as easily be her mother.

But a tap of the mobile's keypad was enough to clarify things. The sender's number was the same as the one that lunchtime. Feeling as though something was tightening around her neck, Beatrice sank down onto the balcony chair.

Cold, completely cold.

The message consisted only of these three words, without any explanation or further comment.

Beatrice remembered the photo of Nora Papenberg holding her mobile pressed to her ear, hand in front of her mouth. *He sent me the text message from this very phone. A Nokia N8, a present from her husband.*

Suddenly, Beatrice felt as though she was being watched. She jumped up and went over to the main door of the apartment, checking to see if it was definitely locked properly. Pulled the curtains shut. Ran back to the balcony and peered down into the courtyard, but no one returned her gaze.

Cold, completely cold. The first association that had shot into Beatrice's mind was the coldness of a corpse's skin, but the longer she turned the words over in her thoughts, the surer she became that the sender of the message hadn't meant that.

She thought back to Jakob's last birthday party, when she had revived all the party games from her own childhood, including a treasure hunt. *Cold, completely cold, warmer now, even warmer, colder, good, warmer, warmer, hot!*

96

Was the Owner trying to tell her that they were on the wrong track?

She resisted the temptation to delete the message, and called Achim instead. In a way, she was relieved that the children weren't with her, but she had to hear their voices and make sure that—

'You? What do you want?' Achim's words perforated her thoughts. There it was again, the utter contempt.

'Hello. Put Mina or Jakob on the line, please.'

'They're busy.'

She wouldn't beg. 'Just for a moment.'

He sighed resignedly. 'Fine, go ahead then. But it would be better if you could look after them properly while they're with you instead and leave them in peace for the little time I have with them.'

She stared over at the corner of the balcony, at a red plant pot in which a small conifer was leading a miserable existence. Nothing she would have liked to say to Achim right now would make the situation any better.

He sighed once more. 'Mina, Jakob, do either of you want to speak to your mother?'

'Later,' called Mina, but Jakob's 'Yes' echoed loudly down the phone.

The sound of running, crashing. 'Hi, Mama!'

'Hello, my darling! Are you having a good time?'

'Yes! Papa really did get us a cat! Mina wants to call her Miley, but that's a totally stupid name! Can we call her Lou? Like Tobias's cat? I think that's much better, but Mina says it sounds like *loo* . . .'

Beatrice listened to him talk, feeling the relief rush through her. Of course the children were fine; what had she expected? Even though the Owner clearly had her mobile number, none of the messages had been personal; no one had threatened her. The messages were a good thing, not a danger. But she still felt safer once she had retreated from the balcony back into the lounge, closing the glass door behind her.

She let Jakob go back to the nameless cat, hung up and looked at the text message again. After staring at the number for a few moments, she pressed the green button. It had barely begun to ring before the recorded voice kicked in. *The number you have dialled is not available right now. Please try again later.*

He hadn't activated his voicemail, which meant Beatrice didn't have the chance to say all the things she wanted to blurt out. That was probably for the best.

She was still holding the phone in her hand when it started to ring, prompting her to nearly drop it in shock. Florin.

'Is there any news? How was this afternoon?'

'We went to the agency. And it seems like the Owner has made contact with me. Three times.'

'What?'

She brought him up to date on the events of the last few hours.

'I'm coming into the office tomorrow,' he said.

'No, enjoy your time with Anneke. Stefan and I have things under control. We'll check out a couple of the choir singers, and if we don't have any luck then we'll see the others on Sunday.'

She heard him sigh. 'You two are making me feel guilty.

And Bea, it worries me that he's sending you anonymous text messages. Are you alone in the apartment?'

The creeping sense of unease from before returned. 'Yes, but you can't seriously think that he'll pay me a visit. That's nonsense, Florin.' Good — she had even managed to convince herself.

'I wouldn't bet on it. We don't yet know what makes him tick. Be careful, okay?'

'Of course.' Seeing her nod reflected in the balcony door, she pulled the curtain closed. 'How was your evening? Was the carpaccio a hit?'

'Don't try to change the subject.' But she could hear from his voice that he was smiling. 'Are you sure about tomorrow? I could come in for an hour or two, at least.'

'There's no need. Really. You always have my back when I need to go and pick up the children, so it's the least I can do to repay the favour now and again. Give my best to Anneke, even though I've never met her, I mean.'

'I will. Have a nice evening, Bea. And remember—'

She interrupted him. 'You, too. Both of you, I mean.'

Ending the call, she collapsed onto the sofa and closed her eyes.

Schubert's Mass in A flat.

A noticeable birthmark on the back of the hand.

Why these particular clues? What was their relevance?

They reminded Beatrice of bad witness statements. Sometimes the strangest things stick in people's memories while they forget the really important ones.

She clapped her laptop shut and went off to bed, not because she was tired, but because she knew she needed the sleep to be able to function tomorrow. She wouldn't unplug the phone this time; she wanted to be contactable in case something was wrong with the children. Presumably Achim would leave her in peace tonight.

She only hoped the Owner would too.

'I have no idea what you want from me, and I have no intention of letting you inspect my hands.' The chubby, angry man in a dressing gown who had opened the door to them was the third Christoph they had called on today, and by far the least cooperative. 'Show me your ID again,' he demanded, looking Beatrice up and down in a leering fashion. The fatty was lucky she was feeling well rested, she reflected. She had slept through the night as if drugged. No calls or messages had startled her awake.

'We're investigating a murder case,' she explained. 'If you don't want to get this over with quickly, we can happily take you down to the station.'

The man made a big fuss of examining the ID, then stretched his hands out. 'If this is some hidden camera thing, you won't hear the end of this,' he grumbled.

'Don't worry.' Gripping his hands a little more tightly than necessary and prompting an involuntary yelp, she looked at his palms. Nothing.

And the backs? Still nothing, even though she pushed up the sleeves of his dressing gown to be sure.

'Thank you, we're done now. Enjoy the rest of your day.'

Clearly the fat man wasn't content with that. 'Aren't you going to at least tell me what murder case this is in connection with?'

'Sorry, but no. Goodbye.'

The next man on their list wasn't at home, and the one after that didn't have any noticeable birthmarks either. Frustrated, Beatrice and Stefan made their way back to the police station, disappearing into their respective offices without another word. As she walked in, Beatrice was surprised to see Florin sitting at his desk.

'Just a couple of hours,' he explained. 'I discovered yesterday evening that if you enter coordinates on Google Maps it shows you the exact location on the map. Look.' He angled his screen so she could see. 'This is the place where we found the hand. More or less exactly. This should make the work easier for us in future, if—'

Stefan rushed into the room, waving a piece of paper over his head. 'This email arrived an hour ago, and you were right,' he cried, thrusting the printout into Beatrice's hand.

The Nokia N8 with the International Mobile Subscriber Identity she had investigated yesterday was registered to Nora Papenberg.

'I knew it!' exclaimed Beatrice. 'He's got her phone, and he's sending us messages from it.'

'Not us, you,' Florin corrected her. 'Which I still find very worrying, by the way.'

'And I still think it's very unlikely he wants to harm me,' she answered, with a conviction that she only half felt. 'He's just trying to demonstrate his superiority.' All the same, she knew she would be double-locking the door and closing all the windows tonight.

Florin nodded, but still looked doubtful. 'It's high time we brought a forensic psychologist onto the case – perhaps he'll read more into the messages than we're seeing. I don't want to risk making mistakes or overlooking anything.'

Midday gave way to afternoon, and the striped pattern on Beatrice's desk cast by the sunlight stretching through the blinds wandered from left to right. At half-past two, an email arrived from the network provider with a PDF attachment listing the connections made by the owner's prepaid card.

The pickings were slim; only one number appeared, and that was Beatrice's own. He had connected to the network cell for just two minutes at a time to send her the two messages, once in Hallein and the second time right there in Salzburg, in the Aigen district. Apart from that, the mobile had been offline the entire time.

'He knows what he's doing,' Beatrice muttered. 'So far he hasn't made a single mistake that could give us anything to go on.' The familiar digits of her own mobile number aggravated her every time the printout caught her eye. 'So are we in agreement that the text messages and note came from him? From Nora Papenberg's murderer?'

Florin stared thoughtfully at the reports in front of him for a few seconds, then nodded. 'Yes. Otherwise it doesn't make any sense.'

Half an hour later, Beatrice tried to shoo him away from the desk. 'You shouldn't even be here today. You have a guest.'

She sounded like her grandmother, but Florin's smile was one of gratitude.

'Okay, okay. But you should call it a day now, too.'

'I will soon.' She started to rearrange the papers on her

desk. 'Just another half-hour.' Seeing the look on his face, she added, 'I have a child-free weekend, so let me make use of it, okay?'

Half an hour turned into two, but beyond that she couldn't make sense of anything; none of her thoughts managed to find a tenable link. Frustrated, she flung her pen across the desk.

She took a deep breath and shut down her computer. After letting Stefan know that she was stopping for the day, and noticing with a guilty conscience that he carried on working regardless, she finally walked out into the sunshine. It hadn't been this warm for a long time. Beatrice pulled her sunglasses and car keys out of her bag, almost making her mobile fall out in the process.

All of a sudden, the thought of driving home, bunging on a DVD and putting her feet up was far less appealing than it had been five minutes ago.

What about living a bit for a change? she asked herself, looking through the contact list on her mobile. A coffee in town, an hour or two chatting to a girlfriend . . . Lisa or Kathrin perhaps?

Fat chance. Both of them had families – children and a husband – so there was no room for spontaneous activities on the weekends any more. But perhaps Gina, who didn't have kids and was recently separated? Without hesitating a moment longer, Beatrice pressed the dial button.

After three rings, Gina picked up. 'Hello?'

'Hi, it's me. Bea. Do you fancy going for coffee in the Bazaar? In half an hour perhaps?'

'What? Oh, sorry, I'm in Rome right now. You wouldn't

believe how gorgeous the weather is! Next week, okay? I'll bring you back a bottle of grappa.'

Beatrice swallowed down her disappointment. It was her own fault; she had let the friendship slip, hadn't responded to emails or invitations for a while now.

You're still afraid, aren't you? Bea, you coward.

Her mobile was returned to her bag. She unlocked her car – no notes under the windscreen wiper this time – and wound down the windows.

There was nothing stopping her going for a coffee by herself, buying a magazine, enjoying the spring sunshine. She drove through the quiet Saturday afternoon traffic towards the old town, crossed the bridge over the Salzach and found a parking space on Rudolfskai.

Walking over to Residenzplatz, Beatrice noticed how the jet of water shooting up from the baroque fountain had been transformed by the sun into a golden fog, completely enveloping the four marble horses which sprang forth from its basin. The tourist season was already in full swing. A living statue in a Mozart costume, painted in glittering silver from head to toe, bowed in front of a Japanese tour group who seemed to have mistaken themselves for paparazzi. Beatrice paused for a moment to take in the scene. Three English students walked past, chattering and laughing, each with a beaker of ice cream in hand.

Ice cream, yes, that was a good plan.

There was a fantastic ice cream parlour a few streets away, with plenty of galleries and boutiques lining the route. Beatrice looked at the fancy clothing in the window displays, but without feeling any urge to shop. There was no point;

the opportunity to wear things like that didn't really come up in her life. Evading another group of tourists, she joined the queue for ice cream.

Hazelnut, caramel and pumpkin brittle in a large beaker, with chocolate sauce. The perfect remedy for her frustration.

Enjoying the explosion of flavours in her mouth, she allowed the first genuine smile of the day to tiptoe across her face.

It didn't even last five minutes. On her way to the cathedral square, where she was hoping to find a peaceful and sunny bench, she saw Florin. From behind, but there was no doubt it was him. His arm was draped around the waist of a tall, slim woman with blonde shoulder-length hair. As they walked, he leant over and said something that made her burst out laughing. A laugh that was much throatier than Beatrice would have attributed to the Anneke in her imagination.

They were crossing Residenzplatz and veering off into the narrow, cobbled Goldgasse. Amongst the crowds, Beatrice kept seeing Anneke's fair hair gleam in the sunlight. Without giving any thought to what she was doing, she followed them, taking care not to get too close. She had completely forgotten her ice cream by now, and only remembered it as the sticky mess began to drip onto her fingers.

'Shit.' She threw the beaker into the nearest bin and tried to pull a tissue from her bag without making everything dirty in the process. In front of her, Florin and Anneke turned in to a lane on the right. Beatrice watched as Anneke put some coins into a beggar's bowl, watched as she stopped with Florin in front of a window display full of shoes, as he brushed a strand of her hair behind her ear and—

Had she lost her mind? What was she doing? Was she seriously stalking her colleague?

She abruptly turned on her heel and ran back down the cobbled street in the opposite direction, as quickly as she could, before Florin had a chance to spot her.

Why, Beatrice? What is it? Why does the sight of two loved-up people torment you so much?

She couldn't answer her own question. It wasn't jealousy, not really; she didn't begrudge them one single minute of happiness. Longing, perhaps . . . that was more to the point. But she couldn't allow herself to lose her composure like this.

She paced hastily all the way back to her car, then took the fastest route home. Browsing her bookshelves, she found a historical novel she had bought two years ago but never opened since. She took it to the sofa with her – that and a glass of Chardonnay. Sleep stalked her with its silent steps; within an hour, it had laid the book down on her chest and pressed her eyelids shut.

The next morning, shortly before eleven, Beatrice and Stefan's search led them to Christoph Beil, a brawny man in his mid-forties who sang Beethoven's Mass in C major with his choir in the Maria Plain basilica. They only noticed the birthmark on his hand after closer inspection – or, to be more precise, the scar from where a birthmark had once been.

'I did used to have one, yes, a naevus, as the doctors called it. It was really dark and looked horrible, so I'm really glad my wife convinced me to have it removed.'

Only an uneven, violet-coloured fleck remained. 'How long ago was that?' Beatrice enquired.

'About two and a half years,' the man explained. He answered cautiously, visibly unsettled by their questioning and the fact that he didn't know what it was about.

Beatrice glanced at Stefan. 'We'd like to speak with you privately, Herr Beil. Don't worry, you're not under suspicion of having committed a crime, but you may be able to help us with a current case.'

Beil hesitated. 'Could you not at least give me some idea of what it's about?'

'Later,' replied Beatrice. 'In private.'

Something resembling protest flickered in the man's eyes, but only briefly. Then he tilted his head to the side and smiled. 'Of course, when would be good for you?'

'This afternoon, around four?' Stefan suggested. 'Florin could be there then too,' he said, speaking more softly as he turned to address Beatrice.

'That's fine. Do you want to come to my house? My wife has been baking, and we could sit out in the garden.'

'You call Florin,' said Beatrice, once they were sitting back in the car.

Stefan raised his eyebrows in surprise, but did what she had asked.

'Four is fine,' he said after hanging up. 'He's dropping his girlfriend off at the airport now, so he can come round to us at half-three.' Lost in thought, Stefan played with the car keys. 'Why didn't you just come out and ask him right away?'

'About what?'

'The year of his birth, of course! I mean, that's what this is all about. Then we could have started working out the coordinates already and might even find what we're looking for!'

'I want to see some form of ID with his birth date on it, preferably his birth certificate, and in general get a better idea of who Christoph Beil is. Or do you think it's just a coincidence that he's part of all this?'

Stefan shook his head, still a little reluctant. 'I know. It's just that our progress feels so slow.'

Slow. The word was haunting her.

'I'm as keen to get the coordinates as you are, but I want to do things properly. Cover as many bases as possible. I don't want to be kicking myself later for stupid mistakes.' Or have Hoffmann rub her nose in them.

Stefan seemed convinced, albeit a little disappointed. 'Okay. It's just that I brought along my GPS device and thought, if we manage to find the guy we're looking for . . .'

An idea sparked in Beatrice's mind. There was still plenty of time before four o'clock, and the opportunity to fill a gap in her knowledge seemed advantageous.

'You know what? Let's go and look for a cache. I want to have done it at least once, and you can show me how it works. Okay?'

He looked surprised, but the prospect of taking on the expert role seemed to have cheered him up. 'Okay, let me fire up my laptop then.'

Christoph Beil stood in the shadow of the basilica, his eyes fixed on the police car. They were leaning over something together, presumably their notes.

With the tips of his fingers, he stroked thoughtfully over

the scar where the birthmark had once been. It was the only thing the policewoman with the honey-coloured hair had been interested in. She had searched for it intently, turning his hands over and around like a doctor.

If only he knew what all this was about, but he didn't dare ask again. He wasn't used to dealing with the police and didn't want to take any risks. It might lead them to ideas it would be better for them not to have. He wasn't under suspicion; the woman had said that very clearly.

Was she the gawky red-haired guy's boss? It seemed so, for the man had stayed silent the whole time, just listening and staring at him attentively.

'Have a good afternoon, Christoph! Give Vera my love!' The hearty slap to his shoulder startled Beil, making his heart skip a beat. Heavens, he would have to be more aware of his surroundings; he didn't want to end up having a heart attack over something like that. Hopefully he hadn't yelped out loud. But Kurt, the man responsible for his now-racing pulse, had headed off without noticing the reaction unleashed by his rough farewell.

It was fine. Everything was okay; he hadn't made a fool of himself. Wiping his hand across his brow, he realised it was wet with sweat and felt annoyed at himself. Where had these sudden nerves come from? After all, he hadn't done anything wrong; he didn't need to worry. Not about Vera, either. She wouldn't leave him – she loved him. And it was very unlikely that the police visit had anything to do with all that. He wasn't guilty, as he had to keep reminding himself.

And if it really turned out to be necessary, he would just come clean.

The caching game was fun – much more so than Beatrice had expected. Stefan logged into Geocaching.com and searched through the maps for a hiding place that was relatively nearby. 'Nothing too difficult, nothing too small,' he murmured. '*Voilà!* Look, this cache is called "The Hole", and it's a regular.'

'A what?'

'A regular. That means it's about this big.' Stefan sketched something the size of a loaf of bread in the air. 'Like the one you found the hand in. And it's also a traditional – which means the given coordinates are also where the box is stashed. No stages, no puzzles. The difficulty rating is two stars, so that means we won't end up searching for hours on end. Although the terrain is three and a half stars, so it'll be more than a light stroll.' He gave her Timberlands an appraising glance, then nodded contentedly. 'Let's head off then.' He connected the navigation device with the computer via a USB cable and clicked 'Send to my GPS'. 'Done. The good thing is that we can drive almost all the way by car, so it won't take too long.'

The GPS device worked with astonishing precision. It led them from their parking space by the edge of the path directly to a wooded slope. Stefan switched into compass mode, and now they could see the distance between them and their target reducing with every step they took. In the end, it was Beatrice who found the entrance to the hole – a gap under a steep crag that she could only reach by lying on her stomach and easing herself along by the elbows.

'If I crawl in there my T-shirt will be in tatters,' she said.

'Yep. That's all part of the fun. Here's a torch.'

She took a deep breath, struggled to contain a fleeting impulse of claustrophobia, and crawled into the darkness. She only switched the torch on when she literally couldn't see a thing ahead of her.

After the narrowness of the first few metres, Beatrice was surprised to see a tunnel open out in front of her. She could even stand and walk along it if she ducked. As she moved forwards, she heard someone following her in the darkness. For a split second, she was convinced it must be Nora Papenberg's killer, that it hadn't been enough for him to simply thank them for the hunt this time – he had picked up their tracks and wanted to trap his prey in the hole.

But it was just Stefan, of course. 'Shine the torch into all the nooks and crannies,' he advised her. 'The box is a big one, so it'll stand out, but any owner worth his salt tries to hide his caches in a well-camouflaged spot so they don't get muggled.'

Hearing the word 'owner' made her jump involuntarily. She shook her head at herself. 'What does "muggled" mean?'

'It's a *Harry Potter* reference. Muggles are people who can't do magic – so in this context, the non-cachers. They've been known to throw cache containers in the bin if they stumble upon them by chance.'

The light of the torch made every protrusion inside the crag throw shadows that could easily be taken for niches, so a good ten minutes passed before Beatrice found the cache, right at the back of the hollow. A plastic container, very similar to the one they had found at the stone chasm.

'Well done,' Stefan praised her. 'Now open the box. That's the logbook, you see?'

She nodded, shone the light on the pages and started to read:

Great cache, found it quickly. Out: Smurf. In: dice. TFTC, Heinzweidrei & Radebreaker

TFTC, Wildinger

All caches should be like this! TFTC, Team Bier

At least half the pages in the small spiral notepad were scribbled full.

'Draw a line under the last comment and write something – whatever you like. People normally leave a note of thanks – TFTC means "Thanks for the Cache". Then sign off with *Undercover Cookie*. We can log our find on the website – it's my eight hundred and sixty-seventh.' Stefan sounded proud.

Beatrice stared at the notepad, wondering whether it was wise to leave handwritten evidence, then shook her head in disbelief. She was thinking like a perpetrator, not a policewoman.

So she did what Stefan had said, drawing a line under the last entry and writing:

I wish all caches were like this. TFTC, Undercover Cookie.

'Is that the right plural for cache?'

'Absolutely. Right, now you pack the logbook back into the plastic bag and see what treasures are in the box.'

A transparent dice, a sticker that clearly belonged in a

collection album from the last football World Cup, a glass marble and a broken Matchbox car.

'Those are the trades,' explained Stefan. 'Normal trades. You can take something with you and then put something else in. Do you want to?'

Even though she couldn't have explained why, she did want to. In her jacket pocket, alongside a rubber band and a tissue, she found a tiny metal heart that had once been part of a keyring. She exchanged it for the glass marble.

'Okay. Now pack everything up neatly and put it back exactly where you found it.'

Having made a note of the hiding place behind the crag ledge, she put the box back, then turned her attentions to the arduous task of crawling back out.

'Right then, I'll have to go and get changed,' Beatrice determined. 'Thank you, Stefan, that was very educational. I think I understand the appeal now.'

'It's good, isn't it?' He beamed. 'The last stage is on the computer. Come on.'

They logged the cache as 'Found', which resulted in a yellow smiley appearing on both the map and the webpage with the cache description.

I really enjoyed it, TFTC, wrote Beatrice as her comment on the site. The abbreviation was flowing from her hand as though it was second nature now.

On the drive home, she contemplated whether she should get one of these GPS devices; perhaps the treasure hunt could be something Mina and Jakob would both enjoy. But thinking back to her very first find made her quickly dismiss the idea. Today, even accompanied by Stefan, she had been overcome by a queasy feeling as she opened the cache box. She wasn't sure if she would ever be able to look at a plastic container like that again without thinking of the severed hand.

They all met in front of the office shortly before four and got into the car, Stefan taking the wheel and Florin – still exhausted from his round trip to Munich – claiming the back seat.

Christoph Beil's house was out in the suburbs, and looked in dire need of renovation. The cracked facade suggested damp in the walls, and the wooden terrace looked unsound even from twenty metres away. But the garden was well looked after, complete with gnomes, clay frogs and a replica of the Manneken Pis.

'We have to be careful – under no circumstances can we give too much away,' warned Florin. 'So not a word about coordinates or caches with body parts.'

They rang the bell at the garden gate. Beil opened it so quickly that it seemed likely he had been watching out for their arrival from the window.

'Would you like some coffee? Tea? Water?' He waved to his wife, who had been waiting in the doorway and now came out bearing a tray of drinks, only to disappear back into the house again straight afterwards.

They all sat down at a massive wooden table, on which a company of ants were forming a long line. Beil wiped them off with nervous, jerky hand movements. 'I've been racking my brains since lunchtime, trying to work out what you might want from me.'

He looked tense, like someone who had to do an exam

without knowing what subject it was in. Beatrice cleared her throat. 'We're investigating the murder of Nora Papenberg. Does the name mean anything to you?' She fixed her gaze on him. But Beil didn't bat an eyelid; on the contrary, he suddenly seemed to relax. 'No, I'm sorry. Although – it's possible that I might have heard about it on the radio. Is this the woman who was found in the cattle pasture?'

'Yes.'

'Hmm. Could you tell me what I have to do with all of this?'

Beatrice wiped her forehead, a tiny insect stuck to her hand. 'We're pursuing every single lead, and one of them led us to you. May I check your ID, please?' Seeing him hesitate, she smiled reassuringly.

Beil pulled a battered black wallet out from his trouser pocket and handed Beatrice his driving licence. She immediately focused her attention on his date of birth.

1964. She noted the day and month, along with the date of issue and licence number, then returned the document to Beil. 'The thing is,' she began cautiously, 'the suspect left a clue that could indicate there's some connection between you and the victim. I'm afraid I can't be more specific.'

'Aha.' He stared at the discoloured spot on the back of his hand. 'But that's not the case. Which means I can't be of any further assistance to you.'

Florin cleared his throat, a signal that he wanted to take over. 'Have you been singing with the choir for a while?'

'Yes, nearly ten years now. I'm a dental technician, so I like to have some artistic balance in my free time.'

'How's business in the dental trade?'

Beil grinned. 'I assume you're referring to the run-down state of the house? It's being renovated this summer. My great-aunt left it to me.'

Florin nodded to Beatrice, who was pulling two photographs from her bag. 'We'd like to ask you to look at the woman in the pictures very closely and tell us whether it's possible that you know her after all.'

Beil took the photos. 'Is that this Nora Pa . . .'

'Papenberg. Yes. Please take your time.'

He laid the picture down on the table, the one of her laughing heartily, and flicked one last confused ant away. It began to scrabble over the edge. 'No. I really am very sorry.'

The second photo was a portrait in which Nora was looking directly at the camera with a serious expression. The jolt that went through Beil's body as Beatrice laid the photo in front of him was subtle, so much so that at first she wasn't certain she had really seen it. But it had definitely been there. No widening of the eyes or sudden intake of breath, but a jolt nonetheless. When Beil handed the pictures back to Beatrice, his hand was completely steady. 'No, sorry. I really wish I could have helped you.'

She kept staring at him, not looking away for a second. 'Are you completely certain that this woman doesn't look familiar to you?'

'Yes. I've got a really good memory for faces, so I would know if I'd ever met her. And the name doesn't mean anything to me.' Beil grimaced apologetically. 'I can imagine that your job is no walk in the park, so I'm sorry you had to come all this way for nothing. And on a Sunday of all days.'

He smiled warmly and looked her right in the eyes without

blinking, but she didn't believe him. He had recognised Nora Papenberg – not immediately, but when he saw the second photo. So it was very interesting indeed that he was denying it.

With a friendly smile, Beatrice took the pictures, tucked them away in her bag and pulled out a business card. 'If anything else occurs to you that you think might be relevant to us, then please call me.'

He put the card in his wallet. 'Of course, but as I said . . .' He shrugged. 'I don't know the woman.'

Beatrice was convinced, even though neither Florin nor Stefan had noticed Beil's reaction to the second photo. If he was lying, then there must be a reason.

'There are two possibilities,' Beatrice pondered out loud. 'First, I'm mistaken, and Beil never met Papenberg. Maybe he's even the wrong choir singer and his birthday will just be leading us off track. For one thing, he doesn't even have the birthmark any more.'

'And the other possibility?' asked Florin.

'My instinct is right, and he did know her. Then there has to be a reason why he's lying to us. If we find something at Stage Two, then we'll speak to him again.'

Back at the office, the three of them sat down on Florin's side of the desk. Florin picked up the copy of the cache note. '"The last two numbers of his birth date are A,"' he read out loud.

'So, sixty-four. Then square that . . .' Beatrice tapped on the calculator and made a note of the resulting sum. 'Four thousand and ninety-six.'

'Okay. Then add thirty-seven.'

'That gives four thousand, one hundred and thirty-three. That should be the northern coordinate, right?'

'Correct. For the eastern coordinates, we need the sum of A's digits – four plus six equals ten. That times ten gives a hundred. Multiply by A and we get six thousand, four hundred.'

Beatrice wrote the number down and looked up. 'Why didn't he just say straight away that we needed to times A by a hundred?'

'To make it less obvious?' Florin suggested. 'To increase the possibility of us making a mistake? Okay, let's keep going. Take away two hundred and twenty-nine and subtract the resulting sum from the eastern coordinates.'

Beatrice calculated, noting the results as she went and then circling them. 'This is it. Shall we drive out there today?' Even as she said it, she realised she wouldn't have enough time before she had to get home.

'Of course!' Stefan had already jumped up, but Florin stopped him.

'I want Drasche to be with us. We'll go first thing tomorrow. Having said that, I'd still like to see where this place is.' He entered the new coordinates into Google Maps. The map appeared on the monitor in just a fraction of a second, prompting Florin to let out a brief and – or so it seemed to Beatrice – pained laugh. 'We've dropped the ball here somehow.'

They zoomed in closer. 'The results are never completely accurate,' said Stefan. 'It'll be a few metres to the right or left of that.'

They would just have to hope he was right. Because the arrow indicating the location of the coordinates they had just entered was pointing directly at the autobahn.

Beatrice arrived home just in time to air the apartment and prepare all the ingredients for ham-and-cheese omelettes. Achim brought the children back on the dot of the arranged time. They were practically bursting with stories about their weekend. The cat was now called Cinderella. She was grey and white and a little bit black. They had gone for ice cream in the afternoon, two scoops each. Papa had been really funny and lost twelve times to Jakob at arm wrestling.

Beatrice smiled, laughed, nodded and suppressed something that, on closer inspection, she identified as melancholy. Did she wish she had been there too?

She shook her head in disbelief, cleared the table and sent the children off to the bathroom. She would read *The Hobbit* to them and have a relaxing evening for once.

'The fires in the middle of the hall were built with fresh logs and the torches were put out, and still they sat in the light of the dancing flames,' read Beatrice. Jakob, who in her opinion was still too young for the book, and for whom she improvised harmless passages in place of the more violent scenes, was staring at the *Buzz Lightyear* poster on the wall, his eyes glistening. Mina's gaze, on the other hand, was fixed on Beatrice; she was smiling and seemed to be at peace with herself and the world for the first time in weeks.

'. . . with the pillars of the house standing tall behind them, and dark at the top like trees of the forest—'

Her phone vibrated, and she heard the first few bars of 'Message in a Bottle'.

Beatrice only realised she had stopped reading and let the book sink when Jakob shook her arm. 'Mama! Keep reading!'

She found her place, started again, tripped over her words.

Stay calm. The message would still be there in a minute, and perhaps it was . . . from Florin. Or from Achim, wanting to relieve himself of some more bitter words. She would find out soon enough, but right now it was the children's time.

'Whether it was magic or not, it seemed to Bilbo that he heard a sound like wind in the branches stirring in the rafters, and the hoot of owls. Soon he began to nod with sleep and the voices seemed to grow far away—'

'Mama! You're not reading properly any more!'

'I'm sorry.' Pulling herself together, she tried to concentrate on the story. Eventually, she even let herself get carried away by it, only looking up again once the children were fast asleep.

To be disabled.

Just those three words, sent from the same number of course. Beatrice stared at her phone until the energy-saving function made the display go dark.

Disabled meant turned off, deactivated. And 'to be' meant it would happen soon. Or perhaps it could also be read in the sense of something or someone being handicapped.

Was the message referring to the mutilated victim? Was the Owner announcing that he was about to start sawing limbs off again?

She sat down on the couch and felt her pulse beating in

her neck and all the way up to her temples. It would be hard to fall asleep now. For the third time that evening, she checked that the door was locked, then fetched a glass of water from the kitchen and turned on the computer. She had left her files in the office, including all the research Stefan had done for her, but she would easily be able to find the list she was thinking of online. She typed *Geocache disabled* into Google, and a list of links appeared. Reading the first two, she discovered that a cache could be 'temporarily disabled'. The term, as she found out two clicks later, meant that the owner had removed the box in order to update it or exchange the logbook for a new one.

No, thought Beatrice, *not that, please.*

In the worst-case scenario, that would mean the coordinates they had gone to such lengths to work out were now worthless. Had the Owner just informed them he was planning to get rid of whatever was hidden at the site in question? Had he already done so? Without hesitating for long, she dialled Florin's number. He picked up on the third ring.

'Listen, I got another message—' She stopped. There was piano music in the background. Erik Satie. Or something similar.

'Is your brother there?'

'No, it's a CD. I was just trying to . . . oh, never mind. What happened?'

She was willing to bet she had interrupted him while he was painting; Florin was a keen artist and said it helped him to wind down. 'He sent me another text message. I don't think it's anything threatening, but perhaps a hint that he's planning to get rid of what he hid for us.'

'What makes you think that?'

'The message says "disabled". That's caching terminology and means the cache will be temporarily removed. Or updated. Maybe he put something new in.' *Something bloody, coagulating.*

For a few seconds, Florin was silent, which made it sound as though he had turned the piano music up. 'Do you think,' he asked eventually, 'that we made a mistake? That we should have gone to the new coordinates right away?'

'I wondered that too.'

'I'll send a few people over there now. We'll keep the area covered for the unlikely event that the Owner really does turn up. Even though—'

Even though he doesn't really believe that will happen. Just as Beatrice herself didn't.

She heard him sigh. 'And if we don't find anything there tomorrow morning, I'll take the fall for it.'

'Nonsense,' she objected. 'If we don't find anything, then it could just as easily mean we have the wrong Christoph. Remember the map, the autobahn.' But she wasn't too keen on that theory. Maybe the others were right; maybe the flicker of recognition in Beil's eyes had just been a figment of her imagination.

N47° 50.738 E013° 15.547

The sundial on the facade of the Thalgau rectory was indicating exactly eight in the morning. They parked the car a few metres away by the side of an unsurfaced road, directly next to the unmarked police car from which their colleagues had kept watch overnight. But apart from two dog-walkers, no one had put in an appearance.

The steady rushing sound coming from the autobahn would almost have been reminiscent of waves breaking against a shore, had it not been for the loud diesel engines of passing lorries. Stefan's comment had been pretty accurate – on the map, it looked as though the coordinates pointed directly at the motorway itself, but in actual fact there was a bridge stretching out across a small valley. They would have to look under it, or in the immediate surrounding area. The autobahn bridge sliced through the landscape just a few metres behind the rectory, separating the house from a gently sloping fragment of forest where the birds were boldly attempting to hold their own against the cacophony of traffic.

'Go ahead until the arch of the bridge, then let us go in front!' bellowed Drasche. He and Ebner were just about to climb into their overalls.

The GPS device Beatrice had borrowed from Stefan that morning was showing another 143 metres to their destination. She hoped he wasn't too disappointed at having to hold the fort in the office instead of coming on the hunt with them.

'What a strange place.' Florin pushed his sunglasses up onto his head and came over to Beatrice to look at the GPS device with her. His proximity filled her with an unfamiliar shyness; the encounter – or rather, the almost-encounter – from Saturday was still playing on her mind. The strange sensation of having intruded into his private sphere.

Drasche stomped over in his blue-plastic covered shoes. 'Which direction?'

'Straight ahead, under the arch of the bridge. Keep to the right just a little.' She pushed the GPS device into Drasche's hand and pointed at the black-and-white destination flag. 'Head towards that. The thing will make a peeping noise once you get there.'

She and Florin walked several paces behind Drasche and Ebner, who were making their way slowly, step by step, towards the indicated location. It was excruciatingly loud beneath the bridge itself, but as soon as they emerged into the daylight again all that remained was the surf-like rushing sound, paired with the babbling of a stream. It was flowing along to their right, dammed up a little further on by a low wall of uneven stones. A miniature waterfall was spluttering out of a hole in the middle of it.

Pretty, but not likely to be a hiding place. Beatrice watched Drasche as he paced back and forth, turning around in circles, before eventually pressing the GPS device into Ebner's hands.

'The bloody thing changes its mind about the direction every other second.'

'That means you're almost there!' she called out to him. 'Look within a five-metre radius.'

Drasche's cursing was only just swallowed up by the combined efforts of the autobahn and stream. 'What am I supposed to do, dig a hole in the ground or something?'

'No . . .' She went forward a few paces and pointed at the wall. 'You have to look for hiding places. Geocaches are often stashed in tiny crevices or holes. You're not supposed to find them at first glance.'

'Then maybe it's in the water,' scoffed Drasche as he lifted a large stone at the edge of the bed of the stream, before climbing up to the small wall with Ebner. 'Just mud, sludge and branches,' he commented. 'Now the GPS is saying we're thirteen metres away.'

Beatrice exchanged a glance with Florin. Had they messed up? Was the cache already gone?

She thought back to yesterday's search, to the hole she and Stefan had crawled into.

'He hasn't given us a terrain rating,' she murmured.

Florin turned to look at her. 'Come again?'

'A terrain rating. Normally each cache has a starring system which shows you how hard it is to find. That way you know whether there'll be any climbing or crawling involved . . .' Her gaze wandered over to the brambles growing around the mouth of the stream. Buttercups, hip-height spiky plants whose name she didn't know, and—

'Gerd!'

Drasche whipped around. 'What is it?'

'Climb down again and come back in my direction. Yes, just a few steps – stop! Is that a tree root there on your left?'

As he leant over, Beatrice moved forwards to be able to see more clearly. He nodded. 'Yes. It's completely overgrown.'

'Reach underneath – there, where the roots are hanging over into the water. From where I'm standing it looks like there might be a little recess.'

Drasche's gloved hands fumbled downwards. It would have been much easier to get access if he had climbed into the slimy riverbed, but he was clearly trying to avoid that. His favourite sentence was: *Your evidence erases their evidence.*

But he couldn't get to it kneeling down, so he lay on his stomach and immersed his arm right up to the shoulder in the cavity between the roots and the bed of the stream.

If I were the Owner, thought Beatrice, *this is exactly the place I would have picked. No one would go rooting around in there just for fun.*

Drasche's triumphant cry made her jump. He pulled his arm back up, bringing out into the daylight a container which was coated in slime and tiny pebbles. An earthworm lost its grip and tumbled down into the grass.

They had been right after all. Relief streamed through Beatrice's body, as welcome as oxygen after being immersed underwater. Florin put an arm around her shoulders.

'Good work, Bea.'

They walked over to join the others. Ebner was already taking photos of the box, the stream, the tree roots and the surrounding area, while Drasche busied himself putting the cache into one of his own transport containers. 'Sorry, but you're not opening anything out here,' he said, turning to Beatrice and Florin. 'For one thing, I'd like to do it in lab conditions, and for another I'm not in the mood to wait for official transportation if it turns out there's another body part in there.'

They struggled to contain their impatience. Beatrice was in no hurry to see the gruesome trade she presumed was inside the box, but the note she hoped it contained was another matter. A clue to the next stage, perhaps a clue leading them to the Owner himself. Or a mistake, at long last.

But they would have to wait while Drasche and Ebner took samples of the mud and searched the surrounding area for any possible traces of evidence. When they finally set off to the lab, the journey seemed to take longer than usual, and even the act of putting on protective clothing in the scrub room was a tortuous exercise in patience. *Slow*, she thought to herself grimly.

Under the light of the blindingly bright investigation lamps, Drasche finally opened the box. He took a note out and unfolded it.

'"Congratulations – you've found it!"' he read out loud. '"This container is part of a game that you are now familiar with. You didn't find it by chance, but intentionally looked for it. The contents won't surprise you as much as last time, but surprises are overrated, believe me. I'm sure you'll soon agree with me on this. TFTH."'

Drasche looked up. 'What an asshole.'

No surprises. It was already clear what was in the wrapped-up bundle that almost entirely filled the container. Feeling vaguely grateful that she didn't have to touch it herself, Beatrice felt her body tense as Drasche carefully pulled it out.

Three additional days in warm spring temperatures hadn't been good for the contents of the plastic film. This hand had expunged significantly more fluid than its left counterpart. Despite the vacuum packing, green and blue discolorations on the flesh were clearly visible.

'Luckily the task of opening it falls to the pathologist,' explained Drasche. Beatrice guessed that his face mask was veiling a sardonic smile. She watched him check the plastic film for fingerprints and shake his head in frustration. Next, he laid the typed note down on the work surface, sprayed it with Ninhydrin and heated it up with the hot-air gun, but this didn't yield any results either.

Commenting that 'all good things come in threes', Drasche pulled another folded piece of paper from the cache container. He spread it out carefully and laid it beneath the lamp to take photos of it under the light.

'I'd hazard a guess that this is the same handwriting as last time,' he established. Instead of waiting for him to read aloud, Beatrice moved closer and leant over the note. He was right. The same looping, rounded letters – Beatrice was sure they belonged to Nora Papenberg. The pen had clearly been shaking at times; the lines slanted slightly downwards like the stems of a withering plant.

Stage Three
You're looking for a loser, and you're the first person besides me to take any interest in him in a long time. Look for scars, inside and out, and an old, dark blue VW Golf. The last three digits of the number plate are 39B. The street he lives in contains a name, which forms your keyword. Transform the letters into

numbers (A=1, B=2 . . .). Take the sum you get from the word, multiply it by 26, add 64 and subtract this from the northern coordinates from Stage Two.

Add the number 1,000 to the house number and multiply the sum by 4, then add 565. Subtract the resulting sum from the eastern coordinates from Stage Two. We'll see each other there.

'A loser,' mused Beatrice. 'That could mean anything. We'll have to go by the description of the car.'

While Drasche checked the second piece of paper for fingerprints, Florin went off to phone the vehicle registration office.

Look for scars, inside and out. The first thing that came to Beatrice's mind was the scar on the back of Beil's hand – that was definitely an outer scar. Her gaze wandered instinctively over to the vacuum-packed hand. The counterpart to their first find – but there was still no body. Presumably inner organs would follow in the next stages, pieces that could fit in mid-sized plastic containers, pieces of a mutilated body . . .

'Bingo!' Drasche leant in closer over the paper he was heating with the hot-air gun. 'We've got plenty of spoils here.' On the letter, particularly around the edges of the page, violet flecks began to stand out. Oval shaped, partly smeared, but clear in some places, almost sharp. Fingerprints.

'Is that a fleck of blood on the bottom right?' asked Beatrice.

'Possibly. You'll get the detailed report when we're done, okay?' For Drasche, that was a consciously polite attempt at kicking them out.

'I'd like the photos right away though,' insisted Beatrice. Ebner promised to email them over in the next ten minutes.

By the time she left the lab, Florin had just finished off his telephone conversation. 'They're sending us a list. All the cars from Salzburg and the surrounding areas which match the last three digits of the number plate.'

Lists. Letters. Reports. Beatrice peeled off her lab coat, threw the gloves in a disposal bin, pulled the protective cap from her head and ran both hands through her hair. When she was trudging through all the paperwork that the case brought along with it, she didn't feel as though they were getting even one step closer to the Owner. She only felt his presence in the notes they found in the containers.

There was another three hours to go before their scheduled meeting with Hoffmann. They hurried back to the office. Beatrice checked her emails immediately in the hope of finding the photos there. Nothing. Instead, a provisional handwriting comparison had arrived from the graphology expert.

'"The two samples correspond in all fundamental characteristics such as size, connectivity, angularity, anticlockwise slant and line spacing,"' Beatrice read out loud. '"This suggests that they originate from the same individual, despite the fact that the second sample shows considerable irregularities which may indicate the subject was under extreme psychological stress."'

Florin had stopped what he was doing to listen. He drummed his knuckles thoughtfully on the desk. 'So Nora Papenberg really did compose the puzzles. And then there's the fact that the blood of the dismembered victim was found on her clothes – Bea, we have to at least consider the possibility that she might not be the victim here.'

He was right, of course; they couldn't rule it out. But it just felt so wrong.

'Two accomplices,' Florin continued, holding a pen in each hand, 'who are in it together, until they argue, and one of them kills the other.' The pen on the right fell onto the desk and rolled towards his keyboard. 'Then the Owner disposes of the helper.'

'Yes, although – nothing we've found out about Nora so far makes her sound like the kind of woman who cuts people up into little pieces.' Seeing Florin frown, she knew what he was thinking. It was impossible to know, taking someone at face value, what they were capable of. Unfortunately. Luckily. She had tried to do it so often, back then, that she had almost lost her mind.

'Have a good look at the photos from the agency dinner. She was carefree in all the pictures, completely relaxed. Until the phone call – then you can almost feel the weight on her shoulders.'

She thought about Christoph Beil. He had recognised Nora. Not her name, but her face. She would speak to him again, hound him if she had to, until he told the truth.

A few minutes before they headed off to their meeting with Hoffmann, word came in that a man had been reported missing. A man who, as the official put it, 'could fit with the profile you have, age-wise'. The individual in question hadn't turned up to work for the last week.

Florin scanned through the report that a colleague had laid on his desk. 'Herbert Liebscher, forty-eight years old, teacher. Divorced, no children.' He looked up. 'Who filed the missing persons report?'

'The school principal. He described Liebscher as being very dependable, and has no idea where he might be. They've tried to reach him on his mobile numerous times, but they just keep getting his voicemail.'

'What about the ex-wife? Has he contacted her?'

'No. Apparently they're not in touch any more.'

Beatrice walked up to Florin's desk and peered over his shoulder. The image showing Herbert Leibscher was a typical old-style passport photo: head dipped slightly, a strained smile, a blurry blue background. A long face with pale blue eyes, a narrow nose and equally narrow lips. Heavy bags under the eyes.

His hands weren't in the picture, of course.

'Send a patrol car over to the school and make sure they get a comb or some other personal article that his DNA might be on,' Beatrice directed their colleague. 'A full-length photo would be good too, one we can see his hands in. And have someone go to his apartment. If he's not there, ask the neighbours when they last saw him. It would be helpful to know as precisely as possible.'

Their colleague – what was his name again? Becker? – raised his eyebrows in disbelief. 'You don't say. We're not idiots you know.' With that, he turned on his heel and left.

Beatrice watched him go, completely baffled. 'What was all that about? Was I – I wasn't rude, was I?' Seeing that Florin was struggling to contain a grin, she couldn't help but laugh. 'Come on, tell me, what's so funny?'

'You treated Bechner like he was still at the police academy.' He stood up and gathered the files for their meeting, putting them under his arm. 'He'll go off to tell the others and confirm your reputation as a control freak.'

'Control freak?'

'Come on. You don't exactly like letting other people handle things, do you?'

'Well, when it comes to colleagues I don't work with very often, I can't know for certain how competent they are.' But at least she knew the man's name now. Bechner. She repeated it to herself a few times, glancing at the clock as she did so. Three minutes past three, they were late – wonderful. She hastily grabbed her notes and joined Florin, who was waiting for her by the door.

'It would do you good to have a little more faith in others,' he said softly. Looking at the picture of the shrink-wrapped hand on the top of his pile of documents, Beatrice wondered if he could really mean that seriously.

Their meeting with Hoffmann went like all their meetings with Hoffmann. He demonstrated his discontent with the results they had produced so far by puckering the corners of his mouth and sighing loudly. Florin was the only one he ever found favour in, so he took over reporting the investigations that they had undertaken so far. And he said she didn't ever let anyone else take control! When Florin got to the part about the text messages the Owner had sent, Hoffmann's attentiveness increased perceptibly. He trained his pale eyes on Beatrice.

'Did you try to call him?'

'Of course. But he had already turned the mobile off again. I'm sure he knows they can be used to locate people. The network he was connected to the second time was about fifteen kilometres away from the one the provider said he used the first time. He's not dumb enough to use the same location twice.'

Hoffmann wrung out a thin smile. 'I see. But nonetheless, you're clearly the one he wanted to make contact with. So I expect you to exhaust all the possibilities that arise from that. Lure him into a trap, provoke him, force him to expose a weakness.' He turned to Florin again. 'I'm sure you'll think of something, right? And you'll soon have a forensic psychologist helping you too, and then it'll be child's play. The killer has given us the fishing rod – now we just have to put the right bait on the hook.'

Drasche was up next, presenting his findings: the fingerprints on the second handwritten document belonged, yet again, to Nora Papenberg. But Beatrice was only half-listening as he explained the details. Hoffmann's last sentence was echoing in her mind. She doubted that a few well-chosen words would be enough to lure the killer out of his hiding place. She would have to give him something he really wanted.

The vehicle registration office had responded swiftly. By the time they got back to their desk from the meeting, Florin's inbox yielded a list of cars, including their owners, for which the last three digits of the number plate and model type matched the clues from the cache. It wasn't a long list: two VW Golfs, one of which was blue – a 2005 model, registered to Dr Bernd Sigart.

'If this is him, then it was pretty easy this time,' said Beatrice. She typed the name into Google, scanned through the first few entries and felt her pulse quicken. One more link and she found what she was looking for. There was no question they had found the right guy: someone who had lost everything. With scars inside and out.

'We've cracked Stage Three,' she said.

'So why do you sound so depressed?' Florin had just stood up to turn on the espresso machine, which came back to life with a gurgle.

'Because when we read the note earlier, I had a different conception of what he meant by a loser.' She cleared her throat and began to read the newspaper article she had found online.

'"Three children and a woman lost their lives last night in a fire near Scharten im Pongau. The blaze, which may have been caused by work in the surrounding forest, broke out around 10 p.m. The now-deceased family were staying in a wooden cabin they had rented as a holiday home, and may have been killed in their sleep by the fire. The husband and father Dr Bernd S., a vet, had been called out on an emergency visit and returned only after the forest and cabin were already engulfed by the blaze. His attempt to push his way through into the burning building left him with smoke intoxication and burns of an unknown degree. He is currently in the emergency unit of Salzburg hospital and, according to the doctors, is out of danger. The firemen were on site until the early hours of the morning."'

She remembered the story. The case had kept the investigators busy for months; it hadn't been possible to unequivocally determine the cause of the fire, but they had managed to rule out arson.

'What a tragedy,' she heard Florin say softly behind her. 'How long ago was that?'

'Almost five years.'

He sat back down at his computer. 'And here we have the next piece of the puzzle,' he announced. 'Sigart's registered address: Theodebertstrasse thirty-three. The street contains a name, just like Nora Papenberg's note said it would.'

They headed over to the address half an hour later, the story about the fire lying heavy as a stone in Beatrice's stomach. She resolved to approach their conversation with Sigart with a great deal of sensitivity. The street name alone was enough to find the cache, so they didn't need to visit him especially for that. But if he had known Nora Papenberg, they urgently needed to hear what he had to say.

Number thirty-three was a multi-storey building with small balconies, just a few degrees away from looking run-down. It seemed a very modest home for a vet. Beatrice rang the bell, and moments later a deep but soft voice came through the intercom.

'Yes?'

'It's the police. We're from the Salzburg Landeskriminalamt and need to speak to you briefly.'

No answer, nor the buzz of the door release.

'Hello?' she persevered.

'What do you want from me?'

'It's about a current case – we have a few questions. It won't last long.'

'Okay. First floor.'

The stairwell smelt of rubber and fried garlic; a baby was screaming behind one of the doors on the ground floor. Sigart was waiting for them at the door of his flat, a haggard man whose jogging bottoms were hanging off him loosely. According to his file, he must have been in his mid-forties, but the deep lines in his face made him look a good ten years older. His arms were crossed in front of his chest, and it was only when he uncrossed them to stretch out a hand in greeting that Beatrice saw the burn scars. Raised, reddish tissue covering his left forearm from the elbow to the fingers, as well as on his neck, stretching up to just under his chin. She took Sigart's hand and returned his firm pressure. 'Beatrice Kaspary, Landeskriminalamt. This is my colleague, Florin Wenninger. We're investigating a murder case and have a few questions we hope you might be able to answer for us.'

The flat was tiny. One room with a kitchenette and a small bathroom. Not a single picture on the walls, no mirror. In the corner, an old portable TV was perched on a stool. Next to it was a wobbly-looking table with just one chair, which Sigart now pointed to. 'Have a seat,' he said to Beatrice.

'Thanks, but . . .' Not wanting to be the only one sitting down, she accepted only when he fetched two folding chairs from the balcony and placed them around the table.

'You may have heard on the news about the body that was found in a cattle pasture near Abtenau,' Florin began. 'It's about that case. There's a detail that led us to you.'

Sigart's gaze wandered across the room. 'A detail?'

'Yes. I'm afraid I can't be more specific than that. You're

not under suspicion – we'd just like to know whether the name Nora Papenberg means anything to you.'

Unlike Beil the day before, Sigart thought for a moment before he replied. 'No, I'm afraid not. But it's hard to answer your question properly.' He spoke slowly, as if he had to check each word was correct before he was able to release it into the room. 'I met so many people every day at the practice that it's entirely possible Frau Papenberg was one of them.' He paused. 'If you like, I can look back through the files. Dr Amelie Schuster took over my practice and all its patients, and I'm sure she'd be happy to help you.'

That wasn't a bad idea. Beatrice noted the vet's name, then pulled the photos out of her bag. 'This is Nora Papenberg. Perhaps you might recognise her face.'

She watched him closely as he studied the photos. But the tiny twitch, the barely discernible jolt that had passed through Beil yesterday, was absent in Sigart. 'No,' he said finally. 'I'm sorry.'

Beatrice tried not to let her disappointment show. 'It's very likely that there's a connection between you and this woman. Maybe there's something that might come back to you?'

He shook his head. 'I hardly ever see people now. I'm sure you researched my background before you came here – in which case you must know—' He stopped abruptly. Then he took a deep breath and continued: 'I don't work, I've sold everything and I'm living off the proceeds.' He stroked his left hand over the scars, as if wanting to explore their heights and depths. 'I only leave this flat when I need to buy food, or to go to my therapy sessions.'

The horror that had distorted Sigart's existence grabbed hold of Beatrice for a split second, along with the irrational fear that his fate could seize her too.

'Is it possible,' she ventured cautiously towards a new thought, 'that your wife knew Frau Papenberg? Was she perhaps in the advertising business?'

A shake of the head. 'My wife worked in the practice with me. She took care of the administrative side. It was easy to balance that with . . . taking care of the children.' Sigart turned his head to the side. 'I'm sorry, but I'm not able to talk about it.'

'Of course. And you don't have to.' A quick glance at Florin, who shrugged helplessly.

'We'll leave our contact details here for you, Herr Sigart,' he said. 'Thank you very much for the suggestion about the client files, and for your time.' He stood up, and so did Beatrice. But as they started to leave, she turned around again.

'Does the name Christoph Beil perhaps ring any bells?'

Sigart, still trying to regain his composure, shook his head. 'No. Who is that?'

'Someone else we hoped might have known Nora Papenberg.'

Whether Sigart had heard them or not was hard to say, for he didn't react. The last image Beatrice saw before she left the flat was of his hunched, trembling shoulders.

As they drove back to the office, Beatrice took out her mobile and dialled the number of the fire investigation department. 'Please send me all the files on the fire near Scharten. Yes, the one the family died in. Sorry? No, it wasn't murder, I realise that, but I still need some of the details for our current case.'

Her colleague promised to bring the files over right away. Returning her mobile to her bag, she leant back in the passenger seat. 'Why did the Owner send us to Sigart? What does he stand to gain from that?'

'Time, possibly.' Florin honked the horn at the driver in front for braking too abruptly at a red light, then drummed his fingers on the steering wheel as he waited for the light to turn green again. 'I think there are two possibilities. One – there's a connection between Papenberg, Beil and Sigart that we're not seeing. Or two – he's keeping us busy by sending us to find people who have nothing whatsoever to do with the murder. But because he's hiding body parts all over the place for us, we're forced to follow his damn blood trail.' He rubbed his hand over his forehead and sighed. 'I just can't stop thinking that the Owner is making fools of us, Bea. He's murdering and dismembering people left, right and centre and leaving clues that no one can decipher.' Florin turned to look at Beatrice. She had never seen his face look this hard. 'I know it's wrong, but I'm starting to take this case personally. If he wants to prove how incapable the police are, I'd rather he didn't use me as a prop.'

Beatrice was just about to put a hand on his shoulder, but then thought of Anneke and stopped herself. 'It's just a question of time until the end of the case is in sight, and the rest will fall into place from there.' It wouldn't do her any harm to be the one to strengthen the team morale for a change. 'It's almost always like that.'

The lights switched back to green and the engine roared as Florin stepped on the accelerator. 'I know,' he said. 'But there's something about this case that doesn't feel right. Those threads you always talk about have been woven into a pattern that's completely alien to me.'

It was as though Beatrice had brought the sensation of heat and smoke home with her along with the reports on the fatal fire. Even though both of the lounge windows were open, she was finding it harder than usual to breathe.

The children had gone to bed half an hour ago. Everything was quiet in the apartment, everything except the water tap in the kitchen, which had been dripping for three weeks now. She opened the file and began to read. The fire had been reported shortly before ten in the evening, by a farmer whose property was a few hundred metres uphill. He had noticed the glow of the blaze; there hadn't been any smoke fumes as the wind was blowing in the other direction.

Beatrice flicked forwards to the photographs. The burnt-down wood. Remains of tree trunks protruded out of the ground like blackened teeth, with charred wood lying around them. In the background, you could just make out the part of the forest which had been untouched by the blaze.

The investigators had been unable to ascertain the cause of the fire. It was July at the time, and it hadn't rained for three weeks. The most likely theory was that the reflection of a shard of glass or mirror during the day had created a smouldering fire, which was then transformed into a raging blaze by the evening breeze. A discarded cigarette couldn't be ruled out, either.

When Beatrice got to the photos of the cabin, she instinctively held her breath. The walls had disappeared; only the thickest wooden beams had withstood the inferno, along with two sections of wall made out of stone.

She lingered longer than necessary over the pictures of the ravaged house, knowing what would come next.

Deep breath. Turn the page. A close-up of the remains of the cracked front door. Turn the page. There.

Four shapeless clumps, as black as their surroundings. Shrunk to a fraction of their body size, no longer recognisable as human beings. Beatrice looked away, then back again. She found details she didn't want to see. A flash of bright teeth behind charred lips. A burst skull. She clapped the file shut and went to the kitchen to fetch a glass of water.

Had Sigart identified his family back then? She searched for the record of his interview. He had returned when the wood was already ablaze, had tried to run into the fire and was forcibly held back by three firemen. He had been taken off to hospital with severe burns; his conversation with the authorities – which was recorded and later transcribed – had not taken place until nine days after the fire.

Every one of Sigart's sentence fragments conveyed utter despair. According to the report, the interview had to be interrupted again and again because he began to scream and the doctors had to be called.

But one thing was abundantly clear from the document: he blamed himself for his family's deaths. He had taken the car on an emergency call-out to a complicated birth at a stud farm, thirty kilometres away. As he drove off, his thoughts were already with the mother animal, which he had been taking care of for four years by then. He considered it possible that he had locked the cabin on autopilot, thereby transforming it into a deadly trap for his family. The investigation had concluded that the door had indeed been locked.

Sigart had initiated legal proceedings against himself, saying that he alone bore the responsibility for his family's deaths, and had refused a lawyer. But of course – given the tragic circumstances – he couldn't be held responsible for what had happened. The psychological report, a summary of which was included in the file, spoke of severe post-traumatic stress disorder, and of a high suicide risk. He was given access to therapy sessions, the ones which he was clearly still making use of today.

Beatrice tucked the files away in her bag and went out onto the balcony. Breathe. The sky was starry and clear, the air cool. Goose pimples pricked her arms.

Why had the Owner led her to Bernd Sigart? What was he trying to show her? Was it possible that . . .?

She sat down and held her face in her hands, trying to think clearly. Was it possible that the Owner wanted to rub one of his own crimes under her nose? Look what I did, and you lot didn't catch me!

But the fire hadn't been an arson attack. It was just very bad luck; fires often broke out in the hot summer months. Was he trying to claim ownership of it regardless? Begging for attention, perhaps? Or, as Florin suspected, was he just doing this to confuse the police?

Perhaps they would know more tomorrow. The name of the street Sigart lived in had given them the new coordinates.

Beatrice unplugged the landline, but left her mobile on. She took it with her into the bedroom and put it on the bedside table. The night passed without interruptions. But in her dreams, she was running through a burning forest to the strains of the Stabat Mater.

N47° 48.022 E013° 10.910

The waterfall crashed down a good twenty metres into the depths, colliding with a shallow pebbled basin and resuming its path as a peaceful, level stream. At its highest point, next to one of the many old mills in the area, Florin, Beatrice and Stefan were leaning over the GPS device.

The task of translating 'Theodebert' into new coordinates had taken a matter of minutes. Finding the cache, however, would be more difficult, for the navigation device was pointing them towards the rocks around the waterfall.

'It could be hidden inside the mill, but that would mean the results are very imprecise,' pondered Stefan. They agreed to clamber down the path to the stream. Drasche stayed close to their heels, lugging along his forensic case and making no effort to conceal his bad mood. He regarded the fact that he was unable to drive his car right up to the location as a personal affront.

They were completely alone here in the forest. At the weekends, the mills and waterfall were popular day-trip destinations, but today they shared the surroundings only with the birds and insects.

The tumbling cascades of water looked even more impressive from below. Beatrice felt a deep sense of foreboding, sensing that the beautiful view was about to be drowned out by something else entirely.

'A little bit further to the right.' Stefan pointed to the crag. A steep little mound, around four metres in height, was huddled up against it, sparsely vegetated with shrubbery. 'One of us should climb up. I reckon that's the spot.'

Drasche peered upwards. 'There's only room for one of us up there, and that's me. Give me the GPS.' Ebner helped him clamber up, handed the navigation device and camera to him and waited for further instructions.

Once again, a rushing sound was providing the soundtrack to their search; even though it didn't come from the autobahn this time, it was still equally pervasive. Beatrice wondered if there was some kind of pattern behind the Owner's choices of location.

'I've got it,' she heard Drasche call. 'It's smaller than the others though.' The cache was hidden in a crevice in the rock, concealed by hard-stemmed plants with nodular blooms. Drasche took some photos in situ and then made his slippery descent, holding the plastic box in his gloved hands.

This time, the container was barely bigger than a cigarette packet, its contents – pressed against the transparent lid and clearly defined – only just squeezed in. It was unmistakable: an ear, possibly two if they were laid on top of one another. 'Fuck,' exclaimed Drasche. 'More body parts. Let's just hope they're not from a different victim. If only the genetic tests could be quicker—'

Beatrice's mobile rang, interrupting Drasche mid-sentence. She pulled it out of her bag, surprised that she even had reception out here. The number was unknown. It wasn't the school, in any case. Nor Achim.

'Kaspary.'

'I . . . I found your card. Your business card.' It was a woman's voice. Her words were rushing into one another; she sounded breathless.

'Who is this?'

'Beil. Vera Beil. You were in our garden on Sunday.'

'That's right. What can I do for you, Frau Beil?'

A trembling intake of breath. 'Christoph has disappeared. Yesterday evening. He said he was just popping out, but he didn't come back all night and . . . I can't reach him on his mobile either.'

'Right, I see.'

'I'm really scared something's happened to him.' Her voice almost cracked. 'He's so reliable – he always lets me know if he's going to be late.'

The connection was cutting out. 'I'll come over to see you, Frau Beil, okay?' Beatrice hurried to speak. 'It may take an hour or even a little bit more, but I'll set off right now. Are you at home?'

'Yes. Thank you . . .'

Beatrice hung up. 'Beil's disappeared. That was his wife. I'm heading over there now.'

'I'll come too,' said Florin immediately. 'Gerd, please investigate the container as quickly as you can. We need photos of the letters as soon as possible – I'm sure there'll be some in there again.'

They didn't speak much on the steep climb up to the mill. Beatrice kept thinking of the moment when she had showed Christoph Beil the photo. Her memory of the jolt that went through his body refused to go away.

147

If I had only kept pushing. If I had pinned him down right away. If . . .

She gave herself a mental rap on the fingers. *The old what-if game won't help; it just drives you crazy. The clock can't be turned back. You can't correct the past.*

And if I could, I wouldn't be where I am today, she thought.

'He was acting strangely the whole of Sunday evening.' The tablecloth beneath Vera Beil's clasped hands was made of plastic. Brown and yellow flowers struggled against each other for dominance, smothering the dingy white background beneath.

'When did that start? Only after we left?'

'Yes. I asked him what was wrong, what he talked to you both about, but he said it was nothing important. He said you just had him mixed up with some witness.' The woman's gaze darkened. 'I sensed that he wasn't telling me the truth. Even though he never normally lies.'

'I understand,' said Florin. He had taken over the soothing, sympathetic role and was leaving it to Beatrice to ask the questions. 'So our visit clearly unsettled him.'

'Yes, you could put it like that.'

'What did your husband do for the rest of Sunday? Did he meet anyone? Speak on the phone?'

Vera Beil thought for a moment, running her right index finger along the stem of one of the brown flowers. 'No, he spent most of it in the bedroom, even though he had actually been planning to watch some crime film. Maybe he did speak to someone on the phone, I don't know. But I do know that he slept badly – he got up at least four times in the night.'

'And how was he yesterday? How long exactly has he been missing, did you say?'

'Well, first he went to work, just like always, but he was back home again by one – he said he was feeling unwell. He lay down and slept a bit, but then at around half-six in the evening, he received a phone call and rushed off. Yes, I think that's the best way of describing it. He literally ran to the car. He called out to me that he wouldn't be long – but that was all he said.'

A phone call. Florin and Beatrice exchanged a quick glance, then she pulled the Papenberg photos out of her bag.

'We'll do whatever we can to find your husband quickly,' she said. 'For now, could you please look at these pictures for us and tell us whether you recognise the woman in them?'

Vera Beil took the tissue that Florin handed to her and wiped her eyes before turning her attention to the photos. 'No. I don't know her.' She said it almost guiltily, as if she felt bad about not being able to be more helpful.

'Are you completely sure?'

'Yes. Please, find Christoph.'

It might have been easier if he hadn't lied to us on Sunday, thought Beatrice grimly. But she kept quiet and was relieved when Florin spoke up.

'We'll do everything we can,' he said. 'And we'll keep you posted, of course.'

Beatrice decided to have Beil's phone calls looked into right away, to find out where the call which had upset him so much the previous evening had come from. It wasn't improbable that it had come from a phone box in Maxglan. Or from a certain mobile phone with a prepaid card.

Until the response from the phone company came back, she hoped to be able to immerse herself in Drasche's findings, assuming that he had already sent the pictures of the new messages. Another puzzle, Stage Four.

But Beatrice didn't manage to find out, because there was someone waiting for her in front of the office. A tall, lanky man with curly hair and glasses that were a little too fashionable to be tasteful. When he saw her and Florin approaching, he jumped up from his chair and stretched his hand out.

'Dr Peter Kossar, pleased to meet you. You must be Florin Wenninger, hello. And Beatrice Kaspary, am I right? I've heard about you – a quasi-colleague, one might say?'

Confused, she returned the firm pressure of his handshake. He didn't break eye contact, and she noticed he had pronounced *Peter* the English way. 'How do you mean, *quasi*?' she asked.

'Well, I heard you studied psychology.'

The penny dropped. 'Are you the forensic psychologist we requested?'

It was as if the man considered blinking to be a weakness of some kind – Beatrice found the intensity with which he was gazing at her physically unpleasant.

'Exactly. Your boss has filled me in on the key details of the case, and the fact that the perpetrator has made contact with you. That's a highly important detail. I've already studied the text messages thoroughly, and I'll soon be able to tell you how to respond to them.'

150

He walked into the office ahead of Beatrice. At last, his gaze had left her, fixing instead on the photos she had pinned up over her desk.

'We will of course make copies of all the relevant files for you,' said Florin. It was quite clear, at least to Beatrice, that he wanted to get rid of the guy as soon as possible.

'Excellent.'

'What happened to Dr Reichenau?' enquired Beatrice. 'Up until now we've always collaborated with him on occasions such as these, and – please don't take this the wrong way – it always worked excellently.'

If Kossar was offended by her question, he didn't let on. 'My colleague is in the process of applying to be the head of an institute and is very busy right now. But I'm sure he'll be pleased to hear that you spoke so highly of him.' He pulled up a chair and sat down next to Beatrice. 'My method of working is different to Dr Reichenau's. He gleans his knowledge predominantly from the written material available, whereas I find that the more closely intertwined I am with the investigations, the better I can assess the perpetrator.'

Just what they needed. Beatrice avoided making eye contact with Florin, but hoped he would say something before she blurted out the words that were poised on her tongue. *You're getting in the way.*

'That sounds very interesting.' She knew Florin well enough to be able to detect the coldness behind his polite words. 'But I'm sure you'll want to catch up on the details of the case first.' He reached for the telephone and pressed a button. 'Stefan? Could you please put together all the important info on our Owner for Dr Kossar? Yes, a copy of the file. No, he's a forensic psychologist, and I'll send him over to you right now. Exactly. Thank you!'

'Well,' said Kossar, ignoring the subtle request for him to leave, 'perhaps I should just tell you a little about myself so that you can get an idea of my qualifications.' He straightened his glasses.

Translated, what he really meant was: *So that you are appropriately impressed.* Beatrice had studied long enough to be able to spot the traits of a narcissistic personality at first glance, and Kossar had them in abundance. While the psychologist pontificated about his additional qualifications and the fact that he had acquired them in the USA, Beatrice's thoughts wandered back to Christoph Beil.

'Impressive,' she murmured, dialling the number of the mobile network provider the Owner was using. 'Excuse me, I have to get back to work now,' she explained to a visibly irritated Kossar, watching out of the corner of her eye as he finally got up and allowed himself to be escorted to the door by Florin.

The technical support assistant she got through to was the same one as the day before.

'You've got a match,' he explained. 'The same prepaid card, registered to a network in Parsch. The number dialled was the exact one you mentioned, and the call lasted around three and a half minutes. From six twenty-four to six twenty-eight. After that, the mobile immediately went offline again.'

'Thank you.'

Florin, who had been trying to reach Drasche while she was on the phone, looked at her with his eyes narrowed. 'He phoned Beil, right?'

'Yes. It's the first time he's made a call on Nora Papenberg's mobile. We need a bugging authorisation.'

Lost in thought, she drew a circle around the notes she had made. Three and a half minutes. She would have given so much to know what was discussed in this short time period. And, even more importantly . . .

'I've got a bad feeling about Christoph Beil,' she said.

Florin frowned. 'Me too. We'll write up a missing persons report – perhaps we'll get lucky.'

She rested her forehead in her hands. 'The worst-case scenario is that the Owner has silenced him.' *And, to make matters worse, after dangling him under our noses like bait, like the promise of a solution to all the puzzles.*

She sent a description of Beil to all stations in the area, along with the instruction to keep an eye out for his car. Florin carried out the necessary calls with a dark expression on his face. He didn't say anything, but Beatrice was convinced he was harbouring the same fear she was: that they would see Beil again sooner than expected. Vacuum-packed in small portions.

That afternoon, they received news from the pathologist's office that the two hands were a genetic match; they came from the same body. Whether the DNA matched that of Liebscher, the missing teacher, would only become clear in the next day or two, but the colleague whom Beatrice had managed to insult – *Bechner, his name was Bechner,* she had it fixed in her memory now – had managed to find a comb in Herbert Liebscher's pigeonhole at the school, next to a tube of cough sweets and numerous packets of antacids.

Florin scanned through Bechner's report. 'It looks like Liebscher was . . . or *is* known amongst his colleagues as being friendly and conscientious. Not very sociable, but reliable. Although somewhat lacking when it comes to a sense of humour apparently. He teaches maths and physics.'

'And there's nothing about any recent changes in behaviour?'

'No, nothing of the sort. He was planning a two-day trip with his class which was supposed to take place next week. The director said the last time he saw Liebscher he was annoyed about the fact that not everyone had paid yet, which meant he couldn't book the bus.' Florin lowered the piece of paper with a shrug.

'Maybe he's not our guy after all.' Beatrice stretched her hand over the desk and Florin handed her the files, including three photos, one of which was a typical class picture. Twenty-six children aged around fourteen, Liebscher standing alongside them with a strained smile. A thin man with thinning hair. Another picture was a portrait shot, and a third had been taken while he was teaching. He was facing the class, a piece of chalk in his right hand, and with the left he was pointing at a functional equation on the blackboard.

Beatrice rummaged around in her desk drawer for a magnifying glass and looked at Liebscher's hands. Was it possible to ascertain whether they were the same ones that had been found in the caches, tinged with blue?

She scanned the picture at the highest resolution and zoomed in on the section showing his hands, comparing what she saw with the photos of the shrink-wrapped dismembered ones. It was certainly possible that they were the same, but she couldn't be sure. The hands in the picture were as unremarkable as the man they belonged to. She suppressed a sigh and tried to get through to Drasche again. This time, he picked up.

'You'll have your written report soon,' he boomed, without a word of greeting. 'It took longer because I had to use every damn method that's ever been invented, but we still only have Papenberg's fingerprints.'

'On a note?'

'Yep. Do you want to know about the ears? It might interest you.' That was probably the closest Drasche would get to a friendly tone in this lifetime.

'Are they from the same victim?'

'They're a matching pair, if that's what you mean. We'll need to wait on the genetic analysis to find out whether they were cut off from the same guy as the hands though.' He inserted one of his typical pauses, indicating that he wanted to be asked for further details.

'Okay.' She decided to humour him. 'Is there anything else of interest?'

'Yes.' Drasche cleared his throat and coughed. 'They weren't cut off with a saw, but a tool with two opposing blades.' He stopped, giving the information time to seep deeply enough into Beatrice's imagination to create a vague image. 'My guess would be a pair of garden shears,' he added.

All of a sudden, the image was crystal clear. Beatrice swallowed. 'I see.'

'That's only half of the story. The ears weren't vacuum-packed together, but individually. The pathologist will have to confirm it, of course, but I'm pretty sure they weren't cut off at the same time. The left one looks much more decomposed than the right.'

Beatrice took a sharp intake of breath through her teeth.

'You've guessed it, right? I think the right ear was cut off while the victim was still alive. One or two days before the left one, in any case.'

'How wonderful. Okay, please send everything over. The photos, particularly the ones of the letters, and the others too.'

'Will do.' He hung up.

A pair of garden shears. Beatrice pictured the monstrosity with steel blades which Achim had always used to trim the boxwood hedge.

'Are you not feeling well?' The concern in Florin's voice made her smile involuntarily.

'I'm fine. It seems our Owner started to mutilate his victim while he was still alive. One of the ears was probably cut off before the man died.'

'Shit,' whispered Florin hoarsely.

'Yep. Drasche is sending everything over now. Including the clues about the next stage.' Realising that she had started to arrange the pens on her desk so they were all parallel and aligned, she gave them an impatient shove before standing up and switching on the espresso machine. Caffeine was a better option than indulging in OCD-like behaviour. 'I wish we had Reichenau in the team instead of that narcissistic fool.' Beatrice quickly tipped the rest of the coffee beans from the packet into the grinder, causing about a quarter of it to spill out and tumble down onto the floor. 'Wow, I'm really on form today.'

'Don't be so hard on yourself,' said Florin. 'And go easier

on Kossar too. We barely know him – perhaps he really knows his stuff.'

'Maybe.' She cleared up the scattered beans and threw them in the bin. 'I'll do my best to be objective, okay? But don't forget he was holding us up from doing our job earlier.'

The coffee eventually helped to reunite her with her concentration. She drank the cup quickly in the knowledge that she would no longer be able to enjoy it once Drasche's photos arrived.

She went through the existing files one more time. Hands. And now ears. Was that purely arbitrary, or was there some symbolism behind it? Had the victim touched something forbidden? Heard something he wasn't supposed to hear? She tried to stop her mind going off at a tangent. Getting to the bottom of questions like those was Kossar's job, not hers.

A few minutes later, Drasche's photos arrived in her inbox. The first data files showed the ears: blood-soaked lobes, one more advanced in the decomposition process than the other. Then the letters.

The first was word-processed, as the previous ones had been, and again started with the same words.

Congratulations – you've found it!

We're still playing the same game; you should be getting familiar with it by now. What do you think of this container? I'd like to know if you draw the correct conclusions from its contents. You may well manage to, but it's unlikely to help you any further.

How are things going with your boss? And the media? Are people getting impatient yet that you haven't come up with anything?

Come on, police! Try harder.

TFTH

The noises from the street outside forced their way in through the closed window, while someone wearing high-heeled shoes could be heard walking along the corridor. *Clackclackclack.* Beatrice waited to see whether Florin would say anything, and when he didn't she cleared her throat. 'He's trying to provoke us.'

'Well, as far as I'm concerned he's doing a very good job of it.' He put his cup down a little too firmly; some of it lapped over the edge and formed a brown lake next to the telephone. 'Come on, police,' he whispered.

Just in time, Beatrice managed to save a pile of interrogation minutes from the spilled coffee. 'He seems to have some personal battle with us. We should go back through all the old files and look for someone who might feel they've been mistreated by the police, someone who blames us for their life being ruined.'

Florin grimaced. 'Well, there'll be no shortage of candidates there.'

'But, you know, sometimes it goes beyond the normal level.'

Suddenly Bechner rushed in without knocking, ignoring Beatrice and addressing Florin. 'Do you have a minute to speak about the statements from the Papenberg relatives?'

'No. Later.'

He waited until Bechner had pulled the door shut behind him, clearly affronted. 'Do you think he's doing this because of us? Torturing and killing people just to get material for his puzzles, to make life difficult for us?'

'No, I don't think that's his motive. But humiliating us and boosting his own ego is clearly important to him. Why else would he write letters like this to us?'

Beatrice clicked on the print icon. With a whirring sound, two copies of the latest cache note peeled out of the printer. Then she opened the next data file from the attachment in Drasche's email.

Once again, the puzzle was composed in Nora Papenberg's handwriting. Erratic at first, almost illegible, but halfway through it looked as though the writer had got a hold of herself.

Even after the first read-through, Beatrice could tell it was going to be exceptionally difficult this time.

Stage Four

You're looking for a key figure. His quota is over 2,000. He never concedes defeat — or so he claims — he has a loud voice and he refuses to tolerate any contradiction. His eyes may be green or blue, but you'll have to find that out for yourself. He makes a living by selling things which, as he himself says, no one needs. He's good at it, too. He has two sons, one of whom is called Felix. Find the man's place of birth and translate it into numbers, just like you did last time. Multiply the value of the first and last letters together, then times the result by 22. Add 193 and add the resulting sum to the northern coordinates from Stage Three. Multiply the tenfold value of the penultimate letter with its sevenfold value and subtract the ninefold value of the same letter from the result. Subtract the resulting sum from the eastern coordinates of Stage Three. We'll see each other there.

'Good God! Someone who sells things no one needs — great. And to top it all off, every other kid in this city is called Felix.' She was just about to reach for the printed copies when the phone rang.

'Wenninger,' Florin answered. 'Really? Where?' His lips

mouthed the word 'car' at Beatrice. 'I understand. Okay, thanks.' He hung up.

'They've found Beil's car, on a forest track near Hallwang. There's a lot of blood in it, but no sign of Beil himself. Drasche and Ebner are already on their way.' Florin's expression was unreadable, but Beatrice suspected he was thinking the same thing she was. The Owner had made it clear he wouldn't stop at two victims.

'Do you know what I think?' she asked softly.

'Hmm?'

'If Beil had admitted on Sunday that he knew Nora Papenberg, if he had explained to us how he knew her, then he wouldn't be missing now.'

'There are too many "if"s there for my liking.'

Yes, thought Beatrice, unfortunately there were. But if she disregarded her suspicions and ignored her instincts, then the case just gaped in front of her like a black hole. A hiding place for which there were no coordinates.

'When I read the last message through again,' said Florin, 'it sounds to me as though Stage Four is close to the final destination. For the first time, we're searching for someone who the Owner admits is important − not a singer, not a loser, but a *key figure*.'

'True.' Assuming there was any kind of concept behind the puzzles.

There was no way around it; they wouldn't get any further without Kossar's help.

'It's fine with me, but have you asked the children whether they'd like to?'

'Of course, Mama. They always love seeing you, you know that.'

They would hurtle around her mother's restaurant like eager young pups, serving the odd salad here and there just like Beatrice had as a child. There was no reason to feel guilty.

Jakob was beaming with excitement; he had packed his apron and was rummaging around in the drawer for a wooden spoon, which he was adamant he wanted to take with him. There was excitement in Mina's expression too, but something else besides. Beatrice sat down next to her on the bed. 'Everything okay, sweetie?'

'Sure. I don't mind that you're offloading us on Oma.'

'That I'm – what?'

'Offloading us. I like going to Oma's – there's always lots of people there, and they're all nice to us.'

It wasn't hard to work out where the new word had come from. Beatrice took a deep breath and tried to keep smiling. No hostile comments around the children; that was the agreement, and she would keep her word even if Achim clearly couldn't. 'Offloading you is something completely different,' she explained. 'I'm taking you to Oma's because I have to work late for the next few days and I want you to be looked after.'

Mina shrugged. 'Like I said, it's okay.'

Beatrice tucked away everything they might possibly need in their bags and tried to suppress the thought that all she ever seemed to do was pack her children's things. Her mobile rang, making her worry that her mother had already changed her mind, but then she read Florin's name on the display.

'We're making progress – the results of the DNA analysis are back. The body parts really do belong to Herbert Liebscher. I'm going to visit his ex-wife this evening – Stefan might come with me . . .'

'If you can wait half an hour, I'll come. I'll hurry – I'm just taking the kids to my mother's first.'

'Good.' His voice sounded flat. 'Then I'll have a brief break and walk around the block. Or have a bite to eat. See you in a bit.'

One last quick glance at the clock. Did they have everything?

'Mina, Jakob, put your shoes on please. We're going!'

Getting the children away from the apartment felt like the right thing to do. The air in Mooserhof was filled with the aroma of home-cooked food and, most importantly, was free from any thoughts of dismembered corpses.

They met at the car pool pick-up station. 'I spoke to Liebscher's ex-wife on the phone. We're driving to her place first, then his apartment – we've got a search warrant from the Department of Public Prosecutions,' explained Florin as he held the car door open for Beatrice. 'Stefan managed to get hold of the spare key Liebscher kept at the school.'

'Is Stefan not coming?'

'He's slept the least out of all of us these last few days. He's about to drop, even though he won't admit it. I sent him home.'

The woman who opened the door of the terraced house to them was pale and, although the evening was one of the warmest of the year so far, wrapped up in a cardigan.

'Romana Liebscher,' she introduced herself. 'Please come in.' Beatrice and Florin followed her into a small living room with pale yellow walls; a little run down, but neat and tidy. In front of the corner sofa was a coffee table from IKEA. They sat down.

'I have no idea what to say . . . I didn't even know that Herbert was missing. And now he's—' She exhaled noisily. 'What happened?'

'We're not entirely sure yet, but we're doing everything we can to find out.' No one could give vague answers with as much conviction as Florin, thought Beatrice.

'How often had you been in contact recently?' Beatrice asked, in an attempt to delay questions which would inevitably lead to vacuum-packed body parts.

The woman's hands wandered over to a tea-light holder shaped like a wooden boat and began to fiddle with it, turning it over and over. Right, left, right. 'Hardly at all. I've been in a new relationship for years now. Herbert and Dietmar don't exactly get on—' She looked up, clearly struck by the sudden awareness that she could have just made her life partner a suspect. 'But they never really argued,' she added hastily.

'I understand what you mean.' Florin's smile had the desired soothing effect, and Beatrice willingly left the remainder of the usual catalogue of questions to him: when had she last seen him, did he have any enemies, debts, shady acquaintances . . .?

The answers Liebscher's ex-wife gave painted the picture of a nondescript life without any particular highlights. A teacher who enjoyed his job, sometimes doing extra tutoring to bring in some extra money, and who went hiking or mountain biking in his free time. He had no debts and was neither loved nor hated by his pupils.

'Why did you decide to get divorced?' asked Beatrice. The answer was no surprise: tedium, monotony. They had grown apart, and then Romana Liebscher had met another man.

'We've been divorced for three years and have seen each other perhaps five times since, the last time was eight or nine months ago,' she said. 'It sounds terrible, but I can't tell you anything about him. Not even whether he had a girlfriend.' Now, and to her own relief it seemed, she burst into tears.

They gave her the time she needed to gather her composure.

'Will I have to identify him?' she whispered.

'No, that won't be necessary.' Florin's answer came a little too quickly and firmly. The woman looked up.

She's not stupid, thought Beatrice. She's realised it would be better not to ask for details.

'It's a complicated case, and we can't allow the details to make their way into the public eye yet,' explained Florin. 'But I promise we'll let you know when we find out who did this, and the circumstances.'

'Could you not at least tell me how it happened? Was he shot . . . or beaten up? Did he go quickly?'

Beatrice thought about the ear. The garden shears.

'I'm sorry.' She filled those two words with genuine sympathy. 'At the moment we don't yet know. But you would be helping us very much with our investigations if you could look at these photos for us.'

Without holding out any great hope, Beatrice fetched the pictures of Nora Papenberg from her bag. But Nora's face was completely unknown to Romana Liebscher.

A sombre mood dominated the car journey to Herbert Liebscher's apartment, even though Florin was constantly searching the radio for a station playing upbeat tunes. It was already getting dark outside. Beatrice looked at her watch; it was after eight. They would have a quick look around the apartment and search for contact details of any friends or acquaintances. Take the computer with them, if there was one. Speak to the neighbours.

The apartment was on the second floor, and there was no lift. As they opened the door, they were met by the smell of kitchen waste in urgent need of disposal.

'I'll go in first, if that's okay with you,' said Florin. A quick glance through the few rooms was enough to clarify that they were alone.

Liebscher had clearly been content with a modest amount of space. A living room, a bedroom, a kitchen with a small table, and a compact bathroom. On the kitchen table stood a full ashtray and the crockery from Liebscher's last breakfast – the half-eaten marmalade on toast had developed mould, while the remains of his coffee had dried up in the mug to form a congealed black layer. Beatrice was overcome by the same sadness she had felt at the sight of Nora Papenberg's unfinished bar of chocolate. She turned away, gave the stinking bin a wide berth and went into the bedroom.

An unmade bed. Wide enough to fit one person comfortably, but too narrow for two. A neat and tidy computer workstation, on which, alongside the keyboard and mouse, there were three piles of books. A bookcase, predominantly stocked with biographies, but with a few travel books and novels too – all the usual bestsellers. Amongst them, Beatrice spotted a small wooden box, like a mini treasure chest. With her gloved fingers, she picked it up off the shelf and opened the lid.

Coins. They were all in transparent plastic coating and displayed a variety of motifs – a ship, a wolf's head, a logo—

'Florin!' Beatrice held one of the coins up into the light to make sure, but there was no doubt – there was the logo, and it was on the plastic coating too. 'He was a cacher. Liebscher went geocaching!'

Geocoinclub: TFTC was inscribed on the copper-coloured coin, with a little stick man, hiking, depicted beneath in white enamel. Engraved on the edge, Beatrice found a combination of letters and numbers, a kind of code. On the other side, the stick man again, followed by another inscription: *Track at Geocaching.com.*

'This is great.' Squinting, Florin looked at the coin and then placed it back in the treasure chest. 'Now we might finally be able to make some progress.'

Hopefully they would, as Stefan's online research still hadn't borne any fruit. He was reading through the geocaching forums on a daily basis and had made contact with a number of their members, but so far without success. There were no clues about anyone having left abnormal objects – like dead animals or excrement, perhaps – behind in caches before. No one had heard of any incidents like that. 'The geocaching scene is incredibly clean and environmentally aware,' Stefan had declared, not without a certain degree of pride.

Beatrice searched through the desk, then went into the living room where there was another bookcase. There was also a sofa suite with a garish brown–green pattern, and in front of it a glass coffee table from which no one had wiped away the water rings. Opposite it was a dusty old-fashioned tube TV left on standby mode.

She didn't see it right away, but her eyes were drawn back to the spot almost involuntarily. She stopped and stared.

TFTH

Someone had written the four letters on the TV screen, swirled through the dust.

'Florin? Look at this!' Beatrice pulled her camera out of her bag and shot five pictures in close-up, then another six from different distances and angles, before grabbing her phone and calling Drasche on his home number.

She heard the TV on in the background as he answered.

'We're in Liebscher's apartment and we've got the computer, but you should come here too. It seems like the Owner has been here.'

After a short conversation with Drasche ('Don't touch anything else and get the hell out of there!') Beatrice retreated to a quiet corner of the apartment and leant on the wall between the kitchen and the bathroom.

Maybe she was about to make a huge mistake. Or maybe it was exactly the right move. But she would only know afterwards. Hoffmann himself had said that she should exhaust all the possibilities, and Kossar hadn't made a single suggestion. She was fed up of waiting. The Owner's messages had been sent to her personally, so it was time to react personally.

She opened the last text he had sent her − Cold, completely cold − and pressed 'Reply'. Debating for a moment exactly what to say, she realised that, given where they were, there was only one possibility.

Herbert Liebscher

It looked like the beginning of a sentence, of a newspaper report, as if she were about to write: 'Herbert Liebscher was murdered in early May; it was a week before anyone noticed he was missing.' Or perhaps: 'Herbert Liebscher: You cut off his hands and ears. We may be slow, but we're getting closer.'

But she didn't write that. She left it at first name and surname, not even adding a full stop, and pressed 'Send'.

The neighbours didn't know anything. Most of them were elderly people who hadn't had any contact with Liebscher, and all they could say about him was that he lived a quiet life. Which was synonymous with: he was a pleasant enough neighbour. Female visitors? No. Friends, colleagues? Very rarely.

By the time they got back to the car it was half-past eleven. Beatrice tried to look discreetly at the display on her mobile. The Owner hadn't replied yet. But believing he would have done was pretty laughable given that he only switched his mobile on for a few minutes at a time. He would get her message when he wanted to send another of his own.

'Any news from the children?'

So Florin had noticed after all. She quickly shoved her mobile back in her bag. 'No. But that's good. If I don't hear anything it means all's well.'

He glanced at her searchingly. 'Why are you so edgy?'

'Am I?'

'You seem to be.' The next traffic light was red. He released the clutch and turned around to face her. 'Have you had dinner yet?'

Food. Now that Florin mentioned it she felt an empty tug in her stomach. 'No, not yet. But it's fine, I've got some bread and ham at home. That'll do me.'

'I disagree.' The light turned green. 'We need to look after ourselves too, you know.' He drove on slowly, his eyes fixed on the road again, but with an expression alternating between thoughtfulness and concern. 'I notice that every time: whenever we're working on a difficult case, you reduce your needs to a minimum. Eating, drinking, sleeping – it's as though none of it matters to you any more.'

'It's good for the figure,' she murmured. But her retort sounded a little pathetic and certainly wasn't an appropriate response for Florin's earnest words. She found herself wishing she could take it back.

'I'm not joking, Bea.' He indicated and veered off into Alpenstrasse. 'Let's take the computer to Stefan's office, then go and get something to eat. A nice relaxed dinner, without discussing the case. Or even better – we can go to my place.

I have roast beef at home, loads of leftover chicken salad, and if you want something hot there's some delicious chilli con carne.'

The suggestion awoke something else besides hunger in Beatrice, something she didn't want to examine more closely, not under any circumstances.

'Thanks, but I'm really tired, and tomorrow we both have to get up early and . . . well, maybe Anneke wouldn't like it.'

He gave her a bemused look. 'Why would she have anything against it?'

Why indeed? It's not like I'm a woman or anything, Beatrice was about to blurt out, but she didn't say anything, laughing instead and hoping it sounded light-hearted and not as awkward as she felt.

Florin parked the car alongside the others in the car pool, turned the ignition off and brushed one of the unruly strands of dark hair off his forehead. 'If I didn't know better, I might think you suspected me of having other intentions than getting you to eat a decent meal.' He smiled, his teeth the only bright thing inside the darkness of the car.

'Don't be silly, I didn't think that for a second. It's just that—'

'It's important to spend at least a few minutes a day enjoying life. Otherwise we'll end up burning out. Come on – some good food, a glass of wine, music and talking about something other than murder for half an hour.'

She closed her eyes. 'Okay.'

Florin's apartment was close to the old town and most definitely not that of your average policeman. When Beatrice had come here for the first time around six months ago, she had asked him if he was taking backhanders to be able to afford digs like this. He had denied it, but the truth was clearly just as embarrassing to him: a rich family and a deceased grandmother who had left him not only money, but this penthouse too.

Walking in, she was met by the scent of acrylic paints. Florin went off to open the windows and terrace doors while Beatrice chose a place to sit from the immense landscape of seating options.

Everything was upholstered in white. Imagining Jakob running around here with his chocolate-smeared fingers, and Mina with her felt-tip pens, Beatrice couldn't help but laugh. No, Florin didn't have any such intentions when it came to her, most definitely not.

She looked at the walls, the ledge over the open fire, the antique bookcases – there was no photo of Anneke to be seen. They were probably in the bedroom, where they belonged. Beatrice stretched out.

'Fancy a splash of champagne?' called Florin. He was standing in the open-plan kitchen, holding up a bottle. 'We're off duty now, so we're allowed.'

'But I still have to drive. Half a glass at the most.'

'Okay.'

He came over to her with two delicate champagne flutes in his hand and passed the half-full one to her. 'It'll kick in quickly on an empty stomach. Do you already know what you'd like to eat?'

'Yes. Roast beef. Please.'

'And salad with avocado and lime dressing?'

She should have realised that Florin wouldn't just serve up the average snack. 'Sure sounds delicious.'

While he busied himself in the kitchen, she checked her phone again. Still nothing. But she was fine with that right now.

'Do you have any paintings on the go at the moment?' she called.

'Yes. Two. But neither is going well. There's not a flicker of life in them.' The clatter of plates. 'Do you want to see? Go on up if you'd like.'

His studio consisted of a chaotic corner one floor up, with an overhead light, two easels, a paint-spattered wooden table and a collection of blank canvases of varying sizes. It smelt of paint and solvents.

'How about some music?' Florin's voice resonated up from below.

'Sure, go ahead.'

'Any special requests?'

She hesitated for a moment. 'Whatever's in the player right now.'

Whatever you put on when you're here alone, painting, reading, thinking about Anneke.

'Okay.'

It was no longer the Erik Satie album she'd heard down the phone the last time. It was Schubert's String Quintet in C major, the second movement. The kind of music that made Beatrice feel as if just one misguided thought would be enough to make her burst into tears.

She drank her champagne down in one gulp and positioned herself in front of the first easel.

Red, bright in the middle, dark around the edges. Silver streaks across the left corner, as though something had splintered. The sight unleashed something within her that she didn't want to face up to right now. She stepped aside and looked at the second easel.

A square canvas, which at first sight depicted an eternity of blue. Towards the middle, the colour darkened until it was almost black, with metallic specks flying through the darkness as if someone had stomped into a puddle of molten copper. The picture was like this evening: a spark of light amidst the darkness.

'Not that great, right?' she heard Florin ask.

'No, they are. Sorry, but I . . .' *I love this one*, she wanted to say, but bit back the words at the last moment. 'I think it's beautiful. Strong – and unfathomable, with a glimmer of hope.'

Florin had come up the stairs and was now standing next to Beatrice, his head cocked to the side. 'Really? Hmm. I think I'll need to take a fresh look at it. But not tonight.' He rotated the canvas ninety degrees. 'It might work like that though. Come on, dinner's ready.' Beatrice felt his arm around her shoulders, the light pressure as he pulled her towards the stairs. 'I'm starving.'

It was a long time since she had been able to enjoy a meal without having to stare at her computer or tame her children at the same time. The roast beef was tender, cut at just the right thickness, and Florin had warmed up a baguette to go with it. Because Beatrice didn't have the slightest desire to let her enjoyment of it be diminished, she drank another glass of champagne, noticing how light-headed it was making her.

'Why are you doing this?' The question slipped out before she could stop it.

'What exactly am I doing?'

'Inviting me round after the working day's over. I would have thought you'd be relieved not to have me under your feet any more.'

He raised his eyebrows. 'I like having you under my feet, as you so nicely put it. And besides—' He stopped, shook his head and topped up both their glasses.

'Carry on.'

'No. It might come out the wrong way. It's the kind of comment which could lead to a misunderstanding.'

She tried to formulate a question in her mind that would encourage him to be more specific, but he shook his head with a smile before she could come up with one. 'Wrong day, wrong time, wrong mood.'

Beatrice put her glass down on the table, suddenly aware of how tired she felt. 'Which door is the bathroom?'

'The second on the right.'

It was spacious, tiled in elegant grey and far too well lit. The mirror confronted Beatrice with her pale face, tired eyes, and the dark rings beneath them. For a moment, she thought about reapplying her lipstick, but immediately dismissed the thought as ridiculous.

Instead, she splashed a little water on her face and looked at the clock. It was already half-past one in the morning.

'I have to get going,' she said as she walked back into the living area.

'Or you could sleep here.' He held his hands up reassuringly before she could respond. 'I have a spare room with lots of space, and no, you wouldn't be imposing.' He pointed towards a door behind him. 'I really would prefer it if you did. After all, we drank more than one glass.'

Beatrice gave in. It was less the thought of the ten-minute drive, and more that of her empty apartment with the nocturnally active telephone.

When Christoph Beil awoke, the world around him consisted of intense darkness. For a few moments, boundless gratitude streamed through him.

He had dreamt it all.

But the very next moment, the pain came back. His sore wrists were burning and throbbing behind his back, and every time he swallowed it felt as if nails were tearing into his larynx. It was all real. He hadn't survived anything.

At least he seemed to be alone now. He held his breath, listening in case he could still hear breathing in the room. He heard something, but it might have been the wind. A gentle, quiet breeze between the leaves.

Gradually, he began to realise that the darkness wasn't necessarily synonymous with night. Something had been bound tightly around his head and eyes.

The noose around his neck was gone, and he was sitting now, but the pain in his throat was still unbearable. He tried not to swallow, but that only made it more difficult. His salivary glands worked as though his very awareness of their existence was spurring them on to hyperactivity.

It hurt so much.

He whimpered involuntarily. Thought about the police-woman with the blonde hair who had given him a chance.

Wished fervently, with all the energy he had left, that he could turn back time.

There. A noise. He raised his head and struggled to suppress a sob. Tried to speak, but his voice was only a rasp and trembled so much that hardly a word he said was decipherable. At the third attempt, he managed to get a whole sentence out.

'Will you . . . let me go?'

He didn't get an answer. Maybe he was mistaken; maybe he was alone after all and his mind was just playing tricks with him. That would be good. Better than the alternative.

It was only when he heard the cough that he realised his senses were still functioning. He struggled against the ties that bound him. 'Please, let me go, I've told you everything.'

A hand on his head, almost a caress. And then the voice.

'That doesn't change the fact that I still don't know enough.'

The morning was sunny and bright, announcing its arrival through the broad slats of the half-shut Venetian blinds. Beatrice awoke gradually for a change, drifting slowly and languidly at the surface of her consciousness.

The shirt she was wearing smelt of unfamiliar washing powder. Because . . . she wasn't at home, but in Florin's spare room. She sat up, feeling as though she had slept too late, but her watch said it was only half-past six. Her next glance was directed at her mobile, and even though she was sure an incoming message would have woken her, she still checked to be sure. Nothing.

Tiptoeing on bare feet, she made her way out to the bathroom. Florin was standing at the hob frying eggs, his hair still wet. 'I've put towels on the stool next to the shower, and you'll find everything else by the sink,' he called.

While she was brushing her teeth, Beatrice wondered why she felt much fresher than she usually did at this time of the morning. And younger. It reminded her of her days as a student, of staying overnight in unfamiliar flatshares after long parties, of—

Pushing the thoughts away, she rinsed out her mouth, got under the shower and started to plan the day ahead. Their main goal was to find the key figure.

'We worked on it all night.' Drasche shot Beatrice a look which implied that she was personally responsible for that fact. 'The apartment wasn't the scene of the crime, that much is clear.'

'Did you find fingerprints? The letters on the TV screen were most likely left by the killer.'

'Who wore gloves, yet again.' He raised his coffee cup to his lips, took a slurp and pulled a face. 'All of the prints we've evaluated so far are the victim's. For which, as luck would have it, we have a variety of fingers at our disposal for comparison.' He laughed. 'The car hasn't been much help either. There are some hairs, presumably belonging to Beil's wife. Unless the perpetrator has long blonde hair – shit!' In the process of gesticulating wildly to depict the hair length, Drasche had spilt coffee all over his shirt. 'So, did you two at least manage to get home at a reasonable hour in the end?'

Beatrice felt herself go red. Of course Drasche didn't know anything about her sleepover – *innocent* sleepover – at Florin's. Each of them had driven to work in their own cars. But she still felt as though she'd been caught in the act.

'There's no need to look so offended. I know you two work hard too.'

Offended. Smiling, Beatrice shook her head. Drasche was in exactly the right job with the forensics. He wouldn't have been suited as a psychologist.

As soon as she was out of the room, the first person she saw — appropriately, given that last thought — was Kossar, waiting in front of the door to her office. She sighed and ushered him in.

'I had a very interesting evening,' he began. 'Where's Wenninger? I think this will interest him too. In fact, I'm sure it will.'

'Florin's with Hoffmann. I'm sure he'll be here soon though, so let's make a start. Do you want a coffee?'

He did. While Beatrice busied herself with the machine, he sauntered around the room, inspecting everything closely as though he was thinking of buying it.

It was only when she sat down that he too pulled up a chair. 'I haven't created a definitive perpetrator profile yet, of course,' he said. 'I'll need to study as many similar cases as I can from the files before I can make a substantiated testimony. But I have managed to establish some first impressions, and in my opinion they should stand up to inspection.' He looked at Beatrice expectantly.

'And?' she asked, a little confused. 'Please go on.'

'Okay. We can assume that we're dealing with a perpetrator who is planning his actions, rather than acting in an uncontrolled way. He's not just killing his victims, but also satisfying other needs, one of which particularly jumps out at me: that he wants to be in contact with us. He sends his messages via the murdered victims — the tattooed coordinates with Nora Papenberg, the notes in the caches, and not least the body parts. He forces us to listen to him, and to engage with what he sends us.'

That was nothing new. 'So you think his main motive is a desire for attention?'

'Without a doubt. He also wants to pit himself against us, to prove himself; that comes across very clearly in his messages.'

'But it's also very clear that he doesn't take us seriously. Why would he want to pit himself against someone who he regards to be incapable?'

Kossar straightened his glasses. 'Well, have you ever been to a boxing match? Before it starts, the opponents often shout abuse at each other, provoking one another. By doing so, they motivate themselves and try to make the other man angry, because then he might make mistakes.' He sipped at his coffee. 'I suspect the perpetrator exhibits strong narcissistic tendencies. He enjoys picturing the police trying to fathom the pieces of the puzzle he's throwing at their feet. I'm sure he'd love to be here in person, watching us come up with theories and pulling our hair out in frustration because none of it makes any sense.'

Florin had arrived in the middle of the last sentence. 'Is that what you think?' he asked. 'Does none of the information in the files make any sense to you?'

'No, on the contrary. But at the moment the information we have mainly draws attention to individual aspects of the perpetrator's psyche.'

'Like what, for example?'

Kossar stared thoughtfully at his hands. 'Normally, when a person is acting like this I would assume he picks his victims at random, studies them for a while and then rips them from their lives. Like God, you see? He watches how his chosen ones contend with their daily lives, drive their cars, care for their families, knowing that he's going to put an end to it all, at a time and in a way that suits him. Like a sadistic child watching an anthill and then plunging a burning match into it.'

Kossar lifted a finger. For a moment, he resembled a pompous old headmaster giving a lecture. 'But unlike most perpetrators who act like that, this one is making a connection between the victims. He leads us from one to the next: Nora Papenberg was the signpost to Herbert Liebscher's body parts. Those, in turn, led us to Christoph Beil and on to Bernd Sigart. Now Beil has disappeared, and you—' he looked at Beatrice – 'have a feeling that he knew Nora Papenberg but kept quiet about it.'

'Yes. And the longer I think about it, the more sure I am.'

'That's very interesting.' He propped his chin in his hand, his forehead furrowed, gaze averted to the side.

Good God, what a show he puts on, thought Beatrice. 'And what do you conclude from that?' she asked, in a tone that left no doubt of her low expectations. But Kossar wouldn't be distracted.

'There was a case in the USA some years ago; a twenty-nine-year-old man who killed people who had a particular breed of dog. They didn't know each other, but they all had this one thing in common. Maybe we'll find something like that with Herbert Liebscher and Nora Papenberg too.'

It was an idea they couldn't immediately dismiss, in any case. 'The best lead so far,' Beatrice summed up, 'is this desire for attention that the Owner clearly has. What would happen if we took that away from him?'

For a moment, Kossar's lopsided smile made him look almost endearing. 'Presumably he would try to force it.'

'Then I think it's time to change the rules of play on our

side,' she said. 'If what you're saying about him is true, and he really does want to be a fly on the wall here, then I'm sure he's following the news and buying the papers to find out as much as he can about how the investigations are coming along. If nothing is being mentioned all of a sudden – then I'm sure he wouldn't like it in the slightest.'

'That's absolutely right.' The smile on Kossar's face deepened. 'It's a shame that you never finished your studies.'

'Indeed.' Beatrice made no attempt to hide the irritation in her voice. 'Anyway, let's make use of these insights.'

Within two hours, following Hoffmann's intervention, the Department of Public Prosecutions had imposed a gagging order on the press, preventing them from publishing details about the case.

The bus rumbled along the uneven road. Bernd Sigart's forehead banged lightly on the pane of glass he was leaning against, which fogged up every time he exhaled. Observing his breathing calmed him down. Every intake and exhalation of breath was one less to contend with. The number was endless.

He closed his eyes. Perhaps, this time, he would just stay seated when his stop came. Keep riding the same route on the bus over and over again, until someone threw him off.

No, he warned himself. Tiredness cannot be permitted as an excuse to let yourself fall, no more than despair and weariness of life could. The appointment would take place, just like every week. And just like every week, it wouldn't help.

As he got off the bus, a woman with a limping Alsatian crossed his path, but it was only when he rang the bell to the practice that he realised he hadn't immediately made a flash diagnosis out of habit.

Another goodbye. He was no longer a father or a husband – and now he was gradually ceasing to be a vet.

Dr Anja Maly's therapy practice was decorated in cream tones which were intended to encourage relaxation, the only real fleck of colour coming from a dense blue meditation picture hanging over the desk. Everything here was designed to promote calm, not least Maly herself. Moving majestically like a tall ship, she came slowly over from the window to greet him, squeezing his hand and gesturing for him to take a seat on the armchair.

Sigart sat down.

'Would you like a glass of water?' She asked him that every time, even though he had never once said yes. This time, too, he shook his head. 'How have you been this week?'

He looked her in the eyes, without smiling. 'I didn't kill myself.' It was the same answer he always gave.

'I'm glad to see that.' The doctor flicked through her files. 'Tell me what's happened over the last few days. We agreed that you should go for a walk for half an hour each day. How did that go?'

He hesitated. 'I didn't manage to go every day. But I went three times.'

She smiled as if he had really made her happy. 'That's a wonderful improvement. How did you feel afterwards?'

He looked to the side, thinking for a moment. 'I don't know. Strange. Once I felt like someone was following me, but it was probably just the thing that's always following me. My conscience.'

184

Maly made a note in her file. 'Did you turn around and see if there was really anyone there?'

'No. Well, not properly, I mean. It was more of a blur, like someone had just ducked into a doorway or disappeared behind a delivery van. Do you know what I mean?' The long sentence had exhausted him. A glance at the clock told him that he had only been here for five minutes, and now he wished he really had stayed on the bus.

'Yes, I can imagine.' Maly's pen scurried across the page. 'Let's come back to the subject of your conscience again.'

He waved his hand dismissively. 'What's the point? I know I didn't set the forest on fire. But the fact is and remains that I didn't see the signs. Miriam asked me not to drive off and she was really upset with me that I was doing it regardless. She was . . .' He put a hand over his eyes.

Then go to hell, Bernd, if you can't even make time for us on holiday.

And that's exactly what he had done. He had taken the most direct and harrowing route to hell imaginable.

When he looked up, Anja Maly's gaze was resting on him, patient and empathetic. He pulled himself together. 'I wasn't there, that's what it comes down to. There's no way that therapy can erase that knowledge from my mind. If I hadn't driven to the stud farm, if I'd sent a colleague instead, my family would still be alive. There's not a shadow of a doubt about that. I could have made sure that everyone got out of the house.' He took a deep breath, but it was as though none of it was making its way into his lungs. 'If you knew how often I dream about it. I smell the smoke and see the flames in the forest, but I don't panic, I just open the door, then I get Miriam and wake the children quickly – Lukas and Hanna run out, and I carry Oskar. We even have enough time to take our most important possessions with us. By the time we're sat in the car the fire is getting closer, but the route down to the valley is clear, and it only takes us ten minutes to get down there. Miriam has phoned the emergency services on her mobile, and they pass us on the road, two big fire engines, their sirens turned on. I park by the church and know that everything's fine. I turn around and see the children on the back seat, and I'm almost exploding with happiness, because I did things right this time, I turned back the clock. Miriam puts her hand on my shoulder, and Lukas says: "Do you think there'll be another fire engine, Papa?" And then I wake up.'

He could feel the tears running down his face, but didn't wipe them away. He didn't have the strength to lift his hand. 'Every time I think – this time it will kill me, that moment when I realise they're all gone, for ever. Do you know what I do then?'

Anja Maly shook her head, looking moved. 'Tell me.'

'I make it worse. In my head, I go back to the moment when I saw what the fire did to my children. Charred, distorted . . . things. So tiny. Did you know that the heat can make limbs explode?'

His words were clearly getting to her. She had children herself, her assistant had told him that, and he could see in her eyes that she was trying to stop the picture he was so vividly describing from seeping into her mind.

'Every single time I think the pain is going to kill me, because it really feels like that. Physical cramps, choking fits.

But it never happens.' He sank his gaze down to the parquet floor. 'Other people die so easily. They have heart attacks, or cancer. My body just keeps living . . . unless I destroy it with my own hands.'

Maly cleared her throat. 'You're punishing yourself for something that isn't your responsibility. I can understand that you make a connection between your absence and the death of your family, but it wasn't in your power to predict such a fateful event—'

He interrupted her with a wave of his hand. 'Let's leave it. There was something unusual that happened last week, as it happens. It might be of interest to you.'

'Oh, yes?'

'The police paid me a visit.'

'Really? Why?'

'It was about some woman who was murdered. It was really strange actually – the police wanted to know if I knew her. But I didn't.'

'So then why is the event significant to you?'

Good question. 'I don't know. Maybe because it was the first time in a long while that I've spoken to the police. A woman and a man, they were both very considerate.' He stopped, trying to formulate a thought, and wondered how Maly would interpret it. 'It was almost a good feeling, somehow, speaking about a murder case that didn't affect me.'

★

His quota is over 2,000. He never concedes defeat – or so he claims – he has a loud voice and he refuses to tolerate any contradiction.

Beatrice read through the description of the 'key figure' for what must have been the tenth time in a row. The word she kept lingering over was 'quota'. What kind of quota could be over 2,000? A hit ratio? Was the man connected with weapons in some way?

She rubbed her forehead. Weren't quotas usually given in percentages? But 2,000 per cent was mathematical nonsense. What was plausible, though, was 2,000 geocaches. In this context, it could be a highly active cacher, a real professional. Someone like that should be easy enough to track down online.

His eyes may be green or blue, but you'll have to find that out for yourself. He makes a living by selling things which, as he himself says, no one needs. He's good at it, too.

So he works in sales of some kind. Perhaps the quota was in reference to that? Wasn't there something like in-house sales statistics in a lot of companies?

It was infuriating: nothing, nothing at all in this clue could be used. Especially not the last sentence of the description.

He has two sons, one of whom is called Felix.

Felix could just as easily be three as twenty-three, and the number of boys named Felix in the surrounding area was probably in the thousands. Exasperated, Beatrice struggled to think clearly. 'The other two clues were child's play compared to this—'

At that moment, her phone vibrated.

Beatrice jumped up and grabbed for her phone, feeling her heart pound throughout her entire body.

It wasn't a message from the Owner, but Achim, who must have somehow found out that the children were at Mooserhof.

You should have custody taken away from you. You're always offloading the kids, and have been for years. You're not fit to be a mother.

Feeling raw inside, Beatrice erased the message. Her gaze met Florin's. He was clearly waiting for her to say something.

'Sorry,' she mumbled. 'It's just another message from my ex.'

She put her mobile away again, aware of him watching her. 'You were expecting something else, right?' he asked.

All she could manage was a shrug. 'Well, it could have been the Owner.' For a few moments, Beatrice was tempted to tell Florin about the lone hand she had played. If you could call it that, but the description seemed to hit the nail on the head. Hoffmann would go mad if he found out she had taken it upon herself to respond to the killer without consulting the others first.

Well, then he would finally have something worth going mad about.

She changed the subject. 'If we're not making any progress on the next stage, then how about with Herbert Liebscher? Has anyone questioned his colleagues at the school yet?'

'Stefan went there with two of our guys. But nothing useful came of it. Three of Liebscher's colleagues knew that he was a geocacher, so Stefan spoke to them for a good while, but unfortunately he didn't find out anything we don't already know.'

Beatrice drew circles on her notepad, lost in thought. 'Liebscher went geocaching, we can take that as a given. But Papenberg didn't, unless her husband was lying to us, which would pose the question of why. And we didn't question Beil about it.' Beatrice didn't say it out loud, but she doubted they would ever get the opportunity to remedy that.

Beil's wife phoned their office for what must have been the fifth time that day – she had been out of her mind with worry ever since hearing that her husband's car had been found. Luckily for Beatrice, Florin took the call, repeating with seemingly limitless patience the same thing he had already said the last few times. That they were doing everything they could to find Christoph Beil. That they would be in touch as soon as they had any news. Then he paused. 'Actually, it's possible you might be able to help us with something. Do you happen to know whether your husband ever went geocaching?' He turned the phone onto loudspeaker so Beatrice could listen in.

'That's . . . the thing with the navigation devices, right?' The woman's tear-choked voice resounded out from the speaker. 'To be honest, I don't know. He had so many hobbies. If he did do it, then he never told me about it.'

'Don't you spend your free time together?'

A hiccoughing sob. 'Not always. He's much more sporty than I am, and I don't mind when he does things with friends without me. He always says a little distance keeps things fresh.'

'So that means you don't know exactly what he's doing when he's not at home?'

'Well, most of the time he tells me. But it's the same the other way around. I have my hobbies too.'

Beatrice, who had just brought up the geocaching website on her screen, was struck by an idea. 'Ask her if her husband had a nickname,' she whispered. 'Perhaps one that his friends gave him at school, or one that she used for him. Something along those lines.'

Florin nodded, but his question was initially met with incomprehension.

'Why do you want to know that?' asked the woman. 'What does that have to do with the blood in his car, and the fact that he's missing?'

Beatrice pointed to her screen, and Florin caught on. 'It's possible that your husband registered on Internet forums with a nickname of some kind. If you can help us a little we can narrow down our search and possibly find some clues. Does your husband have a PC at home?'

The sound of her breathing came through the loudspeaker. 'He has a laptop. And I always call him my Grizzly Bear.'

There was a 'GrizzlyBear' on Geocaching.com, as well as a 'GrizzleBear', but neither of them were Christoph Beil. The first had only registered one found cache, which was back in 2009, in Berlin. The second had registered only five months ago, already logging over 500 finds. 'But all of them in Baden-Württemberg,' Beatrice declared.

Two hours later they had Beil's laptop in their possession – his wife had handed it over without hesitation. Stefan took charge of searching for clues, opening the Web browser and looking through the bookmarks. Geocaching.com wasn't there, not even in the history, which covered the last three months.

'I'll check the emails now,' he declared. 'He has an inbox stretching back four years. If he was sent messages via his geocaching account during that time, then we might find them here, which would give us his username too.'

But not even rummaging through his email folders brought anything to light. The disappointment was written all over Stefan's face, even though he tried to hide it. 'It looks like Beil wasn't a geocacher then. With your agreement, I'd like to go through all the emails from the last few weeks with a fine-tooth comb. Maybe I'll find something useful. Then I'll send the laptop to the IT lab so they can bring any deleted data back from the dead on the hard drive.'

Every single path they pursued seemed to lead to a dead end. The investigation of Sigart's patient files hadn't unearthed anything either: it seemed neither Nora Papenberg nor Christoph Beil had taken their pets to him for treatment. Another idea smothered in the cradle. But there was no time to brood over it: one of Liebscher's colleagues had emailed through some photos taken at a bowling night, including a few close-ups of Liebscher. He was laughing, exposing crooked teeth. Beatrice's attention was drawn to his ears, her hand instinctively lifting to touch her own left ear as she thought about the cache.

'Do you want to come and get a coffee with me?' Kossar had popped up out of nowhere. His question was clearly directed solely at Beatrice.

'Sorry. I'm busy.' The way he looked at her made her feel uneasy. Whenever colleagues tried to approach her about anything other than work, she always felt the acute impulse to run away. She turned her concentration back to Liebscher's photos. Pale blue eyes. They would fit in a very small container. A micro-cache.

Kossar seemed to have noticed her irritation. 'I don't mean to impose.' His tone was significantly more businesslike than before. 'But a chat over coffee might spark off some more ideas about the case. I'm happy to come back later if you—'

Her mobile beeped, announcing the arrival of a message.

With one quick lunge, she grabbed it from her bag and pressed 'Read'.

Just one word. She stared at it, the context slowly dawning on her. But maybe she was wrong. Hopefully.

'Bad news?'

She had to get rid of Kossar. Showing him the message right now would just bring on another of his gusts of hot air. She would tell him about it later. Once she had worked out her own thoughts on it.

'It's a family matter. With all due respect, I really must ask you to let me get on with my work.'

He stared at her for a moment. 'Family, I understand. Yes, Hoffmann mentioned that you had a messy divorce behind you. If you'd like—'

'Sorry if I didn't express myself clearly enough, but I really don't have much time and I have to work.'

'How about the two of us go get some coffee?' Florin stood up, walked over to Kossar and clapped him affably on the shoulder. 'I could use a quick break. Let's go.' Beatrice, having known him for so long, was the only one to hear the edge of sharpness to his voice.

Kossar's laugh sounded forced, but Beatrice barely noticed. The word on the screen of her phone was taking up all her attention:

Archived.

With one click, she found the caching dictionary under her favourites on the browser, opened it and confirmed that her suspicion was correct. An archived cache was one that had been taken out of operation. It was gone and wouldn't be replaced.

First *disabled*. Then *archived*.

Presumably the Owner didn't mean the container he had hidden for the police. He was being abstract. It was clear he was referring to something they were looking for, and right now, first and foremost, they were searching for Christoph Beil.

Archived. In the unusual peace and quiet of her empty office, Beatrice wondered whether the Owner was trying to tell them, in his own particular way, that Beil was no longer alive.

That evening, she drove to Mooserhof and found the children being kept very busy. Jakob – dressed in jeans and his pyjama top – was sweeping the floor, singing and distributing little packets of sugar among the tables, while Mina was in the process of serving a bottle of water and two glasses on a tray. Her gaze was fixed with the utmost concentration on the load in her hands, as if hoping that through hypnosis she could prevent them from falling.

Beatrice's mother was standing behind the bar, pulling a pint of beer. 'I didn't expect to see you!' She waited until the foam top was at the right thickness, then put the beer krug down and hugged Beatrice. 'You look tired. Are you hungry? Hang on, I'll tell André to bring you a portion of stuffed cabbage leaves – they're delicious!'

Beatrice was about to protest, but didn't have the energy. Besides, she really was hungry. Her stomach was practically screaming out for nourishment. 'Okay. I really just came to see the children quickly though.'

'But you're not taking them with you today, are you?'

'No. It'll probably be another few days. This new case is . . . very unusual.'

Her mother looked indifferent to the explanation. 'That's fine. I love having them here, you know that.'

'Thank you.'

'Sit down at table twelve, I'll bring you a drink in a moment.'

Jakob shot over to her, giggling, placed an open sugar sachet on her knee and hugged her. 'Are you staying here tonight?'

'No, sweetie. I really wanted to see you, but I have to get up early tomorrow, and it's going to be another long day.'

He nodded, his eyebrows knitted together, the very personification of understanding. 'I earned some pocket money. Three euros and forty-five cents. For clearing plates and putting out the sugar. Oma said I'm a really good helper.'

'You certainly are.' She squeezed him against her, seeing

Mina come towards them carrying water and a glass of apple juice.

'You're not picking us up yet, are you?' She looked really worried.

'No. Although I'd really love to. I miss you guys.'

'Yeah. We miss you too, but you can hold out a bit longer, right?'

'A bit.'

'Good,' replied Mina contentedly, going back to the bar. Jakob fidgeted around on Beatrice's knees.

'Uncle Richard told us that you're going to have a . . . a burn-ow . . . soon. What's that?'

It took her a moment to understand what Jakob meant. 'No, sweetie, I'm not going to have a burn-out. Where is Uncle Richard anyway?'

'He's over there playing cards.'

Beatrice looked over her left shoulder. Yes, there he was, her darling brother. Shuffling cards and laughing about something the brawny man next to him was saying.

'You two should go to bed – it's already past eight,' whispered Beatrice in Jakob's ear. 'I'll tuck you in, okay?'

'Okay!'

The bedroom up in the loft was still as cosy as it had been when she used to sleep there herself. She put Jakob and Mina to bed, listening to their stories of the day and trying to push everything about the case to the deepest recesses of her mind. No, she wasn't going to burn out. Three days' holiday once the Owner was caught would be enough to recharge her batteries; it always was.

When she went back downstairs to the restaurant, there

were two things waiting for her: cold stuffed cabbage, and a critical brother. 'Surely they can't be paying you so much that you just let everything else go to hell?' His blond hair clung to his sweaty forehead – and he had put on weight since the last time she saw him.

'It's not a question of money, Richard.' She started to eat. Even though it was no longer hot, it tasted good.

'No, of course not. You're saving the world, right?' He winked as he said it, but she still felt like plunging the prongs of her fork into the back of his hand. Just as she'd always wanted to back when they were kids, when he used to pinch food from her plate.

'Achim was here this lunchtime – we had a long chat.'

The fork nearly dropped out of her hand. 'What?'

'Yep. He's in a really bad way, Bea. He comes here a lot, whenever he's sure he won't run into you. I think he's hoping that one of us can explain to him why you wanted a divorce.' Richard looked at her thoughtfully. 'Maybe you'll at least explain it to us one day? You had it good, Bea. He was crazy about you, and if you ask me, he still is.'

She almost spat out her half-chewed mouthful of cabbage. 'Yeah, sure. Listen, he doesn't even talk to me when he picks the kids up. He looks at me as if I'm a stinking pile of rubbish that someone forgot to take out.'

Richard wiped a serviette across his forehead. 'I believe you. But only because you're the one who took everything he cared about away from him. If you were to give it back—'

'You can't be serious.' She put her knife and fork down. 'We're not good for one another, Achim and I. We never were. He wants someone who enjoys the same things as him, who laughs at the same jokes. Who likes cooking and only works to bring money in.' She snorted. 'You would probably get on much better with him than I ever could.'

'But it would make your life so much easier.'

'Except it wouldn't be *my* life any more.'

Richard twisted the serviette between his hands as though he wanted to strangle someone with it. 'It's because of what happened back then, right? You've become so much harder since then, Bea. You have to move on at some point, you can't bring someone back to life by—'

'That's enough, okay?' She pushed her plate away; at least she had eaten half of it. 'I'm really grateful that Mama always helps out when I need it, and that you look after the children too. Really I am. But when it comes to Achim and what happened back then, as you put it, you don't get a say.' Without giving him a chance to react, she stood up, ruffled his hair and gave him a hug. 'Everything's fine. I'm not on the brink of burning out, but thank you for teaching Jakob a new word.'

'You're welcome.' He held her at arm's length for a moment and gave a sigh. 'Is there anyone who understands what's going on in your head, Bea?'

She smiled and shrugged.

Not that I know of.

She drove home slowly, the car radio turned up louder than usual. Once she got back, she would have a shower and then try to look at Stage Four with fresh eyes.

The car behind her seemed to have its headlights on full

beam, because the reflection in the rear-view mirror was blinding her. Aggravated, she stepped on the accelerator to put some distance between them. But by the next traffic light, he was right behind her again. And at the next, and the one after that.

An uneasy feeling started to creep over Beatrice. She turned around. Was the car following her? It was impossible to see the driver's face, but maybe she could at least make out the model of the car . . . No, she couldn't.

At the next crossroads, she turned left, then right at the one after that. The car was still behind her. It was keeping to the same speed, not even overtaking when she slowed down and gave it the opportunity to.

There were two more turns before she would be back home. Then she would park and get a better look at her pursuer. But when she turned right at the next crossroads, the car drove straight on. She tried to catch a quick glimpse of the driver's profile, but couldn't see clearly enough; even the number plate was too dimly lit to be made out. She shook her head. She didn't normally get so worked up about things. What was it that Richard had said about a burn-out?

Nonsense. She had all her wits about her and would only worry about it if she saw the car again in the next few days. It had been red, four-door – a Honda, if she wasn't mistaken.

A thought rushed into her mind.

A red Honda Civic. The car Nora Papenberg used to drive. She sat at the living-room table, searching through her notes. It was probably just a coincidence; there was always a time in the midst of the investigations when it was common to overanalyse everything, and Beatrice was very familiar with this phenomenon.

Had the car following her really been a Civic? She had only seen it briefly from the side – it had been red, yes, and definitely a Honda, but other than that?

She filed the thought away for the time being and took the photos from the most recent cache out of her bag. For the next two hours, she sat there studying the photos and letters, staring at Nora Papenberg's writing and trying in vain to find someone on Geocaching.com whose profile would prompt that familiar 'click' in her mind.

His quota is over 2,000. He never concedes defeat. Was there a way of filtering users with over 2,000 finds? Apparently not. That night, in spite of all her efforts, Stage Four refused to reveal its secrets.

The news reached Beatrice on a cool morning from which the drizzle had slowly but persistently washed away all colour. She arrived in the office at the same time as the phone call: a male body had been found near the Salzach lake. Three fishermen had pulled the corpse from its hiding place after spotting a naked foot protruding from the reeds at the water's edge.

On the way to the scene, Beatrice thought about Beil's wife. She would now have to identify the man she had affectionately named Grizzly Bear. The description given by the police officers at the scene seemed to fit his profile.

The third victim. She looked across at Florin, who was driving. 'We should arrange some police protection for Bernd Sigart.'

*

Beil's body had been laid out on the shore of the lake, and it was a horrific sight. Naked down to his underpants, his body was covered with wounds, some of them deep, narrow and jagged, as if a small animal had been trying to burrow something out from beneath his skin. Blue strangulation marks ran around his neck, and the face above it was already bloated. But there was no doubt that it was him.

'Do you know what instrument the cuts might have been inflicted with?' asked Beatrice, but she didn't receive any answer from Drasche, who was busy taking Beil's fingerprints. Typical. She spotted the medical officer standing just outside the cordoning tape, making notes whilst he leant over the bonnet of his car.

'Good morning, Doctor. I know I'm impatient, but I need all the information you can give me.'

He nodded, without breaking the contact between his pen and the paper. 'The man has been dead for roughly three days, but he was brought here a good while later. He has grazes and deep scratches all over his body, and a stab wound on the left side of his ribcage. That could be the cause of death, but the victim was definitely strangled as well. He was found lying on his stomach, but the livor mortis is on his back, which means the corpse must have been in another position for a good two days.' He shrugged his shoulders. 'That's all I can tell you right now.'

'The scratches and cuts – what do you think they were inflicted by?'

The doctor sighed loudly. 'I don't know. Presumably it was a jagged instrument, something like a blunt saw that both scrapes and cuts the surface.'

'While he was still alive?'

'Yes, that's very likely.'

Beatrice glanced over her shoulder back at the dead body. Beil had been tortured, and she would bet anything that someone had been trying to force information out of him. Presumably the same information he hadn't wanted to tell her.

Florin spoke to the uniformed policeman who had been the first one on the scene, while Beatrice went over to the three fishermen who were waiting, palely and silently, by the squad car.

'The guy over there had a go at us about moving the body,' said one of them. 'But we wanted to see if he was still alive, whether there was anything we could do.'

'Of course. Don't worry,' Beatrice reassured them. 'My colleague is a little quick-tempered – it's nothing personal. Did you notice anything else that might be significant? Did you encounter anyone on your way down to the lake, for example?'

The three men looked at each other, then shook their heads in consensus. 'It was half-five in the morning, and there's hardly ever anyone here at that time,' said the oldest man, whose grey-flecked hair came down almost to his shoulders. 'But there was something I noticed – well, nothing really compared to the dead body, but still –'

'Yes?'

'Twigs.' He looked at Beatrice almost apologetically. 'A few metres away from where we found the man, there were these short twigs on the ground, and they formed a word—'

'Not a word,' interrupted one of the two younger men. 'Just meaningless letters. TFTL, I think.'

'No, it was TFTH,' said the third man.

'Are they still there?'

'No, we dragged the body across them when we pulled it out.'

'I see.' *How incredibly helpful.* 'Nonetheless, if you could please show me where the twigs are.'

The spot was just inside the cordon, directly on the river bank where the ground was soft. Beatrice waved Ebner over, who collected the twigs up one by one and stowed them away carefully.

'The Owner left us his usual message,' she said to Florin, after pulling him a few steps away from the uniformed policemen. 'Thanking us for the hunt. We'll have to . . .' She closed her eyes, trying to bring some order to her thoughts. 'We'll have to speak to Konrad Papenberg again. Tell me if you disagree, but I believe Beil was killed because of something he knew. The Owner tortured him to find out exactly what, then killed him. Whatever it was – this information he had – must be connected to Nora Papenberg.'

'The accomplice the Owner disposed of.' Florin was gazing off over the lake into the distance. 'That seems the most likely explanation to me. Maybe Beil even knew why they murdered Herbert Liebscher.'

Twenty minutes later, Hoffmann's car drove up while Beatrice was asking the fishermen some further questions. Out of the corner of her eye, she watched Hoffmann look at the body, pace around the scene, then speak briefly with Drasche before heading over in her direction. 'You knew the victim, is that correct?'

'Yes. Christoph Beil. We questioned him last Sunday, and two days later his wife reported him missing.'

Hoffmann nodded gloomily. 'The third murder in such a short period of time – this is ruining our safety stats for the entire year. I expect this case to speed up, Kaspary. For heaven's sake, the murderer is giving you clues, communicating with you – there must be a way to work with that! Why aren't you following Kossar's suggestions?'

Beatrice was silent. Letting herself get drawn into an argument would be just as futile as pointing out Kossar's overly relaxed approach. Any attempt at self-defence had a tendency to spur Hoffmann on to self-opinionated tirades. More often than not, they started with the words: *If I were in your position, I would have* . . .

'You'll attend the autopsy today and report back to me afterwards.' Before she had a chance to respond, he marched over to Florin, who was kneeling down at the edge of the cordoned area talking to Drasche, the body firmly fixed in his sights. She watched Hoffmann go, allowing herself to daydream for a moment that it was his autopsy she was attending instead.

'Male corpse, 184 centimetres tall and weighing 93 kilos, in a healthy state of nourishment with a strong build.' Dr Vogt's scrawny figure moved around the autopsy table with measured steps as he talked into his Dictaphone. 'The subject's back – with the exception of the area which was in contact with the ground – reveals fixed, reddish violet livor mortis that doesn't fade when finger pressure is applied.'

As Vogt continued with the external examination of Beil's corpse, Beatrice reached for her mobile, which she had tucked into the pocket of the white coat lent to her by the forensics unit. *Archived* had been the Owner's last message. He still hadn't responded to her reply. Did he not care that she knew who he had been dismembering and hiding away? Did it please him, unsettle him?

'Rigor mortis has set in, the eyelids are closed. There are dotted traces of bleeding around the upper and lower lids. Moving on now to the skin injuries –' Vogt stopped next to Beil's shoulder. 'There are abrasions around the inside of the upper arm, four centimetres wide and six centimetres long, which have penetrated the upper layers of the dermis. The wounds are uneven in depth, which suggests they were inflicted by a serrated object. Lesions of the same sort are also located to the left of the navel, in both armpits and on the inner left thigh, five centimetres above the knee.'

As Vogt detailed one injury after the other, Beatrice closed her eyes, trying to picture a tool that would create wounds like that. Maybe a blunt saw blade? It was possible, but the cuts seemed too small in surface area for that.

'There are sharply outlined wounds around the ankles and wrists, suggesting that the subject was forcibly restrained. On the back of the left hand is a violet-pigmented scar, two centimetres in diameter, which predates the victim's injuries and death.'

The scar which had enabled them to find him. The Owner had led them to Beil with his clues, waited until they had spoken to him, then attacked almost as soon as their backs were turned.

But why not sooner? Was it all about provoking the police, was that really part of his motive? It felt as though they were just running around haplessly, dashing to wherever he wanted them to go. Yet the Owner was always there in front of them.

A thought that had occurred to her when she arrived at the scene earlier that day reared its head again with renewed force: if that was the killer's trick, then they would have to keep an eye on Sigart.

The autopsy lasted two and a half hours. It seemed Beil had died as the result of a stab to the heart. A sharp object, presumably a knife blade, had penetrated the front wall of the thorax and the pericardium, as well as the anterior and posterior walls of the heart. He had died of internal bleeding.

'What about the strangulation marks?' Beatrice pointed at the blue marks which ran around Beil's neck in ring formations.

'There are two choke marks which suggest he was hanged, but not fatally,' Vogt explained.

'Aha. And what do you make of that?'

'Either he tried to hang himself and failed, or his murderer couldn't decide which method to use. Are you familiar with Mozart's *Abduction from the Seraglio*? "First beheaded, then hanged, then impaled on hot stakes . . ."' He sang with an astonishingly full and deep voice.

Beatrice knew a few pathologists and was familiar with their unique sense of humour, but the sight of Vogt singing in front of the corpse while the liver was being weighed by the assistant pathologist was almost enough to make her flee the room.

'Two choking marks, you say?'

Vogt interrupted his performance. 'Yes. So either the rope slipped or someone tried to hang him twice.' He shrugged, looking at Beatrice with his head tilted to the side. 'I'll leave it to you to make sense of that one.'

It was just before five in the afternoon when they rang Sigart's doorbell, and it took him a long time to answer.

'You'll have to excuse me. I was sleeping.' He was shockingly pale, and a deep red crease stretched diagonally across the right side of his face, clearly the imprint of a pillow. 'Come in.'

He sat down on the edge of the couch, awkwardly pulling on a pair of socks.

'Sorry that we woke you,' said Florin.

'Don't worry. Maybe I'll be able to get a few hours' sleep tonight now.' He looked up. 'It's the pills, you know? My doctor prescribed me new ones which make me very tired, but unfortunately only during the day.' He gestured towards the folding chairs, which, it seemed, were still at the table from their last visit.

'Herr Sigart, we'd like to know whether you've noticed anything unusual in the last few days,' Florin began. 'Anything unsettling?'

Sigart looked at him quizzically. 'What do you mean by unsettling?'

'Well, have you received any strange phone calls? Were there perhaps anonymous messages in your letter box? On your mobile?'

Sigart's expression indicated that he found Florin's questions strange, but he was clearly still dazed with sleep. 'No.'

'Good. I'd like to ask you to contact us right away if something of that sort happens. Only open the door to people you know and trust. Inform us if anything seems even the slightest bit suspicious.'

Sigart was fully awake now. 'Why? What's going on?'

It had been obvious that this question would come, and they had already agreed during the drive over to cause him as little worry as possible. Beatrice took a deep breath.

'It's possible that the person who murdered Nora Papenberg takes a perverse pleasure in the act of killing, so it's important to us that all people who are connected to the case exercise caution.'

He nodded slowly. 'What happened?'

'As I already said, there are signs that the man could continue to be dangerous.'

Sigart seemed interested, but not excessively so. 'What kind of signs?'

'That's not relevant, but the important thing is that . . .'

'Earlier on, on the news —' he interrupted her, pointing the scarred index finger of his left hand to an old portable radio — 'they said that a body was found in the Salzach lake. This morning. Is that what you mean by "signs"?'

The latest murder had of course been reported in the media, albeit without any reference to the Papenberg case. But Sigart wasn't stupid. Reading the answer etched on their faces, he nodded. 'That's quite a clear sign. And now you're worried that he'll come after me next?'

'That could tie in with his weird logic, yes,' answered Florin. 'We don't know enough about him and his motives, but he — how do I put this? — led us to you, just like the man we found today. That's why we'd like to put you under police protection.'

'Me?' He seemed genuinely amazed. 'I can't think of one single reason why anyone would kill me,' he said. 'After all, I hardly even exist any more. Whether I'm sitting here in this hole of a flat or lying in a coffin under the earth doesn't make a difference to anyone. Not even me.'

'I don't doubt that you feel that way,' said Beatrice. 'But that won't protect you if the killer's mind works the way we suspect it does. Please think for a moment. Is there someone who might stand to profit from your death?'

'Only the funeral director. I've stipulated in my will that any remaining funds are to go to the Association for Psychological Crisis Intervention.' Something almost resembling a smile crept across his features.

'It doesn't necessarily have to be a material motive. Is it possible that you know something that could hurt someone else?' She held his gaze. 'It seems like that may have been the case with the most recent murder. Is there anyone you could prove to be dangerous for if you were to divulge some information?'

His eyes were already rejecting the notion even before he shook his head. 'If you like, I can tell you the names of people who feed their dogs chocolate because they think of them as children. Or others that keep their parrots in criminally small cages. But I don't have any information more damaging than that. What do you want from me? Do you want me to make something up just so I have something to tell?'

Florin laid the portrait from Christoph Beil's missing persons report out on the table. 'Have you ever seen this man?'

A resigned sigh. Sigart looked at Beatrice as if he wanted to ask for her help, but then shrugged his shoulders and leant over towards the photo. He looked at it for a long while – so long that they started to get hopeful.

'No,' he said. 'The face doesn't ring any bells. And I really tried to recognise him, believe me.'

'And what about this man?' Florin pulled out another photo, this time of Liebscher. 'Do you perhaps know him?'

'Why? Does he belong to the circle of potential victims too? Or is he already dead?' He pushed the photos away. 'To be honest, I don't know what you want from me. I have nothing to do with your case. I don't know the people who were murdered, and I don't feel threatened. And even if I did, my life ended when my family died. Leave me in peace.'

Sympathy and irritation fought for the upper hand within Beatrice. It just wasn't possible that every single one of their attempts to make progress led to a dead end. There *had* to be some connection between the victims.

She held her breath. Was that really true? Was it not equally plausible that the murderer was picking names out of the phone book at random and finding out about them, just to look on gleefully as the police desperately tried to establish a connection between them? The thought paralysed her. If that were the case, then the hunt could last a very long time.

She looked at Sigart, who was hunched over on his chair, staring out of the window at the grey concrete wall opposite. Over time, most heavily traumatised people either found a way to deal with their lot, or they committed suicide.

'You know,' he said, with a barely perceptible smile, 'it would save me the effort. A murderer, I never thought of that. Stepping in front of a bus, a scalpel, injecting myself with an overdose – sure.' He looked up. 'I've put lots of animals to sleep, and I'd like to die like they do. Calmly. At peace.'

There was no doubt about the sincerity of his suicide wish, but they weren't making any progress here. 'As my colleague has already mentioned, we'd like to put you under police protection, but we need your approval for that.'

'I appreciate your concern.' His comment sounded genuine, at least. 'But I don't want that. I want my peace and quiet and I don't want policemen at the door.'

She had feared that kind of response. 'Do you have a mobile phone?'

He looked at her, confused. 'Of course.'

'I'll give you my mobile number, and my colleague's too. If you feel under threat or even suspect someone is watching you, call us. It's better to call us than the emergency line, because we'll know what it's about.'

Sigart blinked as though he had something in his eye, then turned his head to the side. 'Thank you. But I can't promise I'll take you up on your offer.'

He saved the number in his phone regardless. Beatrice tried to discreetly sneak a glance into his existing contacts, but without success.

'We'll send a squad car over to check on you now and then,' said Florin, getting up from his chair. 'But please do us a favour and watch out for yourself.'

Sigart's shoulders twitched. It was futile; he would do as he pleased. They were almost out through the door when something occurred to Beatrice. The idea was an unusual one, and she was intrigued to see how he would react. 'If you're in agreement, I'd like to speak to your therapist. I need your permission though.'

He hesitated. So there *were* some things he still cared about. 'What do you hope to achieve from doing that?'

'I'm grasping at any straw I can think of, you know? You're connected to this case in some way, and I want to understand how.'

With his scarred left hand, he kneaded the unscathed fingers on the other.

'You're ambitious, aren't you?'

The question startled Beatrice for a moment. 'I would say I'm more . . . persistent, I think.'

Again, that crippled version of a smile. 'Good for you. I can remember how that used to feel.' He swept his pale tongue slowly over his lips. 'You can speak to my therapist if you really want to – her name is Anja Maly and her practice is in Auerspergstrasse. I'll tell her to expect you.'

'You were very quiet towards the end,' said Beatrice as they went back to the car.

'I know. I was concentrating on Sigart. He was different to our last visit and I was trying to work out exactly how.'

'And?'

Florin hesitated. 'I've never studied psychology, but he reminded me of someone today. An uncle who's been dead for a long time now.'

Beatrice opened the passenger door, but didn't get in. Instead, she glanced back at the small balcony belonging to Sigart's flat. 'Your uncle committed suicide, didn't he?'

'Yes. By the end he was so calm, giving all his things away. He just let go of everything. I think Sigart is almost at that point. Shouldn't we have him sectioned?'

It was a tempting thought — Sigart would get help, and at the same time no longer be accessible to the killer. A tempting thought indeed.

Back at the office, they worked late into the night. The photos of the three puzzles lay spread out on the desk in front of Beatrice, each one the Owner had given them so far. A singer. A loser. A key figure. She looked for parallels, differences, hidden messages. By half-ten, her eyes were stinging. 'I'm going to head off home. I'm—'

—*dead tired*, she had been about to say, but Sting interrupted her; sending his SOS out. The phone was in her bag and Beatrice's attempt at opening it resulted in knocking it from the table and spilling half the contents across the floor. The message tone continued.

Hopefully everything was okay with the children, and hopefully the Owner hadn't—

She read the message and froze. But some kind of noise must have escaped her, for through the thick, dirty haze veiling her mind, she sensed Florin's sudden attentiveness, his concern.

'Bea?'

She didn't respond. She had to get her thoughts straight first. By now, she could recognise the number at first glance; it was the prepaid card in Nora Papenberg's mobile. Then she realised: this was the response to the last text she had sent.

Spirit of Man,
How like water you are.
Fate of Man,
How like the wind.
Let's look for a victim.
Evelyn R.
R.I.P.

The ball had been returned. It was as if he was saying, *You know something? Then look at this — so do I!*

She resisted the impulse to delete the message. *Let's look for a victim,* my God.

'Bea? What's wrong?'

Speechless, she handed him her mobile. She watched as he immediately recognised the sender's number, then scanned the message with a frown.

'Goethe.'

'Yes. "The Song of the Spirits over the Waters".' She rested her forehead in her hands. How had the Owner found out?

'Who's Evelyn R.?'

She's the end of innocence. The caesura. The volte-face.

'She's dead.' It didn't answer his question, but it was all she could manage right at that moment. How could the Owner know about Evelyn?

She thought about the car that had followed her, the one with the headlights turned up too brightly. Suddenly, the thought of spending the night at home alone was yet another threatening shadow in her world.

Forbidding herself from thinking longingly of Florin's

spare room, she started to pack up her things. 'Could you give me my phone, please?'

'Bea!' He hadn't taken his eyes off her for a second. 'Explain to me what this is about. This isn't caching slang – it's to do with you personally, right?'

'So it seems.'

'So it seems?' He pushed his hair back from his brow, clearly exasperated. 'Look, of course you're under no obligation to tell me everything about your life, but this is about a case we're working on together. It would be really helpful if I was also able to interpret the messages the suspect is sending us.'

She had to collect her thoughts. Everything was rushing, colliding inside her. She needed to be alone. 'I sent the Owner a message, and it seems this is his answer.'

Florin's eyes narrowed. 'You did what?'

'Yes. I know. I played a lone hand, without discussing it first. It was a spur-of-the-moment decision, when we were in Liebscher's apartment and found the writing in the dust. I made it clear to him that we knew the identity of the man whose body parts he was putting in the caches. "*Herbert Liebscher*", that's all I wrote. I wanted him to know we're getting closer, that we're open to a dialogue. The more often he gets in touch, the higher the probability that he'll slip up and make a mistake.'

She searched Florin's face for understanding, but it was expressionless and – despite the tiredness in his eyes – harder than usual. 'You do realise,' he said slowly, 'that by doing that you're playing his game, not yours. Let's forget for a moment that you didn't inform anyone else in the team

– you accepted his invitation by sending that message, Bea. Now you're his official opponent. And I don't like that one bit.' He held her mobile out towards her. 'You can see how personal he makes things. He swotted up, and clearly knows more about you than the people who see you every day.'

That was one way of looking at it. His official opponent. Her eyes were burning; she closed them and pressed her fingertips against her eyelids. 'Evelyn was one of my friends at university,' she said, watching the dots and streaks that appeared in the darkness of her self-imposed blindness. 'We shared an apartment. Then she died.' Beatrice opened her eyes again and looked directly at Florin. 'She was doing German philology, and I was studying psychology. Neither of us graduated.'

The question he wanted to ask her was clearly written on his face, but he didn't voice it. 'Under the circumstances I think it would be better if you don't stay by yourself until we've caught the Owner,' he said instead. 'My apartment is big enough, so why don't you—'

'No.'

He blinked, then turned away. 'Fine. But do me a favour and call me once you're home and you've locked up. Leave your mobile next to the bed. Have you got the emergency number on speed dial?'

'Yes. Of course.' She stood up and slung her bag over her shoulder. 'You should head home soon too. It's been a long day.'

On her way out to the car park, Beatrice turned to look back several times, but there was no one behind her. Nor

216

was there during the drive home, throughout which she spent more time looking in the rear-view mirror than at the road.

She did as Florin had asked: double-locking the door behind her and even sliding across the bolt she had never used the whole time she had lived here. It would be completely useless if someone was really intent on getting in, but it still felt reassuring to limit the possibilities. She checked that the windows were locked and pulled the curtains. Then she kicked her shoes off, sank down onto the sofa and stared at the ceiling.

Evelyn. Anyone could read about it in the newspaper archives if they made the effort, but establishing the connection to Beatrice was a lot more difficult. Her surname had been different back then, and she hadn't spoken to a single journalist. And yet the Owner had still managed to draw the correct conclusions.

She felt her eyes start to close, then opened them wide. Was that a noise?

No. She was being silly. Nonetheless, she still felt better after doing a round of the rooms, not finding anything apart from the usual blend of order and chaos. Only then did she call Florin.

'Did you get home safely?' He was still at the office; she could hear the clatter of the keyboard in the background.

'Yes. No one followed me, and there was no one lying in wait when I got here. Everything's fine.'

'Good. And remember, if anything unusual happens—'

'I'm a police officer, Florin. I know how to look after myself.' The words sounded convincing, even to her. For the first time since arriving at her apartment, she started to relax.

The night passed unbelievably quickly. Her head had barely touched the pillow before her alarm clock went off again. She had slept deeply, as if drugged, and her mobile had stayed silent.

'Make sure a squad car goes round to check on Sigart. They just need to briefly make sure that all's well.' Beatrice leant on Stefan's desk, pointing at the address on the note she had just given him. 'And then could you try to make some sense of Stage Four? I can't make head nor tail of it, so it would be good to have a second pair of eyes take a fresh look.'

Stefan ran a hand through his red hair, looking mildly offended. 'Do you seriously think I haven't been going over it already? I've requested a list from the records office on all residents in the state of Salzburg named Felix who are under the age of forty.'

That's exactly what Beatrice would have done a few years ago. But she had learnt through experience that lists like that only helped if you at least had some vague idea of what you were searching for. Still, it wouldn't hurt.

Seeing Kossar approaching out of the corner of her eye, she sighed. 'See you later, Stefan.'

Kossar waited in the doorway to her office, glancing longingly over at the coffee machine, but she didn't want to offer him anything that might lengthen his stay unnecessarily. It was bad enough that she would have to talk to him about her past. 'The Owner sent me a new message yesterday. Here it is.' She had typed up the message and printed it out.

Kossar scanned the words, nodded, sat down and read it through once more. 'Can you tell me who Evelyn was?'

'A friend. We lived together.' For some inexplicable reason, it felt easier to tell Kossar about it than Florin. It felt less personal, at least as long as she was just talking about the bare facts.

'So my assumption would be that she didn't die of natural causes. Am I right?'

He was pretty good at his job when it came to direct conversation, at least. Which meant all she needed to do was nod, not explain anything.

'I understand. The fact that the Owner knows about it is one thing, the fact that he's shoving his knowledge right under your nose is another entirely. That supports our theory that he wants to demonstrate his superiority. And — correct me if I'm wrong —' he looked at Beatrice as if he was searching her face for something — 'but it seems like he's hit a raw nerve. Am I right?'

She hesitated, then nodded.

'He wants to show he can hurt you. He'd probably also like to see how you react, so don't rule out the possibility that he might try to get close to you.'

Beatrice was pleased Florin was out of the office and not around to hear Kossar's words. He was already on the brink of putting her under the personal protection Sigart had refused. 'Okay. So, a tentative prognosis then — what will he do next?' she asked.

'Well.' Kossar took his glasses off with a sweeping flourish. 'He will continue to pursue his plan — unfortunately, at this point, no one can say what that plan consists of. To me, it looks like an opus, a production, a kind of psychopathic work of art. There were a few cases in the US that showed similar patterns. I've spent the last two days looking for possible parallels.' Looking pleased with himself, Kossar leant back in his chair and put his glasses on again. 'By the way, that means you're not in danger. You're the audience – it would be counterproductive to kill you.'

That's good to know. Beatrice forced a smile. 'Thank you for your comments. So what do you suggest I write back to him in response?'

Kossar took a long time before he answered, even for him. 'Only reply if you have something clever to say, something that will interest him. Something on a level with the surprise he dealt you yesterday.'

Even though she wasn't hungry, Beatrice went to the canteen for lunch and picked up a sandwich. On the way back, she ran into Stefan.

'Some of the guys checked on Sigart, everything's okay. They said he looks ill and seemed absent-minded, but apart from that he was fine.'

It sounded as though he was a step closer to ending things. They had to initiate the process for institutionalisation.

'I've also been pondering what the comments about the key figure's career could refer to. Selling things that no one needs – he might be an insurance salesman.'

She burst out laughing, and was suddenly unable to remember the last time she had done so. 'Stefan! That's a serious career path you're calling into disrepute.'

'If you say so. But that's what came to mind – knocking on people's doors, cold calling – see what I mean? Or maybe he sells something completely different – like stain removal products or newspaper subscriptions, or maybe just hot air . . .'

Hot air – in other words, mere rhetoric. Maybe he was in the advertising industry. If that was the case, there could be a connection between him and Nora Papenberg.

'That's not a bad idea. Keep at it, Stefan.'

He beamed and disappeared into his office. Beatrice went off to hers and found Florin there with his eyes closed and the telephone held to his ear. Within just a few moments, Beatrice worked out he was talking to Vera Beil. She had identified her husband yesterday, and had collapsed right there on the spot. Severe shock and circulatory failure, the doctors had said when she had been taken to hospital. Presumably she was phoning from there; she had already called twice today, but only ever wanted to speak to Florin.

'Anything,' he was saying. 'Try to think back, Frau Beil. What did your husband say as he left the house? Or before that, on Sunday evening?'

Beatrice turned her attentions to her computer. The mobile provider had emailed saying that the last connection via the prepaid card had been made at 22.34 yesterday, at which time the mobile was located in Salzburg's historic quarter. She was relieved: no one had been following her; she could rely on her instincts after all. Unfortunately, though, it seemed she could also rely on the Owner's caution: he hadn't yet connected to the same cellular network twice.

The afternoon crept up slowly and doggedly, leading to a gloomy evening and, shortly after 8 p.m., an equally gloomy evening meeting. No one in the team had any great flashes

221

of inspiration to offer; no one was in the position to lay new ideas on the table.

'We're stuck,' said Florin. 'Stage Four is a hard nut to crack – neither Beil's wife nor Papenberg's husband know anyone who meets the criteria of the key figure. So we're going to have to do the painstaking work and translate the two clues.'

Beatrice's phone interrupted him. It wasn't the melody announcing a text message, but the one for incoming calls.

'Sorry,' she murmured, pulling the phone from her bag and heading towards the door. She didn't know the number on the display, which was a good thing, implying it would be quick to resolve.

'Kaspary.'

A wail, followed by a whimper. Crashing in the background. She gripped her phone tightly. 'Who is it?'

'Help me!' The man's words were hoarse and faltering, squeezed out between sobs, but Beatrice was sure she could recognise Bernd Sigart's voice.

'Herr Sigart, is that you?' Everyone in the room turned to look at her. Florin gesticulated frantically with his thumb, as though he was pressing something. She understood and switched to speakerphone.

'Help me!' Sigart was sobbing. 'He's trying to—' The word culminated in a scream, followed by a crash which sounded like a bookcase falling over. Another crash, then the whimpering was muffled; someone must have put their hand over the microphone. It crackled, rustled, then the sound became clear again, and Sigart's cries cut shrilly through the air in the meeting room. 'Stop! Please! No!'

'Where are you?' shouted Beatrice.

There was no answer, just a dull thud, more pain–racked screams, then the connection was abruptly broken.

'Shit! Florin, Stefan, we need to drive to Sigart's flat right now!' She clapped Bechner on the shoulder. 'Tell all available squad cars in the area to get over there, Theodebertstrasse thirty-three. Quickly!'

She estimated the driving time in her mind: they would need at least fifteen minutes, twenty more realistically, even if they went through the red lights. Florin jumped behind the wheel, stepping on the accelerator even before all the doors were shut. His lips were pressed into a thin line, all his concentration directed on the road. Meanwhile, from the back seat, Stefan offered his analysis of the call.

'Sigart said "he", which means it's just one guy. So now we at least know that the Owner is a man—'

'We don't even know for sure if it *was* the Owner,' Beatrice interrupted him. Her throat felt dry with nerves. Sigart does value his life after all, she thought. We all do, as soon as someone wants to take it from us, as soon as things get serious.

Hopefully became her mantra for the next ten minutes. *Hopefully* we won't get there too late. *Hopefully.*

The walls of the building in Theodebertstrasse were reflecting the blue lights of the two squad cars that had arrived before them. The street was narrow, so one single car up at the crossing was enough to block access to traffic.

Four male and one female uniformed officers were standing at the front door, talking into walkie-talkies. Seeing Beatrice and Florin arrive, the policewoman came running over to them.

'We've already been in,' she called breathlessly. 'It looks pretty bad in there.'

Florin voiced Beatrice's thoughts before she managed to. 'Is Sigart dead?'

The policewoman shrugged. 'Probably. It's hard to say.'

'What does that mean?' The entrance lay in front of them, and even though dusk was already turning to darkness and the street lamps were only giving off sparse light, the dark smears and flecks in the hallway were unmistakable. Bloodstains ran down the stairs, as if something heavy had been dragged along the floor. They led down to the cellar.

'It certainly seems like whoever did this got a look at the house beforehand and worked out the best escape route,' explained the policeman holding the walkie-talkie. 'The cellar leads to a rear exit, and the suspect must have had a car parked there, because the traces of blood stop abruptly.'

'But what about Sigart?' asked Beatrice impatiently.

'We haven't found him.'

They ran up the stairs, taking care not to disturb the bloodstains. Beatrice noticed a large shoe print in one of the smears and hoped fervently that the Owner had finally made a mistake. The story told by the bloodstains was a clear one. They had come too late.

'Was there any sign of a break-in?'

'No.'

Now she saw for herself: the door was open, but undamaged. He must have let the killer in.

The inside of the flat looked like a slaughterhouse. Most of the blood was on the floor, on the wall next to the couch and by the table, which had been knocked over. The bookcase lay diagonally across the room and had buried a folding chair beneath it; the legs jutted out from under the heavy load like those of a squashed insect.

As expected, there was no sign of Sigart, but they still called out for him, checking the bathroom and finding nothing but blood and more blood. The patterns on the wall suggested an intensely spurting wound. Sigart must have been badly injured, unconscious or even dead before the killer dragged him through the building out to his car.

'He acted pretty damn fast.' Florin's gaze had stopped at the pool of blood next to the table. 'The patrol team said they arrived seven minutes after the emergency call, and both Sigart and the killer were already gone.'

That at least increased the probability that, in his haste, the Owner had made a mistake. The bloody shoe print on the stairs, for example. Tiptoeing cautiously, Beatrice crossed the small living area and glanced into the kitchen. Compared to the rest of the flat, it was quite clean. 'But we warned him. Why would Sigart just open the door like that?'

'The Owner isn't stupid. Maybe he disguised himself as a policeman, a handyman, or a postman. Or maybe . . .'

Beatrice nodded, fighting against the sense of helpless frustration rising inside her. 'Or maybe they knew each other.'

It was a mild evening, and most of the neighbours hadn't been home at the time the crime was committed. While Drasche and Ebner inspected the flat and stairwell, the others tried to find someone who might have seen the Owner.

An old woman living in one of the ground–floor flats reported that she had heard a dull thud: 'As though someone had dropped something heavy.'

'That was it? No screams?' Florin probed.

'Yes, but I thought they were coming from the TV.'

The neighbours who lived next to Sigart were only arriving home now, and were clearly horrified. By 10 p.m., the residents from the other flat downstairs still hadn't come back.

'It must have been very loud. There was a struggle – we heard part of it on the phone,' Beatrice explained to the tenants in the flat above Sigart. 'Did you not hear anything?'

The man lowered his gaze. 'We did. He was screaming and banging against the walls, but, the thing is – that was nothing new. In the last few years I've rung his bell again and again whenever he had those . . . incidents, but he never opened up, and I knew, you see . . . I mean, the thing with his family.' He looked back up. 'I didn't want to be a nuisance. He always made it clear that he wasn't interested in any contact or help.'

We were too slow, thought Beatrice, feeling the hate well up inside her, a feeling that had no place in her work. She balled her hands into fists and burrowed her fingernails into her palms; normally that helped.

'Wenninger? Kaspary?' Drasche's muffled voice echoed out of Sigart's flat. 'Come here, but be careful!'

When they got there, he was kneeling next to the upturned table and pool of blood. With his gloved hand, he pointed at something light and oblong amidst the red. 'The killer left us some body parts again.'

'What is it?' They leant forwards towards Drasche.

'Except this time he didn't package them up for us. Do you see?' He turned the oblong shapes around carefully.

Fingers. Beatrice went cold as she thought of Sigart's screams. *Stop it*, he had yelled, his voice racked with pain and fear.

'The little finger and ring finger of the left hand,' Drasche clarified. 'They must have been cut off at the same time, possibly hacked off, because the wound is sharp and the bone was severed too, I think.' He put the fingers into one of his evidence bags and held it out towards Beatrice.

She took it, noticing a detail that turned her suspicion into certainty. 'They're Sigart's fingers, for sure.'

Drasche's eyebrows climbed up to his hairline. 'And you know that how?'

'I recognise the burn scars.'

They closed off the street, called the inhabitants out of the surrounding houses and questioned them about a stranger who had entered building number 33 between eight and half-past that evening. Maybe a little earlier. But no one had seen anything.

Perhaps a parcel carrier, a policeman, a pizza delivery boy? No.

They worked until long after midnight, receiving a steady supply of updates on Drasche's discoveries: the footprints in the stairwell were a size 45, while Sigart was a size 43. The blood in the flat couldn't just stem from the severed fingers, as the fan-shaped patterns on the walls suggested injury to a large blood vessel. 'At a height of around one hundred and sixty centimetres from the floor, it was probably Sigart's carotid artery. Or the other man's, but if that were the case he wouldn't have been able to get away.' It was clear from Drasche's expression that he hadn't seriously considered that possibility, but wanted to state it nonetheless. 'I'll be able to tell you relatively soon whether the blood comes from two different people or just one.'

Finally, in a dark corner next to the cellar exit, Ebner found Sigart's mobile, smeared with blood. He had clearly been trying to cling onto the connection with Beatrice. That night, the thought haunted her into her sleep.

It happened the next morning, just after she had brushed her teeth, and without any warning. Beatrice huddled on the floor and tried not to lose consciousness, opening and closing her fingers to bring the feeling back, forcing away the image of Sigart's severed fingers as she did so. That would only make it all worse.

She hadn't had a panic attack this bad in years, and even though she knew what was happening to her, the thought remained that – this time – it could be something serious.

A heart attack, cardiac arrest, sudden death. She gasped for air, trying to bring her pulse back under control with the strength of willpower alone. She followed the leap-frogging of her heartbeat with a mixture of amusement and despair.

Breathe. Breathe. Think about something else.

Back then, the psychologist had advised her to accept the fear, to greet it and let it go again.

Hello, fear.

It was there, pounding inside her chest, her temples, her neck, her stomach, but it didn't respond to Beatrice's greeting. Didn't reveal where it had come from so suddenly.

But Beatrice knew what had awoken it. She lay flat out on her back, closed her eyes and tried to stay perfectly still. It felt as though her lungs had withered to hard, walnut-sized clumps.

She pictured Evelyn's face, her green eyes, her deep-red curly hair. That throaty voice. Everyone had always turned to look at her whenever she laughed.

I'm so sorry. So very sorry.

The cool tiles of the bathroom floor were pressing hard against her shoulder blades. The image of the living Evelyn faded, the disfigured features of the dead Evelyn engulfing it with all its horrific force. Beatrice tore her eyes open, concentrating on the bathroom ceiling, the dusty milk-glass lamp directly above her head.

She had to get up; there was so much to do. They had to find Sigart.

His corpse, you mean.

She managed to silence the inner voice by humming 'I'm Walking on Sunshine', a song that left no room for panic. *Ten to fifteen minutes*, she thought. It had never lasted any longer than that. *You'll make it. Of course you will.*

'Could you please tell me what on earth is wrong with you?' They could probably hear Hoffmann's voice even on the floor above, word for word. 'Did you go shopping, get a manicure? Do you realise we have a case here that's more important than your fingernails?'

229

Beatrice waited until she was sure she could keep her voice steady. 'I'm sorry I'm late, but—'

'No buts!' yelled Hoffmann. 'Four dead bodies in one single week! Nothing else is important right now – you don't have a private life!'

Four? Had Sigart's body already been found?

'And then on top of all that you go and disobey my orders. There'll be consequences, Kaspary, you mark my words!'

There was no doubt what he was referring to. She looked Hoffmann in the eyes, those silt-coloured, murky-puddle eyes, and waited to see if there was more. When he just shook his head silently, she left him standing there and walked past him to the office, where Florin appeared at the door with a vexed expression.

'There are three bodies, not four.' He gave her shoulder a quick squeeze. 'Are you okay?'

'Yes, of course,' she said softly. 'Just forget it.'

'I can't. Sorry.' Florin pressed past her. She hung her bag over the back of the chair and turned the computer on. His voice filtered in from the hallway, pointedly calm, but as sharp as splintered glass.

'It's not very helpful when you demotivate us for an entire day because of a twenty-minute late start. We're all pushing ourselves to the limit here, so I would be very grateful if you could recognise that and not put on additional pressure.'

'Well, what kind of pressure do you think I'll be under if we can't show any results? You must realise that, Florin.' Hoffmann's voice now had the chummy, conspiratorial undertone that irked Beatrice so much. Not that he had ever used it with her – heaven forbid.

'I know you're fond of Kaspary,' Hoffmann continued, now considerably quieter. 'But recently she's seemed very jittery and distracted, and that's just not acceptable in a case like this. Kossar thinks she made contact with the killer without waiting for his advice.' Hoffmann raised his voice again. 'She's blatantly disregarding my orders, and if she thinks she's going to get away with it—'

'She discussed making contact with the Owner with me. We had to act, and Kossar takes too long with things. If we've overstepped the mark, then you'll have to hold both of us responsible.'

Beatrice closed her eyes and tried to suppress the protest that was trying to force its way out of her.

'Is that so?' The rage had drained away from Hoffmann's voice. 'Then you should have told me that before, Florin.'

'You're right. But I can assure you it was a clever move on Kaspary's part. The Owner has already responded. You won't find an investigator better than her, I can promise you that.'

'Oh, come on. She has her qualities, no question of that, and she's been successful on a couple of cases, but . . . I'm wondering whether I should partner you with someone else, someone without acute personal problems, because they seem to be consuming all her energies right now.'

Beatrice stared at the login screen on her computer. It was only once her jaw began to ache that she realised she was grinding her teeth. If Hoffmann thought he could sideline her he was mistaken, but she should have realised he would try.

'No, absolutely not,' she heard Florin say with a certainty

that left no room for politeness. 'That would be a big mistake. I don't have the time or the energy to explain the case to another colleague, and besides—'

'Oh, come on. Not the same old story about her oh-so-wonderful powers of deduction.'

'You know full well I'm right.' Florin had lowered his voice again. 'Think back to the brewery murder. Or the two dead women on the train tracks. She was always the first one to put the pieces together.'

A dismissive click of the tongue, quite clearly from Hoffmann. 'I think you're exaggerating a little.'

'Not in the slightest.'

'Fine, have it your way. But I want to start seeing results, not just a steadily growing number of murder victims. I'm serious, Wenninger.'

'You know full well that no one can force these things. Neither you, nor I, nor Beatrice Kaspary.'

Hoffmann snorted. 'Does the girl know how much you stick up for her? People will start getting ideas, you know.'

'If it's okay with you, I'm going to get back to work now.'

'Right then, good luck.' Was that an ironic undertone in his voice?

Footsteps in the corridor betrayed Florin's return. Beatrice hastily typed her password and didn't look up from the screen even when he stormed into the room and sank down into his chair.

She could feel him looking at her.

'Don't pretend you didn't hear that,' he said.

She looked up, tried to smile and failed when she saw his serious expression. 'Thank you. You know it makes me uncomfortable when you stick your neck out for me like that, right?'

He raised his eyebrows. 'Well, that's the same way I feel when you send text messages to serial killers behind my back. But you were right about the time pressure. Waiting won't get us anywhere.'

She rested her head in her hands. 'I'm just worried that Hoffmann won't buy the thing about my powers of deduction . . . or perhaps I should say former powers. I mean, not even I do.'

'Well, you should. I wasn't making it up, Bea, you've always been the one to have the flash of inspiration in the end.'

'That's teamwork. I was the first one to see it, that's all. You might have had the same thought two hours later.'

'Or two weeks later. You know, any other boss would be happy to have you.' He shook his head. 'Do me a favour and don't let Hoffmann wind you up. Or bring you down. I'll try to keep him away from you.'

She nodded silently, wondering how she was going to manage to concentrate on her work – she would have to ignore not just Hoffmann, but also Achim, her memories of Evelyn, this morning's panic attack and her bad conscience regarding the children.

Hoffmann may be a bastard, but he's right: I've got no end of personal problems. They're like a millstone around my neck.

She pulled the files in front of her. On the top lay a note from Stefan, who had worked until four in the morning. *I'll be back in the office by ten. Goodnight*, he had written.

There was also a preliminary written assessment from

233

Drasche, who described the loss of blood indicated by the traces in the flat as potentially life-threatening, adding that, in all probability, Sigart was already dead.

That was very bad news. But in spite of it, for the first time that day Beatrice felt as though she had solid ground beneath her feet again. She worked well with facts, even if they were unwelcome ones.

A canine unit had been called out the previous evening and had searched the area surrounding the building in Theodebertstrasse, but they hadn't been able to pick up any scent beyond the spot where the trail of blood stopped.

The times between the victims' disappearances and their deaths varied. Why?

With Nora Papenberg, it had been just over four days. With Herbert Liebscher, at least a week, if they assumed he was already in the grip of his kidnapper the first time he didn't turn up to class. Christoph Beil had lived just another three days.

If Sigart hadn't already bled to death or had his throat cut by the Owner, how much time did they have left to find him?

Realising that she was chewing on her pen, she pulled it from her mouth. The Owner had done things differently this time: instead of luring his victim away with a phone call, he had made a personal visit. Why? Had Sigart not answered the phone?

' And why such brute force at the scene? Beatrice leant back and closed her eyes, trying to visualise the situation.

The Owner rings the doorbell, perhaps disguised as a deliveryman. Or Sigart knows him, and opens up. Do they talk to one another? Maybe the killer tries to drag his victim away immediately, but Sigart manages to make the phone call. That's why the Owner attacks there and then, severely injuring him, and drags him out of the house.

'Florin?'

'Yes?'

'We have to speak to Sigart's therapist.'

Dr Anja Maly gave up her lunch break to speak to them. She had sounded genuinely aghast on the phone when Beatrice informed her that Bernd Sigart had gone missing.

'I'm very concerned,' she said, closing the door of the consultation room behind her. 'I wouldn't rule out the possibility that Herr Sigart may be a danger to himself.'

'That's the least of our worries right now,' replied Florin. 'It looks like he's become the victim of a crime, and that's why we need to ask you if he mentioned anyone during his sessions – any friends or acquaintances.'

'The last time we saw him he was planning to release you from your confidentiality clause,' Beatrice added. 'There's a chance that he's still alive, and we're using all the means we can to find him, but we need some leads to go on. Can you give us any?'

They could see from Anja Maly's face that she was deep in thought. 'He told me about your visit and said it was connected to investigations for a murder case.' She pointed towards a sand-coloured sofa and waited for them to take a seat before she herself sat down. 'My God, the poor man. I presume you know his history? He comes to me once or twice a week, and we're trying to work on what happened, to find a way for him to accept it as part of his life – but I have to admit we're making very slow progress.' She clasped her hands around her knees and shook her head. 'And now he's a victim again. It's unbelievably tragic.'

Let's look for a victim echoed in Beatrice's mind. She had been convinced that the Owner was alluding to Evelyn, but maybe she was wrong. Maybe he had meant Sigart, and had been announcing what he was about to do. A loser, a victim – the two were closely linked.

'We have reason to believe that he knew the suspect and opened the door to him,' said Florin. 'Sigart mentioned to us that he almost never leaves the house and doesn't have contact with anyone. Are there any exceptions?' He smiled at the therapist. Even though Maly barely moved a muscle in her face, Beatrice could tell that the smile was having the desired effect.

'Wait a moment, I'll just get my notes.'

She pulled a thick blue ring binder out of a lockable cupboard and opened it towards the end. 'The last few times he was here we mainly spoke about his sleeping problems and the fact that he was going to try to leave the house more often.' She flicked forwards. 'He was having nightmares a lot, and increasingly suicidal thoughts. But he never mentioned any acquaintances. I don't think he even knew his neighbours by name.' She looked at the next page, read some more, then shook her head. 'It's very sad. He was living in complete isolation.' She stopped for a moment, laying her index finger on the page she had in front of her. 'Wait, this could be of interest to you. In his last session he told me he'd felt like someone was following him on one of his walks. When I tried to find out more, he just shrugged it off and said it was probably his guilty conscience.' She looked up. 'His feelings of guilt were always a major topic in our sessions. He was convinced he was responsible for his family's deaths, and resisted all attempts to relativise it.'

Beatrice leant forwards. 'You said he thought he was being followed?'

'Yes. But not threatened, it seems. He didn't think it was worthy of anything more than a brief mention, and also said he didn't see or recognise anyone. I think he thought it was just his imagination.'

Like I did the other day, thought Beatrice. The blinding lights in the rear-view mirror.

'Did he mention any phone calls? Was there someone who might have got in touch out of the blue, a new or old acquaintance perhaps?'

Maly shook her head emphatically. 'No. From time to time the vet who took over his surgery would call, whenever she had questions. Sigart's parents aren't around any more, and he completely broke off contact with his former friends. He didn't want—'

She was interrupted by Beatrice's phone beeping.

Beatrice quickly pressed the red button in order to stop the message tone. 'Excuse me for a moment, please.' She turned away, recognising the Owner's number, and felt her face start to burn up.

This time it was a picture message. The text said **NM**. Just those two letters, nothing more. The attached picture took around three seconds to load, but even once it appeared

Beatrice wasn't sure at first what she was looking at. She rotated the phone a little, then suddenly everything became clear. She suppressed the noise that was trying to force its way out of her, something between a curse and a groan.

'Something urgent?' asked Florin.

'Yes. I'm afraid we're going to have to excuse ourselves, Dr Maly. Thank you very much indeed for your help.'

The therapist accompanied them to the door. 'Could you let me know when you find out where he is?'

'Of course. Thank you again.' Beatrice practically pulled Florin out of the practice, down the steps and over to the car, where she leaned against the driver's door.

He stood next to her. 'I take it that was from the Owner.'

'It certainly was.' She opened the picture and handed Florin her mobile. 'You tell me whether that's good or bad news.'

'Oh, God.' He looked closely at the picture, then gave her the phone back. 'It looks terrible.'

The image was sharp, and in spite of the small display, new details jumped out at Beatrice every time she looked. The pale arm with the dirty sleeves, pushed up to the elbow. The pile of bloody gauze bandages, crumpled on the brown tabletop. And the hand. Three fingers and a gruesome wound where the little and ring finger had once been. Dark red, almost black in places.

'Let's drive back to the office and enlarge the photo as much as we can,' said Beatrice. 'Some of the background is visible, so maybe it will give us some clues.'

'NM.' Frowning in concentration, Florin pointed at the message attached to the photo. 'Could it be initials this time? Is he giving us clues to his name, or perhaps the next victim's?'

'I don't think so. If I remember rightly, it's another geocaching abbreviation and means "needs maintenance".'

'This guy has a pretty sick sense of humour,' muttered Florin. He flung open the car door and sat down behind the wheel. 'Let's go. We need some extra people on the case to question the neighbours again, shine a light on the other victims' social circles and search through the geocaching sites. We have to find Sigart before the Owner kills him.'

The photo was easy to enlarge and revealed further chilling details. They had summoned Vogt from the pathologist's office, and he was now sitting in front of Beatrice's computer, his hands folded into a steeple in front of his mouth.

'I can't be completely certain, but I suspect the fingers were severed with one single blow. Have a look for an axe or a sharp kitchen knife as possible weapons.'

Florin pointed at the image. 'The man is likely to also have a neck wound and has lost a lot of blood. I know you can only see the arm in the picture – but do you think he's still alive?'

Vogt zoomed in further on the section showing the hand and moved his face so close to the screen that his nose was almost touching it. 'Well, he at least lived for some time after the fingers were severed, because the edges of the wound seem slightly inflamed, and you can see the first stages of the healing process.' He pushed his glasses right up to the top of his nose. 'It also looks as though the hand muscles are tensed. So it's likely that he was still alive when the photo was taken. I can't give you any guarantees though.'

Guarantees weren't necessary. For Beatrice, Sigart was alive until proved otherwise. 'We'll speak to Konrad Papenberg again,' she said after Vogt had left. 'This whole thing started with his wife – her handwriting is on the cache notes and Liebscher's blood on her clothing. In one way or another, she must be the key to this case.'

'But she's not the key figure, at least not according to the Owner,' Florin interjected. His fingers were drumming out a speedy rhythm on the surface of the desk. 'He hasn't yet given us any false information in his messages, have you noticed that? He doesn't lie to us, so if he says someone is the key figure, then we should identify that person as quickly as possible.'

'Yes, except that might take for ever,' answered Beatrice. 'I think Sigart is our priority, and the path to him is via the other victims.'

Konrad Papenberg's face had turned a deep red and was just ten centimetres at most from Beatrice's. 'Get out of my house right this second! I won't allow you to slander my dead wife under my roof!' A drop of spit landed next to Beatrice's right eye. She didn't wipe it off. Instead of backing away from Papenberg, she took a tiny step towards him. It had exactly the desired effect: he stepped back, putting more distance between them.

'I understand that you're upset,' she said in a decidedly calm voice. 'Nothing has been proven, of course. But there was someone else's blood on your wife's hands and clothing, and we've since been able to match that blood to another victim. I hope you can understand that we have to investigate this.'

'Perhaps she was trying to help him!' roared Papenberg. 'Had you thought of that? No, you'd rather believe that Nora is a murderer, my Nora, my . . .' His voice failed him and he sank down onto the couch, burying his face in his hands.

Beatrice nodded to Florin. It was a silent request for him to take over the questioning. She hadn't counted on such an extreme reaction, and although she felt sorry for Papenberg, his lack of control didn't necessarily have to mean an end to the conversation if Florin took the right approach.

Florin sat down next to the man on the sofa and spoke to him softly. Beatrice removed herself from his line of sight as much as possible, positioning herself over by the window in an attempt to let him forget she was there.

It was clear that nothing had been cleaned or tidied in the apartment since their last visit. There was dust on the furniture, clothing scattered on the floor, newspapers, unemptied ashtrays – all evidence of how Konrad Papenberg's life had been turned completely upside down.

'Of course your wife was a victim,' Beatrice heard Florin say. 'We're just trying to understand what happened. I'd like to show you photos of two men, perhaps you might know one of them. Would that be okay?'

Papenberg didn't answer. Beatrice could hear the sound of papers being shuffled, so presumably he had nodded.

'No, I've never seen them before. Which of them is Nora supposed to have murdered, according to your colleague?'

'This man here, Herbert Liebscher.'

'I don't know him. I swear to you – if I did, I'd tell you.'

Beatrice looked around and saw that the photos were shaking in Papenberg's hands. His face was wet. 'No one wants the murderer to be found more than I do. I want to help you, but when you say things like that about Nora . . .' He fumbled around in his pocket, pulled out a crumpled tissue and blew his nose. 'She was the most gentle person I've ever known. She could barely hurt a fly, and felt bad about the silliest of things. Sometimes she would burst into tears when bad news came on the TV, and then would be inconsolable for hours. About car crashes, for example, even if she didn't know the people. She was so compassionate, you know?' He scrunched the tissue up in his hand. 'She could never have been an accomplice to murder.'

Beatrice turned around from the window. 'Was she always that way?' she asked. Her question was one of genuine interest.

'Ever since I've known her, yes. She did a lot of charity work, like for Children's Village, Médecins Sans Frontières and organisations for disabled people. Not just donations, I mean personal stuff too. She always said that when she . . . died, she wanted to feel like she had made a difference.'

A woman with a social conscience, empathy and a dedication to giving something back. But perhaps there was a darker side to Nora Papenberg, even if her husband had her up on a pedestal.

Beatrice tried to fight the feeling of frustration welling up inside her. She was familiar with this phase from previous cases. The aimless stumbling around in the darkness; being in the wrong place at the wrong time. It required the utmost patience, something she struggled with even in normal circumstances. But the fact that someone's life depended on her work this time made it almost unbearable.

'You look exhausted,' said Florin as they got back in the car. 'Let's go and get something to eat, sit on a park bench and have a quick break.'

'I'm not hungry.'

'Bea, it's quite clear that you've already pushed yourself to the limit.'

A sharp retort twitched on her tongue, but she controlled herself. Usually she liked it when Florin looked out for her, but not when she was under as much pressure as today. 'It'd make me feel sick, can't you understand that? I won't be able to stomach more than a coffee and a few biscuits, and we have all of that back at the office.'

Florin started the engine without saying another word. She looked at him from the side, feeling guilty for her harsh tone, but then fixed her gaze on the road. She knew she was taking this case more personally than any other. By mentioning Evelyn's name, the Owner had stirred up an old guilt within her.

She knew she would do it; the only question was when. Since Florin had dropped her back at home, Beatrice had pulled her phone from her bag again and again, her fingers hovering indecisively over the buttons, trying to formulate a message in her mind. Something clever that would interest the Owner, that's what Kossar had said.

Shortly before eight, she drove to Mooserhof to see the children. She felt a fleeting moment of relief that they were both happy and didn't seem to be missing her too much. Mina hugged Beatrice for longer than usual, reporting that she'd got a good mark for her dictation. She also seemed to know exactly how many mistakes each and every child in the class had made.

Jakob had renewed his friendship with the neighbours' son, and was spending most of his time on their farm with the chickens. He presented Beatrice with an egg he had personally collected from one of the hutches.

'I got a present yesterday too,' he said proudly. 'A little world that lights up when you press a button.'

'A globe, you mean?'

'A globe, that's what I said. And Mina got a really pretty mirror with sparkly flowers around the edges.'

From Achim of course. 'Was Papa here for a while then?'

'No, he hasn't come.'

'So who's giving you such lovely presents? Oma?'

'No, not Oma!' He sounded almost outraged. 'But the guests are all so nice to us, a few of them give us euros if we bring them their food. And sometimes we get stuff too. The man with the globe had all kinds of toys with him, a whole sack full, and he was going to sell it all at the flea market.'

'And he just gave you some as a present?'

Sensing the hidden accusation, Jakob reacted with lightning speed. 'I asked Oma if I was allowed to take it and she said yes. And today a woman gave me a pen, with penguins on it! Look!'

Beatrice admired Jakob's new acquisition enthusiastically. He tapped his index finger on the tip of the egg which he had put on the table. 'Make yourself a scrambled egg from it, okay?' he said, rubbing his nose against her cheek.

Later, as she drove from her mother's restaurant back to

the office, she was almost expecting someone to be following her again, but the street behind her was practically empty. The egg lay on the passenger seat, and Beatrice made an effort to brake carefully at every crossing. She felt strangely protected, somehow, by the mere presence of Jakob's fragile gift.

'I want him to give me Sigart,' declared Beatrice. She had the telephone receiver clamped between her ear and shoulder, had taken off her shoes and was sitting on the revolving chair with her legs tucked beneath her. By night, all was peaceful in the murder investigation department. There was no one else there except Florin, who sat wearily in front of his computer, an enlarged version of the photo of Sigart's mutilated hand on the screen.

From the other end of the line, Beatrice could only hear heavy breathing. Had Kossar fallen asleep already? 'What can I send to the Owner as bait? What can I offer him?'

Kossar cleared his throat. She could picture him setting his glasses straight. 'That's risky, my dear,' he said. 'We don't yet know enough about him and his motives, and we don't want to provoke him.'

My dear? Beatrice mouthed the words silently. 'Listen, I have a chance here. I can't just throw it away. We've been waiting for your input for days now, and time is running away from us. So, what would you do?'

She looked up, saw Florin's surprised expression and shrugged her shoulders. She needed some expert advice. And if Kossar was the only one available, she had no choice but to turn to him.

'Well,' said the psychologist slowly, 'the Owner has made a personal connection with you by referring to your deceased friend. Try to answer in an equally personal way. It's not necessarily without danger, but it's probably the only possibility of establishing some common ground with him. And that would be an immeasurable win. Show that you're curious about what he's doing. Be a good audience.' She heard him chuckle softly. 'Just don't applaud too loudly.'

He tried to open his eyes, but the blindfold was so tightly wrapped around his head that his eyelids remained firmly shut despite all his efforts.

He was shaking from the cold, and from fear. With every cramped, trembling movement of his body, the ties cut deeper into his wrists. 'Hello?' he whispered. 'Is anyone there?'

No answer.

He swallowed down the panic surging within him and tried to get his bearings.

It was in vain. He could have been here for an hour or even twelve; losing consciousness had taken away any sense of time.

But it hadn't taken away the pain. His pulse was racing, a rhythm beating against the inside of his skull with the merciless sharpness of a pickaxe. His wrists were burning, but he couldn't feel his hands. They were completely numb. He tried to move his fingers, but couldn't work out whether they were responding.

'Hello?'

He waited, trying not to breathe, trying to sense the presence of another person, but everything around him was quiet, empty.

He only had himself to blame. He had been warned and hadn't taken one single word of it seriously. And now . . .

The fear swelled, breaking through the thin layer of control that had been holding it in. Even though his head felt close to bursting, he yelled, screamed with panic.

But no one came, and after a while he quietened down again, waiting silently. He tried to think about his family, but that just made everything worse. Behind the tight blindfold, tears began to well up. The mucous membrane in his nose was becoming swollen.

'I see we're ready now,' he heard someone say behind him. He reacted instinctively, trying to turn around, but the ties just burrowed deeper into his flesh.

'What do you want from me?' he croaked.

'Answers.'

He swallowed a sob, not voicing the question in his mind – *Answers to what?* 'If I tell you what you want to know, will you let me live?'

The silence was as complete as before, as if the man behind him wasn't even breathing. Then he felt a hand on his head.

'I'll tell you how it's going to be. First, you'll lie. Then you'll tell the truth. Then, at the end, you will die.'

The clock on her computer said 01.26. Little by little, the space around Beatrice was losing its sharp contours. She had planned to drop by the office only briefly after visiting the children, to pick up a few files, but she had discovered two new reports. They had drawn her into some research, and now four hours had passed. She resolved to go home as soon as she had sent the text message. Let us help you, she typed into her mobile, only to delete it again. It was roughly her twentieth attempt at formulating a message which would provoke the Owner into conversing with her. But she couldn't find the right tone. The messages she came up with either sounded ridiculous or overbearing. The last one topped them all, as it implied he was crazy.

'Although he is, of course,' mumbled Beatrice.

'Pardon?'

'Sorry, Florin, I was just talking to myself.' She tried to smile, but it felt like a pathetic attempt. 'Shall I make us some coffee?'

He glanced at his watch and raised his eyebrows. 'Suicide by caffeine, eh? I could actually do with one too, though. Stay where you are, I'll do it.' The espresso machine rumbled back to life. 'You're still battling with the text message, right?'

'Yep.'

'We should come up with one together.'

'I'm not so sure.' She looked out of the window into the darkness, but her own pale reflection in the glass obstructed her view of the night. 'Kossar advised me to be authentic and honest. And personal too, but I don't want to mess around – this is about saving Sigart's life.' She tossed her mobile onto the table. 'Maybe there are some magic words, some code that will unsettle the Owner so much it stops him from committing another murder.'

The steam pipe made hissing, spitting noises, transforming the milk into a cloudy froth.

'I think the Owner's going to see through the message no matter what you write. He'll know what you're trying to achieve, so you might as well spell it out.' He placed a cup in front of her. 'But forget Kossar – don't go in for anything personal, Bea. Don't give him any incentive to get to know you better.'

She let his words go in one ear and out the other, then pulled the mobile back towards her. *That's what I want*, she thought, *one to one*.

I'd like to speak to you and understand why you're doing what you're doing.

Now add something personal.

21 May, 08.41 a.m.

She drank the cup of coffee down in three long gulps and sent the message off before she had the chance to change her mind. He wouldn't know what to make of the date; a little puzzle for the Owner, for a change. Yawning, she stretched her arms. 'I'm going to head off, Florin. And yes, I will let you know when I get there.'

The memories filled her mind as she got in the car, summoning up images that Beatrice hadn't pictured this vividly in a very long time.

She turned the car radio on and allowed the music to chase the ghosts from her head at eighty decibels.

The answer came at 5.43 a.m., as the gleaming red display of the radio alarm clock betrayed when Beatrice opened her eyes. The text message tone had haunted her dreams, so she didn't realise at first that her phone really was making a noise.

Her hand fumbled around, grasping the mobile and nearly knocking it off the bedside table. She managed to get a grip on it just in time, then held it up in front of her face.

If you want to talk, then you come to me, said the Owner's message. You'd be able to if you drew the right conclusions. An interesting date – a shame that you omitted to mention the year, but I think I recognise it all the same.

From one second to the next, Beatrice was wide awake. She read the text again and again. The right conclusions, sure. If they had already reached them, then any conversation between them would be taking place in the interrogation room. But at least the Owner had responded to her message, and with an answer that referred back to what she had written. They had entered into a dialogue.

Feeling slightly dizzy, she got out of bed and padded into

the kitchen. She filled a glass with cold water and drank it down in long gulps.

He liked taking things literally. And he wasn't willing to admit that he didn't know what the date referred to. If he had even an inkling of what significance it held for Beatrice then his message would have read differently, she was sure of that.

In the hope of being able to get back to sleep, she lay down in bed and closed her eyes. She had set the alarm for seven. But sleep had now escaped her, and unfortunately without taking the tiredness along with it. Beatrice stayed in bed regardless, mentally scanning every single word in the Owner's message.

What would he say if she asked him about Sigart, whether he was still alive? Or if she asked him for another clue for Stage Four?

He would continue to be cryptic, just the same as always. *You come to me* – how original.

With a deep sigh, Beatrice turned onto her side. Her instinct was urging her to forget the search for Stage Four temporarily, to leave Liebscher's remaining body parts to their vacuum-packed fate. Because if there was any conceivable pattern at all, it was that the Owner waited until the police made a find before he pounced. In all likelihood, the best thing they could do to protect the people he had chosen was to play dumb.

'I have a used-car salesman, a sales coach and a calendar salesman, each of whom have two sons including one called Felix.' Stefan beamed as he held some papers under her nose.

'Now, is that good work or what?'

'It's –' Beatrice glanced quickly through the pages – 'wonderful, Stefan.'

'I carried on researching from home until I found them. Who do you think we should start with? Look, here are the addresses, so if we visit the calendar guy first—'

She held her hand up to interrupt him. 'Not today. We'll discuss it with the team, but I think we should hold off with Stage Four for now.'

'What? Why?'

His obvious disappointment made him look even younger than he did already. She patted him gently on the shoulder. 'We need to be cautious. It didn't turn out too well for Beil and Sigart after we spoke to them.'

'You think—?'

'I'm not sure. But it seems like the Owner just wants to shove people under our noses before ultimately killing them. So we're not going to play that game any more.'

Stefan mumbled something that sounded both dejected and acquiescent at the same time.

'Come to the office for a bit.' She pulled him gently along the corridor. 'I'll make us some coffee.'

Kossar agreed with her entirely. Their new approach was not giving the Owner what he wanted, but instead luring him out of his hiding place. The psychologist was wearing different glasses today: blue frames with a dark red pattern. They clashed intensely with his green eyes.

'This is the most personal message he's sent you yet, Beatrice. He's spurring you on, reacting to the date you gave and inviting you to come and find him. That goes far beyond merely transmitting information.'

'It's just that I don't believe I can coax him into giving up Sigart, no matter what I write, and that's really—' She saw Stefan and Kossar exchange a brief glance. 'I see. You both think he's already dead.' The memory of that April night twelve years ago fought its way back into Beatrice's mind. The memory of Evelyn's face – first alive, then dead. She pushed the image away, forcing herself to think of Sigart, his pale expression, devoid of all hope. She cleared her throat. 'I'll repeat myself as often as I have to – so long as we haven't found a body, I won't give up on him.'

'Neither will I,' she heard Florin say as he entered the room. 'If he was alive yesterday, then the chances aren't bad that he's still alive today.'

The only problem was that they didn't have the faintest idea where to look for him. Further questioning of his neighbours hadn't brought any results. But how was that possible? Had the noise really not startled anyone, had no one even looked through the peephole in their front door?

'We heard the struggle ourselves on the phone, and know that at least one of the witnesses in the building heard it too, even though he misinterpreted it.' Florin was propping up his chin with one hand while doodling in a squared notepad with the other, drawing snake-like lines that ended in crooked fingers. 'Okay, Sigart lives on the first floor, so the route to the cellar isn't far, but the Owner must still have been incredibly quick.'

Beatrice's eyes followed the intertwining lines and picked up on his thoughts. 'He grabbed him by the arms and pulled him down the stairs. The bloody shoe print —' she pulled the corresponding photo towards her — 'was pointing up the stairs. So either the Owner went down the stairs backwards, or he went back up again.'

'Backwards,' Florin surmised. 'He was pulling Sigart down behind him.'

The telephone rang. Bea's contact in the mobile provider's technical department reported that the text message earlier that morning had been sent from a location near Golling, around twenty kilometres south of Salzburg.

'It wasn't even 6 a.m.' Beatrice tapped her pen agitatedly on her notepad. 'The Owner must have to sleep at some point too; after all, he's got a hell of a workload. If he gets too tired he'll make mistakes, which he won't want to risk, so it's very likely he lives near Golling. Or that he's at least staying there temporarily.'

'Unless,' Stefan interjected, 'he's not alone. I mean, you agree that Nora Papenberg may have been his accomplice. It's possible that there are more.'

They had discussed this idea a number of times, with differing results. Kossar rejected the theory every time, and today was no exception. 'The person composing these puzzles is clearly conceited. The Owner wants to prove he's better than us, but his success will only be fully satisfactory if he, and only he, can take all the credit. I'm absolutely convinced that we're looking for a lone perpetrator.'

'So then how do we explain Nora Papenberg's role?'

Kossar only needed a few seconds to answer. 'It's possible

that he needed help at the start. But at soon as things were going to plan, he—'

A knock at the door interrupted his flow. One of the secretaries came in – *Jutta, Jette, Jasmin?* Beatrice cursed her appalling memory for names – bearing a bunch of flowers wrapped up in paper, their scent mingling with the aroma of the coffee.

'These were delivered for you, Frau Kaspary.' She winked, laid the flowers on the desk and headed off.

'Just a moment!' Beatrice called after her, but the woman had already pulled the door shut behind her. Kossar was grinning as if the bunch had been sent by him personally.

'Come on then, show us!'

Beatrice slowly pulled the cellophane off the paper. For a brief moment, the thought occurred to her that Florin might have sent them. But why would he send flowers? A quick glance revealed that he seemed as confused as she was.

She dispatched the first layer of cellophane into the waste-paper bin, admitting to herself that she was just trying to buy time with all the fumbling, then ripped the packaging open.

White calla and violet lilies. Three spruce twigs. Baby's breath. All tied together with a white-and-gold ribbon.

Her body reacted more quickly than her mind. She rushed out of the office and got to the bathroom just in time. She threw up her breakfast and the coffee she had only just drunk, still retching even after her stomach had nothing left to give. But not even the smell of vomit was enough to drown out the scent of the flowers, still clinging mercilessly in her nose. It had been a mistake to believe that 21 May would be a date just like any other to the Owner. He knew what role the day played in Beatrice's life, and that clearly wasn't all he knew.

She straightened up, waited until the black spots in her vision had disappeared, and then flushed the toilet. Her shock and disgust had now been joined by shame. Losing the plot like that at the sight of a few flowers didn't exactly make her look very professional; how was she going to explain it to the others?

A few sips of water chased the acrid taste from her mouth. She opened the door leading back out into the corridor, bracing herself for questions from her colleagues – and ran straight into Hoffmann.

'On a break, Kaspary?'

Her first instinct was to dodge around him without a word, to run away like a child, but she had already exhibited enough weakness today.

'Why would you ask that? You can see exactly where I've been.' The words came out quiet and forced; the hollow feeling in her stomach had returned.

Hoffmann came a step closer and sniffed the air. 'Have you just been sick?'

It took all the control Beatrice had to stand still and not break eye contact. 'Yes.'

'Are you pregnant or something? For heaven's sake, what next?'

She couldn't hold back her laughter. 'No, most certainly not.'

He looked her up and down. 'I see. Well, that doesn't make it much better, but—'

'If you say so,' Beatrice interrupted him. 'I don't really think that concerns you though. I'm feeling much better now, by the way, thank you for asking.' Without waiting for a response, she left him standing there.

Kossar and Stefan were still in the office when she walked back in, and so was Florin. 'Are you feeling better?' He stood up and came over to her. 'You're really pale. If you don't feel well, you should go home, okay? It's not going to help anyone if you collapse, Bea.'

The bouquet of flowers was still on her desk. Someone had freed them from the rest of the paper.

'I'm not ill. Sorry that my reaction was so extreme – it's just . . . these flowers.'

'So I gathered.' Florin held up an envelope, white with a black edging, like a death notice in a newspaper. 'Shall I open it for you?'

She shook her head and swallowed down the stomach acid rising up in her throat again. A death announcement, what else could it be? Sigart was dead, and the Owner had found his own unique way of telling her. She sat down, pushing the flowers far away from her, and steeled herself for the sight of more horrific pictures. She opened the envelope.

A white card without any adornment. Beatrice read it through, and tried to make sense of it but failed.

Everything that is entirely probable is probably false.
N47° 26.195; E013° 12.523
You know everything, and yet you find nothing.

Speechless, Beatrice handed the card to Florin.
'We've already phoned the flower delivery company while you – while you were outside,' explained Stefan. 'They said

the order came from a young woman who spoke very poor German.'

'We need a more detailed description.' She averted her gaze from the flowers, staring into the distance. 'Stefan, could you—'

'Drive over there? Of course.' On the way to the door, he waved his phone in the air. 'Keep me posted. I'll do the same.'

Beatrice looked back at the card. New coordinates. Was this Stage Four? A little extra help from the Owner so the game didn't grind to a halt?

Florin pushed a glass of water over towards her. 'Are you feeling better?'

'White calla and violet lilies,' she said softly, 'were the flowers on the wreath I bought twelve years ago for my friend's funeral, the one who was murdered. The Owner keeps making references to Evelyn.' She pushed sweaty strands of hair off her forehead. 'Even the colour of the ribbon is the same.'

'I wonder why he picked you, out of all of us.' Florin's gaze was full of sympathy, and Beatrice couldn't handle that right now.

'No idea.' She gestured towards Kossar, who was standing at the window with a thoughtful expression on his face. 'Why don't you ask the expert? And while you're at it, ask him how the Owner knows the inscription on her gravestone.'

Spirit of Man,
How like water you are.
Fate of Man,
How like the wind

The quote had been chosen by Evelyn's mother, a pretty, friendly woman who had collapsed during the funeral and had to be taken away in an ambulance. Beatrice had only seen her twice after that, and she had looked smaller and greyer each time. Not just her hair but her skin and eyes, too, seemed to lose their colour. She had been as friendly as ever, but the friendliness had become absent-minded. Even though Beatrice had fully intended to, she had never managed to tell Evelyn's mother about what had happened back then. About how easily Beatrice could have prevented it.

No one from her new life knew about it. Or so she had thought.

'Right then,' said Kossar, interrupting her thoughts, 'what seems evident is that the Owner wants to establish a strong link with Frau Kaspary. She's the only one receiving his text messages, and now flowers, and he put a note under her windscreen wiper too – a little like lovers might do, don't you think?'

Beatrice looked away. If Kossar carried on like this she would have to run off to the toilet again.

'Was the man who killed your friend ever caught?'

She shook her head, convinced she knew what Kossar really wanted to ask.

'There's no way it's the same killer! The behavioural patterns are completely different. For a start, the Owner doesn't commit any sexual offences.' She gestured towards the photos of the severed hands and ears that lay in front of Florin. 'The dismemberments aren't in any way comparable, and nor are the weapons, as far as we know. Besides, the Owner has predominantly killed men, so there aren't any parallels there either.' She raised her chin, staring defiantly at Kossar. *Hold your head high, even if your neck's dirty* had been one of Evelyn's favourite sayings. When Beatrice continued to speak, her voice was quieter than before, but also fiercer. 'I would have thought you knew that. No serial killers change their pattern just like that.'

'No, of course not,' responded Kossar gently. 'And I can't remember having suggested that. I only asked whether your friend's murderer was ever caught because I think it would have helped you considerably in dealing with the trauma.'

His response felt like a blow to the stomach. He was right; she had simply pushed her own interpretation onto him. She would have to apologise for questioning his competence. But right now she was too angry to be fair. 'More important than my so-called "trauma",' she snapped, 'are these coordinates. Let's not fool ourselves – we know what we're going to find there.' Sigart's blood-covered mobile came into her mind. The prospect that his painful life had now come to an end wasn't comforting, not even in the slightest.

'I wouldn't be so sure.' Florin pointed his pen at the computer monitor in front of him. 'The quote the Owner sent you this time is by René Descartes, and he was a mathematician.'

'Like Liebscher!'

'Precisely. So it's possible that the Owner hasn't sent us the location of Sigart's body, but the coordinates to Stage Four, as a gift of sorts. Leading us to another one of Liebscher's body parts. It's as if he knew we were planning to stop playing his game.'

★

The location was directly at the intersection of two busy roads near Bischofshofen, where a bridge stretched over the Salzach. Water and scenic spots – the Owner clearly had a weakness for them.

They made their approach with a backup team: three dog handlers, and four squad cars to immediately block off the street if they found something. Drasche and Ebner had been called away to a break-in at a jewellery store, but two colleagues had been sent in their place.

The coordinates directed Beatrice and Florin right towards the bridge, the arches of which were accessible on foot – stone steps beneath the road led from one arch to the next. The three officers with their dogs were already down there, while four others were searching the surrounding area within a radius of thirty metres, so far without any success.

Down below, the river rushed northwards towards the city. Beatrice stood at the edge of the bridge, leaning over the stone wall and trying to ignore the pungent stink of urine rising up towards her. If the Owner hadn't been careful, the river might already be carrying what they were looking for off towards the border. It was damp within the arches of the bridge; a plastic box could easily be dislodged by a strong gust of wind and fall into the water.

And it seemed that Beatrice's fears were to be confirmed, for three hours later they still hadn't found anything. The dogs had dug up a perished squirrel, but that was all. No body, no cache. At around two in the afternoon, they gave up the search.

'He's making fools of us,' said Beatrice bitterly. 'He tosses us a few coordinates and we run off and do exactly what he wants.' She sat down in the grass near the roadside and watched the dog handlers working their way through the arches of the bridge one more time.

What if it was a mini-cache? An eye, vacuum-packed in an old photo film cartridge, hidden away in one of the numerous niches in the wall. Would the dogs be able to sniff it out?

Probably. But so far the Owner had hidden his containers in such a way that, with a little patience, they could always be found.

'I wish I knew why we're here.' A cool wind had started up, prompting Florin to pull his jacket closed across his chest.

'Me too. Why is he luring us out here? Maybe it's to get us out of the way. If all the attention is focused on Point A, it leaves him in peace to do whatever he wants at Point B.'

You know everything, and yet you find nothing.

What did the Owner mean exactly? That they knew everything, knew the coordinates, and still weren't finding anything? Or were his words meant to be read figuratively?

For the duration of the journey back to the office, Beatrice went over the messages she had received from him again and again in her mind. A text message and a card today alone – he was astonishingly eager to communicate. Which gave her reason to fear they were moving towards the culmination of his bloody production.

Achim was waiting in the car park next to the entrance of the office building. Judging by his posture, he had already been standing there a long time. For a few moments, Beatrice felt yet again as though her lungs were refusing to take in any oxygen.

It's fine, she reassured herself. If he were to get loud and offensive then she wouldn't hesitate to call for help this time. After all, there were enough law enforcers on hand.

Florin had noticed Achim too, and groaned with irritation. 'That man's got perfect timing. I can get rid of him for you if you like.'

'No, it's fine. I'll deal with it.' She took her time getting out of the car and waited until the others had disappeared into the building. Achim looked at her. A few strands of blond hair stood up from his head, windswept.

'Hello, Beatrice.'

She stopped silently in front of him, her arms folded. He tried to smile, but it was a less than convincing attempt. Seemingly aware of that, he looked down at the ground.

He wants something from me, thought Beatrice, feeling the muscles in her shoulders start to relax. *Otherwise he would just come straight out with it.*

'You've got a lot on at the moment, haven't you?' An understanding tone. It sounded almost genuine.

'Yes. We're under a lot of pressure.'

'I understand. Well, this is the thing . . . I know the children like being at your mother's, and that she likes having them around, but . . .' He was clearly finding it difficult to maintain a calm tone; Beatrice was very familiar with the slight redness creeping up his neck.

'But I see them so rarely. And I'd love to have them with

me if you don't have time. Even at short notice. It would help us both.'

At this moment, here and now, Achim really meant it; there was no question of that. But she still couldn't let him off that lightly. 'For you that would be like a double jackpot, wouldn't it?' she said. 'You'd get more time with the children, and each time it happened you'd get the opportunity to use my job against me.'

He raised his hands. 'This isn't about us and our issues – it's about Mina and Jakob. I know they'd like to spend more time with me.'

She felt a sharp stabbing sensation in her gut. 'Did they say that?'

'Mina did. Does that bother you so much? That they miss their father?'

Yes. No. Of course not. 'Of course not. What bothers me is that you speak badly of me to them. It was only the other day that the expression "offloading them" came up when I took them to Mooserhof.' Realising that her tone had become sharper, she tried to calm herself down. 'Mina certainly didn't learn the expression from me, at least not in this context.'

It was clear that a retort was on Achim's tongue, but with some effort he managed to suppress it. He pulled an open pack of Camels out of his shirt pocket, but on looking at her he seemed to think twice and put it back. 'It's possible that I blurted it out once, but that's only because I haven't yet got used to everything being . . . different. And I didn't want things to be like this. I still don't.'

Sure. So everything's my fault then, thought Beatrice. 'It's an

265

adjustment for all of us. Listen, I have to get back to work – but you're right. The next time I need some help, I'll call you first.'

He smiled, with genuine happiness this time. Beatrice would have smiled back had there not been a glimmer of triumph in his eyes.

'Have a good day, Achim.' She held her hand out, which clearly surprised him, but he grasped it nonetheless.

'I mean it, Beatrice, I want us to get on better again.'

'Okay.' She pulled her hand back. 'I'll be in touch.'

'The woman who ordered the flowers was brunette and slightly overweight. She paid in cash.' Stefan was reading from his notepad. 'The saleswoman couldn't place her accent. Turkish or Hungarian, she said.'

'Well, I'm not surprised, they're practically the same,' remarked Florin sarcastically, leaning back in his chair. For the first time since they'd started working on the case, he seemed anxious.

Beatrice was only half-listening to the conversation. Her enquiry with the provider hadn't revealed any new information. Since the text message that morning, the Owner had kept the mobile turned off.

Sensing that the ball was in her court again, Beatrice opened a new message on her mobile.

Thanks for the flowers, she typed. I'd like to compliment you on your attention to detail and ask you to answer just one simple question for me: How is Bernd Sigart?

Would the Owner think the message was ridiculous? Probably. But she wasn't in the mood for playing it safe with subtle hints any more.

For a moment, she contemplated mentioning the coordinates and the bridge, but decided against it. She didn't want to distract from the main thrust of the message.

She sent it and went off to fetch a bottle of iced tea from the vending machine. With the drink in her hand, she looked for a peaceful spot outside. The tea was unbearably sweet and so cold that pain shot to her temples with every sip.

She needed to take a break for half an hour, so she drank slowly. She wanted to give him time – if he hadn't connected to the network so far, then he might do so soon. Then she could respond immediately. The exchange of messages pleased him; that was quite obvious. He enjoyed the innuendos, the surprises he gave her. He would want to see her reaction.

But it wasn't until three the next morning that the strains of 'Message in a Bottle' announced the arrival of a new message. Wide awake from one second to the next, and with her heart pounding at a worrying speed, Beatrice sat bolt upright.

You want to know whether Sigart is alive? He is. So far. But he's in a bad way. If you're that fond of him, I'll keep him for you until the end. I hope you'll appreciate it.

Until the end. If ever a piece of information was a double-edged sword, then it was this. So there was still a chance of

267

saving Sigart, but at the same time the Owner was saying he wasn't yet done with the murders. Stage Four was still unsolved, of course, the puzzle they had refused help with. Stefan was continuing with the research, but even if he were to find something, and something quite definite, they wouldn't question the key figure, but instead have him watched around the clock. If the Owner was lurking somewhere in the vicinity of his next potential victim, waiting for the police to show up, then they might have a chance of catching him.

Would there be a Stage Five?

She read through the message again.

The next thing to find its way into Beatrice's consciousness was the peeping of the alarm clock. She had managed to go back to sleep after all, her mobile phone clasped tightly in her hand like a talisman.

Kossar didn't agree with her theory. 'Keeping him until the end could also mean keeping his corpse until the end. Don't let him lull you into a false sense of security.' The gaze behind the slender lenses was full of the psychologist sensitivity Beatrice had found so abhorrent in her lecturers at university. 'Remember the state of the flat – he lost an awful amount of blood, and I'm sure he carried on bleeding after he was bundled into the car.'

He could spare her the know-it-all tone. Beatrice had no intention of arguing with him. She waited until she was alone with Florin in the office, then called Drasche.

'Without medical care it would be unlikely he'd survive,' he said dispassionately. 'Maybe he didn't die immediately, but I wouldn't hold out too much hope.'

'Was all of the blood his, then?'

'Yes.' The answer came without hesitation. 'AB negative, and you don't get much rarer than that. The finger and all the traces of blood originate from the same person. I compared my lab data with Sigart's medical file, and all the parameters match. His finger, his blood. No traces of anyone else's blood. The perpetrator clearly didn't sustain any injuries.'

'Thank you,' said Beatrice quietly. The small amount of optimism that had visited her in the early hours of the morning had trickled away at Drasche's words. For the rest of the day, she hoped for a message from the Owner, for another picture message showing that he had answered truthfully, that Sigart was alive. But her mobile remained silent.

According to her kitchen clock, it was just before midnight. When the phone rang, Beatrice was standing in front of the fridge in her bathrobe, her hair still wet.

'We've got another body.' Florin's voice sounded incredibly weary. 'And three guesses as to where it was found.'

'Oh, shit. Sigart.' So the Owner had gone against his word and killed him – or let him die of his injuries.

'No, it doesn't seem like it's Sigart, going by the description. But it's definitely one of our Owner's victims.'

'How do you know that?'

'The body's at the bridge, at the coordinates where we searched yesterday morning. I'm already on my way. It would be good if you could come too.'

N47° 26.195, E013° 12.523

The red-and-white cordon tape fluttered in the night wind, while dazzling floodlights illuminated the foot of the bridge. *Cold, completely cold*, thought Beatrice as she got out of her car. She was shivering, but put that down to her wet hair. She had tied it into a low ponytail, and now felt as though she was carrying around a small, drowned animal at the nape of her neck.

Stefan came running over the bridge towards her. 'Florin's down below with the body. There's not much room to move and they're all stepping on each others' toes down there, so I'm pretty sure they'll bring the guy up soon. It's unbelievable, Bea. He looks terrible.'

She nodded silently and pulled him along with her to the bridge wall, next to the floodlights.

Pale skin and a stocky body which bore no resemblance to Sigart's gaunt frame. Twisted legs, naked feet. Beatrice couldn't make out much more than that, because both Florin and Dr Vogt were leaning over the body, clearly struggling to keep their balance on the sloping embankment. Drasche was there too, more lying on the ground than sitting, busy grappling with the lock of his evidence case.

'It looks like the Owner just pushed the guy off the bridge,' Beatrice pondered out loud. He wouldn't have had the time or the opportunity to place him down there – the road was really busy even at night. Had he not been able to find a better location? Had he decided to give up on his former principle of seclusion when selecting this one?

'Do we have any idea yet of the dead man's identity?'

'No. There aren't any new missing persons reports. But he was married. Drasche has taken the wedding ring for examination.' Stefan shrugged. 'It must have been a really gruesome way to go though. Even Vogt says he's never seen anything like it.'

The three men were now clambering up the embankment one after the other, while a few uniformed officers got ready to haul the corpse up to the top. Drasche was the first to step over the low wall, holding out a plastic evidence bag towards Beatrice. The wedding ring.

'Graciella, 19.6.2011,' he said. 'Our grieving widow.'

She made a note of the information; the unusual name was a gift that would make their work easier.

'Hey, Bea.' In the glare of the floodlight, Florin looked almost as pale as the corpse. He took the cigarette offered to him by Drasche – an absolute first.

'I'll come along to the autopsy,' he said, taking a deep drag of smoke. 'I want to know what the body looks like internally.'

Why? Beatrice wanted to ask, but the two policemen had just lifted the man over the wall. They laid him down on a tarpaulin, and Beatrice signalled for them to wait before covering him up.

The very next moment, she regretted her decision, but forced herself not to look away.

A red-and-black crater was located where the man's right

eye would once have been. Festering lava had oozed out, burrowing deep grooves and exposing raw flesh.

The dead man was baring his teeth like a bulldog about to bite, and it was only on closer inspection that Beatrice realised the contorted expression wasn't due to scorn or pain, but a missing lower lip. It was as if it had melted away. The stained tongue protruded out from between the teeth, an oversized, blood-bloated leech. The inside of his mouth was a darkly encrusted wasteland.

'How did that happen?' she asked Vogt, who had come over to stand next to her.

'My guess would be acid, perhaps acetic or hydrofluoric. Do you see the dark crust on the mucous membrane? That's a typical sign of it.'

'You mean he drank acid?'

'Or was forced to, more like. I can only say for sure after the body's been opened up, but I'm expecting to find a corroded oesophagus and perforated stomach, as well as mediastinitis. We'll see. We also found marks around the hands and ankles indicating that he'd been restrained, similar to those on Christoph Beil, but cutting in more deeply this time. Cable tie, if you ask me.'

Beatrice's mind recalled the image of Nora Papenberg, lying face down on the meadow, her hands tied behind her back. Cable tie, as white as the dead skin beneath it.

Vogt nodded to the policemen to cover up the body, and this time Beatrice didn't stop them. 'What about the eye?' she asked.

'The same thing. And downright horrific, because it was ante mortem.' He saw the unspoken question in her face.

'The eyelid was corroded. He must have tried to close it in order to protect the eye. Not too pleasant.' He left her standing there and went over to his car, where he pulled out a muesli bar from the glove compartment.

On the opposite side of the street towered the stone figure of a saint, a woman in long robes holding a tower in her hands and staring down to the ground. Florin was sitting at her feet, another cigarette between his fingers, looking over at Beatrice.

'Don't make a habit of that,' she said.

'I won't. Anneke hates it when I smoke.' He took two more deep drags, then stubbed the cigarette out next to him in the grass. 'I'd like to call on Konrad Papenberg again. Let's see if he has an alibi for tonight. Who else is there – Beil's wife? Would she be capable of hauling along a guy like that?' He looked at Beatrice, his head cocked to the side. 'Would you be able to manage it?'

'Not alone. And besides . . .' She tried to formulate her thoughts into comprehensible words. 'I don't think it was Papenberg or Vera Beil. Or Liebscher's ex-wife. It just doesn't make sense.'

'That's not a strong enough argument.'

'I know. But that doesn't necessarily mean I'm wrong. If you look at the messages the Owner's sent me so far, can you really imagine them coming from Konrad Papenberg? Or from Vera Beil? It's just not her tone.'

Florin didn't answer right away. He stared at the crumpled cigarette, clearly regretting having smoked it. 'That's irrelevant. We've distanced ourselves much too far from our normal method of working. We've let the Owner force his

273

games on us and stupidly believed that he'd keep to the rules he himself made. Initially he waited until we'd found his next victim before attacking. But now he's lost patience – either that or he's just having too much fun. Who knows, for fuck's sake!'

A jolt went through Beatrice. For a split second she had grasped onto an important detail, something had locked into place, but then the thought slipped away again as quickly as it had come. At first the Owner had waited, but now he was there ahead of them . . . there was something behind that, something important. She repeated every one of Florin's words in her mind, but the thought refused to come back, like a shy wild animal hiding in the undergrowth.

Florin had already stood up and was walking towards the pathologist's vehicle, which had finally turned up. He stood there, a black silhouette against the floodlight, watching as the unknown dead man was put into a body bag.

We all end up in containers eventually, thought Beatrice.

'Am I dealing with a bunch of amateurs here, or what?' Hoffmann's spit flew right across the table. Even though the day had only just begun, all the people around it looked utterly exhausted.

'Four dead bodies, possibly five, and in just two weeks! There must be suspects, witnesses, something!'

With that last word, his voice had taken on a pleading tone. He seemed to have heard it himself, as he frowned and crossed his arms in front of his chest.

'Kaspary! Maybe you could make a contribution for a change. What do we know so far about the new victim?'

She squared her shoulders. 'Male, between forty and forty-five years old, of stocky build. According to Dr Vogt the cause of death was probably the intake of a strongly corrosive fluid.'

'I mean his identity! Is there anything to go on yet?'

'He didn't have any ID on him, and we don't have any recent missing persons reports, but we do have a wedding ring and what's likely to be the wife's forename.'

'You've been lucky then. So get on with it, okay? Do you have any idea what kind of pressure the Department of Public Prosecutions is putting me under? And several times a day at that!'

'We've already started looking for witnesses who may have driven over the bridge at the time of the crime,' Florin interjected. 'It's virtually impossible that the perpetrator would have been able to park there and get rid of the body without being spotted by someone. And we're also applying for a search warrant for Konrad Papenberg's house.'

'Okay.' Hoffmann wiped a hand over his sweaty brow. 'What about the last puzzle? The key figure? Have you found someone who fits the description?'

Stefan raised his hand. 'We've found three people where the most important points match up, but the clues are unfortunately very vague—'

'And? Check the people out then! For heaven's sake, don't be such a girl, Gerlach!' With an expression of exaggerated suffering, Hoffmann leant back in his chair. 'As soon as you have something, come straight to me. The press have already got wind of the latest murder, so that means I'll have to give a press conference tomorrow. And God help you if I have to stand there with empty hands.'

★

The online telephone register was a speedier source of information than the public registry, so Beatrice started with that, finding only three Graciellas in the entire district of Salzburg. She printed out the telephone numbers and tried to work out which of them was the most likely. One Graciella was listed in the phone book alongside her husband – a Carlos Assante.

The dead man from yesterday hadn't looked Mediterranean or Latin enough to be called Carlos Assante, so Beatrice moved this number to the bottom of the list. The two other entries only had mobile numbers listed.

'Hello?'

'Good morning, Frau Perner. This is Beatrice Kaspary, Salzburg Landeskriminalamt.'

A shocked intake of breath. 'What's happened?'

'I'd like to know where your husband is.'

'What?'

'Your husband. Do you know where he is?'

'Yes. He's in the bathroom, shaving. Do you want to speak to him?'

'No, in that case everything is fine. Have a good day!' Without waiting for the woman to respond, she hung up. Two more numbers, and if neither of them brought results then she would need the registry after all. It would probably be a good idea to look for Graciellas outside Salzburg too, and maybe even across the border in Bavaria.

'Hello, who's speaking?' The woman's voice was throaty and cheerful.

'Beatrice Kaspary, Landeskriminalamt.'

'Oh.'

'Are you Graciella Estermann?'

'Yes, but . . .'

'Could you tell me where your husband is?'

In the background, Beatrice could hear children's voices, then a dull crackle as the woman covered the speaker of her mobile. A few seconds later, the tone was clear again and the clamour silenced.

'What do you want from my husband?' The question didn't sound unfriendly, but cautious.

'Nothing special. I just need to know where he is.'

'I can't tell you precisely. He's been away for the past week, on business.'

Beatrice's pulse quickened. 'When did he last get in touch with you?'

Graciella Estermann took her time answering. 'A few days ago, I think. No, Saturday. Could you please tell me what this is about?'

Beatrice brushed the question aside. 'And you haven't heard from him since then? Isn't that unusual?'

'No.' This time the answer came promptly. 'He's often like that, only getting in touch when he needs to. I want to know what this is about!'

'Of course. I'd like to come by with my colleague. In an hour's time, would that be okay?'

'You want to come here?' For the first time, the woman sounded unsettled. 'He's in trouble again, isn't he? I don't know anything about it though. I mean, I hardly ever see him.'

There wasn't yet any proof that Beatrice really was speaking to the victim's wife, but she was becoming increasingly convinced. 'This will probably sound like a strange question,' she said, 'but could you tell me when you and your husband got married?'

The woman's silent confusion didn't last as long as she expected. 'It was . . . in June 2001. On the nineteenth of June.'

'Thank you. We'll be with you in an hour. Please wait for us.' Beatrice hung up. She typed *Estermann* and *Salzburg* into the text field on Google. The first couple of results brought up a Walter and a Rudolf.

Rudolf Estermann sold plant-based slimming drops and figure-shaping moisturisers to chemists' shops all over the country. He was a travelling sales representative. *Bingo.*

Alongside that, it seemed he also ran a small online shop. *Five kilos in ten days!!!* promised the garish red writing on the homepage. What a load of nonsense.

She pushed her chair back and stood up. Heading out of the office to look for Florin, she found him with Stefan, going through the data on Liebscher's computer.

'There doesn't seem to be anything here,' sighed Florin. 'Stefan has already read back through the last three months' worth of email correspondence, but hasn't found a thing. No connection to Beil, Papenberg or Sigart.'

'But I've got something.' Beatrice held up the printout with the telephone numbers. 'I'm ninety-nine per cent sure that the unidentified dead man is called Rudolf Estermann. He's a rep for some dubious slimming products and—'

She stopped short. It must be because of how exhausted she was, but the connection had only just occurred to her.

'Bea?'

She was already out of the door, running along the corridor towards her office and debating feverishly the quickest way of getting the necessary information.

Back at her computer, she typed *Felix Estermann* into the text field on the search engine. 'Things that no one needs,' she whispered.

Felix was nine and a member of the Sport Union Judo School. At the last club tournament, he had won third place in his age group. Beatrice clicked on the club's photo gallery and found him in the fourth image. A slim child with dark hair, tanned skin and a beaming smile.

From left to right: Felix Estermann (9), Robert Heiss (9), Samuel Hirzer (10), said the photo's caption.

'He has two sons, one of whom is called Felix.'

'Excuse me?'

Beatrice spun around. Why on earth did Florin always have to creep up like that?

'Sorry, I didn't mean to startle you. I thought you were talking to me.'

No. She had been talking to herself a lot recently; it was as if she could only understand her own thoughts if she voiced them out loud. She rubbed her hand against her forehead and tried to sort through her findings in her mind.

'He's the key figure. Rudolf Estermann.' She rummaged frantically through the photos that were lying next to the computer screen in a disorderly pile. She bit back a curse as some of them slipped down to the floor. '"Here – listen. He makes a living by selling things which, as he himself says, no one needs. He's good at it, too. He has two sons;

one of whom is called Felix.'" She held the picture out towards him and tapped her finger on the section she had read out. 'It all fits.'

He caught on right away. 'This Estermann guy is a sales rep, you said?'

'Yes. He sells diet pills to chemists. His wife hasn't heard from him in a few days. It all fits, Florin!' Beatrice pointed her pen at the screen. 'And that's the son called Felix. I phoned the wife and told her we'd be coming round.'

'Good. Vogt wants to start the autopsy at twelve, so we've got two hours.' He picked his keys up from the table. 'Let's go.'

They weren't even out of the door before Beatrice's phone beeped. The tone was making her skin crawl by now; she would have to change it. As soon as the case was over.

FTF. But don't let it get you down, chin up.

That was all. And it was yet another caching abbreviation; she remembered having seen it on the list. On their way out, she flung open the door to Stefan's office.

'Call the telephone company and find out which network the Owner was connected to two minutes ago.'

He looked up. 'Okay.'

'And remind me what "FTF" means?'

'First to find. If you find a cache first, then—'

'Great, thanks.'

First to find. He had been quicker than her, had worked out that they would use all the means they had to protect anyone his clues led them to from now on. But he didn't want that; he had wanted to pour acid into Estermann . . .

And then those sarcastic words of consolation. *Don't let it get you down, chin up.* What a sadistic bastard.

'I think things are about to get even more gruesome,' she said, as Florin steered the car out of the car park.

He glanced at her sideways. 'Not necessarily. Nora Papenberg died quickly, but before that he cut Liebscher's ear off, and we don't yet know how he killed him in the end. Sigart has already lost two fingers. Who knows what else he did to him before . . .'

Even though Florin didn't say it out loud, Beatrice read the message between the lines. He no longer believed they would find Sigart alive.

Five dead bodies in just a couple of weeks. *My God.*

Stefan phoned shortly before they reached Graciella Estermann's apartment. 'Bea? You won't believe this! The last text message from the Owner – he was connected to the UMTS cell on the roof of police headquarters.'

'Shit.' He couldn't have disappeared again that quickly. Had they driven right past him? Beatrice suppressed the impulse to ask Florin to turn around. There was no point now. 'Thanks, Stefan. Could you have a walk around and keep an eye on who's in the building? Just to make sure, I don't really believe that the Owner is still there, but—'

'But it can't hurt just in case. Of course.'

She told Florin what Stefan had said. 'He's lurking nearby. It seems like the news blackout is having the desired effect – he's hungry for information.' She turned around and peered through the rear window. Behind them was a white Vauxhall Astra with a dark blonde woman at the wheel. 'When we park let's pay attention to whether anyone else stops nearby.'

'Or,' Florin replied slowly, 'whether someone's already here. I mean, I'm sure he's worked out that we'll have found out the dead man's name by now. It's the logical next step to go and see the widow.'

For the last five minutes of their journey, Beatrice stared silently out of the window. She would have to speak to Kossar again. The Owner's increasing proximity was an opportunity they couldn't allow to slip through their fingers.

There wasn't anyone suspicious around when they got out of the car in front of the house. Nor did anyone seem to be paying them any attention whatsoever. A woman with a shopping basket in one hand and a whining child in the other made her way past them, but that was all.

Graciella Estermann turned out to be a pretty, dark-haired woman in her mid-thirties, who evidently found it difficult to stay sitting down for even a minute. 'After your call I took the children to school, then tried another five or six times to reach Rudo, but it keeps going straight to voicemail.' Her accent was audible, but her grammar was faultless. She crossed her arms in front of her chest and fixed her gaze on Florin. 'What's going on?'

There were no photos of Estermann on the wall or any of the shelves, only pictures of the two children – as babies, as clumsy toddlers, as school kids with gaps in their teeth.

'Before we continue, we'd like to ask you to show us a photo of your husband.'

'Why?' Rather than showing any signs of concern, she seemed intrigued. Cool, that was it.

'We'll be happy to explain once we've seen it.'

It was quite clear that she wasn't happy with the order of the proceedings, but eventually she shrugged and went to rummage around in the bookshelves, pulling out a small photo album.

'*Madre de Dios*,' she mumbled, laying it in front of Florin and Beatrice on the coffee table.

Wedding photos. Even the first photo was enough to confirm that they wouldn't need to keep searching. The Rudolf Estermann in the picture looked very much like the dead man, even though he had been younger and slimmer at the time the photo was taken, as well as having two eyes and a lower lip.

Beatrice and Florin's silence clearly lasted a little too long, and Graciella Estermann immediately caught on.

'Something's happened to Rudo, hasn't it? Are you going to tell me what's going on now?'

'We found a dead body last night, without any identification papers. It seems that it may unfortunately be—'

'Rudo?' Her voice had become louder, as if the thought made her angry. 'Was he drink-driving again? What was it – did he drive into a tree this time?'

'No. There's a possibility that he may have been murdered.'

That silenced the woman. She slowly lifted her hands to her mouth, as if to make sure that no sound would escape from it.

'What happened? Was he killed in a brawl? An argument?' she asked.

A strange question.

'Is that something you might have expected?'

A look of slight regret crept across Graciella Estermann's

face, as if she would have liked to retract her question. 'Not expected, no, but it wouldn't have been a great surprise.'

Beatrice leant forward. 'Tell me about your husband.'

'He drinks a lot and can't keep his hands off other women.' She stood up and walked over to the window, then from there to the bookcase. She took a book out, looked at it, put it back again, then picked up another. 'He isn't a good man. You can ask everyone who knows him.' She suddenly froze, holding her breath. 'But I didn't kill him, in case you think that!'

They didn't get the opportunity to respond, as Gabriella Estermann just kept on talking. Within ten minutes, they knew the majority of her life history, particularly the story of her marriage. Estermann had met Graciella in Mexico, where she used to work in a hotel. Everything had happened quickly: love, disillusionment, alienation, resentment. Two children.

'Well, you don't look too surprised by the news,' said Beatrice finally. 'With a murder case, that does tend to make us a little suspicious.'

'You wouldn't be surprised either,' the woman retorted. 'Rudo had more trouble in his life than any other man I know. If anyone so much as looked at him funny, that was enough to set him off. If someone nabbed a parking space from him, he would smash up their headlights. He once even punched a waiter who brought him the wrong side dish with his steak.' She looked at the book in her hands.

Trying to be discreet, Beatrice looked for any bruising on the woman's arms or face. Nothing.

'He hasn't laid a hand on me in a long time, nor the

children,' said the woman with a sad smile. She was really sharp; clearly she had picked up on Beatrice's train of thought despite all her attempts at discretion. 'Not like that, and not in the other sense either. He was hardly ever at home.' Her smile disappeared. 'To be completely honest, I am a little surprised. I always thought Rudo would end up killing someone one day. Not the other way around.' Her upper body suddenly seemed to sag, a trace of grief visible in her eyes for the first time.

So the man must have had enemies, and had maybe even been involved in criminal activity of some kind. Even though Beatrice was sure to find the information in his file, she asked all the same. 'Could you tell me where your husband was born?'

If the question had taken Graciella by surprise, then she didn't let on. 'In Schaffhausen. His father was Swiss.'

Back in the office, it was time to decipher the coordinates for Stage Four. The 'S' had a value of nineteen, the 'C' three, and the 'H' eight. With an endearing eagerness, Stefan turned his attention to the task. He was perfectly capable of doing it alone. Beatrice tried not to disturb him, speaking quietly into the phone.

'I think the Owner's trying to get close to us. He sent me a message today, and his phone was connected to the network directly in this area. Why is he doing that? Does he want to look up at my window while he types?'

'It's very possible,' replied Kossar after thinking for a moment. 'On the one hand he feels safe enough to risk it, but on the other he enjoys the thrill that it might go wrong.

He's the stranger who lays his hand on your shoulder in the darkness, then disappears again without being caught.'

An icy shiver passed over Beatrice's arms and back. 'That doesn't sound good to me.'

'No. The Owner picked you as his contact, Beatrice. I think that before his game comes to an end, he'll seek out a personal encounter with you.'

'But why?' She instinctively turned to look out of the window. Everything looked just as it always did. Nothing stood out or caught her attention. Stefan hadn't noticed anything on his circuit around the building either.

But the Owner wants to show us that we're slow, thought Beatrice, *he wants to send his FTF victory messages and then thank us for our efforts, full of sarcasm. TFTH.*

'Maybe he's not turning to me as an individual, but as a representative of a group. The police.'

'We shouldn't rule that out. Nor should we discount the idea that he finds you attractive, and perhaps that's the reason why he wants to play his game with you rather than with Florin or even Hoffmann.' Kossar cleared his throat. 'If that's the case, you need to be careful, Beatrice. I know I told you to lure him in with personal information, but that may not have been one of my best ideas.'

Was Kossar admitting to having made a mistake?

'Don't worry, I only gave him a date. Even if he understood what I meant, it won't enable him to get any closer to me.'

'Good.' He seemed genuinely relieved. 'Let's leave it at that, okay? Don't give him anything of a private nature.'

As if that would make any difference. As if he didn't already know much more than I want him to.

★

Florin returned from the autopsy looking pale and grim-faced. The same hard look from the night before was in his eyes again, but this time there were no calming cigarettes within reach.

'Estermann's gullet was black inside. The tissue was completely dead, the stomach perforated. Vogt thinks he died from sepsis, so it would have taken two to three days of unbelievable pain. The whole of the chest area was inflamed and the gullet had developed festering sores.'

'And the eye?'

'Corroded away with forty per cent hydrofluoric acid. The substance Estermann drank was the same kind of solution, just less concentrated. Otherwise the Owner wouldn't have been able to have his fun with him for as long.' Florin laid both his hands on the table, spreading out his fingers, and stared at them as he spoke. 'Hydrofluoric acid was a really good choice. In high concentrations, it can dissolve glass. But even strongly diluted it can eat through everything – skin and flesh. It even corrodes bone. Not very quickly, mind, but over time. Day after day, it eats away at the whole body.' Taking a deep breath, he balled his hands into fists. 'Do we have any new information?'

The change of subject made Beatrice lose her train of thought for a moment, but then she recovered herself. 'The coordinates. Stefan did the research. This is Stage Five.' She passed a printout of the Google Maps page across the desk to him.

'Am Wallersee.'

'Yes. A no-through road by a small wood, surrounded by fields. The nearest house is half a kilometre away.'

They set off forty minutes later. The way Florin was driving began to worry Beatrice just a few blocks down the road. He was driving much too quickly. Much too angrily.

'Shall I take over?' she asked, trying to sound casual as her hand gripped the armrest on the passenger door.

'No.' He beeped at a taxi driver who had swerved out of the bus lane.

When Florin was in this mood, it was futile trying to reason with him. Beatrice turned around to Stefan, who was slouched back in the rear seat, his arms behind his head and eyes closed. If he managed to get a few minutes' sleep, even like this, it would do him good.

'It's really starting to get to me, Bea.' She could only just make out what Florin was saying; his voice was almost entirely swallowed up by the cacophony of traffic. 'When was the last time it took us this long to at least find a suspect?' He was driving at a normal speed again now, only accelerating once they reached the autobahn.

'You can't compare this to other cases. Until now we've never had to deal with killers that act anything like this one.' Even if she couldn't manage to reassure him with her words, then at least she could reassure herself. 'The Owner is organised and extremely well prepared. He's . . . like a director, staging his own play.'

Florin didn't respond. She looked across at him, his profile, the furrowed brow, mouth slightly open. Suddenly she felt the intense urge to stroke the hair off his forehead. She pulled herself together.

Wonderful timing, Bea, incomparable. So typical of you.

'If we decided not to play by his rules, and not to follow

his clues,' she said, persevering, 'then we would just be standing around empty-handed. Say if you think I'm wrong.'

A dark look was Florin's only answer.

'He's not making any major mistakes. The only one I can think of so far is the bloody footprint in Sigart's building. And even that hasn't been of any use so far.' She was silenced as Florin made a foolhardy attempt to overtake, cutting up a Jeep Cherokee with a Viennese number plate.

'Are the victims just collateral? What do you think, Bea? Is he like the Washington sniper in 2002?'

A singer. A loser. A key figure.

'No, he's not. He . . .' She tried to make sense of her thoughts. 'He sees a link between his victims. Perhaps it's a link that only he sees, and maybe it's completely crazy, but for him, it exists. I'd bet anything on it.'

And he sees a link with me, she thought, *even if it is one of a different kind*. Kossar was right. Sooner or later, the Owner would make himself known to her.

N47° 54.067 E013° 09.205

A light wind swayed the grass in the field where the police team had gathered. Drasche, who had installed navigation software on his mobile especially for this case, was engaged in a heated discussion with Stefan, whose Garmin GPS was showing a location that was around fifteen metres away from Drasche's results for the exact same coordinates.

So far, neither of them had found anything, and the search dogs weren't due to arrive for another half-hour.

Bushes, trees, a lake. There were no rocky crags or hollows that offered themselves up as hiding places. If the Owner had sunk the container in the water, then the coordinates they had worked out were useless anyway, regardless of whether they went by Stefan's or Drasche's results.

Cautiously, putting one foot in front of the other, Beatrice walked along the stretch between the two possible spots. The trees were dense, the ground soft. But there weren't any indications that someone could have buried something here.

She took a few paces towards the lake, hearing the splash of the small waves which were being pushed by the wind against the water's edge. With every step she made, her colleagues' voices became quieter, their words less comprehensible. Beatrice stopped by a tree stump and sat down.

If I wanted to hide something here, how would I go about it?

She tried to focus on her surroundings, to shut out

disruptive thoughts. *Water. Trees. Earth.* Yes, burying it was the most likely option.

Just a moment – the trees. Beatrice touched the raw bark of the tree trunk rising up directly next to her. There had been something on that list of caching abbreviations. She closed her eyes, concentrating. *JAFT.*

Just another fucking tree.

Tree hiding places were popular and common, and during her research Beatrice had stumbled across some very creative ideas – preserved roots, hollowed-out branches, nesting boxes mounted especially for the purpose of hiding a cache. It was certainly worth pursuing the idea.

The inspiration came completely out of the blue, at the very moment when Beatrice stood up to go back to the others. *You know everything, and yet you find nothing.*

We do know, she thought, *but only because he's telling us.*

'Florin!' Twigs and dry leaves crackled beneath her feet. 'We have to look upwards, to the treetops! We'll probably need ladders.' She positioned herself on the spot Stefan had marked and looked up at the branches of the nearest tree.

'Why up there?'

'The Owner told us. I just didn't understand it.' She turned to Florin. '"Chin up", he wrote. Does anyone have binoculars with them?'

They discovered the cache – much to Stefan's pride – directly by the coordinates he had dictated, fastened a good eight metres up a beech tree. The container was bigger than all the ones they had found so far, a box with the dimensions of a small television.

Stefan offered to retrieve it. He clambered up, accompanied by Drasche's detailed instructions.

'It's attached to the trunk with gaffer tape,' he called down to them from above. 'I'll cut it loose, then lower it down to you on the rope.'

Beatrice watched with mixed emotions as the container swayed its way down to them. Even before it had touched the ground, she was pretty sure what it contained. The size was about right, and the Owner's words . . .

Even Drasche was impatient this time, and declared that he was prepared to open the box on location. 'Without taking any risks and destroying important evidence, of course,' he growled as Beatrice started to edge closer.

The box had four snap locks, which he undid one after another until the lid was open and the contents revealed.

She had guessed right. *Chin up* could be interpreted in more ways than one.

The part of Herbert Liebscher's body which had once steered his thoughts, housed his memories and directed his senses was now wrapped in the same strong plastic film that had surrounded all the others.

Beatrice and Florin silently exchanged looks. Vogt wouldn't need to ponder over the cause of death this time. Half of Liebscher's head had been shot clean away; a large chunk of the right temple was missing, grey brain mass clinging to the inside of the plastic film.

Less obvious, but noticeable nonetheless, were the missing ears. On one side, the wound was dark red and scabbed, while on the other it was smooth and pale. The uneven teeth, stained a brownish yellow, were bared.

A tea drinker, thought Beatrice, *or a heavy smoker.*

Gases had collected under the film, swelling out the plastic and threatening to burst it in the not-too-distant future.

'We've nearly got the whole guy now,' observed Drasche. He carefully pulled the usual two notes out from under the head.

'You'll get the photos this afternoon, and the information as soon as I get back. Watch your backs, guys, this is getting more gruesome by the day.'

'No, stop.' Beatrice went over to him. 'I want to read them now, see the handwriting.' She ignored Drasche's groan and peered over his shoulder.

Nora Papenberg's handwriting again, now almost as familiar as that of an old friend.

Stage Five

You're searching for a torn woman. Indecisiveness has made her sick, and one day it will cost her her life. She is both guilty and innocent at the same time, like most of us, but she bears her guilt more heavily than most.

Look for dark hair and a name to match, for talent in flute and composition.

Once again, the year of birth is the key: add 15 to the last two digits of the number and multiply by 250. Add 254 and subtract the result from the northern coordinates from Stage Four. Multiply the first two digits by the second two digits of the birth year, add the number 153 to the result and then add the resulting sum to the eastern coordinates.

We'll see each other there.

A woman, for the first time. No, that wasn't entirely true – the case had begun with Nora Papenberg, but there hadn't been any search leading to her.

Could it be that the Owner placed significance on symmetry? A woman at the start, four men, then a woman again at the end? No, he'd said he planned to keep Sigart until the end.

Drasche was now reading out the cache note – *Congratulations, you've found it! This time it was worth it, don't you think?* – but she was only half-listening. Flute and composition. That sounded like a student or teacher at the Mozarteum. Dark hair and a name to match.

Florin already had the car engine running. This time, they would beat the Owner to it.

Torn woman sounded quite worrying, particularly as the Owner seemed to be developing a fondness for the literal. While she and Florin were in the car, Beatrice requested a list of female students studying composition and flute from the Mozarteum. She also requested a second list of the names of the teachers, and a third of alumni.

'That's a good start.' They were the first words Florin had uttered since they drove off. 'Don't forget the private academies.'

'I won't. But first there's something else I want to check out.' She looked through her notes for the telephone number of the conductor for the choir Christoph Beil had sung in.

'Kaspary here, LKA. Could you tell me where you normally hold your choir practice?'

'In the church. There are set times when we're allowed to use the space.'

'I see. And you never hold them anywhere else?'

'Well,' said the man hesitantly. 'Occasionally, ahead of really important concerts, we use one of the rooms in the Mozarteum.'

'Thank you.' Feeling that she finally had something important within her sights, Beatrice tucked her phone away. 'You'll see,' she said to Florin. 'We'll find what we're looking for at the Mozarteum.'

But when the lists arrived, Beatrice's suspicions weren't confirmed. Dark hair and a name to match – she had hoped for an obvious choice: something Mediterranean, or literal, like 'Schwarz', for example. She hadn't reckoned with the large number of students from Japan and China studying music in Salzburg. They were particularly prevalent in the flute classes, regardless of whether it was the transverse or wooden flute.

'Shit,' groaned Beatrice, leafing through the printouts. 'It's going to be impossible to check them all out. The ex-alumni have long since moved away, and the others . . .' She rested her head in one hand, closing her eyes for a moment. What if she discounted the international students initially? The clue could refer to one of them, of course, but so far all the victims had been locals.

Using this approach, she looked through the list again, but the darkest name she came across was 'Wolf'. Alexandra Wolf. Dark in a mystical sense, perhaps? She requested the girl's details, but instinct told her she hadn't yet found who they were looking for.

She read through the Owner's message once more, and then again. *A torn woman.* Sick with indecisiveness, both guilty and innocent. Perpetrator and victim?

Look for talent in flute and composition. Talent, not qualifications.

A picture began to form in Beatrice's mind. Someone haunted by a past event, someone who felt guilty and distraught. Torn. Or perhaps they had been torn *from* something – their studies, for example. Beatrice picked up the phone.

'It's Beatrice Kaspary again. Do you happen to have any records of female students who interrupted their studies there at the Mozarteum? I'm thinking in particular of the flute and composition classes.'

The woman at the other end of the line sighed. 'That's a difficult one. We can of course find out who quit, but it's a time-consuming task when you don't know who you're looking for.' It seemed quite clear that she wasn't contemplating making the effort. 'Do you at least know when the girl in question broke off her studies?'

'No.' *Don't get discouraged*, Beatrice told herself. 'Send me the files from the last ten years. That should be enough.'

Another sigh. 'I'll see what I can do.'

'His nickname was "DescartesHL" and his password "skyblue".' The air in Stefan's office was sticky. Bechner, who he shared the room with, had an issue with open windows – a pollen allergy.

'He found over nine hundred caches, most of them here and in Bavaria, but it seems he used to go caching while he was on holiday too.' Stefan scrolled down the page to a bar chart that showed which countries Liebscher had gone cache-hunting in: Italy, France, Great Britain. Even the USA.

'Most geocachers love their statistics,' explained Stefan. 'Look, there's a percentage calculation of which days of the week he was most active on. Sunday is at the top, which is no surprise.'

'This is great work, thank you.' Beatrice noted the details down on a scrap of paper.

Descartes. *Everything that is entirely probable is probably false.* The Owner knew the nickname and had built it into his game; he had known about Liebscher's hobby. Is that why he'd hidden his body parts all over Salzburg, as if his corpse was a puzzle they had to piece together?

No. That was too simple. Too banal.

'DescartesHL,' she reported to Florin shortly later. 'It's pretty clear that HL stands for Herbert Liebscher. And Descartes, well, it seems he couldn't let go of the mathematician in him even on his days off.'

That evening, Beatrice left the office earlier than usual. She drove over to see her mother and the children first, then headed home and set her laptop up on the living-room table.

Name: DescartesHL.

Password: skyblue.

One click of the mouse and Liebscher's geocaching profile page was in front of her. The finds from the last thirty days were shown first, listed under the *Geocaches* link, and it seemed Liebscher had been active until shortly before his death. The most recent entry was twenty-two days old, a multi-cache near the Traunsee lake.

Challenging, but worth it! he had written in his online logbook. *TFTC!*

Three days before that, he had gone on a lengthier expedition, logging eight finds. None of the entries revealed any unusual observations. He praised original hiding places or the beautiful scenery the search had led him to, and expressed his gratitude on every one.

Beatrice worked backwards chronologically. There was a tricky mystery cache which Liebscher was very proud to have solved; according to his comment he had left a coin behind, presumably one of the special caching ones they had found in his apartment. He had also logged three multi-caches and twenty-four 'traditionals', in other words, caches without difficult additional puzzles.

She had now reached mid-March of this year, and had almost given up hope. The most exciting comments had been along the lines of: *Looked by the wrong rock to start with, but the hiding place became clear after a quick look around. Coordinates are a little off!*

But then came the entry from 12 March. It was just a 'traditional', but it made Beatrice's inner divining rod lurch. The cache was in central Salzburg, hidden in a park near the Leopoldskron Palace.

Original idea! Liebscher had written. *Discovered along with Shinigami. TFTC!*

It was the only entry so far that made reference to a fellow cacher. And the same applied to the other three finds Liebscher had logged on 12 March. He and Shinigami seemed to have spent the whole day together on a collaborative treasure hunt.

She scrolled on. On 10 March there were two caches, but

no reference to a companion. But four days before that, on 6 March, Shinigami was there again:

Great hiding place, but the logbook is almost full! Found together with Shinigami. TFTC!

Okay. Every finder documented his success on the page of the cache in question, so Shinigami's comment should be recorded there too. She opened the link and looked through the comments to 6 March. There was DescartesHL, and directly above him Shinigami, who had not made his entry until three days later.

She read, realising at once that there was something she could put her finger on here. Or rather someone.

Found with DescartesHL. Sometimes we find, and sometimes we're found, isn't that true? TFTC.

And to the rest of you: TFTH.

The rest of you, thought Beatrice. *That's us.*

Shinigami's profile was empty. Of course it was. The only information on there was his registration date and cache finds. The list was short: seven caches, all discovered in March and April this year. Shinigami had registered on 26 February. Barely a week before he first went on a hunt with DescartesHL.

It took Beatrice no more than three minutes to confirm her suspicion. Shinigami had found all seven caches together with Herbert Liebscher, and in all seven entries he had not only expressed his thanks for the cache, but for the hunt too.

She managed to catch Florin while he was still at the office; he picked up straight away.

'Has something happened?'

'What? No, everything's fine. But I found something.' She took a sip of cold coffee from the sorry remains of her breakfast still on the countertop, then grimaced. 'I'm ninety per cent sure that the Owner went geocaching with Liebscher. I'm sending you the link. Take a look.'

In the blink of an eye, the mail was sent. Down the line, Beatrice heard Florin click on it. Then another click.

'It's the entry above DescartesHL, the sixth of March.'

'Shinigami.' Florin's voice was as clear as if he was sitting right next to her. 'Sounds Japanese.'

The overseas students at the Mozarteum came into her mind. *Maybe we'll have to check them out after all*, thought Beatrice resignedly. Nothing could be ruled out, nothing at all.

'We'll look into it – I'll check whether Stefan or Bechner are still here. We need the real identity behind the pseudonym. This is great progress – thanks, Bea.'

It was unusual for him to thank her, and it left a strange aftertaste. Was he trying to counterbalance Hoffmann's attacks?

'Don't mention it.'

'Now go and get some sleep. I'm stopping soon too.'

'Soon.' In the background, she heard his mobile ring, the tone he had programmed for Anneke. He would be in a hurry to go now anyway. 'See you tomorrow, Florin,' she said, hanging up before he could.

Liebscher's first cache find was almost seven years ago, meaning that he must have gotten a taste for the treasure hunt long before it had become a trend. His enthusiasm was clearly audible in his log entries, and he had gone out geocaching practically every weekend. Most of the caches he'd found back then didn't even exist any more: a red line through them meant they'd been archived. Only a small number of caches seemed to last more than four or five years.

Treasure hunting by GPS had clearly been one of Liebscher's favourite pastimes for a number of years, and then . . .

Beatrice stopped. She scrolled up, then further down, checking the dates. No, she hadn't been mistaken. After a weekend in Vienna that had brought him eighteen new finds, there was a break of a year and a half. Not one single cache. Nothing.

Had he been ill? Or had the divorce sapped too much of his energy? She would have to ask at the school.

After the gap, his approach seemed more hesitant. There was around one registered find a month, two at most, and the log entries seemed less detailed than the older ones.

Quickly found, TFTC. Aside from the ones she had read earlier, most were very brief indeed.

But why? Beatrice looked at the clock. It was half-past ten, much too late to phone Romana Liebscher now. Tomorrow.

She clapped the laptop shut and went to the kitchen, where she found herself unable to decide between sparkling water and the last bottle of beer which had been sitting in the fridge door for months on end now.

Water. She drank it straight out of the bottle, enjoying the prickling sensation of the bubbles in her mouth, her throat, her stomach. She suppressed a burp, then wondered who she was trying to be polite for.

Intent on enjoying just ten minutes of free time before going to bed, she walked over to the window and looked

301

out at the night sky over the city. There was almost a full moon, another three days to go at most.

'Shinigami,' she whispered to the moon. She took a long slug of water and pulled the curtains shut, just in case she was being watched. Then she smacked herself on the forehead in disbelief and ran back over to the coffee table.

Why hadn't she checked right away? Now she'd have to start up the laptop again, the rattling old heap.

Google was generous with its answers: A *shinigami* was a Japanese death spirit, regarded as a bad omen. Beatrice fumbled blindly behind her, grasped the lint-covered blanket from the reclining chair and pulled it around her shoulders.

The Owner had made his intentions clear from the very moment he registered on the geocaching site. He would bring death. But no one had understood his message – not least Herbert Liebscher.

Dagmar Zoubek was one of those women who command respect at the very first glance. Tall, with a taut back and an equally taut bun at the nape of her neck, she reminded Beatrice of the ballet teacher who, with her impatient, bony hands, had pushed Beatrice's toes outwards when she was six years old. But Zoubek taught the flute, not ballet.

Beatrice had made a spur-of-the-moment decision that morning. The thought of having to plod through endless lists of names had been so unbearable to her that she had decided to go for the direct route. She would look for a torn woman, not a dark-haired woman with a dark name.

They were sitting in one of the small practice rooms, where a Steinway dominated the space.

'Many students go through difficult times,' explained Zoubek after giving it some thought. 'The pressure here is bearable, but some just aren't up to it. I'll need you to narrow it down a little more for me.'

'She was likely to have been studying composition too. And she probably had dark hair.'

To her credit, Zoubek tried to hide the flicker of mockery in her eyes. 'Dark hair? Do you realise how many girls here change their hair colour on a monthly basis?'

It was hard to imagine Zoubek being popular with her students. A schoolmarmish nature seemed to be inherent to this woman's character, as firmly rooted as the nose on her face.

'The problem is,' explained Beatrice, 'that I can't even narrow down the time period. It's just as possible that the student in question left the institute six years ago as six months. It's even possible that she's still here. The information I have is very vague.'

'I'm inclined to agree with you there.' But Beatrice's admission seemed to make Zoubek more sympathetic. 'Personal crises. Let me think . . . yes, one student lost her parents in a car crash last year and then went back to Munich. It was very tragic.' The woman stopped for a moment and lowered her gaze. 'A very gifted young woman. Although her second subject was singing, not composition, and her hair was always blonde.'

'Could you tell me her name anyway?'

'Tamara Kohl.'

If the subject and hair colour had matched it would have been worth a try, but given they didn't Beatrice could probably rule her out. The Owner was always very precise with his clues.

'Can you think of anyone else? Was there a suicide attempt, perhaps? Self-harming behaviour? Or aggression towards others?'

The way Zoubek glanced away told Beatrice that her questions had struck a raw nerve. 'Was there?' she persevered. 'Please tell me anything that comes to mind – it could be exactly the information I'm looking for.'

'There was this shy girl . . . a little plump and always on a diet. She had dark hair, yes. I taught her in flute, and if I'm not mistaken composition was her second subject. She worked very hard – not as gifted as the others, but she was very diligent.'

Diligence was, if Beatrice had judged her correctly, an indispensable virtue in Zoubek's universe. 'What happened to her?'

'It was such a long time ago now. She wasn't even in my class at the time it happened – she had switched to my colleague Dr Horner's group, but I think she had some kind of breakdown. She was picked up by an ambulance and unenrolled from the university shortly after.'

'Can you remember what kind of breakdown it was? What it was caused by?'

Zoubek shook her head briskly. 'I wasn't there. I just heard that she started to scream and cry and that no one was able to calm her down. Maybe it's better if you speak to Dr Horner – he'll be able to tell you more.'

I certainly will, thought Beatrice. 'Could you please tell me the girl's name?'

With a demonstratively thoughtful expression, Dagmar

Zoubek pursed her lips. 'It was a long name, not an easy one to remember – I'd have to check.'

'That would be very helpful, thank you.'

Clearly a little disgruntled, the teacher got up from her chair and left the room. Ten minutes later, she came back with a blue ring binder.

'Here she is. Melanie Dalamasso. Flute and composition. There's a note here – ex-matriculated due to health reasons, roughly five years ago.'

'Thank you.' Beatrice shook the woman's hand and went out into the fresh air of the Mirabell Gardens, where the sun was shining hazily. She found a bench and stretched her legs out in front of her.

Bingo. There was no need to look any further; Dalamasso was an Italian name, which fitted the dark hair the Owner had mentioned. And Beatrice didn't even need to bother Google in order to solve the rest of the puzzle. As a child, she used to have a dictionary of names, and would always flick through it eagerly whenever she met someone new.

Her own name had often been cause for amusement, as Beatrice meant 'Blessed'. Her best friend at school had been called Nadine – meaning 'Hope'. Sitting a row in front of them in class back then was a Melanie, a girl with strawberry blonde hair and freckles on her face, neck and arms. They had always had fits of giggles about the fact that Melanie meant 'Dark'.

It seemed that Melanie Dalamasso hadn't just stopped studying, but had also shelved her entire life of independence. She was now living with her parents, and spent from eight in the morning until half-four in the afternoon in a psychiatric day clinic.

'She's under observation around the clock, but we won't question her, not yet.' Florin looked at each of them in turn, pausing when he came to Hoffmann. Eventually, their boss nodded.

'Anyone who attempts to get close to her will be checked out by our guys. I've spoken to her parents and her doctor, and we're getting full support from both sides. Unfortunately there's no information that could be of use to us – no one knows what caused Melanie's breakdown.' He took the glass of water Stefan handed to him and sipped at it. 'Apparently she was always quite difficult growing up, with a tendency for depressive moods.'

Beatrice had read through the parents' statement before their meeting. They were at their wits' end. They described Melanie as a silent, withdrawn girl, who had hidden herself away with her flute from a young age. She was eight when she first went to a psychotherapist, because she'd stopped eating after two girls from her class had come up with the idea of nicknaming her the 'Italian Hippo'.

What might have prompted other children to run in tears to their teacher or parents, or to kick the bullies in the shin, left Melanie reeling for weeks on end. She insisted that a change of schools be the condition for her agreeing to eat again. Her parents gave in and registered her at a private school which specialised in music. A few years followed in which they believed she had 'grown out of' the problem, as her mother put it. But when puberty set in, Melanie began to suffer from extreme mood swings that led to renewed anorexic and bulimic episodes. Her parents were convinced that, had it not been for the flute, she would probably have died. Once again it led to psychotherapeutic intervention, and a three-week hospitalisation during the summer holidays.

Six years ago, at the age of eighteen, Melanie had passed the entrance exam for the Mozarteum. She moved into a tiny studio apartment near the Salzach river, dreamt of a career as a soloist and fell in love with a fellow student who, although he didn't return her feelings, let her down very gently and became a close friend. He introduced her to a group of students who went on hikes, to cafés or the cinema in the evenings, and who also studied together for music theory exams. For a while, Melanie even lived with two of the girls from the group in a student flat share.

'She wasn't at the centre of everything, but she was at least part of it, and she was doing so well,' Melanie's mother was quoted as saying in the report. What happened next, no one can really explain. She turned her back on the group and went her own way. She retreated into herself again and started another of her numerous missions to lose weight. Questioning and probing her hadn't helped; it never had. One of the mother's friends had reported seeing Melanie with a man old enough to be her father. They had apparently been strolling through the Christmas market in Hellbrunn, their arms wrapped around each other, oblivious to the rest of the world.

Melanie's mother had been torn back and forth between happiness and worry. Her child was in love and happy – but hadn't thought to introduce or even mention the man to her parents. She stormed out of their regular Sunday lunches any time they tentatively tried to bring the conversation around to him.

Six months later came the breakdown. Frau Dalamasso received the call at ten in the morning, right before the start of the summer holidays. They told her that Melanie had suddenly started screaming during orchestral rehearsals for an upcoming concert, and that she had been inconsolable ever since. When her mother arrived, the ambulance was already there, and Melanie had been sedated by the doctor.

'She's been in a completely different world ever since. She hardly speaks any more, and if she does then only sentence fragments that don't make any sense. The doctors suspect she's suffered from a kind of autism since birth, and that it's only now reached its full force,' concluded the father.

Why would the Owner want to kill someone like Melanie Dalamasso?

'. . . speak to the woman anyway.' Beatrice only heard the last half-sentence of Hoffmann's objection. 'Kossar could do it. He's a psychiatrist, he knows how to handle sick people.'

'He's a forensic psychiatrist,' objected Florin. 'I don't think Melanie Dalamasso's doctors would take too kindly to that. I suggest we leave it for now and instead concentrate on trying to protect Melanie. So far our conversations with the Owner's targets have brought us either very little or nothing.' Florin interlaced his fingers and nodded briefly at the photos spread out in front of them on the conference table. 'I've shown the parents the pictures of the other victims, from Papenberg to Estermann. There was no sign of recognition in their faces at all. In order to show the girl the pictures we'd need the approval of her doctors, but even if we get that, we may do considerable damage without accomplishing anything from it. Melanie hasn't spoken in five years, and that's not going to change just because we show her a few pictures. So as long as she can't tell us what she knows, or what she's thinking . . .' He shrugged his shoulders.

A torn woman. Back in her office, leaning over the desk, Beatrice laid out the photos of the victims in front of her, adding a new one: Melanie Dalamasso. Her dark hair framed a round face. Heavy-lidded brown eyes, a nose that tilted slightly upwards. A pretty mouth, the contours of which were out of focus, making it look a little lopsided.

Papenberg. Liebscher. Beil. Sigart. Estermann. Dalamasso. An unsolvable puzzle. With a few brief hand movements, Beatrice shifted the photos around, letting the new order take effect. Papenberg was in the middle now, Beil next to Dalamasso, Estermann on the outside right, Liebscher above him. Sigart's photo was a little askew, the upper right-hand corner of his photo touching the corner of Papenberg's mouth.

Beatrice laid the photo of the last message down. The Owner, expressing himself through Papenberg's hand.

Something connects you all, Beatrice thought. *A puzzle behind the puzzles*.

But the photos stayed silent. Just like the dead.

N47° 28.813 E013° 10.983

There was no doubt about Dalamasso's birth year – 1985 – but there was about the accuracy of the coordinates. The members of the team found themselves right by the Bundesstrasse again, just a few kilometres away from the bridge where they had found Rudolf Estermann's body. A narrow fork in the road led past detached houses, up an incline, then tailed off approximately a kilometre into the forest.

'He can't have hidden anything here.' Drasche was stalking up and down with the GPS device in his hand. 'This is a residential area. Unless he buried the body parts in someone's front garden.'

'Or perhaps he didn't keep exactly to the coordinates.' Squinting, Beatrice turned around slowly on the spot. The surrounding area had a number of potential hiding places – at distances of roughly fifteen, twenty and fifty metres there were trees (*fucking trees*, she thought to herself), crash barriers and an area of greenery. But there, right on the spot they had calculated, there was nothing but the road and a traffic sign limiting the speed to thirty kilometres an hour.

They must have made a mistake. The Owner had always been very precise. 'Where's the second GPS device?'

Stefan had taken the day off, on Florin's strict advice. 'Your eyes are so red they're competing with your hair,' he had commented, prescribing him a twenty-four-hour break.

Their younger colleague had given in with a mixture of reluctance and relief, pressed his navigation device into Florin's hand and set off home – by bus rather than car, as he was worried about falling asleep at the wheel. But even Stefan's Garmin, tried and tested on so many caches, still came up with the same answer as Drasche's mobile software.

With the last coordinates, it had been the right place but the wrong time. They'd got there before the Owner had dumped Estermann's body. Would he do the same thing again?

Beatrice tried to tune into the surroundings, looking from the wet asphalt up to the sky. Until just now, thin threads of rain had woven a grey cloth across the landscape. Now the clouds were slowly starting to break apart.

Dalamasso is the solution to the new puzzle, she thought. But it was virtually impossible that the Owner could kidnap her, kill her and dump her here. Two armed guards were keeping an eye on her around the clock, both in the day clinic and at home. When Melanie first noticed them she had burst into tears, a wordless howl. After that, at her mother's request, they had relinquished uniforms for plain clothes and kept their distance. Now Melanie just stared right through them, as if they were invisible.

The sun came out, making the road glisten. Beatrice shielded her eyes with her hand, not having reckoned on needing sunglasses. Something was blinding her. A round, reflective sticker on the traffic sign, placed right in the middle of the zero, beside to three. Next to it, someone had scrawled '*Don't eat animals*' with a black marker.

'Maybe we've thwarted his plans this time.' There wasn't much hope in Florin's voice, but Beatrice nodded all the same.

'Yes. Maybe he thought we'd take longer to find Melanie Dalamasso, or didn't predict that we'd put her under police protection.' But she didn't believe that one bit. The Owner must know that they wouldn't – couldn't – let the young woman out of their sight for a second. They should have acted sooner and convinced Sigart of the necessity of accepting police protection.

'Search everything within a hundred–metre radius,' Florin ordered. 'We're keeping a lookout for containers, paper, anything that could be a message. It's possible that it's very well disguised.' Three officers from the dog team set off obediently with their animals. If there were any body parts hidden around, they would find them.

But something was different this time. She felt her mobile vibrate in her pocket. Her heart skipped a beat. There it was, his next text, his next move in the game – but then she saw the number and sighed, rejecting the call.

It had only been a matter of time until her ex-husband got back in touch. But now wasn't the time for an argument.

The clouds were chased across the sky by the wind, blocking the sun again. Beatrice put her mobile back in her jacket pocket with the same guilty feeling she always had when she ignored a call. Maybe it had been important. An emergency.

Evelyn jumped into her mind. But she couldn't allow her mind to be clouded by what had happened back then. She had to focus. To concentrate. This was a different story, and it would have a different ending.

The dogs didn't find anything. 'Liebscher's body parts are old enough by now and the temperatures high enough for the plastic film to inflate and eventually burst,' Drasche had prophesied. 'And even if they haven't – the dogs would smell the caches anyway. We did some tests.'

'But what would the Owner be hiding now?' Beatrice interrupted the despondent silence that had so far dominated the drive back to headquarters.

Florin turned his head slowly in her direction without taking his eyes off the road. 'What do you mean? We're far from having found all of Liebscher. There are still the feet, the limbs, the torso – if the Owner wants to he still has enough for another twenty or thirty caches.'

'But we already have the head. So there's no more suspense. It's more essential than any other part of the body and clearly answers the question of his identity. Would you play the feet or even inner organs after you've already done the head? It would be like taking a step back.'

'Play?'

'Yes.' She hadn't intentionally chosen the word, but it hit the nail on the head. He plays a hand, they play a hand. And given that he didn't have to play by the rules, he was always at an advantage. It was costing them one round after the next.

She thought about the puzzle spread out on her desk. She would make the next move alone.

'My daughter is being driven home by your colleagues. I get the impression she doesn't feel entirely comfortable about it, but I tried to explain to her that it's important.' Carolin Dalamasso was a pretty woman, not much older than fifty. She had willingly agreed to Beatrice's request to stop by, and had clearly used the time to bake a cake. The sweet aroma filled the apartment.

Beatrice tried to smile through her guilty conscience. Strictly speaking, the visit to the Dalamassos wasn't necessary – Florin had asked all the important questions and compiled the information into his report. But he hadn't spoken to Melanie, hadn't even caught a glimpse of her. That wasn't enough for Beatrice. She wanted to – no, not wanted, *had to* – get some impression of the young woman. A torn woman. Could you sense it just from standing opposite her?

'Would you like some coffee? I have decaf too.'

She had neither the desire nor the need for her fifth coffee of the day, but she had to play for time. If necessary, she would make small talk until the daughter arrived home. 'I'd love one. With plenty of milk and a little sugar, if that's okay.'

The woman nodded and smiled. There was a watchfulness in her eyes, which Beatrice suspected wasn't new, but rather stemmed from constantly looking out for her psychologically ill daughter.

It was 4.40 p.m. Melanie could arrive home any moment now, depending on how busy the traffic was.

'What can I tell you that I haven't already told your colleague with the lovely dark eyes?' With swift energetic movements, Carolin Dalamasso cut three slices of cake and put the cups on the table. Then she sat down.

'I'd like to know how Melanie was doing before her breakdown. Were there any events that, in hindsight, could be interpreted as warning signs?'

The woman's smile was suddenly streaked with pain. 'Of course. You always know better afterwards. Carlo and I have

314

thought of dozens of situations in which, looking back, we should have sought medical assistance for Melanie. But back then we thought she was just a little sensitive because she was in love for the first time. She had a boyfriend, you see? Unfortunately we never met him, and my theory is . . .' She sighed and looked out of the window, where a blackbird had settled on the balcony railing. It looked around jerkily, then flew away again. 'I think he broke up with Melanie. She was still living in the flat share back then, and one evening she called us, but we couldn't make out a single word. She was sobbing, almost howling. We drove over there right away of course, but she was in her room and didn't want to talk to us. Her flatmates were just as clueless as we were. They were relieved in the end, I think, when she was admitted to the clinic. That was five days later.'

'And there was never any clue as to what might have caused it?'

'No. But I've already told your colleague all of that.' The vigilance in her eyes increased in direct proportion with the narrowing of her smile.

'Did you give him the names of Melanie's flatmates?'

'Of course.' She took a sip of her coffee.

Beatrice decided to push further. 'The case we're working on is exceptionally challenging. I hope you understand. For that reason, communication between the investigators is not as thorough as we'd ideally like it to be.' Was that the sound of a car stopping in front of the house? Hopefully. 'I do know, however, that Florin Wenninger showed you these photographs.' She pulled the photographs of the Owner's victims out of her bag. 'I also know that you don't believe you know any of these people. But sometimes a day's distance can help, and maybe something might occur to you, even if it's about only one of the faces.' She laid the photos in front of Carolin Dalamasso on the table. The unsolvable puzzle.

'We're convinced that these people had some connection to your daughter, but we just don't know what kind. So far no one has been able to help us with this. That's why I simply have to ask you once again. I hope you don't mind.'

With a helpless shrug, Carolin leant forwards to look at the photos. 'And these people have all been murdered?'

'Four of them, definitely. One of them could still have a chance.'

'My God.' She picked up the photo of Nora Papenberg and stared at it intently. Then she shook her head and put it back down on the table. 'I'm so glad you're protecting Melanie,' she said softly. 'I just can't understand why anyone would want to harm her. Her, of all people.'

'We're doing everything we can to find out. Absolutely everything.'

Beil's photo, Sigart's photo. Always the same shake of the head.

'Does Melanie still play the flute, by the way?' asked Beatrice.

'Yes. But not like she used to. The sounds she produces now are a long way from being music, they—' The woman paused and listened. Beatrice heard it too, a muffled whirr, then a metallic, rushing sound. The lift.

'I think that's them now.' Carolin stood up. 'You can't question Melanie, you know that, right? She's stable right now and the doctors are hopeful that her condition will improve. It was much worse, you see, far worse, and—'

The doorbell rang. The woman went into the hallway and opened the door. Beatrice gathered the photos up. Her guilty conscience was making her feel sick, but she had to do what she had come to do.

She heard the police officer's affable voice. 'Everything's fine, no incidents. Have a nice evening!'

Beatrice knew the two policemen would now take up their position in their car in front of the building, nourish themselves on hot dogs and Red Bull, and wait for the night shift to come and relieve them. They were the good guys, and Beatrice envied them.

A girl with a chubby face appeared in the doorway, stopping abruptly as she saw Beatrice. Her dark hair was tied in a ponytail at the nape of her neck. Her eyes spoke of confusion, an impression that her lopsided glasses only intensified.

'We have a visitor, Melanie.' Carolin Dalamasso grasped her daughter gently by the shoulders and pulled her towards her. 'This is Frau Kaspary.'

Beatrice pulled her bag over her shoulder and stood up, the photos in her left hand. The girl's gaze flitted over to her, away, then back again. *Although she's not really a girl*, thought Beatrice, *in a few years she'll be thirty*. 'It's nice to meet you, Melanie.' She stretched her right hand out, but Melanie didn't take it. She didn't say a word.

'I think I'd better go then, but it's possible that I might come by . . .' *Now*. Beatrice unclasped the fingers of her left hand. Felt the photos slip away from her, heard the soft clatter as they fell to the floor.

'Oh, I'm sorry.'

317

She bent over. The photos of Papenberg, Estermann and Beil were lying face up. The others had turned rear-side up as they fell. Beatrice acted as though she was trying to collect them together, but Carolin Dalamasso must have realised by now that she was taking too much time over it, that she was hoping—

A gasp. Beatrice looked up, directly into Melanie's face, which was distorted into a grimace. She stared at the pictures and let out a howl, a long-drawn-out noise, like an animal. Her glasses fell to the floor.

'Get out!' hissed her mother furiously.

'I didn't mean to—'

'Out!'

Melanie's howl transformed into something more high-pitched, something more shrill. She covered her face with both hands, and her mother had to stop her from banging her head against the door frame.

'I'll be making a complaint about you!'

Beatrice closed her eyes and nodded wearily. 'Contact Walter Hoffmann. He'll welcome you with open arms, believe me.'

She practically ran from the apartment, the building, down the street, but she couldn't shake the feeling of nausea.

There was no doubt that Melanie had recognised some-one, and she hadn't liked it one bit.

But there was nothing Beatrice could do with this information. She sat in her car, the photos still in her hand, the taste of bile forcing its way upwards into her mouth. She had no idea which of the photos had unleashed Melanie's reaction. Had it been one of them, several of them, all of them? One thing had become completely clear: the Owner wasn't killing his victims at random. The connection between them, however, was still enshrouded in darkness. And there was little hope that Melanie would be able to offer any explanations.

'I might well have done the same thing.' Florin was trying to comfort her, but she knew him better than that. From the very start he had only wanted to protect Melanie, not question her. His work had never resulted in a screaming girl. Or the threat of suspension.

'Shinigami,' she said, without responding to his words. 'When is Stefan planning to come with the information?'

'Any moment now. The site's admin team is being very cooperative,' he said. 'They're sending us the email address the Owner used for his registration, as well as the IP addresses he logged on with. If it takes a while then that's because the last login was over three months ago. The geocaching website gets a huge amount of traffic.'

Perhaps, thought Beatrice, *this is a trace the Owner forgot to erase. We're due a bit of luck.*

Stefan indeed appeared just five minutes later, beaming contentedly: 'The email address is gerold.wiesner@gmx.net. I found a Gerold Wiesner registered in Salzburg – he's fifty-eight years old and works on the national Bundesbahn railways. Looks like we've hit the bull's eye, people!'

They were tentatively hopeful, but even that was short-lived. Beatrice knew only too well how simple it was to open an account with geocaching.com. And creating a fake email address wasn't exactly tricky either. They went through the police records and soon found the information they needed: whoever had concealed himself behind the nickname 'Shinigami', it certainly wasn't Bundesbahn employee Gerold Wiesner. On 25 February this year, he had fallen onto a power line while carrying out maintenance work at the central train station, just a few months before his retirement was due to begin. He was survived by a wife and two grown-up daughters.

25 February. Shinigami had registered on Geocaching. com on the 26th. He must have been sitting in front of the computer, the newspaper open next to him, and seen the report. He hadn't even needed to make up a fake name. So simple. So unremarkable.

Her hope now rested on the IP address, but the Owner hadn't shown any weakness there either: the computer he had used was in an upmarket Salzburg hotel, available for guests to use around the clock without having to pay.

'Of course, people who visit the hotel café could theoretically use it too,' explained the hotel manager. 'It's part of our service, you see?'

'And if I were to ask you who used the computer on the twenty-sixth of February at 15.42, would you be able to tell me?'

'I'm afraid not.' If the manager's regret wasn't genuine, he at least acted it well.

'I understand. The man we're looking for must have also used the computer on the ninth, fourteenth and twentieth of March, and then a final time on the third of April. So it's possible that someone may have noticed him.'

'That's true. I'll check right away who was on duty in

the café on those dates, then give you a call back.'

They were clutching at straws, nothing more than that.

And to the rest of you: TFTH. The Owner had known three months ago that he would kill Liebscher at the very least. He had thanked his pursuers for the hunt before they had even begun.

To Beatrice's surprise, the hotel manager called back twenty minutes later. When the telephone rang she was talking to Bechner, asking him to check whether there might be another Gerold Wiesner who could be a suspect – she seemed to automatically assign all the menial tasks to him.

'On two of the days you mentioned, Georg Lienhart was on duty,' explained the manager. 'He said he did notice someone. The dates may match up.'

'Excellent!' Beatrice signalled to Bechner, who was trying to use the opportunity to head back to his own office, that they weren't yet finished. He sighed demonstratively; she beamed at him equally demonstratively.

'Can I speak to Herr Lienhart?'

'Yes, he's right here.'

The waiter sounded very young, but on the ball. 'There was this really tall man with a beard, and he never took his coat off even though it's really well heated here. He ordered coffee and drank it really quickly, each time at the table next to the computer. Then he paid right away and left much more of a tip than most guests do.' The boy fell silent for a moment, perhaps thinking about his unexpected financial windfall from the stranger. 'Then he sat down at the computer and went to great lengths to spread himself out as much as he could, if you see what I mean. I thought right away that he'd kept his coat on for that reason, so it would be easier for him to keep the screen hidden.'

'You didn't happen to catch a glimpse of it regardless, by any chance?'

'We're told to be discreet.'

Beatrice could almost picture the young waiter in front of her, including his grin. 'But you did it anyway, in keeping with the need for discretion, of course?'

Georg Lienhart hesitated. 'No. Although I was of course curious about what all the secrecy was for. That's why, after the man came back the second time, I opened up the browser history and had a look.'

Fantastic. 'And?'

'I couldn't find anything, unfortunately. The whole session was erased.'

Beatrice ran her hand through her hair and tried to suppress the irritation welling up inside her. But it didn't matter. It spoke volumes that the man had erased everything which could provide clues as to what he was doing.

'You've been a great help. Now I just need to ask you for a description of the guest, as precise as you can be. Any detail you remember could be very important.'

The young man gathered his thoughts. 'The coat he had on was dark blue, and his shoes were black. I noticed that because they didn't match, although the items looked very expensive. He had pale gloves on, and a pale scarf.'

'Can you remember his hair colour?'

'He was bald. Completely, as if he was ill. But his beard was brown with a bit of grey. He had a full beard, a really thick one.'

If only all our witnesses had such good memories. 'You're doing a great job, really. Is there anything else that stood out? Birthmarks, warts, tattoos?'

He thought again before giving his answer. 'No. All I really saw was his head and face, so if he had a tattoo on his arm, I don't . . .'

'Of course.'

'He said something strange though. Probably that's why I remember him so well . . . and because it fits in with what's happening now. At the time I thought he was crazy.'

Beatrice leant back. 'Yes?'

'He said: "It's possible that they might ask about me. If they do, tell them they could be making life much easier for themselves. And tell them: *Thanks for the hunt.*"'

The sky above him was blue, and the swallows were soaring high. The weather was good, and would probably hold for another two or three days.

Days of waiting. His thoughts wandered to the policewoman, as they often had recently. It couldn't last much longer now, if she had followed his clues, if she had finally understood them.

Looking up at the sky made him dizzy, almost making him stumble. *Take it easy, be careful*, he reminded himself. The thought wasn't without a comic element. It was a shame he couldn't share it with anyone.

Except the woman, perhaps. Everything was ready. He was throwing the fingerless man out as bait. His predators would fall into the trap; they had no other option.

He waited until his senses were obeying him again, then looked upwards. Directly above him, an aeroplane was sketching its white line in the perfect blue, a long minus sign which frayed out at the end, dissolving, dissipating. Five minus two was three, minus one . . .

It couldn't be avoided. With a shrug of his shoulders, he let the sky be sky and turned his attention to more earthly matters. Severity. Blood. Pain.

The past weeks had been filled with those things. The most surprising realisation he had drawn from his experiences was just how much reality could differ from imagination.

Not when it came to the plan itself. That had gone perfectly. But in practice, the action felt so different from any fantasy.

He looked around one more time before he went back into the darkness, smiling into the strengthening breeze. *So beautiful.*

Someone sighed, and it took him the duration of a heartbeat to realise it had been him. A man who had to go back to his work. Brutal, harsh, gruesome, painful. Not willingly, never willingly – how could he? But it was the safest way. Everything was ready; there was no reason to wait any longer.

After he had done what was necessary, just two hours had passed by. He was getting better at it. It wasn't even that difficult any more.

He cleaned up, using three buckets full of water to dispose of the blood. *Good.* Now just the message. The picture had turned out well, even though the sight of it almost winded him. He gasped for air and waited until he felt better, then put the mobile in one pocket and the battery in the other. Looked for and found the car keys. There was no rush. He could take his time. Ten or fifteen kilometres would be enough. Then back. And sleep, at last.

Jakob kissed and hugged her before he disappeared back to the neighbours' farm, but Mina was querulous. She reminded Beatrice of herself at that age, almost thirty years ago now. Or even just thirty minutes ago. *She's a smaller version of me. Maybe that's why we clash*, she thought.

'If you don't have any time for us, you can give us to Papa. He likes having us there, he told us.'

'I thought you liked being with Oma?'

'I do. But . . .' She panted for air, and for the words. 'You always say it's just for a few days, and then it's always much longer, every time.'

If this was Mina's way of telling her mother she missed her, then she was doing her best at hiding it. Everything she said came out as an accusation.

'You're right,' said Beatrice. 'It's already taken far too long. But now we're nearly there, I'm sure of it. And this weekend Papa will come and get you, and you might be going sailing if the weather's nice.'

The idea seemed to appeal to Mina, as she summoned up a nod and a half-smile. 'That might be nice. So when are we going to do something together?'

'Once the case is over I'll take some time off and you guys can pick what we do. Is that a deal?'

'Anything we want? And we can do it?'

'If I can afford it and it's not illegal, then yes.' She pulled Mina close to her, feeling resistance at first, then little arms around her waist.

'I don't think it is,' mumbled her daughter from down by her stomach.

Richard, in a gracious mood today, found some reassuring words once Mina was out of earshot. 'She's perfectly happy here, don't worry. And if you were to come more often in the evening, instead of just phoning, then that would be—'

He broke off as her mobile beeped loudly.

'Shit.' Beatrice rummaged around in her handbag, found the phone and muted the sound. A picture message. At first, all she saw was the number – *the* number – then the picture appeared. Beatrice heard herself gasp for air.

'What is it?' Quickly, too quickly, Richard was beside her, catching a glimpse of the screen. 'Oh, God, Bea, what *is* that? A person? Or . . . yes, look, that's an arm! Horrific. It looks like something in an abattoir.'

She freed herself from his grasp on her wrist as he tried to get a closer look at the photo.

An abattoir.

'I have to go.' She grabbed her bag and rushed out to the car without saying goodbye. She turned the engine on, the phone slipping from her fingers. She picked it up and dialled Florin's number. 'Are you still in the office?'

'No, I just got home, why? Should I—'

'I'll come to your place, see you in fifteen minutes.'

A severed middle finger, swimming in blood, next to the

mutilated hand. A fresh wound, a bloody stump. The amputation cuts on the ring and little fingers seemed to be inflamed rather than healing. The thumb and index finger, the only ones still attached, were crooked towards each other like the two halves of a pair of crab scissors. Or the tips of a croissant. Beatrice took a deep breath, in and out.

Enlarged on Florin's laptop, the picture showed details that hadn't been visible on the small screen of her mobile phone. There was a newspaper, partially saturated with red, and when they zoomed in today's date was visible on it.

'Sigart's still alive.' It was hard to tell whether Florin saw that as good news or bad. Without tearing his gaze away from the photo, he scrolled from the top to the bottom and from left to right. 'It's a wooden table, and the background is quite dark. The photo was taken with flash.' He pointed at a light reflection in the pool of blood. 'The killer put something underneath, it looks like a white plastic tablecloth. He's doing everything he can to maximise the impact of the picture.'

Although it could have been even more horrific if Sigart's face had been in the shot. But, like last time, the picture ended at his shoulder.

Was that because Sigart had actually long since died of blood loss? 'Can you zoom in on the wound?'

On closer inspection, Beatrice's theory didn't stand: the flesh where the fingers had been severed was pink, not sallow. The hand was pale, but not grey. And it was definitely Sigart's hand, unless another of the Owner's victims also had severe burn scars.

Florin reached for his phone and instructed Stefan to find out where the mobile was at the time the message was sent.

He forwarded the photo, and then sent it to Vogt and Drasche. All the usual actions that had so far brought them zero results.

'Why isn't he showing us Sigart's face?' murmured Beatrice.

'I'd prefer to know why he's sending us these pictures at all. No, I'll be more specific – why is he sending them to *you*?'

'Because it's possible he thinks we have something in common.' The thought felt like ice on the back of her neck. 'Because he thinks I'm a perpetrator too, in some ways.'

Until now, she had kept quiet about the text the Owner had sent to accompany the picture, as if she were concealing a flaw she didn't want Florin to see. She pulled her phone back out of her bag and read the words to herself once more, silently, before uttering them out loud.

'"Omission to do what is necessary, Seals a commission to a blank of danger."'

Now her own wound was almost laid bare. But Florin didn't yet catch on.

'He sent that with the picture? Is it Goethe again?'

'No. Shakespeare. It doesn't matter anyway. The important thing is what the Owner means by it. And he means me.'

Florin turned to face her, took her hand in his and held it tight. 'He means you and Evelyn?'

'I don't know who else he could mean.'

She hasn't noticed that dark has fallen outside. David is still lying on top of her, his mouth buried in the curve of her neck. He's humming or murmuring; she can feel the vibration on her skin. A moment of complete and utter contentment. *Thank you*, she mouths silently, feeling as though she's about to laugh. Or cry.

'Beabeabea,' whispers David, rolling off her and pulling her with him, holding her head close to his shoulder. 'Let's stay here for ever. Just the two of us. We can shut the world out and make our own.'

She lays an arm across his chest, breathing in his scent, never having smelt anything better. 'For ever isn't long enough.'

'You're right. Beautiful, clever Bea.' David's kisses on her closed eyelids are so gentle, just a whisper, not enough. She seeks his lips with her own, sinking into them.

'I'd fetch us something to drink, but for that I'd have to let you go,' he says when they surface again.

'Dying of thirst isn't a good idea,' answers Bea, nudging his shoulder affectionately. She doesn't take her eyes off him as he stands up and crosses the room, naked and beautiful, much too beautiful for her. She's always thought that, keeping to friendly kisses on the cheek whenever they met and said goodbye, only wondering occasionally in her daydreams what it would be like. What it *could* be like. With him.

Until last night. When his hand had suddenly rested on hers. She had spread out her fingers, and his plunged into the space between, tearing the blue-and-white checked paper tablecloth at the pizzeria.

'He's been crazy about you for months, sweetie.' Evelyn had followed her to the bathroom, of course, pulling silly faces as she touched up her mascara. 'Was I right or was I right?'

'Okay, okay!' Something inside Beatrice had jumped around in excitement, and if she wasn't careful she would join in, like a little kid who had just been given a lolly. 'And you really think . . . I mean, you reckon it's not just a whim?'

'This is David we're talking about, not me,' Evelyn had grinned, ruffling Beatrice's hair and then pulling a hairbrush out of her bag. 'He's just a tad too respectable to be my type, otherwise you'd have competition.' She plucked out a few long, deep red hairs that were entangled in the brush.

'Here you go, sweetheart, make yourself pretty for him. And don't feel like you're lucky to be with him, okay? If anything it's the other way around. You're gold, don't forget that.'

Beatrice hums the Spandau Ballet hit to herself as David walks back from the kitchen. He has a tea towel over his arm like a waiter, and he's carrying a bottle of cheap sparkling wine and two mismatched water tumblers.

'Not very stylish, I'm afraid,' he says, pressing the prettier of the two glasses into her hand. 'But I hope you can see the charm in it.'

She can. Paradise is now a badly ventilated bachelors' pad with unwashed dishes in the sink and piles of dirty washing in the bedroom. But she doesn't care about any of that.

For a while, the cork is reluctant to leave the bottle. They struggle with it, giggling, and once they're finally victorious a good third of the contents shoot out. But they don't care about that either, snuggling up to one another, drinking from the old glasses and each other's mouths, kissing each other's bodies.

Then her phone rings.

'I'm not answering it.' She holds her empty glass out towards David and he fills it up halfway. They drink. The phone continues ringing – beeping, to be precise – boring shrill holes in the mood.

'Fine then.' Beatrice swings her legs out of bed. Where was her bag?

'Why doesn't your answerphone kick in?'

'Because I deactivated it. Otherwise I'd never receive any calls – by the time I've found the phone the mailbox has always picked up.'

Evelyn. Oh, God, yes, the stupid party. She'd completely forgotten.

'Hi, Eve.'

'Hey, sweetie, where are you?'

'I'm . . . um, I'm busy.'

'Busy . . . oh, I get it, with Michelangelo's David. Understood. How long will you be there for?'

'That's hard to say.' He's behind her now, lifting the hair from the nape of her neck and kissing the sensitive spot. 'It's likely to be a while. A very long while.'

'Does that mean you're not coming to Nola's? I'm already there, and I can tell you you're missing a good party.'

She suppresses a blissful sigh. 'I very much doubt that.'

'Oh, come on. Just bring him with you. Make everyone else jealous of how happy you are.'

'That's a good idea in theory, but . . .' Did she really have to spell it out?

'Fine then, stay in bed for all I care. The only thing is, I don't know how I'll get home later, this place is in the middle of nowhere. I was counting on you.'

Just like you always do. For the first time that day, her elated mood is starting to deflate. *I'm the one with the car and the driving licence, and you're in absolutely no hurry to get yours. That way, the question of who's drinking and who's the designated driver never even comes up.*

'There are loads of people there. I'm sure someone will give you a lift.'

'Yes, probably.' Evelyn giggles. 'There's a really cute blond guy with dark brown eyes, so let's hope he lives near us.' She hangs up.

'Evelyn?' asks David. 'The fiery-headed flatmate?'

'That's the one. I stood her up, and she's not used to that.' Smiling, she goes back to bed, into David's arms, into the space beyond the passing of time, into the chaotic paradise.

Four hours later, the phone rings again. 'Hi, sweetie. Listen, I can't get a lift home. Some people left early and the others are sleeping here.'

Beatrice had been sleeping too – not for long, maybe fifteen minutes or so. Her mind is foggy and she's barely able to grasp what Evelyn is saying. 'Then sleep there too.'

'No way. There's no space left, apart from on the floor. And there are two drunken, annoying guys I want to get away from. Would you be an angel and pick me up?'

You can't be serious. 'I'm sorry, but I'm tired and I've been drinking and—'

'And David is about to ravish you again.' She hears Evelyn sigh. 'I'm happy for you, really I am. It's just a difficult situation – but I know it's my own fault. I really have to get around to doing my driving licence. Never mind, it's been a while since I hitch-hiked. So, hopefully I'll see you tomorrow and hear all the dirty details?'

For a split second Beatrice considers giving in. Getting dressed and driving twenty miles through the night to pick up her friend from a party and take her home. Then David's hands win out, on her back, around her waist, on her buttocks, moving down and in between.

'Sure. See you tomorrow.'

'Don't do anything I wouldn't.' Evelyn blows her a kiss down the line before hanging up.

Their night comes to an end shortly after seven the next morning. David has to get up and start work at the call centre job with which he's financing his medical studies. She leaves the house with him, breathing in Vienna's morning air and scraping together a few coins to buy croissants for breakfast. She plans to brew some fresh coffee at home, hoping that there is still some of the raspberry jam left that her mother had sent her.

'Will I see you this evening?' David whispers into her hair. She's happy that the question comes from him; otherwise she would have had to ask. She nods, kisses him and is still warming herself with his words even once she's sitting on the metro.

Five stops on the U6. David's place is in Vienna's ninth district, her flatshare with Evelyn in the sixth. She can still smell David on her. She closes her eyes and smiles, breathing in his scent. In the small branch of one of the large bakery chains, she buys four croissants, pleased to find they're on offer. As she skips down the narrow Turmgasse towards her home, she feels like bursting out into song.

Evelyn is evidently already back and awake. Pink Floyd's *The Wall* is blaring out into the hallway, and old Frau Heckel glares at her as they meet at the main door. 'I'm going to call the police at some point, you know, if you keep making such a racket all the time. It's been on for hours – it's just not acceptable!'

'I'm sorry, Frau Heckel. It won't happen again.' She feels the urge to hug the old woman, wanting her to be cheerful too. Her happiness won't tolerate any sullenness today.

She dashes up the stairs to the third floor, feeling as though she could run for ever, *The Wall* accompanying her on her climb. She and Evelyn have been listening to the CD constantly over the last few weeks, and know every song by heart. 'One of My Turns' is a favourite, even though its sombre lyrics are laughably inappropriate this morning. She spins around as she reaches the front door, her eyes closed, smiling indulgently at Roger Waters's depressing contemplations on life.

She fumbles her key out of her bag and puts it in the lock. Frau Heckel did have a point; the music was on really loud. Luckily the other flats in the building are rented to students, so hardly anyone ever complains.

The door now open, the song blares out into the hallway.

Beatrice sings along to the words. She holds the paper bag filled with croissants up in front of her face like a microphone.

She smells it before she sees it, and wonders why her heart has suddenly begun to beat faster, why something within her wants to turn back.

Ignoring the feeling, she closes the door. It smells . . . smells of . . .

'Evelyn?'

No answer. She passes through the tiny kitchen and is about to knock on Evelyn's door, but it's already standing ajar so she pushes it open.

Evelyn isn't there. The room has been trashed and it looks as though an animal has been slaughtered on the bed, splattering the walls with blood, dripping all over the floor, all over the room.

The thing, whatever it is, is splayed out on the bed amongst the duvet and pillows. It's well disguised amidst all the red, glistening in parts.

Something smacks against Beatrice's head. The door frame, but why? She grabs onto it, the breath streaming out of her body with a whistling sound. Now something hits her left knee. The floor. A speck of red is just a few centimetres away; she can't tear her eyes away from it. What if it creeps and flows over to her, touches her?

Summoning up all her strength, she lifts her gaze to the bed.

There! Silver. It glistens and shines, brought to life by a beam of sunlight.

Nail varnish.

Evelyn's . . .

nail varnish.

The floor comes closer and everything falls, falls slowly towards the red: first the croissants, landing in a saucer-sized puddle, the red eating greedily into the paper bag, the printed image of the baker grinning away as it reaches his mouth, his eyes . . .

She only realises she's screaming when someone grabs her from behind, turns her around, pulls her in towards them. Her screams are smothered by a sweaty body in a washed-out T-shirt. She hits out, bites and scratches until she catches a glimpse of the face above the T-shirt. Holger from next door. His hands tug at her, trying to drag her into the kitchen, *MyGodmyGodohmyGod*, he cries.

She tries to close her eyes but it won't work, she can't, she's forgotten something. But what?

The croissants.

One of them has tumbled out on the floor, the left tip saturated with blood. Raspberry jam, thinks Beatrice, vomiting on the kitchen floor.

The policewoman speaking to her is focused and friendly, but Beatrice can see her own horror reflected in her eyes. She hates her for that. And for the fact that every single one of her words confirms something that should never have happened.

'You lived here with Frau Rieger?'

Rieger, pronounced like Tigger but with a long 'e' instead of 'i' and Rrrrr, says Evelyn in Bea's head. 'When did you last see her?'

337

'Yesterday lunchtime. We were planning to—' She stops as she sees two men in white overalls walk into Evelyn's room wearing masks and gloves. Anonymous, veiled figures.

'They're my colleagues,' explains the policewoman. 'You were just about to say you were planning to do something together?'

Go to a party. Again, Beatrice's body reacts more quickly than her mind, crumbling into sobs.

The policewoman is patient. 'Take your time.'

Gradually, Beatrice manages to choke out words. The address of Nola's house, where the party was held. The rough times of Evelyn's first and last call.

It is around this time that Beatrice's brain begins the 'what if' game. For years to come, it will be her constant companion. The 'what if' game can last hours, and never fails to unleash its exhausting impact.

If I had picked her up, if I had driven there with David, if I hadn't left her alone, if . . .

'We'll get you some counselling,' says the policewoman as Beatrice breaks down yet again.

In the end, it's an injection which erases the red images in her head and stops the 'what if' game. For a short while. After that, the whole thing starts all over again.

The police reconstruct Evelyn's last night. The party guests provide detailed statements, and it soon becomes clear what must have happened. The phone call at half-past three, the one that reached the sleepy and love-drunk Beatrice, was the last Evelyn had made in her life. She hadn't tried to call a taxi or any other friends.

'She said she was going to hitch-hike,' sobbed Nola on the phone. 'But she could have stayed here – the first bus into town would have left at five.'

New what-ifs for Beatrice's game. *If Evelyn had waited, if she had been more careful . . .*

But it was Beatrice, and only Beatrice, who Evelyn had asked for help.

She can no longer bear David's presence; he has become an accomplice. She hardly eats and sleeps very little, walking through the streets and staring into people's faces. Which of them could be capable of it? Maybe it's the man standing next to her in the metro, or the man letting her go ahead of him at the supermarket checkout. Maybe it's the young guy on the other side of the street pushing the blue polka-dot pushchair, or the bald man with the worn-out trousers reading the newspaper as he walks along. *Of course. He's looking for reports about what he did.*

Beatrice besieges the investigators with phone calls. The policewoman gave her the direct line in case she thinks of anything else that might be relevant, and she calls three times a day. She reports minute details from Evelyn's life, things that suddenly seem to be full of significance. But above all, she just wants to know, know, know.

No one tells her anything. All she finds out is the same information that's in the paper. That the murder of Evelyn Rieger resembles another case from three years ago which was never solved. On that occasion, too, the victim was raped, slashed and practically disembowelled.

Alongside the article, they always print the same photo of Evelyn, taken by Beatrice barely two months ago. Such a beautiful picture of her. An angel with deep red locks and bright green, knowing eyes.

I miss you so much.
I'm sorry.
If I had known.
If I had listened to you.
If.

At the funeral, she tries to imprint the face of every man present on her memory, but the crowd of people is too big. There are two policemen there too, but they keep their distance, looking on awkwardly.

Her mother and Richard have come, even though they barely knew Evelyn. They've closed Mooserhof for two days, which Beatrice is very grateful to them for. She told them about her guilt. *I could have prevented it. So easily.*

'There's no way you could have known,' said her mother. 'The only guilty party is the man with the knife. The knife killed her, and the man who used it. No one else.'

The thought comforted Beatrice for a mere five minutes, but then it became stale, like over-chewed gum.

David comes to the funeral too, wearing a black polo-neck jumper despite the twenty-four-degree heat outside. He comes over to stand next to Beatrice and tries to hold her. She pushes him away.

'There's nothing I can do to change what happened,' he says sadly. 'And neither can you.'

He has no idea what's going on in her mind, but he does seem to have genuine feelings for her. And that just makes it worse. She avoids looking at him, punishes herself by looking at Evelyn's mother instead. She lets Rheinberger's Stabat Mater soak into her, trying to swallow away the metallic taste in her mouth. Guilt tastes like blood.

In the weeks that follow, she waits. The case gradually disappears from the news, and the police don't arrest anyone. David has given up on trying to see her again, while she has given up on trying to finish her studies. After a while, Richard turns up on her doorstep to take her back to Salzburg.

She doesn't try to protest. She calls the policewoman in Vienna just once a week now, and there's never any news. She hates the police. At some point, four or five months after Evelyn's death, she tells the woman, 'You're an incompetent waste of space.'

Hearing the policewoman's sharp intake of breath, she prepares herself for a strong retort. But the answer, when it comes, is totally calm. 'You know what?' she says. 'You try and do a better job, you know-it-all.'

'Fine, I will!' Beatrice hangs up. But the thought sticks in her mind. Every time she thinks about it, it lifts a little of the weight off her shoulders. After six months of therapy, when she finally makes the decision, she is welcomed with open arms.

It happens during the first year of her training. Along with five of her colleagues, she's on duty at a ball at the Hohensalzburg Castle. A blond man in a tuxedo keeps strolling past her, smiling. She can see his hesitation.

'There are hundreds of women dressed in expensive dresses

in that ballroom, but none of them look as beautiful as you in your uniform.' Achim Kaspary is the junior manager of a saw factory just outside Salzburg. He treats her well, doesn't rush things. He's not anywhere near as exciting as David, and he's not the kind of man she would let down a friend for.

He's a good man to marry.

The flame of the tea light on the coffee table had almost drowned in liquid wax. Beatrice pulled her hand from Florin's grasp to push the hair away from her forehead. He hadn't interrupted her even once, but by the end she had felt his fingers clasping more tightly around hers. She searched his eyes for sympathy, or condemnation, but to her relief found neither.

'You don't think we're dealing with Evelyn's murderer here, do you?'

She shook her head firmly. 'No. Evelyn was the victim of a sexual crime.' My God, she sounded like she was quoting a newspaper article. As if that made things more bearable. 'She was raped, vaginally and anally, and with all kinds of utensils. Then he slashed her with a kitchen knife that her grandmother had given her.' *Red.* Beatrice's mouth was dry. 'No one ever questioned the motive. The Owner, on the other hand, has shown zero sexual interest in his victims. Neither the men nor the women. His motive is still completely unknown.'

Her last words were accompanied by the sounds of a violin. Anneke's ringtone.

'I can call her back later,' said Florin. 'No prob—'

'No, it's fine, take the call, I have to . . .' She gestured towards the bathroom.

Even through the closed door, she could still hear Florin's voice; earnest and tender. She couldn't make out the words, and she preferred it that way. He laughed twice. For a few seconds, Beatrice felt betrayed.

Only when she could no longer hear his voice did she flush the toilet and leave the grey-tiled refuge.

'Are you okay?' He had made some tea; the dark, fragrant leaves swam on the surface of the shimmering water.

'No,' she said, honestly. 'And I won't be until we find Sigart. I keep picturing his mutilated hand right in front of me.' She stopped there, hoping that Florin would understand. *He called me because he needed help – does that sound familiar?*

'I'm going to drive home,' she decided, giving the tea a longing look. 'I'll do some Internet research. We've got the latest coordinates, so I'm sure there must be something there,' she added.

'But you're not planning to drive out there by yourself, are you?'

She snorted. 'What would I do out there in the middle of the night? Hope I stumble across something that we missed during the day?'

Florin hugged her and let her go. For a moment, she felt disappointed he didn't try to persuade her to stay.

It was stuffy in her apartment; the windows had been closed all day. Beatrice longed to be able to go out on the balcony, but every time she went out there she felt as if she was being watched. It was just her imagination, of course. But she felt more comfortable inside the apartment, with the doors double-locked. She set up her laptop on the coffee table and entered the Dalamasso coordinates into Geocaching.

com. There was no cache within a two-mile radius. Then she logged into Liebscher's account and read through his entries, without knowing what she was actually looking for.

Half an hour later, she turned the computer off and exchanged staring at the monitor for staring at the lounge ceiling. Melanie Dalamasso's reaction had been so clear. If only she could speak to her, show her the photos one by one—

A wish that was certain not to be fulfilled. Beil had been her only chance, the jolt when he had seen Nora Papenberg's photo. She shouldn't have let it slip by. Beatrice could hold no one responsible for that but herself.

'Well, you've got yourself into a fine mess now, haven't you?' From Hoffmann's expression, anyone would think it was his birthday. He must have been lying in wait for her behind his office door. Now he was sitting there on his pigskin chair, and she was standing before him like a school pupil who had been called to see the headmaster.

'I have a complaint here about you, from Carolin Dalamasso. She said you confronted Melanie with photos of the victims. Is that true?'

'They fell out of my hand.'

'Then that was very clumsy of you, Kaspary. The girl's condition has worsened considerably since yesterday, the doctors are worried and her mother's on the warpath.' He paused. 'My God. How could you? Tormenting a sick girl like that! You're a mother yourself. Would you really use any means to get results in spite of your complete lack of competence?'

She didn't answer. Anything she said would just make it worse.

'So what did you achieve through your clumsiness? Any new clues? Did the girl tell you a story?'

'No.'

'No.' Hoffmann rotated a pencil between his fingers. 'Do you have any idea how much you've damaged our reputation by doing this? The reputation of your colleagues, who play by the rules? I'm really disappointed in you, Kaspary. There will be consequences, you mark my words.' He waited, but when Beatrice just stared at him in silence, he waved her out with his hand.

When she got back to her own desk, Kossar was there, smiling as she approached. He pointed to two folders, a yellow one and a red one.

'There's a lot to read here, Beatrice. I went to great lengths to prepare everything for you, but a lot of it is in English. I hope that's okay.'

'What is this?'

'In the red folder, you'll find everything you need to know on the case of Raymond Willer, a serial killer from Ohio. The most interesting document is probably the interview my colleague from Quantico conducted with him. Willer selected his victims at random, but left behind encrypted messages to make the police think otherwise. He said it was a competition, him against a huge machinery of power. He was highly intelligent, with an IQ of one hundred and forty-seven. He was only caught after the twelfth murder.'

Beatrice shrugged. 'But the Owner isn't killing random victims.'

'The yellow folder,' continued Kossar as if he hadn't even heard what she had said, 'is about the Mike Gonzalez case.

He killed nine people with the sole intent of saving them. There are a few cases like that. Religious delusion – the selection of victims only *seems* to be at random. In the interview, he said he saw a light above their heads and knew they were ready for the kingdom of God. So he wanted to help them get there as quickly as possible. And the fact that he made them suffer beforehand was apparently just to save them from the fire of purgatory—'

'Our case doesn't have random victims!' Beatrice heard herself shout, immediately regretting how loud she was. Losing her nerve was bad, very bad. But at least she had succeeded in halting Kossar's narrative flow. 'They knew each other. Not every one of them, perhaps, but Beil knew Papenberg, and Dalamasso knew at least one of the victims. I'm sorry you had to do all this work for nothing.'

'That's assuming you're right.' It seemed nothing made Kossar lose his cool. 'And that's not certain yet,' he said.

'It is. You can bet your fucking glasses on it.'

You know everything, and yet you find nothing, the Owner had written. *You know everything, and yet you find nothing.*

I know that you're Shinigami. I know that you knew Liebscher, that you went hunting for hidden plastic containers together. And I know you've informed yourself about my history, but when? When you realised I was one of the people looking for you? And why?

'Perhaps you're connected to the motive in some way,' Florin had pondered the day before. Beatrice had considered the idea, turning it over and over before discarding it.

No, she didn't believe that. But he had made her a part

of his production, and his messages were predominantly directed at her. Now it was up to her to decipher them.

I've overlooked something, she thought. *I should go right back to the beginning, but I don't have time for that, and the most important figures are already dead.*

But why not look back at the first appearance of the Owner himself, as least in so far as Beatrice was familiar with it?

26 February, enter Shinigami. He registers with the geocaching website – *why?* Just to make contact with Herbert Liebscher, or so it appears. For after seven collaborative finds, the website doesn't seem to interest him any more.

The caches are part of the solution. Otherwise all the hiding places, abbreviations and coordinates would just be pointless.

Would he really do all that just because it was Liebscher's hobby? Beatrice's instinct protested against this theory; it wasn't that, it couldn't be that.

She rummaged through her notes, a thick folder of them by now, looking for her jottings from Konrad Papenberg's first interview.

There it was: Nora had been a nature lover. She was sporty and loved going hiking. But geocaching hadn't been one of her hobbies. Not if her husband was telling the truth – and presumably he was, because even after a thorough search there had been no sign of a geocaching membership on Nora's computer. The site owners had confirmed it too: there was no Nora Papenberg registered with them. And that was key, because without a computer, without registering with the online community, geocaching was pretty much impossible.

Something made Beatrice linger over this thought, preventing her from moving on. *What if . . .*

She read through the husband's statement once more.

Married for two years, they had known each other for three. Nora's computer was three years old, which by today's standards made it practically a Methuselah in the world of technology, but still—

A glance at the clock revealed it was technically too late to call Stefan, but she didn't care – it was important. She dialled his mobile first, then his landline, but every time it just went through to a mailbox with a recorded message of Stefan asking the caller to leave their details.

Damn it. She wrote herself a note so she wouldn't forget any of her thoughts.

We haven't found anything, but that doesn't mean there isn't anything, thought Beatrice, as she laid down her pen. *It's much more likely that we were looking for the wrong thing.*

'Passwords, nicknames, forum pseudonyms – make me a list, please.'

Stefan's hair was standing up at a strange angle, as if he had only just woken up. His unshaven chin supported this theory, but his eyes looked wide and alert. 'For Papenberg? Sure.'

'For Beil and Estermann too. Sigart and Dalamasso don't have computers, but we should check out Dalamasso again just to make sure.' She reached out and tried to tame the unruly strands of his hair, but they resisted all of her efforts. 'I didn't wake you last night, did I?'

He shook his head, grinning from ear to ear. 'No. I put my phone on silent. I wasn't at home.'

Aha. 'Are you going to tell me her name?'

The left corner of his mouth wandered upwards, followed by the right. 'I think you'll have to content yourself with Nora Papenberg's nicknames for now.'

She had the office all to herself. Florin was leading another interrogation marathon. Someone had seen a red Honda Civic parked by the Wallersee lake two weeks ago, late in the evening.

Nora's car. Had she gone there with the Owner in order to hide Liebscher's head in the treetops? Nora, alias NoPap1; Norissima; radishes_are_red.

Beatrice raised her eyebrows as she looked at the last lexical invention – how did someone come up with something like that?

FrankaC. Wishfulthinker28.

These were all Nora's nicknames, as found by Stefan so far. Names she had used online. There were possibly more to come. 'But five is quite a lot, already too many to keep track of,' he had observed. He was right, as Beatrice realised a few minutes later. She could no longer remember what nickname she had used to register on Geocaching.com, until she eventually thought of Jakob's cuddly owl. Elvira the Second.

She logged onto the site and went to *Find User*. NoPap1 didn't bring up any results, and nor did Norissima. FrankaC had one hit, but she was clearly in excellent health and had found her most recent cache just two days ago. There was a detailed profile, including photos showing her at a number of different locations – particularly around Hamburg, where she lived.

Wishfulthinker28. Type and enter. Beatrice crossed her fingers. *Bingo*.

There was no information on the profile, nor any photos – maybe it had never been updated, or even deleted. But the user clearly existed. There were 133 smiley faces denoting 133 successfully found caches.

Feeling as though she'd finally found the hidden door leading to the right path, Beatrice opened the list. As always, the most recently logged find was at the top.

Wishfulthinker28 had been out caching near the Mondsee lake. The entry was red and crossed out, meaning that the cache was now archived, as were the majority of the user's finds. No wonder, for the last one had been five years ago. Wishfulthinker28 had clearly found another hobby.

Okay, thought Beatrice. *Let's go with this for a moment. Let's assume this is Nora Papenberg's account.* The area was correct, as most of the found caches were in or around Salzburg. Five years ago, Nora Papenberg hadn't even met her husband – so she would have had a different surname then.

Within seconds, she reached Stefan on the internal line. 'Before she got married, Nora Papenberg's surname was Winter, if I'm not mistaken. I need the site admin team to tell us whether there's a Nora Winter behind Wishfulthinker28.'

Beatrice circled the cursor around the last entry. *Great view, I'd definitely come back. The hiding place for the container is really inventive, but I still managed to find it quickly. Had fun! TFTC!*

It didn't sound like a farewell comment, nor did it suggest she had lost her enthusiasm for geocaching. Okay, there were a number of reasons why someone might give up a hobby

– a new boyfriend, a new job, a pregnancy or illness. But she didn't believe that, because . . .

Following a sudden flash of inspiration, Beatrice opened Herbert Liebscher's profile and scrolled through the entries that DescartesHL had made at around the same time. Inside her mind, something began to lock into place.

There it was, the connection. Barely perceptible, but it was there nonetheless, like a thin strand of light in the darkness.

Nora Papenberg's last entry was on 3 July. Herbert Liebscher had been in Vienna between the 6 and 8 of July that same year, had found eighteen caches – and then stopped. For one and a half years. Papenberg had stopped for ever.

That's no coincidence, no doubt about it. There has to be a common cause.

Beatrice printed out the profile pages and compared the caches listed on each – yes, there were overlaps, but that was no surprise with two people who lived in the same city. There wasn't a single entry, however, where one of them referred to the other. With the caches that came up in both DescartesHL and Wishfulthinker28's lists, there were months, if not years, in between each of them finding the same cache. There was nothing at all to indicate that the two of them had known each other.

'You were spot on,' announced Stefan shortly before midday. He was still very chirpy, and had even managed to clamp down the rebellious strands of hair. 'Wishfulthinker28 is a Nora Winter with an Austrian postal address – I just got the confirmation through.' He laid a printout on Beatrice's desk, shaking his head slightly as if trying to chase away an unwelcome thought. 'Do you think we're dealing with someone who's targeting and killing geocachers?'

'It's too early to say. But could you please do something for me? Ring Carolin Dalamasso and ask her whether her daughter used to be a geocacher before—'

She stopped. Of course. It all fitted.

'Before the breakdown, you mean? Of course, will do. What's up?'

The dates. 'Sorry, Stefan, I have to check something.'

Melanie Dalamasso's breakdown. Yes, that was it. The same summer. Twelve days after Nora Papenberg had found her last cache.

Four cups of coffee later, Beatrice was no longer sure whether her agitated state was a side effect of the caffeine or whether she really was on the brink of what she and Florin called the 'last twist of the kaleidoscope'. One more detail, one more piece of information, and the chaos would give way to meaning: the picture would become clear. Beatrice could feel the moment drawing close, just as she did every time. She wished the realisation would come, but at the same time she was afraid of it. Because, in most cases, the final picture was a particularly ugly one.

When she packed her bag at around half-past nine that evening, the moment still hadn't come. If anything, that afternoon it had taken a step backwards. It may have been surprisingly simple to find out Nora Papenberg's cacher alias, but their attempt to do the same with Christoph Beil and Rudolf Estermann had been fruitless.

Beil had been active on very few Internet forums, and he

hadn't concealed his identity in the slightest. The different combinations of forenames and surnames he had used online hadn't brought up any results on Geocaching.com. And nor had Grizzly Bear.

When it came to Estermann, it seemed he had only used his computer for business purposes. His browser history was a mix of the homepages of pharmacies and beauty salons.

'Rudo', as his wife had called him, had been a damp squib too, regardless of the combinations they tried. Beatrice had got tired, worrying that her dwindling concentration might make her miss something if she continued to push.

She was just putting on her seat belt and about to turn the key in the ignition when her phone rang.

'I'm taking the children to my place tomorrow,' said Achim, without a single word of greeting. 'What on earth goes on in that head of yours? Do you really think you can just shove them aside whenever it suits you?'

The goodwill he had shown during their last encounter had clearly evaporated.

'I'm not shoving them aside. I'm battling one of the most difficult cases I've ever worked on. This isn't normal day-to-day life.' She sighed. 'This is an exceptional circumstance. I thought you understood that.'

When he replied, his voice was less cold, but flat and toneless. 'This is all so messed up, Bea. I think I could provide Mina and Jakob with a more stable life, one without any exceptional circumstances. The only thing standing in the way of that is your egotism.'

If it hurts to hear it, does that mean it's true?

'You're being unfair.' She closed her eyes. 'Fetch the

children tomorrow then. I'll tell my mother. Then I'll come see you the day after tomorrow and we'll discuss everything. It's possible that everything here will have settled down by then anyway.'

He laughed, sounding genuinely amused. 'As if that were ever true. Who are you trying to kid, Bea? If it's me, then don't bother. That train left the station a long time ago.'

Half-past ten. She showered – hot, cold and then hot again – but the raw feeling in the pit of her stomach remained.

No more Internet research for today. She lay down naked on the bed, feeling the cool linen against her back and wishing the children were asleep in the next room.

A blurry shape moved on the ceiling. A spider's web? She resolved to clear it first thing tomorrow with the broom; it would be good to be able to clear something up in a quick, uncomplicated manner . . .

Her mobile ringtone catapulted her out of a deep sleep. Her heart was beating fast and frantically against her ribs, something must have happened—

'Did I wake you, Frau Kommissar?' His enunciation was slurred.

'Achim, I swear I'll report you.'

'I don't care. I spoke to my mother, she—'

Beatrice ended the call and put the mobile down next to her on the bed. She looked at her shaking hands in the light of the bedside lamp, which was still shining brightly.

To hell with it. She would call in sick tomorrow and spend the day with the children. Bring the exceptional circumstances to an end. Things couldn't carry on like this.

Her pulse was beating far too quickly and far too hard. Damned coffee. After a glance at the clock — it was only half-past midnight, thank God — she curled up, pulled the blanket over her shoulders and closed her eyes. Some breathing exercises would steady her pulse; she just had to concentrate on not letting any other thoughts come into her mind, and then she would be able to switch off.

But in the darkness behind her closed eyelids, Melanie Dalamasso appeared, screaming, trying to bang her head against the door frame . . .

No. Enough.

She couldn't get Dalamasso out of her mind, though. She was the one they were looking for, the torn woman — so why hadn't there been anything at the coordinates? Were they just a clue to future events, as they had been once before? Had the Owner planned to dump Dalamasso on the Bundesstrasse?

Beatrice turned over in bed. *Shut up*, she ordered her inner voice.

Dalamasso's breakdown had occurred, Liebscher hadn't gone near a GPS device in a year and a half, Papenberg had given up geocaching for ever. Caesuras, both small and large, within a short space of time.

But not on the same day.

Beatrice gave up. The chance of sleep had retreated from her like the sea ebbing away from the shore. She pulled on a T-shirt, fetched a glass of water from the kitchen, and turned on her laptop.

The green of the geocaching website banner shone out into the darkness of her living room. Without knowing what she was looking for, she opened Nora Papenberg's profile page. Some users entered their home town under *Location*. Wishfulthinker28 hadn't, and nor had Herbert Liebscher.

She would go through the 133 caches in reverse order, reading every entry closely. Maybe she would stumble across something, maybe there would be a meeting with Shinigami or a clue about other cacher friends. Christoph Beil, for example.

A very amusingly disguised container, my compliments to the owner! Nora had written about her penultimate find. *I almost gave up, but a flash of inspiration at the last moment pointed me in the right direction. TFTC!*

Next entry, 18 June: *Simple, but not entirely without its challenges − TFTC!*

Another one that same day: *Tricky, but we were victorious in the end. Woohoo! TFTC, Wishfulthinker28.*

There was no indication of who 'we' referred to. Beatrice clicked on the page of the archived cache and found a certain BibiWalz who had also entered the find on 18 June. She was still active, with the number 1877 in brackets next to her nickname and a gallery containing over thirty photos, which Beatrice looked at one by one. BibiWalz was blonde, freckled, chubby and a complete unknown. But she made a note of the name just in case.

Working backwards the next cache was from 15 June. Nora's entry conveyed sheer excitement. *My first night cache! Found together with CreepyCrawly. We set off on our adventure armed with chocolate, crisps and a torch, and arrived at our destination in just over an hour. The path signs reliably showed us the way, and we weren't afraid for even a second. Compliments to the owner of the listing. TFTC times a thousand!*

CreepyCrawly? Beatrice searched for the owner of this strange pseudonym, but his or her profile was just as sparse as those belonging to Nora and Liebscher. Again, she made a note regardless.

The next cache, a week before that: *This was a really great cache; I never knew this beautiful church was here, TFTC!*

Gradually, the tiredness began to creep back into Beatrice's body. Ignoring it, she clicked on the next link in the list. Blinded by the ceiling light, she leant back and squinted.

A memory returned to her mind with the force of a hammer. Light. Reflection. Where was it again? She looked for the right page. Yes, there it was; Nora's enthusiasm about the adventure . . . there were even photos of the cache, not from her, but taken by other cachers. *View the Image Gallery of 25 images.*

One click and it all became clear. Beatrice clapped her laptop shut, pulled on her jeans and a jacket over her T-shirt and was already at the door by the time she realised she'd forgotten the most essential tool: a torch.

Achim had given Jakob one for his birthday, an LED torch in which the batteries were alleged to last for ever. Where was it again? Hopefully he hadn't taken it . . .

No, here it was. Beatrice put it in her bag and grabbed her mobile as she left.

Once she was sitting in the car, she remembered that she'd only be able to reach the emergency team at this hour. Which was possibly for the best – her intuition probably didn't hold up to closer inspection.

Nonsense. You're right and you know it. We know everything, and yet we find nothing – the Owner made himself very clear.

But nonetheless, Beatrice wasn't comfortable about going in without any backup. No one would give her an approving pat on the back for playing a lone hand again; quite the opposite, in fact.

It was 1.45 in the morning. She phoned Florin, preparing herself for drowsy disorientation. She let it ring twice, three times, five times, then hung up before the mailbox kicked in.

Never mind. It was better that he got some sleep. She wouldn't put herself in any danger; she would just drive out there to see if she was right. It was entirely possible that her hunch was just a figment of her imagination.

She hadn't even driven 500 metres by the time her phone rang.

'What's happened?'

She almost laughed out loud with relief. Florin sounded wide awake and completely alert.

'Did I wake you?'

'Yes, but it doesn't matter. What's going on?'

'I'm driving out to the Dalamasso coordinates. We found something there – we just didn't realise.'

'What?' She heard him take a deep breath. 'But why now? In the middle of the night?'

'That's the only time it will make sense. Trust me.'

She picked him up fifteen minutes later. He had insisted on coming, and she hadn't protested for very long.

'Morning,' he said as he opened the passenger-side door. He didn't seem to have had enough time to brush his hair or button up his polo shirt, but he did have his gun with him.

'Thanks for calling me back. It feels better if there's two of us.'

'No need to thank me. But it would be even better if there were twenty of us, so we'll phone the base once we've made sure you're right.'

'Okay.' She turned the radio on. Phil Collins was singing 'In the Air Tonight', the song with the best drum intro of all time. Evelyn used to play along to it with her cutlery and plate at every opportunity she got.

Speed limit: 30 km/h. The reflective circular sticker in the middle of the zero was illuminated by Beatrice's torch, a tiny full moon in the darkness.

'A night cache.' Beatrice pointed the beam of light down the road. 'It starts here. If I'm right, we need to find another reflector nearby . . .'

'And then another and another.' Florin turned slowly around on his own axis, holding his torch at head height. 'There!' He pointed towards a tree at the edge of the road, a good fifty metres away. Behind it, a pathway forked off.

'We're not waiting until tomorrow,' said Beatrice as she saw Florin's hesitation. 'It'll be dark for another four or five hours, so maybe we'll be able to find Stage Five before sunrise.'

Without giving an answer, Florin went over to the marked tree. He nodded. 'Call Stefan. If he's awake, he should come join us. I'll report back to base and say we'll check in at hourly intervals.'

Stefan's mobile went straight to the mailbox. 'You're missing something here,' she said in her message. 'Stage Five is a night cache. I'll bet you've never done one of those before, have you?'

They parked the car in a clearly visible spot near the fork in the road, then set off. The path was narrow and zigzagged up the hill past cattle pastures and farms. Beatrice discovered the next reflector on the wall of a wooden barn. 'The owner is marking all the turn-offs,' she realised. 'We have to go right here.'

They followed the trail of shining clues into isolation. The beams of light from their torches danced along the path, intermingling against a grey, brown and green background. They heard the muffled sound of a cowbell nearby. Beatrice couldn't help picturing Nora Papenberg's corpse again, on her stomach in the meadow, the cows alongside her. Was the tinny clang of a cowbell the last sound she had heard in her life?

The path plunged into the even deeper darkness of the forest. A reflective gleam from the knothole of a tree trunk confirmed that they were on the right path. Something scurried past them, disappearing with a rustling sound into the bushes to their left. Birds protested the disturbance at such an unusual hour.

The path wound its way steeply upwards, and Beatrice began to regret not bringing along anything to drink. The gentle sound of a nearby stream could be heard amidst the nocturnal rustle of the leaves, but to find it they would have to fight their way through the undergrowth.

After an hour, they stopped for a rest, and Florin called back to base to report that everything was under control. 'I've only got two bars,' he said with a frown after hanging up. 'How's your mobile reception?'

'Not much better. There aren't very many radio masts out here.'

Nor were there many houses or farms. Beatrice and Florin had passed the last one about twenty minutes before, and since then they hadn't seen any signs of human dwellings. But at least the path was in good condition, albeit not tarmacked, as it had been at the start of their climb.

Before long, they found themselves searching around another fork in the path, and for a few moments Beatrice felt as though she was deep underwater, too deep to ever get back to the surface. They shone their torches into the forest, but the beams only penetrated the first row of trees; behind it, the world was absorbed by darkness. Above them, rustling sounds and the gentle sway of the treetops in the night-time breeze. Beatrice was freezing beneath her light jacket. Where was the next damned reflector? To the right, she hoped, for the path there seemed fairly even. But of course they soon realised they had to go left, where it looked much steeper. She was the one to spot the small shining disc, impaled on a thorny bush.

They spoke only when necessary now, battling their way further into the solitude. Something around them had changed in the course of the last few minutes: the forest had taken on a new form of darkness. It wasn't so dense any more. It was bleaker, sparser. Beatrice pointed her torch at the trees. Stunted, dark trunks, interspersed with young spruces and their vibrant green. Then, the blackness again.

It reminded her of something. Some painful research she had undertaken.

He's mocking his victims. He's mocking us. He wants us to find

Sigart's severed fingers and some witty message about how strange life can be.

Without realising, she had quickened her pace. Her breath came out in gasps and her heart was racing, but she didn't stop. Florin caught up with her. She felt his questioning look and shook her head. First they had to get there. First, certainty.

They almost missed the next reflector. They had just emerged from the forest and it was there, right in front of them, fastened to a flat stone at the edge of the path.

Beatrice was convinced the cache must be hidden beneath it, but she was wrong. The only things they found as they lifted it up were a worm and two beetles, who fled in panic from the beam of light. A loud, snapping sound, like the lashing of a branch against wood, announced that they had probably startled even more wildlife.

'I think the path must go down there.'

'Here? But there's nothing.' The terrain sank down before them, densely overgrown with bushes and hip-high brambles. 'We'd need a machete to get through there.'

'Then we'll have to manage without.' Florin looked at his watch and pulled his mobile out from his trouser pocket. 'Hi, Chris.' He spoke in hushed tones. 'We're okay, we're leaving the path now and heading off into the thicket. In an hour . . . Hello? Can you hear me? Okay, yes, I'll call again in an hour.'

Florin took a tentative step forward into the undergrowth. 'Come on, Bea, we can go through here.' He stepped down a little and took her hand. 'There must have been a path here once.'

A step. Another. A third. They made their way slowly, unbearably slowly, down an overgrown slope, until Beatrice got her foot caught in a tree root. She dropped the torch and grasped around for something to hold onto, feeling a searing pain shoot from her right palm to her elbow as she finally found her grip.

At first she thought it was barbed wire, but it was only stinging nettles. Florin pulled her up, and that was when she saw it.

A shining number five. She pointed towards it in silence, then groped around on the ground for her torch. The number was fixed to a small wooden shed, and seemed to be swinging back and forth.

'Stay behind me.' Was it a gust of wind that had set the '5' in motion, or someone who was lying in wait for them here? Florin pulled out his gun, and they both listened into the night. Wind. The gurgling of the stream. The sounds of birds, more distant than before. And the soft scraping sound which accompanied the movements of the swaying number.

They walked over to it. *Slowly*, thought Beatrice. Yet, unfortunately, not without making a noise. Dry twigs and rustling leaves betrayed their every step.

'It's just the wind,' said Florin, as they reached the wooden shed. A cut-out of the number five was affixed onto a battered tin container, which in turn was dangling from a thin, rusted wire. Beatrice pulled a pair of silicon gloves from her jacket pocket.

Fingers, she thought, like before. *Eyes, toes. What else could fit in a tobacco tin?*

She carefully pulled the looped wire from the wooden ledge it was wrapped around. The wire wouldn't relinquish its grip on the tin itself; it was wound around the entire cylinder and fixed with several layers of thick tape.

'It doesn't look new,' observed Florin.

'No.' Beatrice struggled with the screw cap, twisting several times before it loosened with a grinding sound. Preparing herself for what was to come, she lifted the lid. For the first few moments, she couldn't comprehend what she was looking at in the beam of torchlight.

A pale blue hairband. A one-yen coin. A key. A heart-shaped stone. Beneath all of that, a plastic bag with something orange inside. 'The logbook.' Beatrice pressed her torch into Florin's hand and pulled the small book out of its wrapping.

It was a little damp despite the packaging, but the pages could still be turned without needing to be prised apart.

'It's just a normal cache,' she said, reading through the various thank-yous. 'Why is Stage Five suddenly the odd one out?' She flicked further back. The cache was old; the first entries had been made over six years ago.

Following her instinct, she turned the pages without reading, on and on, until she found the last entry in the logbook.

There it was. The connection they had been searching for all this time, in black and white. Nora Papenberg's handwriting was unmistakable.

12th July
Two hours of hiking in the searing heat and then a hiding place like this! But it was worth it! TFTC, Wishfulthinker28, AlphaMale, GarfieldsLasagne, DescartesHL, ChoristInTheForest.

'On the twelfth of July five years ago, they were all here, all the Owner's victims.' Beatrice spoke in hushed tones, trying to order her thoughts. 'Since then, no one else has found the cache. Except us. Nora Papenberg gave up her hobby afterwards, just like Herbert Liebscher, although he did start up again later. And do you know what, Florin? Neither of them registered having found this cache.' Something must have happened, and it must have been after Nora wrote the note in the logbook. She held it up, 'ChoristInTheForest' – that must be Christoph Beil, no question . . .'

Blackened trees. Destroyed lives. Beatrice went through the signatures. Five stages. Five names.

That's one too few.

She shook her head. Did she know what had happened, or did she just *think* she knew? 12 July: she would have to check the date, but it was possible – no, probable – that it had been the day of the forest fire.

Five deaths. Five names. The joker in the pack.

The words of the logbook entry hammered inside her head as she shone the light towards where the slope began to even out. There was something there, something angular, stony. 'Down there.'

Step by step by step. Beatrice thought she would recognise the place as soon as she was standing before it, but she would have walked straight into it if Florin hadn't pulled her back by the arm.

A foundation built of stone, half in, half outside the forest. In the middle was a cover of sorts, square and made of metal. It was pushed a little to the side, just far enough for someone to be able to put their hand through. From the space beneath, a faint shimmer of light forced its way out, making the opening a pale grey gash in the blackness of the night.

They communicated with a quick glance. It had been a mistake to assume they would only find a cache container. There was someone here, and he must have been listening to them. Florin pulled out his gun.

'We're not going in without backup. Two cars, maybe three. No risk-taking,' he whispered.

They retreated back into the forest, into the darkness between the trees. Mobile reception here was bad, but at least there was some. Beatrice listened to the dialling tone and her own breathing, both of which seemed much louder than usual. 'We've found something, send us some backup. There's a cellar with a light burning, and we have reason to suspect someone's down there, even though we've seen no signs of life yet.'

While she described their location, Beatrice replayed her own words in her mind. *No signs of life.* She remembered the mobile photos of the hacked-off fingers, only half-listening as the base announced that there would be three cars with them in around twenty minutes.

'You know what that cellar is, right?' she whispered after she had ended the call.

'I think so. There are still scorch marks in the forest.'

The moon shone above them, the clear sky saturated with stars. In comparison, the shimmer of light making its way up to the surface from below the ground was hazy and milky. Beatrice didn't take her eyes off it for a second, waiting for it to expand and then darken behind a looming figure. But no one appeared.

The minutes seemed to pass at a painfully slow pace. Everything within Beatrice wanted to creep towards the crack, open it wide and climb down. *If it is the Owner's hiding place, then we'll probably find Sigart there too.*

The thought intensified her impatience. Florin's hand grabbed her wrist, and she realised she had already started to crawl out of the thicket. He pulled her back and laid an arm around her shoulder. 'No going it alone this time.'

'But what if Sigart's down there?'

'Then he'll have to hold on for another five minutes.'

Beatrice fingered the round metal cache tin through her jacket pocket. Its contents shed new light on the events, although she couldn't yet figure out how, not conclusively at any rate. She closed her eyes and counted the minutes. Was that the sound of someone whimpering? The wind carried a quiet, feeble noise towards her – but maybe it was just the sound of the wind itself, a plaintive, restless whisper.

By the time the three police cars were parked on the path, Beatrice was already kneeling down by the cellar opening. She had heard the approaching engine sounds, and from then on had been deaf to Florin's warnings.

Could she hear anything? A voice, breathing?

She laid her ear against the crack, recoiling involuntarily as a puff of air wafted out of the cellar towards her.

All of a sudden, she was back in Evelyn's bedroom with the smell of blood – but here it was mixed with the stench of putrid flesh. Beatrice sat down, took a deep breath and tried to banish the unwelcome images. Images of red.

Shadowy figures armed with lights climbed down the slope. Whispered instructions, hushed voices.

Then Florin was standing next to her. 'Let's go in.'

They were only halfway down the steps before Beatrice cursed herself for having waited so long.

Sigart was lying on the floor, shaking. He was pressing his maimed left hand to his chest, his mouth moving silently.

'Call an ambulance!' Florin shouted to one of their colleagues.

Beatrice knelt down next to Sigart. There was a cut on the side of his neck, but they didn't need to worry too much about that as it seemed to be healing well. She ignored the stench coming from his hunched-up form. And she only half took in the surroundings: the noose hanging from the ceiling, the wooden table she recognised from the Owner's photos, the saws on the wall. She concentrated all her attention on Sigart, touching his forehead gently. He flinched away from her as though she had electrocuted him. Then he lay there, motionless, wheezing and trying to say something.

I have to calm him down. Explain that we'll talk later. But her curiosity was stronger. She leant over to him, tried to breathe evenly and put her ear next to his mouth.

'Please,' he whispered. 'Not . . . another . . . one. Please don't . . .'

Ashamed, Beatrice sat back up. Florin had come over to her side. 'What's he saying?'

'Nothing that can help us. He's pleading with us not to cut another of his fingers off.'

★

When the ambulance arrived, the emergency doctor diagnosed wound inflammation and severe dehydration. 'He probably hasn't had anything to drink for two days now. But if he doesn't get sepsis then he has a good chance of surviving.'

Only once Sigart had been taken away did they pay more attention to the cellar. It was roughly twenty square metres. Around the wooden table were three chairs, and towards the back of the room Beatrice discovered a device which was roughly the size of a laser printer. She only realised its purpose – the wrapping of food products – when she saw the vacuum bags lying next to it. In a corner, half covered by bloody muslin bandages, was a pair of red women's shoes.

Drasche arrived as dawn was breaking. He worked silently, and they left him in peace. He did the same, knowing that they had to get an impression of the place where Liebscher, Beil and Estermann had been killed. On a small stainless-steel bottle which Drasche was in the process of sealing away in his evidence bag, there was a sticker with the letters *HF*. Hydrofluoric acid.

The table's surface was ploughed with notches and covered with red and brown flecks. If Beatrice stood in front of it, a little to the side, the perspective was exactly the one she knew from the picture messages, only without the hand and severed fingers.

The noose on the ceiling brought to mind the strangulation marks on Christoph Beil's neck.

So this was where it had all happened.

Drasche had taken the tobacco tin cache, but the signatures in the logbook were firmly etched in Beatrice's memory: Wishfulthinker28, AlphaMale, GarfieldsLasagne. DescartesHL, ChoristInTheForest.

Five.

The feeling of having stumbled upon a critical gap in her line of thought, the feeling which had crept chillingly up her spine the first time she read the entry, was no longer as intense as it had been initially, but it was still there. It lurked, ready to be summoned, in the recesses of her mind.

At the hospital, they were optimistic. They had treated Sigart's wounds and he was responding well to the antibiotics they had given him. His psychological condition, however, was described as critical, veering from distracted and depressed to completely apathetic. 'You'll have to wait a little longer to speak to him,' explained the doctor.

So Beatrice immersed herself yet again in online research. Stefan had already explained a while back that profiles set up on Geocaching.com couldn't be erased: once you were registered, that was it. And true to his word, the pseudonyms from the cache log were all still there. AlphaMale – such a humble codename could only belong to Estermann. His quota was indeed over 2,000 caches. 2,144, to be precise – not a single unconquered find. In comparison, Christoph Beil's 423 finds seemed downright modest. GarfieldsLasagne – had Dalamasso been witty enough to name herself after a plump cartoon cat and his favourite meal? Her profile showed only twenty-four caches; according to the log entries she had found them all with ChoristInTheForest.

They were a couple, thought Beatrice. Christoph and

Melanie; they must have met at the Mozarteum, after a choir rehearsal perhaps.

A man old enough to be her father, as Carolin Dalamasso had put it. And married, so no wonder Melanie hadn't wanted – or been able – to introduce him to her parents.

She was the last one, the one who had remained unharmed. It was hard to imagine the Owner would give up now, but so far no one had tried to get close to her. Her watchers hadn't reported any unusual events.

'Blood traces from Liebscher, Beil, Sigart and Estermann. And small amounts from Papenberg too. The saws were used to cut up Liebscher's body, and Nora Papenberg's fingerprints were found on the handle. A vacuum-packing machine has been taken off for investigation. The bags match those we found in the caches.' Drasche stood in the conference room, leaning against the back of his chair as if he couldn't carry the weight of his body without help. 'So it's as good as proven that the cellar was the scene of the crimes. You'll have to work the rest out yourselves – all the evidence is there.'

'And you say the Owner imprisoned Sigart in the building his family burnt to death in?' Hoffmann's question was directed at Florin.

'In the cellar of the building. Yes, it looks that way.'

'A particularly perfidious form of sadism?' That, in turn, was addressed to Kossar.

'I'd interpret it like that, yes.' Beatrice noticed, not without a degree of satisfaction, that he had become more cautious since his 'random victim' theory had been proven so grossly inaccurate.

'It would also be supported by the fact that he let Sigart live longer than the others. In his mind, they're all connected with the fire – the five geocachers who passed through the area on the same day, and Sigart, who blamed himself for the deaths of his wife and children, both to himself and to anyone who would listen.'

Hoffmann nodded. 'Then we're dealing with someone who was also affected by the fire, in some way or another.' His gaze slid from one person to the next, skipped Beatrice and stopped at Florin. 'You're working closely with the guys from the fire service, right, Florin?' Without waiting for an answer, he smacked both hands down on the table to signify their dismissal. 'Good. Then the case will soon be closed.'

The first detective to exchange a few words with Sigart was Florin. He managed to catch him at a good moment during a routine visit, and had a five-minute conversation while two doctors sat alongside, ready to usher him out immediately if their patient's condition worsened.

'I asked him about the Owner, but he said he didn't know him. He described him though, as well as he could. The description matched fairly precisely with the one given by the hotel waiter. Bald, a full beard, medium height. Sigart wasn't sure about his eye colour. Blue or green, he thinks. He said he spoke without any regional accent, and the voice was neither particularly high nor deep. He wore gloves the whole time. That's as much as I got in five minutes.'

Florin's disappointment was clear to see. If Sigart had known the man and been able to name him, the case could have been closed very quickly indeed. Hoffmann's ideal scenario.

'If I were a man,' said Beatrice slowly, 'and I wanted to disguise myself without using wigs and false teeth, then I'd grow a beard and shave off my hair. Everyone who sees me would then remember me as a bearded bald guy, even though I'm normally clean-shaven with a full head of hair.'

A smile twitched across Florin's face. 'Hoffmann would be very happy if you grew a beard. "Don't be such a girl, Kaspary."'

They laughed, and it did them good. 'But you're completely right,' Florin continued. 'The description doesn't necessarily help. The Owner isn't making it easy for us.'

She sat on Sigart's bed and waited for him to wake up. He'd been in the hospital for three days now. His condition was stable, according to the doctors. They had allowed Beatrice to pay him a visit, but now he was sleeping, while the IV released one drop of electrolyte solution into his veins per second. The sight nudged something within Beatrice, something like the precursor to a realisation. She waited, but it didn't come.

Sigart stirred. His eyelids fluttered softly before they opened. He turned his head and looked at her, and Beatrice knew that he had recognised her right away.

'It's good to see you alive, Herr Sigart,' she said.

He didn't smile, but looked at her steadfastly.

'Can you speak?'

A shrug of the shoulders, followed by a pain-filled grimace. He cleared his throat. Had the tilting of his head been a nod? Beatrice decided to interpret it as such. 'That's good. I don't want to disturb you for too long, but there are so many things on my mind. I'm sorry we didn't get there soon

374

enough to prevent you from being kidnapped. We came as quickly as we could, but the perpetrator was unbelievably fast.'

Sigart's eyes closed again. His breathing sounded worse; the memory was clearly causing him distress.

'The thing is,' Beatrice continued, 'I'd like to know why you ignored our warnings. We offered you protection, and when you didn't want it we pleaded with you to be careful. Not to open the door to anyone. But the killer still got to you, and there was no sign of forced entry.'

She gave him time to process her question. His eyes were still closed, and after a few seconds he turned his head to the side, away from her.

'That's why we have the theory that you must have known the killer,' she continued. 'And there are a number of additional reasons why I still believe that's the case. But you told Herr Wenninger he was unknown to you.'

He didn't stir. Beatrice felt impatience welling up inside her, and counted silently to five. She gave herself, and him, time. Took a deep breath. Sigart no longer stank of blood, vomit and urine, just of disinfection fluid.

'If you didn't know him, why did you open the door? I just don't understand.'

Had he gone back to sleep, or were her questions too painful for him? Beatrice tried again, as gently as she could, but Sigart was no longer reacting.

The Owner hadn't been in touch since the picture message showing Sigart's severed middle finger. The dog team had searched the woods around the cellar where Sigart was discovered, but hadn't found anything. Drasche had been completely baffled by the prints found in the cellar. 'We found fingerprints from all the victims, but not a single one from the killer. He must have worn gloves the whole time.' That, at least, matched Sigart's statement.

Lost in thought, Beatrice worked through the Owner's text messages once more, reading one after the other.

Slow.

Cold, completely cold.

Was his sudden silence connected to Dalamasso? Was he frustrated that he couldn't get close to her?

No, she thought. *He could have got to Melanie before we solved the puzzle that led us to her. Like he did with Estermann.*

Melanie. Beatrice had saved her mother's number in her mobile. She'd have to act fast, otherwise she'd lose her nerve.

'Dalamasso.'

'Good evening, this is Beatrice Kaspary from the LKA.'

A deep sigh. 'Yes?' Just one syllable, filled with contempt. But at least the woman hadn't hung up.

'I'd like to apologise for my behaviour. It was unacceptable. How is Melanie?'

'She's . . . she's doing a little better. But she's still trying to self-harm, and is hardly sleeping at all, except with the help of strong sedatives.'

'I'm very sorry.'

No answer this time.

'Did you want anything else?' asked Carolin Dalamasso eventually. Curt, icy, clearly hoping that she didn't.

'Yes, to be honest. I'd like to ask you something.' She took the silence at the other end of the line as consent. 'Did Melanie used to react to things that extremely? Were there any events or triggers that upset her as much as those photos?'

She was expecting a dismissive answer, or none at all, but she was wrong.

'Children.'

'Sorry?'

'She had strong reactions to children a few times, particularly loud ones. But only in the first year after her breakdown, and then it seemed to pass.' Carolin Dalamasso sighed. 'When she was at school, there were some children who bullied her a lot. The doctors think these memories might have been triggered by the sight of children.'

'I understand.' *Yes, I really believe I do, but not in the way you think.* 'Thank you, Frau Dalamasso. I wish Melanie all the best. My colleagues will continue to look out for her.'

'I know. Are we finished now?'

'Yes. Thank you again. Goodby—' The rest of the word was swallowed by the beeping of the disconnect tone. Carolin Dalamasso had hung up.

The suspicion which Beatrice carried around with her that evening and the whole of the next day was much too vague to be uttered out loud to the others. When Florin questioned her on how quiet she was, she fobbed him off with an answer as brief as it was nondescript, and after that he left her alone with her thoughts.

Several times, Beatrice caught herself sitting and staring at the surface of her desk. To any onlooker, it must have seemed as though she wasn't doing a thing, but inside her mind the kaleidoscope was turning incessantly, equipped with a few new fragments.

Drasche's surprise about the fingerprints. The Owner's silence. An IV needle.

The varying difficulty levels of the puzzles. And what was the point of them anyway?

Then the references to Evelyn, which she should have understood a lot sooner.

'Coffee?' Florin was standing next to the espresso machine, holding up two cups.

She stopped herself from snapping at him for interrupting her train of thought. 'Yes, please. Strong.'

He pressed the buttons. 'When are you going to tell me what's going on in your head?'

'When I'm sure it's not just nonsense.'

'Okay.' It was clear he wasn't content with the answer. 'But I'd really prefer it if we could all discuss new approaches as a team. Or at least between the two of us.'

'We will. When I'm ready.' He would just have to be annoyed at her. Some threads of thought are so delicate that they tear and blow away if you try to put them into words. 'Give me another few hours.' In her mind's eye, she saw the needle stuck into Sigart's vein. It seemed inconceivable. *If you're that fond of him, I'll keep him for you until the end.*

The end, thought Beatrice, *can't be that far away now.*

She left the office earlier than usual; Florin's probing looks were too off-putting. The feeling that her thoughts were going round in circles evaporated as soon as she stepped out into the fresh air.

The children were spending the evening at Mooserhof again; Achim had to take a client out for dinner. In those circumstances, of course, handing over the children was completely fine. Everything was always fine if he did it. But at least he had taken them to her mother's, where they would be content.

When she arrived at the restaurant, Jakob clung to her like a monkey on a tree. 'I want to go home,' he mumbled. 'Are you taking us with you tonight?'

Soon. Next week. Tomorrow. She pulled him close and buried her face in his hair. 'We're almost finished. Listen – either we catch the guy in the next three days, or I'll tell Florin that he has to keep looking by himself. Then I'll just do a few smaller things and I'll even be able to pick you up from school every day too.'

'Honest?'

'I promise.' The thought of giving up the case she had been so intensely involved in from the start made a painful hole in her pride. But it had already had too much of an impact on the children.

'Cool!' Jakob jumped down to go and tell his Oma the happy news.

Beatrice hugged Mina. 'I'm so looking forward to having you both back with me,' she said, feeling Mina nod against her chest.

They spent the evening eating and playing cards in the restaurant. Beatrice tried very hard to lose at Mau-Mau, and ate fried beef and onions in gravy, realising with surprise that she was incredibly hungry. Richard served her a taster dessert plate, of which she didn't leave a single crumb.

'Three days?' Jakob checked, as she put him to bed.

'Three days and not one more.'

On the way home, she tried with all her might to convince herself that she wouldn't mind taking a step back. Stefan could take over her tasks and pass his own to Bechner. *And then I'll do Bechner's stuff*, she thought. *All those menial tasks I give him*.

Before she had a chance to smile at the thought, her mobile rang.

'Sigart has disappeared.' Florin sounded fraught. 'The hospital has already been searched. Theoretically it's still possible that he just pulled the IV line out and decided to go for a walk, but no one has seen him for two hours.'

The information sank in Beatrice's stomach like a stone. The kaleidoscope turned yet again. 'Okay, I'm near Theodebertstrasse right now, so I'll drive past his flat and see if there's a light on.'

'Okay. Keep me posted.'

Beatrice looked at the clock. It was just before 10 p.m. She could park the car opposite the postal depot and walk across to Theodebertstrasse on foot.

At number thirty-three, it was dark behind the windows of the first floor. She stopped in front of the entrance and thought of the blood they had found here last time. AB negative, rare and precious. Her thoughts raced on. Blood transfusions. IV needles.

A car drove past, and for a few seconds the headlights blinded her, making her feel strangely vulnerable. Then the beam of light fell on something else.

A red Honda Civic, parked diagonally opposite.

It wasn't a rare model of car by any means. But it was an interesting coincidence nonetheless. Beatrice quickly crossed the street and could already feel the disappointment bearing down on her shoulders as she approached. It couldn't be Nora's car; it had Hungarian number plates. But just to make sure she wasn't overlooking anything, Beatrice leant down to peer into the passenger-side window. The hazy street lighting fell on two empty, crumpled-up water bottles, a newspaper and a leather bag.

She squinted, trying to see more clearly. So perhaps it was Nora's car after all. It wasn't yet hard proof, of course, she would need to break into the car and—

'How convenient. I was just on my way to you.'

She didn't get a chance to turn around towards the voice. A blow to her neck, a sharp, burning pain, and the world disappeared into a racing vortex, a whirlpool tugging her away into nothingness.

Blows all over her body. Her legs, her back, her behind. As if through thick cotton wool. Everywhere but her head. Then emptiness again.

Come up for air. Time has vanished. Open eyes . . . can't. Darkness. Drifting in and out of consciousness.

Her breathing was slow and heavy. It was the first thing she became aware of, and it filled her with a vague sensation of gratitude at still being alive. She tried to grasp what had happened, wanting to remember, but the thoughts slipped out of her mind like wet soap through her fingers.

At least her body was obeying her. She flexed her toes, coughed. She wanted to hold her head, but her hands wouldn't move. Beatrice opened her eyes.

She knew this place. But where from? She didn't like it, but she knew she had been here before. With . . . a man. Not her ex-husband, another man – Florin.

As if his name had been the password to her memory, everything rushed back to her, not neatly ordered, but in a torrent. She swallowed, with difficulty, and deliberately ignored the ridged, filthy wood of the table in front of her. Once again, she tried to move her hands away from her body.

A dull pain shot through her; she still couldn't do it. *I'm tied up*, she thought, picturing the woman in the cow pasture in her mind, the cable tie around her wrists. She just couldn't remember the woman's name. Everything was blurry and out of focus, as if she was floating through murky water. But she was sitting down. On a chair, and her hands were . . . behind her.

Nora Papenberg, she finally remembered. That was her name.

She closed her eyes, trying to find her way back into her mind. But now the pain was breaking out of the thickly insulated room it had been lurking in. It bit hard into her back. Into her hips. Her wrists. Beatrice tensed her shoulder muscles. It was bearable, just about. A small price to pay for a clear head. She listened.

Someone was here. Quiet footsteps in the background, a rustling sound. If she twisted her upper body just a little, she would be able to see him. But it was too soon for that; she had to get a grip of herself first. If he gave her enough time, that was.

'Good evening,' said a voice behind her. Quiet and polite. So she had been right.

'Good evening, Herr Sigart.' She waited for him to come over and sit opposite her at the table, but he didn't move. No footsteps on the stone floor.

She tried to remember what was behind her. The noose hanging from the ceiling. Nora Papenberg's shoes, as red as the picture in Florin's atelier, as red as the blood on Evelyn's bedroom floor. Dried bandaging fabric in crusted waves.

No, of course not. The forensics team had taken all that with them.

The saws were gone now too, but Drasche had left the table and chairs, still speckled in places with forensic powder.

On the floor, at the foot of the steps, there was something new: the doctor's bag Beatrice had seen on the passenger seat of the Honda Civic.

'How are you feeling?' Sigart asked the question as if he was a surgeon who had just operated on her.

Beatrice decided to play along. She just had to break free from her ties, then she would have an advantage over him. He was weakened; there was no way he could use his left hand.

'I'm relatively okay,' she answered. 'Still a little blurry in the head. And my hips feel bruised.'

'Yes, unfortunately that couldn't be avoided.' Finally, Sigart stepped aside, far enough for her to be able to see him. He was still pale, but he seemed taller than he had before. His left hand was bandaged, the dressing stretching all the way to his elbow. 'I wasn't able to carry you, so I had to drag you. I'm afraid that gave you a few bruises.'

'I see.' Was he still on painkillers? Probably. 'You're clearly doing much better than before. When I saw you in the hospital, I thought—' *I thought what I was supposed to think.* Beatrice left the sentence unfinished.

Sigart walked all the way around the table, then sat down. In his right, healthy hand, he was holding a gun, which he now laid on the scratched table, the barrel pointing at Beatrice. 'I'm pleased that we finally get to talk alone.'

The dull, cotton-wool-like sensation in her head still hadn't completely disappeared. What did Sigart want from her?

I'm his audience, as Kossar had put it. Hopefully he had been right on that point at least.

'You probably want to hear that I'm surprised,' she said. 'But I'm afraid I'll have to disappoint you there.' She held his gaze, even though fear was now stretching its cold feelers out towards her throat. Whatever narcotic Sigart had injected her with, it was losing its effect.

He cocked his head to the side. 'How long have you known?'

'Since I went to see you in the hospital. With all the blood you lost, we expected you to be on the brink of death. I might have thought of it sooner if you were a doctor, but you're a vet.' She saw a smile creep across his face. 'But of course you still know how to take blood, how to store it, and how much there had to be to make us draw the right conclusions. Or, rather, the wrong ones. What did you use to create the drag marks in the stairwell? A sandbag?'

'Something like that.'

'From the very first time we met you, you were always so pale. But in the hospital, you looked healthier – and it was because you had more blood in your veins than in the previous weeks. The spray pattern on the walls – did you compress the bag of blood and then punch a hole in it?'

'Precisely. Bravo, Beatrice.'

Something in the tone of his voice unsettled her, but she carried on regardless. 'You also know how to carry out a local anaesthetic – probably better than any hospital surgeon, who always has an anaesthetist on standby for that. But I still don't know how you managed to cut your own fingers off.'

He lifted the bandaged hand off the table a little and put it back down again carefully. 'By imagining this moment, right here and now. Tell me what else you worked out, Beatrice.'

She thought for a moment. 'That you know about Evelyn and think we have something in common. Guilt as a result of bad decisions. Where did you get your information from?'

'You have quite a talkative brother. I'm sure you don't know this, but my wife and I used to eat at Mooserhof quite frequently. We both read about Evelyn Rieger's murder, and knew from your brother that you were friends with her. Every time I asked about you, he quite willingly opened his heart to me. You were still in Vienna then, trying to get back on your feet, but your brother was convinced you wouldn't manage. My wife and I had many conversations about guilt back then.' He shifted his gaze to the two remaining fingers on his left hand. 'At the time, I was of the opinion that the only person to carry guilt is the one who intentionally harms someone. Miriam disagreed. She said that guilt never falls on just one person alone.'

Beatrice could see that he was withdrawing into himself, hearing his wife's voice in his mind as if she were right next to him.

'After her death, I knew she was right. I was immensely guilty. My wrong decisions, my skewed priorities. You know the feeling, don't you, Beatrice? That's why I put my case in your hands.'

'What do you mean?'

'I made sure you would be on duty when Nora Papenberg was found. That granted her an extra day of life.'

A day of fear and despair, of futile hope. She hoped he would give her an extra day, too. 'Keep me posted,' Florin had said. When would he expect to hear from her? After an hour? Two? Maybe even sooner? He was probably already pulling out all the stops to find her.

She shifted her weight, trying to feel whether her mobile was still in her jacket pocket. If it was, her colleagues would be able to find out her location.

But she couldn't feel anything. Perhaps it had fallen out when Sigart had dragged her down the steps, or outside, in the forest. That would be just as good – no, even better, as he would have no chance of finding it . . .

Then she saw it. On a pile of bricks that someone must have left in the corner of the cellar. It lay alongside Nora Papenberg's Nokia, and next to it, like small, rectangular playing pieces from a board game, were the batteries.

Sigart followed her gaze. 'Yes, unfortunately you are un-contactable,' he said. 'But you still managed to send your colleague a text from Theodebertstrasse. "Driving home now, I'm shattered. See you tomorrow." That should have won us a little time.'

She wanted to scream, not knowing whether it was out of rage, panic, or just to lose herself in her own cries. Instead, she bit down on her lower lip until it hurt. *Driving home now, I'm shattered.* But no word as to whether she had found Sigart. Maybe that would have made Florin wonder. If so, he would have tried to call her back, only getting the mailbox. Was *shattered* enough to make him leave it? Or would he persevere, maybe drive to her place just to be sure?

She didn't know.

'Nonetheless,' Sigart continued, 'we don't have all the time in the world. I asked you what you've understood of what's happened, but you haven't yet given me your answer. I need you to concentrate.' He picked up the gun in his right hand, almost playfully. The mouth pointed at the wall, then at Beatrice, lingering briefly, then gliding to the side. After a few moments, Sigart put the weapon back on the table, frowning as if he wasn't sure quite what he was doing.

'You lost your family in a forest fire,' Beatrice began hastily. 'That was here. We're in the cellar of the building you rented.'

He nodded. 'Correct.'

'You got called away by a client, and that's why you hold yourself responsible for what happened – but not just yourself.'

'Another point.' With the two remaining digits of his left hand, he traced the line of a long cut in the wooden table. 'To start with, admittedly, it was different. Back then I thought I was the only guilty one, just me alone – but then . . . what happened then, Beatrice?'

She remembered the tobacco tin. *TFTC.*

'Then you stumbled upon the cache and found out that five people must have been here on the day of the fire.'

'Not just that. Think, Beatrice, you know everything. Draw the correct conclusion. Don't disappoint me.'

She thought. Struggled to swallow. 'And . . . there was a key in the cache. It was . . . the key to the cabin?'

'Yes. Which had been used to lock it. From the outside, as I now know.'

Against her better judgement, Beatrice struggled to accept the conclusion that logically followed. 'But they were just geocaching! Didn't you read the entry? What makes you think it was those five who locked the cabin? What would they have gained from doing that?'

'We'll get to that in a moment. But for now let's just leave it as this — it was them.' He took a breath, short and sharp. He tentatively touched his bandages, checking the amputation wounds. 'I asked myself the same thing at first, of course I did. Was it just a coincidence? Was there really a connection? After all, I didn't want to make any mistakes. So I looked at the accounts on Geocaching.com, one nickname after the other. Once you're registered on there, you can't delete the account, did you know that?'

'So did one of them log the discovery of the tin and write something incriminating?'

Sigart shook his head. 'No. But they all deleted the information from their profiles. Only DescartesHL remained active. From the remaining four, there wasn't a single entry after that day in July. So I knew they had to have had something to do with the fire. And when I spoke to them they all confirmed it, here at this very table.' Sigart suddenly closed his eyes, as if he was in pain. 'Please excuse me for a moment.' He took a small bottle of serum from his medical bag, drew some up into a syringe and injected it into his left arm. 'The last few days have been rather painful, as I'm sure you can imagine.'

She watched him, every one of his practised movements. Her mouth was bone dry, and she wanted to ask him for something to drink, but she knew he wouldn't take too kindly to his carefully staged finale being interrupted to fetch water from the well. And there didn't seem to be any down here in the cellar.

'Why did you bring me here?' she asked quietly, once he had put his utensils back in the bag. 'Are you planning to kill me too?'

He didn't say no, but instead tilted his head thoughtfully. Regretfully, almost. Beatrice's blood ran cold. 'You're going to kill me?'

'Calm down. You have a chance of getting away alive. Not a particularly big one, admittedly, but it exists. Are your colleagues on the ball? Are they bright? Then you don't need to worry.' He smiled. 'First and foremost, you're here so I can thank you. Thanks for the hunt, Beatrice. Thank you very much indeed.'

'You're the first person to ever thank us for hunting them.'

That seemed to amuse Sigart. 'You still don't get it, do you?' He leant over, as if he wanted to confide something in her that no one else was supposed to hear. 'You didn't hunt me.' He looked at her, his gaze full of expectation.

Was this a new game? 'We were hunting the man who killed Nora Papenberg, Herbert Liebscher, Christoph Beil and Rudolf Estermann,' she said. 'Presumably, Melanie Dalamasso was supposed to be his last victim. And it certainly seems like you are this man. The Owner.'

'That's what you call me? How sweet. And yet so ironic, for I own hardly anything now.' He propped his elbows on the table, about to put his fingertips together into a steeple when he suddenly seemed to realise it was no longer possible. 'I thought you would call me Shinigami. I was very particular about my selection of nickname, but then you can't control everything.' He sighed, yet this time it had a contented tone to it. 'You weren't hunting me. Think about it, Beatrice

– you know everything you need to figure it out. So, I found the cache and was on the brink of finding out who was guilty for the death of my children, right? I found out the most important details.'

'Yes. The names.'

'Correct.' He smiled at her, like a teacher who knew his best pupil could do better. He was eagerly awaiting what she was about to say.

And all of a sudden, Beatrice realised what had happened, what Sigart had been thanking them for all this time. The realisation lay in front of her like a steep precipice she was slipping helplessly towards.

The cable tie cut deeply into the skin of her wrists, but she still wrenched against it. It refused to give by even a millimetre.

'Please don't.' Sigart lifted his claw-like left hand. It was probably intended to be a calming gesture. But only when the pain became really bad, the unrelenting material chafing away at her skin, only then did Beatrice give up her futile attempt at freeing herself.

Sigart responded with a contented nod. 'I knew you wouldn't take it very well.'

'We played right into your hands,' whispered Beatrice. 'You had the names, but not the real ones. Only pseudonyms, and you couldn't do anything with those.'

He didn't say a word, but his eyes demanded that she keep talking.

'We solved the puzzles for you, from the few little details you knew about the five. We found out their true identities so you could kill them. You . . . you used the results of our investigations for your own revenge. You followed us, didn't you? And that's how you knew who we were questioning.'

His face spoke volumes. She had hit the bull's eye. *But what else could we have done? Not work on the case? Not look for the people in the puzzles?*

She thought for a moment, her mind still foggy, then remembered her previous discovery. 'But you found one of the cachers without any help – Herbert Liebscher. He was stupid enough not to leave the caching scene and you contacted him.'

'Yes, by email, via his geocaching account. Descartes, what a joke. I told him I was a new member and that I wanted to do my first outing with an old hand. I said we were both from Salzburg and that his nickname suggested he was an intelligent guy. He took the bait right away.'

And you took your time, lulled him into a false sense of security . . . for the duration of seven whole caches.

'Did you knock him out to bring him here? Or drug him with something?'

'The latter, like I did with you. I wanted his head to be unharmed, I wanted all of his memories from the twelfth of July, all the names.'

The kaleidoscope had come to a halt; the picture was now clear. 'But there was a problem with that. He didn't know the others.' Beatrice groped around for ideas. 'He only knew – Nora Papenberg.'

Sigart's eyes reflected genuine admiration. 'Bravo. That's exactly how it was. The two of them had arranged at some caching meet-up to go on this trip together. It was quite a trek, and they didn't even find the cache. They were already halfway back when the other three turned up, GPS device in hand. So they all returned together. There wasn't much time to chat, and people hardly ever remember names the first time they hear them.'

But Liebscher had known Papenberg, at least by her maiden name, and maybe he also knew the name of the ad agency where she worked. He had told Sigart, filled with fear, probably screaming in pain . . . and then Sigart had gone to fetch Nora. Used some ruse to call the agency, find out her current surname and maybe even her mobile number. None of that was too difficult; if he had trodden carefully it would probably have taken just twenty minutes.

The photos from the agency meal were still clear in her memory. Nora's shocked face as the past came back to haunt her.

'What did you say to her, that night on the phone?'

'That Herbert Liebscher had told me what had happened on the twelfth of July five years ago. That I knew what role she had played in the whole thing. That I would keep quiet if she gave me ten thousand euros, a very modest sum for being able to keep everything hidden. If not, I said I would have no qualms about sending the evidence to her husband and boss — and to the police too, of course.'

'What did she say?'

'She tried to placate me. She said she didn't have ten thousand euros, that she didn't believe there was any evidence because she hadn't done anything. We arranged a place to meet, and she came.' He shrugged. 'She was terrified of losing everything she had worked so hard for. I told her I could understand that, and that the loss would be a hundred times worse than she could ever imagine. Once she was unconscious, I took her car and brought her here.'

Just like that. Beatrice inhaled deeply and felt a stabbing pain in the muscles of her right shoulder.

'Was this a prison for your victims?' she asked. 'The whole time, when you were in your flat or with your therapist?'

'I couldn't have found a better one. The stone walls swallow up every scream, every cry for help. And even if they didn't – hardly anyone ever comes out here. There used to be two farms, just a few hundred metres away.'

'Which also burnt down that night.' Beatrice remembered having read it in the report. No victims, but immense damage to the properties.

'Nora,' she continued. 'The puzzles we found were written in her handwriting.'

Sigart shrugged. 'She was an ad woman. I liked the way she phrased things. You could almost feel the mystery behind the words. She also knew the most about the other three – women pay much more attention to these things than men do. For two days, the three of us had an intense brainstorming session. Liebscher wasn't much use, except as a means of exerting pressure on Nora.'

She swallowed. 'Is that why you cut his ear off?'

'It certainly sped things up. After that, she suddenly remembered the birthmark and the Schubert Mass. It turns out people do share the odd detail about their lives when they spend an hour hiking together.'

The birthmark. A piece of recently studied choral music. A casual comment about an unfulfilling job, children's names.

Beatrice went through the letters in her mind, including the one about Sigart. *A loser.*

'You made it very easy for us to find you.'

'Why waste time? I was eager to meet you, Beatrice. And you gave me something even at our first meeting, by asking me if I knew Christoph Beil. I had already followed you when you went to his house to question him. The next morning, I walked up and down his street, waiting for him to come out, and then asked him for directions. But I couldn't see a birthmark. I was unsure, but then when you mentioned the name I knew you would have checked everything and that he was the one. So that enabled me to identify the third person.'

We did his work for him. Looked for the victims. Although . . .

'What about Estermann? We didn't find him, the clues weren't specific enough – no, wait. Of course. Beil knew him.'

Sigart's gaze wandered over to the hook that the noose had been hung on. 'Christoph Beil filled in most of the blanks that Papenberg and Liebscher left open. He was loosely acquainted with Estermann – they had chatted over a beer at a couple of caching events. They spoke on the phone after you questioned Beil, so to a certain extent Estermann had been warned. But just about the police, not about me.' Lost in thought, Sigart began to tug at his bandage. 'At the very end, Beil told me a great deal about everything that happened.'

'You tried to hang him, didn't you?'

'I hauled him up there, but then brought him down again. I was never the sadistic type and it wasn't enjoyable for me, in case you think that.'

'Where did the graze wounds on his thighs come from?'

Sigart leant back in his chair. He stroked the barrel of the gun over the scarred flesh on his left forearm. 'He claimed never to have seen the key. So I introduced them to one another.' He inserted a strange little pause, as if he was trying to work out whether a laugh would be appropriate at this point. 'He loved his wife a great deal, did you know that? Loved her and betrayed her, but there's no need to tell her that.'

She didn't know what he was getting at. He loved his wife? 'Is that why you killed him with a stab to the heart? Did you give all your victims a symbolic end like that?'

'After a fashion.'

All of a sudden, the unwelcome memory of Estermann's corpse leapt back into her mind, and Beatrice wondered whether he had been sitting in the same chair as her when the acid was trickled into his eye.

'So why the acid with Estermann?' she asked softly.

Had Sigart not heard her? He was staring past her, at the floor, his expression numb.

'Because I wanted him to burn,' he said eventually. 'From the inside out. And he did.'

The key figure. 'Was he the one who locked the cabin?'

Sigart didn't answer. Judging by the look on his face, Estermann was dying again right now in his mind's eye.

'What about Melanie Dalamasso?' Maybe this name would make him carry on talking. 'She's severely ill, and you know that. A torn woman. What would you have done with her – cut her up into pieces?'

Wherever he had been in his thoughts, the last few words brought Sigart back to the present. 'I'm the only one I tore to pieces.' He raised his mutilated hand. 'I wouldn't have killed Melanie Dalamasso. I wouldn't have touched even a hair on her head.'

'Because she had already been punished enough by her illness?'

'Wrong.' He sighed. 'Don't do that, Beatrice. No half-baked theories. Stay on safe ground.'

Was he losing patience? That would be bad. She needed time; the conversation could be made to last all night if she played it right. Her mind grasped for the first scraps of certainty it could find. 'Nora Papenberg had traces of Herbert Liebscher's blood on her person. So you forced her to kill him? And then to . . .' Her gaze twitched over to the place where the saws had been just a few days ago.

'Correct.' Sigart's healthy hand played with the gun, turning it round and round on the table, always anticlockwise. 'Tell me why,' he demanded.

'So that we came to the wrong conclusions. It gave you more time.'

'That was certainly a welcome bonus.'

Beatrice was struggling to drag her gaze away from the gun. The thought that he could wound her or kill her if she gave the wrong answer suddenly didn't seem so far-fetched any more. It was in his eyes. Vengeance for his family might include killing her, even though she didn't understand why.

'It's all connected to guilt,' she said carefully. 'I just don't know what Nora did to make her so guilty that you would do that to her.' The tattoos on the soles of the woman's feet came to her mind, the first coordinates that Sigart had left

397

for them. And on such a sensitive spot; every step must have been incredibly painful.

Every step.

Beatrice looked up. No half-baked guesses, Sigart had said. But she risked it.

'Nora ran away, that day. She could have fetched help or taken the key and opened the cabin, but she ran off.'

A muscle twitched in Sigart's face. 'Not bad. And why did I leave Liebscher to her?'

She tried to think, but none of her ideas seemed even the slightest bit logical. 'I don't know,' she whispered.

Sigart leant over the table, gripping the gun tightly in his right hand. 'She wasn't very decisive. She wasn't the kind of person who acts when it's necessary. So I gave her something to do and left the decision to her. No, two decisions – gun or knife. Him or her.' He leant back again. 'In the end she chose *him* and *gun*. Nora Papenberg's personal choice.'

He stretched, a little awkwardly, as if he had cramp. 'It's time for us to go up now.'

That was a surprise. And an unexpected opportunity – he would have to untie her hands for that. As soon as her circulation was flowing again, she would have an advantage over him, at least enough for her to flee.

'Please don't get your hopes up.' The mouth of the gun wandered to the right again, until it was pointing at Beatrice's chest. 'I have a very precise plan for how this will play out. If you try to deprive me of it by running away or putting up a fight, I'll shoot you on the spot. Reluctantly, but I'll do it.' He pushed back his chair and stood up. He looked taller than ever. 'If you do force me to do so, you won't be the only one to die. I went back to Mooserhof recently, and Mina brought my coffee. She's a pretty little girl. And she's already starting to know it. From all the toys I brought with me, the only thing she wanted was Hanna's mirror.'

Beatrice gasped for air. The memory rushed back. *Mina got a really pretty mirror with sparkly flowers around the edge.*

'And you gave Jakob a little globe.' Was that her voice, that hoarse rasp coming from deep inside her throat? Beatrice struggled against the sensation of falling into an abyss, saw Mina and Jakob in front of her, sleeping in the loft, the loft which was entirely made of wood . . .

'I thought that since your children and mine might have to share the same fate, then they might as well share a few toys too.' Sigart looked at her searchingly. Was he waiting for a reaction? If her hands had been free, she would have attacked him right there on the spot.

'That's not what I want, of course,' he continued in a friendly tone. 'I just want to make sure you cooperate. If you do, then nothing will happen to your children, I promise. If not, everything is already prepared for my Plan B. I think it's only fair that you know that.'

It took some time before the black flood of panic in Beatrice's mind began to ebb away, leaving her able to think clearly again. She would have to wait until there was a fail-proof chance of overpowering him. 'Okay. I'll do what you ask.'

'Until the end?'

What end? she wanted to ask. *Mine? Yours?*

But she swallowed all her questions and took a deep breath.

So deep it was as if she was scared it might be her last. 'Yes. Until the end.'

He cut through the cable tie with the help of a Stanley knife, a task which took some time as he only had the two remaining digits on his left hand to work with. In his right hand, he was holding the gun against her head. Beatrice felt the steel pressing against a spot behind her ear. She didn't move, taking shallow breaths and fully expecting the knife to slip and plunge into her palm, but he worked slowly and carefully until her hands were freed. The cable tie clung to the wounds on her right wrist. Beatrice pulled it off carefully, having to make several attempts as her fingers were completely numb.

Sigart stepped to the side, withdrawing the gun from her head. 'Tell me when you can grip things properly again,' he said, 'because you'll be responsible for the torch.'

'Okay.' Beatrice bent and stretched her fingers, sensation gradually returning amidst stabbing pain. She massaged one hand with the other and avoided looking at her raw, grazed wrists, concentrating instead on Sigart and his weapon. *If I quickly duck away, push him over or pick up the table and throw it at him . . .*

It was too risky. She wouldn't be able to take him by surprise. The concentration with which his gaze was fixed on her didn't falter for even a second.

Once her fingers felt as though they almost belonged to her body again, Beatrice nodded at Sigart. 'I'm okay now.'

'Good. If you turn around, you'll see a woollen blanket in the corner, and a torch on top of it. Take the torch and go up the steps ahead of me.'

It was an LED torch with black aluminium casing. It wasn't heavy and hardly qualified as a weapon. *But what if I blind him with the light?*

They were just wild thoughts. She wouldn't do anything unless she could be sure she would succeed in incapacitating him.

Holding the torch in one hand, she used the other to open the hatch door. Cool night air rushed towards her.

Turn the light off and run. But she dismissed that thought immediately, too. She wouldn't have a chance on this terrain in the darkness; she wouldn't be able to orientate herself, while Sigart knew every tree and every stone.

'It's hard to believe, isn't it?' she heard him say behind her. 'So much open space all around, and yet it's still a prison.'

She knew he didn't just mean for her. 'What happens now?' she asked. The beam of the torch moved across tree trunks and bushes, searching for the path from which help would come. If it came.

'Now let's fill in the gaps in your knowledge. Do you remember where you found the cache? The tin with the shining five on it?'

'Yes.' She pointed the torch at the wooden shed. Unlike last time, today it was open. Inside it lay something low, something stony.

'The cache was originally hidden there. In the well, you see? The tin had wire wrapped around it and had been lowered almost two metres deep into the well. That's why it wasn't destroyed by the fire.' Sigart came over to stand next to Beatrice, but not near enough for her to be able to surprise and overpower him. 'On the twelfth of July, Nora

Papenberg, Herbert Liebscher, Christoph Beil, Melanie Dalamasso and Rudolf Estermann were here shortly before six in the evening. It was a hot day, and the weeks leading up to it had been very warm. All five of them were tired, but in good spirits and intent on finding the cache. Nora showed them all the nooks and crannies and trees they had already searched in vain, including the shed surrounding the well, which was the first thing to catch the eye. But only now, together, did they find the cache hidden down it on the wire. They all laughed, happy to have finally found it. Dalamasso took out some snacks and shared apples and pretzels with the others. We're on safe ground so far, for all their stories are unanimous up to this point. Now, shine the torch a little further to the left.'

She did what he said, but there was nothing there except dense shrubbery, raspberry bushes, twines and the stinging nettles she had already made her acquaintance with.

'From now on their accounts differ a little, but the main point is that someone had a full hip flask with them. Beil said it was Estermann, while Estermann said it was Beil. The only thing they agreed on was the contents: pear schnapps. They sat right where you're pointing the torch, Beatrice. Except back then there was a meadow, with bluebells, marguerites and wild dianthus. Then Lukas came running out of the forest.'

'Your son.'

'Yes. Beil said he had a bow and arrow with him, and that he was covered in dirt. They chatted with him for a bit, apparently. He told them he was on holiday here, that his parents had just argued and that's why he wanted to go hunting in the forest instead. Then Estermann offered him a sip from his hip flask.'

Sigart's voice had become quieter now, then he cleared his throat and continued in a normal tone. 'Estermann said it was Beil, of course. The others may not have noticed, because they were sitting some distance away, although Papenberg said she remembered the conversation between Lukas and the two men getting a little loud. In the end, he drank some and then ran back to the cabin.'

Beatrice pictured Jakob in Lukas's place, then hastily shook away the image.

'Miriam, my wife – she was a wonderful woman. But when she got angry she was so unpredictable. I had already annoyed her a lot that day, and then Lukas came in the door and told her some man had just given him alcohol . . . so you can imagine how she reacted. Papenberg described what happened next very precisely: she said Miriam came storming out of the cabin, shouted at Estermann, grabbed the flask from his hand and emptied the contents onto the grass.'

Had Sigart's attention waned? He seemed to be lost in his thoughts, in the images that his story was summoning up, but at the same time he reacted immediately to every one of Beatrice's movements, and still had the gun pointed at her. She decided to wait.

'Estermann didn't take Miriam's outburst very well. He screamed back at her, saying that she'd stolen his property and would have to replace it. Fifty euros and they could call it quits. Miriam said the only thing he would get from her was a report to the police for bodily harm, for giving alcohol to a child.'

All Beatrice could see in the beam of the torchlight were the thin, swaying branches of a young spruce, but the scene was almost tangible. *He isn't a nice man*, Graciella Estermann had said.

'Threatening him with the police was Miriam's big mistake,' Sigart continued. 'She went back into the cabin and he jumped up and followed her. The others may have tried to placate him. Beil and Liebscher both told me they tried to hold him back, but apparently Estermann just shoved them aside. He ripped the door open, turned the cabin upside down, and only came out once he had found Miriam's mobile. "You're not reporting anyone," he said, smashing the phone up with a rock. That was something else that everyone remembered very clearly.'

Almost without realising, and without prompting any protest from Sigart, Beatrice had turned around, pointing the torch at the place where the cabin used to be.

'By now the children were crying, all three of them. While Christoph Beil, the only one who knew Estermann a little, tried to calm him down, Melanie Dalamasso spoke to Hanna and Lukas, trying to sing them a song, but she was shaking all over. Miriam was busy with Oskar, who was screaming his head off. Liebscher and Papenberg kept their distance – could you please shine the light to the left? A little more? That's it, thank you. Round about there.'

On the spot indicated by Sigart, a raspberry bush and mulberry bush were fighting for supremacy.

'Papenberg just wanted to get away. She thought the "arsehole in the checked shirt", as she called Estermann, was repulsive and the situation made her feel sick. Liebscher agreed with her, but said they should make sure the woman from the cabin wouldn't report them. He was a teacher, and his principal didn't take any nonsense when it came to disciplinary actions. He hit a sore spot with Nora by saying that, because she had just started her job at the ad agency and there was no way she wanted to risk being involved in something unpleasant. They decided that as soon as Estermann left, they would talk to Miriam and try to find a way to compensate her for the damaged mobile phone.'

A good idea, thought Beatrice. So what went so terribly wrong?

'Estermann cursed and grumbled for a little while longer, trying to provoke Miriam, ruffling his feathers – but he was close to letting it go and leaving. "She can't report you," Beil kept saying to him. "She doesn't know your name." In one of our long conversations, he said that Miriam must have heard him. She came out of the house, pale with rage, and ran up the hill saying that she was going to fetch help from the neighbours.'

Sigart's voice started to falter. Suddenly he looked smaller, hunched, as if he had sunk into himself. The gun was still aimed at Beatrice; he was supporting it in the crook of his left elbow, where it lay peacefully. Just one shot would be sure to reach its target.

But still. This is the first viable opportunity.

She took a breath, tensing her muscles, but Sigart's attention snapped back to her, almost palpably. 'No,' he said. 'We're not finished yet.'

'Of course. I know that.'

'At the beginning, when I only had Liebscher with me and

405

he told me how Miriam had stormed off, I wondered whether he had made it up, or at least exaggerated things. To reduce his own responsibility. But later all of them described it the same way, every one of them. I always knew it was true deep down. Miriam was like that. Always so impulsive, with no consideration for what the consequences might be. If she had calmed down and waited until they were all gone, or if she had at least not told them what she was planning to do—'

If.

If I hadn't driven to Sigart's alone.

If the children weren't with my mother, if . . .

She hated this game. 'Did Estermann stop her?'

A cold look swept momentarily across Sigart's features. 'No. He grabbed Oskar and put a thumb against his eye. He said he would push it in if Miriam didn't come back to the cabin. The others said they pleaded with him to stop. Apparently Melanie Dalamasso started to cry, loudly – too loudly for Estermann's taste, and he ordered her to shut her mouth, saying that she could start sewing an eye patch for the little one if she didn't.'

An eye for an eye. Pushed in or corroded away. Beatrice's stomach cramped up. Estermann had children himself, how could he be capable of something like that? 'So did Miriam come back?'

'Of course. Estermann locked all four of them in the cabin and pulled down the window shutters. Wooden shutters, painted green and white. You could pull them down from the inside, but they were secured on the outside. He sealed the whole place tight, then sat down next to the well. Beil said it was the first time he looked truly content.'

She had only seen Estermann as a corpse, that horrifically disfigured body, but now she had to actively fight against the hate welling up inside her. *No, don't let yourself be manipulated. Even though he was the one who locked them in, Estermann is still a victim along with the other three.*

'By that point, it was all too much for Papenberg. She said she was leaving, and ran off right away without paying any attention to Liebscher, who she had come with and who wasn't as swift to react. Melanie called after her to contact the police as quickly as she could. According to Beil she was clamping her hands against her ears to block out the sound of the hammering on the wall and the children's cries. But as soon as anyone took a step towards the cabin, Estermann positioned himself in between. "They can come out once the old bitch has learnt her lesson," he said. And he reminded Beil that it was in his interest too to put this unpleasant event behind him without any outside interference. "Or do you think your wife will be pleased when she finds out you've found yourself a younger woman?" Beil told me he hadn't thought of that. He was suddenly in just as much of a hurry to get away as Nora had been.' Sigart looked over at the narrow path that ran above them, the path Beatrice kept glancing at in the hope that the blue light of the squad cars would make itself seen through the trees.

'Nora had shouted out a few words of reassurance to them as she ran off, saying she would get help, and not to worry, that she would hurry. Beil took the same line, but Melanie thwarted his plans. She wanted to stay until the children were safely out of the house. And then Liebscher joined in. He had stood on the sidelines the whole time, Nora said later, as if he was in denial about what was happening. When he rejoined the others, he was clearly nervous. He tried to convince Estermann to open up the cabin, saying that there must be some sensible way of resolving the argument. In response, Estermann took the key from his trouser pocket, pulled the cache out of the well and put the key in it. Then he lowered the tin back down almost two metres.'

'But they could have brought it back up, couldn't they? If it was on a wire?'

'Yes. I think Melanie would have done that if there had been enough time.'

Another 'if'. She couldn't bear to hear any more.

'Liebscher was still talking to Estermann, using all his usual teacher's tricks, but he was just running up against a brick wall. While he was talking, he lit a cigarette. He told me later at least a hundred times how much he regretted that afterwards. He was concentrating only on Estermann, he said. Beil, on the other hand, realised at once how dry the forest and surrounding area were. He tore the cigarette from Liebscher's hand and threw it on the ground to stamp it out.'

Beatrice guessed what had happened. 'On the spot where Miriam had emptied out the schnapps?'

'According to what they all said, yes. When I held the glass of acid to his lips, Estermann cried out that he was completely innocent. After all, Liebscher was the one who had lit the cigarette, and Beil had caused the fire. Until the very end, he was convinced I was doing him an injustice.'

Because he hadn't meant for *that* to happen, at least. Beatrice felt sick, from Sigart's story, from her own fear, and from the images of charred and corroded corpses she was picturing in her mind. 'My colleagues' reports made no mention of fire accelerants. But alcohol is one.'

Sigart shrugged. 'And that surprises you? It must be obvious to you by now that the police weren't exactly thorough in their investigations.'

Something threatening flashed up between his words, something that applied directly to Beatrice. 'So did none of them try to put out the fire?' she asked hastily, trying to change the subject.

'The well wasn't in use any more. There wasn't a bucket they could have drawn up. They tried to put out the flames with their jackets, but that just wasted valuable time. It must have got very hot very quickly, and the flames were so close to the well that no one dared to go after the key. Apparently Melanie tried, but Beil pulled her away with him.'

The torchlight was now dancing over the wooden shed surrounding the well again, which someone must have rebuilt after the fire. Presumably Sigart himself. She looked into his face; it was wet with sweat and tears, but showed relief at the same time.

'Why didn't you content yourself with just killing Estermann?'

'Isn't it obvious?' He waited, only continuing when she shook her head. 'After all, you read the file. The call to the emergency services was made by one of the two farmers whose farms burnt down that night. Before and after that – nothing.'

For a moment, it seemed as though Sigart was about to break down; he lost control of his facial muscles, but then gathered his composure again after a shaky breath. 'They knew who had been trapped up there amidst the flames. But not a single one of the group reported the fire. Not even anonymously. Not a single one.'

There was nothing that could be said in response to that. Silently, she wondered what would have happened if Nora had informed the police as she had promised, if Liebscher had been less worried about his job, if Beil had been less worried about his marriage. If . . .

'But Melanie,' she said. 'Why did she keep quiet? Was she so sure that Nora would get help? I mean, Nora didn't even know about the fire.'

She thought back to the moment when she had let the photos fall, remembering Melanie's horror.

'She struggled out of Beil's grip again because she couldn't bear the screams from the cabin. She wanted to go back and warn the neighbours, but Beil and Estermann wouldn't let her. That's how Liebscher told it. Melanie was screaming like crazy, he said, and Estermann slapped her; then Beil was trying to persuade her to leave and practically carried her down the hill.' With his bandaged hand, Sigart stroked the barrel of the gun. 'I don't know exactly what they did with her then. Presumably Beil told her they could never see each other again if she didn't keep her mouth shut. And Estermann's threats would have been a lot less subtle than that. But those are only my presumptions.'

Melanie, torn between her love for Beil and her conscience. It was entirely possible that Estermann had turned up at that rehearsal for the Mozarteum summer concert, thought Beatrice.

'Why did you cut Liebscher up into pieces?' she whispered. 'Surely not just because it was his cigarette?'

A brief laugh. 'No. But you see – the others at least felt guilty enough to feel incapable of going caching any more. Or let's call it a fear of being discovered. Either way, none of the others were still active when I compared the entries from the logbook with the profiles on the website. But Liebscher was. So because those cursed little containers were clearly so important to him, I thought it was only logical that he ended up in them.'

The arm with which Beatrice was holding the torch was slowly going numb. 'And what about the parts that didn't fit in the caches? Legs, arms, torso?'

Sigart's lips were parted by something which was almost a smile. 'Burnt,' he murmured.

Of course. Every one of Sigart's actions told the story they were rooted in; not a single decision had been made at random.

The torch in Beatrice's hand trembled, painting loops of light in the forest. If he was finished telling his story, then it was now time for what he had referred to as 'the end'. Straining her ears, she listened into the night. No engine sounds, no sirens. It seemed that the text message Sigart had sent from her phone hadn't aroused Florin's suspicions.

She cleared her throat, trying to sound confident. 'I think I can just about follow the steps you took. But I don't fit into the pattern. I wasn't there that day, I had nothing to do with the case.' *Let me go* were the unspoken words hanging in the air.

His silence gave her hope, but at the same time haunted her with fear. Was he contemplating sparing her? Before, in

411

the cellar, he had told her she had a small chance of surviving. *At least that means he's not going to shoot me point blank in the head.* Beatrice tried to drag her gaze away from the gun and look at Sigart instead.

When he finally spoke, it was in such a quiet voice that it was almost drowned out by the whisper of the trees. 'Four years,' he said. 'That's how long I asked myself whether I could have locked the cabin myself. By accident, because my thoughts were already with the pregnant mare. The fact that I wasn't here at the decisive moment to tackle Estermann, that will haunt me as long as I live.' He looked at Beatrice thoughtfully. 'Can you imagine what it's like to ask yourself, for four long years, whether you set the trap that your wife and children burnt to death in with your own hands? Every single day, I tried to remember each movement I made from the moment I left the house to when I got into the car. Do you know what it's like to never come to a clear conclusion? Sometimes the cabin door was open in my memory, other times it was closed, the keys were in my hand – or were they in my bag after all? Every day, endlessly. I could have spared myself all that if the police had just been more thorough in their investigations.'

Behind her, Sigart took a step closer. Beatrice expected to feel the barrel of the gun at her head or against her neck, but all she could feel was his breath. 'I found the cache in the well. So why didn't your colleagues? I questioned the suspects, uncovered the circumstances leading to the deaths of my wife and children – I did everything that should have been the police's job.'

She couldn't help but retort, even though she wasn't sure

if it was wise. 'But by using methods that we would never employ.'

'You have other ones, better ones. A whole infrastructure of technicians and labs, with all the equipment that money can buy.' He placed his mutilated, bandaged hand on her shoulder, making her jump.

'But I didn't work on that case,' she said, suddenly enraged with the injustice of the situation. 'I had nothing to do with it!'

'Correct. But there was a time when you felt just the same as me,' whispered Sigart. 'Your brother said you were so angry with the police that you swore at them down the phone and then eventually decided to take matters into your own hands. That's why we're here today. Because you can understand me.'

What did he want? Did he need an ally? A kindred spirit? She had to concentrate, had to make sense of what he had just said. 'You're right. I can understand that you want to speak to someone who lost a loved one in an equally brutal manner, and I'd be happy to talk to you about it.'

He laughed softly. 'No, Beatrice, we've talked enough. Now we're going to do something different.'

The barrel of the gun bored hard into her spine. Instinct was threatening to overpower her common sense; she needed all her willpower just to stop herself from running away. He would shoot her in the back just as he had warned, and she would have lost her chance. In despair, she looked over at the top of the hill; maybe Florin wasn't coming with squad cars, but on foot, stealthily, just with Stefan, or two or three others?

But there were no shadows, no footsteps, and still no engine sounds.

'It's like a bet, you see? You're relying on the skill of your colleagues, and I'm betting against them. I'm intrigued to see who will win.' He pushed her, just a light shove with the gun, and she took a step forwards.

'The police didn't find the tin in the well — but fair enough, it was small and inconspicuous. You, on the other hand, Beatrice, are not.'

A further shove made it clear to her that she had understood the significance of his words correctly. 'You want to—'

'Hide a cache, that's right. A big one in place of a small one. One that should be more worth your colleagues' efforts than an old tin can with a key in it. Unfortunately though, this cache is a little less robust. So let's hope the police are more resourceful this time.'

He directed her towards the shed, the light of the torch flickering over the planks. *My coffin*, thought Beatrice. When would someone next pass by here? Forensics had done their work; there were still a few yellow partition tapes here and there, fluttering in the night breeze. Would anyone think of looking for Sigart here? It was unlikely. Why would he go back to the place where his life had been destroyed for ever — his prison, the hiding place the Owner had clearly relinquished?

Beatrice had stopped in her tracks. The path was becoming steeper now, and she felt as though she couldn't take another step. 'How deep is it?'

'About four metres to the water's surface. There's an old iron ladder fixed to the wall, and after that I'm afraid you'll have to jump.'

She would stand in the water. But that would be the best-case scenario, she told herself. In the worst case it would be too deep and she would have to swim on the spot. 'Please. Don't do this. You have your certainty now, and you've had your revenge. Let me go, I'll—'

'You'll make sure I get help,' he interrupted her, 'and a fair judge. The exceptional circumstances of my situation will be taken into account, my disturbed state due to the severe loss I suffered – that's what you wanted to say, right?'

Yes. That, and that she had children who were waiting for her to pick them up tomorrow. No, today. It must be well past midnight now. *You can forget about telling him that. He knows you have children.*

She took another step upwards. Another and another, then her foot got caught and she stumbled. She held tightly onto the torch with her right hand and managed to break her fall with the left. Something sharp bored into the ball of her thumb.

'Have you injured yourself?' Sigart sounded genuinely concerned, which almost made Beatrice burst into hysterical laughter.

'A little.' The desire to laugh vanished as she assessed her bleeding hand in the torchlight. 'It must have been a stone.'

'Yes, there's certainly enough of them around here.' With a brief jerk of the gun, Sigart ordered her to keep climbing.

Beatrice struggled to her feet. There were just another few steps to their destination. This was her last chance – if she fell over again, on purpose, and dragged Sigart with her, if she could get to the gun.

He must have sensed her intentions. 'The gun is pointing right at your back,' he said abruptly. 'If you turn around now, I'll shoot you. It's not an empty threat, Beatrice. I'll see this through to the end.'

His serious tone made her abandon her plan. Another step, then another. The wooden shed was directly in front of her now, and she could smell the musty air. Four more steps, and she felt the rough wood. Thinking quickly, she pressed her bleeding hand against it. It was a quick, sweeping movement, all she could manage. Hoping that she had managed to leave a mark, she avoided shining the torch nearby, trying not to draw Sigart's attention to it.

In order to go into the shed, she had to duck. The cover was already lifted up; the well came up to knee height. 'Climb down the first two rungs,' ordered Sigart, 'then give me the torch.' The mouth of the gun was now pointed directly at her face.

She did what he said, pushing away her fear and trying to heighten her senses. If she memorised every detail inside the well, every spot she could get a grip on, then it should be possible to climb back up again. If she could make it up to the iron rungs, then she would be able to get out.

Holding tightly onto the edge, Beatrice stepped onto the first rung. It was rusty and crooked. Then the second. She handed Sigart the torch. 'Are you going to light my way?'

'Of course.'

The third iron rung. The fourth. Now her head was below the edge of the well. The smell of cellars and mould engulfed her. Half an arm's length to the left, Beatrice discovered a stone protruding out of the wall which she would be able to grip onto. Good.

★

The next rung and the next. Then the last. Even though Sigart was still shining the torch, it had become difficult to make out the details of her surroundings. Her own shadow was darkening the shaft of the well.

'You'll have to jump from there.' Sigart was now just a silhouette behind the beam of the torch.

She had known what was awaiting her, but it was completely different from how she had imagined it. Beneath her lay a dark, narrow abyss, which could just as easily be bottomless as two metres deep. She hesitated.

'It's only water. You won't hurt yourself.'

He must have been a good vet once, thought Beatrice vaguely. *He has the kind of voice that makes it easy to trust him.*

But she didn't jump, instead grasping the last iron rung with both hands and lowering herself down carefully. Yes, there was water all right; her ankles were immersed in it.

'You have to let go.' Sigart's voice echoed through the well shaft, followed by an unmistakable click. He had released the safety catch on the gun.

Beatrice loosened her grip and dropped. The icy water pressed the air from her lungs, completely enveloping her.

There! There was ground under her feet; she pushed against it, reached the surface again, gasped noisily for breath.

'Take care, Beatrice.' A drawn-out scraping sound from above. Sigart closed the lid of the well. No light any more, nothing. Just the sound of her own breathing and the gurgling of the water in absolute darkness

N47° 28.275 E013° 10.296

For a moment, Beatrice was tempted to weep, to mourn for everything she would never see again – the sun, the sky, her children's faces. But crying took too much energy and clouded the mind.

'Save that for later,' she told herself. Her voice echoed dully against the well shaft, sounding comforting and sensible. That was exactly what she needed right now, all of her wits and senses.

The water was too deep to be able to stand up in. If she stretched and immersed herself up to her nose, she could just about feel the ground beneath her feet, but it was slimy and soft. She would have to try to swim on the spot, with sparing movements, which would keep her warm at the same time. Or at least ensure that her temperature dropped less quickly.

Underwater, she pulled the shoes and socks from her feet. Good. Now feel around the wall, systematically, the way a blind person would.

There were little protrusions here and there, but none of them big enough to grip onto. The walls were slippery with moss. Even when Beatrice managed to find a stone that was sticking a little further out than the others, her fingers slipped when she tried to pull herself up on it.

But she didn't give up. The well's diameter wasn't that

big; if she stretched both arms out to the side, the palms of her hands easily reached the opposite sides of the shaft.

She would be able to lie down diagonally and support herself with her back and feet if she needed to rest. And she *would* need to. Soon. If she didn't manage to climb up—

All of a sudden, she realised she no longer knew which part of the cylindrical well shaft the iron rungs were on. She had turned around several times and lost her orientation in the darkness.

But even if I did know, she thought, *even if I did – they're much too high up. I couldn't jump up to them. The only way up is to climb, and the walls are too slippery for that.*

She tried regardless. Tried to imitate the way free climbers negotiate chimneys, their hands and feet propped to the left and right, but she couldn't get a grip. After four attempts she was exhausted, paddling in the water and wheezing. A fast pulse was throbbing in the wound on her left hand.

She had no choice but to wait, ration her energy and hope that Sigart was underestimating the police.

One. Two. Three. Four. Five. Six. Seven. Eight.
One. Two. Three. Four. Five. Six. Seven. Eight.

Beatrice counted her breaths. If the time was passing down here, it would be up there too, up where the darkness was endless.

But it couldn't possibly be as slow as down here. She counted on, counted and wished she had a watch so she could see how long she had already managed to hold out.

The worst thing was the cold. Her teeth were chattering uncontrollably and her fingers and toes had long since gone numb, which meant that any more attempts at climbing would be futile. She had already tried, again and again.

I'm so tired.

But going to sleep meant death. Not moving meant death. Despite that, Beatrice turned over onto her back in the water and propped herself against the shaft with her shoulders and knees, still paddling her hands to keep herself awake. She looked up and wondered if she would be able to tell when the sun rose. Whether a beam of light would push its way through the seams of the well cover.

That would give her some hope.

She paddled on half-heartedly. Once the world woke up again, someone would miss her. Florin would wonder why she hadn't come into the office. He would probably call her at around nine or half-past. *So late.*

Unless there was news. Then he might get in touch sooner, maybe even around eight.

She flexed her fingers. Open, shut, open, shut. Were they even responding? She couldn't feel a thing.

She tried to float. It didn't work; it was much too narrow here. But her arms hurt so much.

Suddenly her mouth was full of water; she spluttered, gasped, spluttered again. Had she drifted off? The cold was paralysing her body and her thoughts; she had to keep herself awake somehow.

Beatrice began to sing. The first song that came into her mind was 'Lemon Tree' by Fool's Garden. Her voice was loud, louder than she had expected, presumably because of the well shaft.

If someone was out there – maybe they would hear her?

She sang whatever songs she could think of, holding her

breath now and then so as not to miss any sounds that might make their way down from above.

No. There was only silence, and the endless gurgling of her movements in the water. The world was a long way away and had no idea she was down here.

Beatrice only stopped singing when she realised it was using a dangerous amount of energy. But she could hum at least . . . the first English song that Jakob had learnt at school came into her mind.

Twinkle, twinkle, little star
How I wonder what you are
Up above the world so high
Like a diamond in the sky . . .

He had sung it to her in the kitchen, hopping around with a beaming smile, and when he got to the words 'diamond in the sky' his eyes had got so big and round and . . .

Was she crying now after all? Her eyes were burning, and her nose felt swollen. The hum stuck in her throat like a cold, half-chewed lump of food.

One. Two. Three. Four. Five. Six. Seven. Eight.
One. Two . . .

Mina doing a cartwheel on the living-room carpet. 'Look at me, look at me!'

Jakob pulls three squashed dandelion flowers out from behind his back. 'I picked them for you.'

'Chin up, sweetheart,' laughs Evelyn, and Achim says, 'None of them look as beautiful as you in your uniform.'

Five. Six.

A croissant without jam. Crooked fingers. 'Don't do anything I wouldn't do,' calls Evelyn cheerily. 'Hold your head high, my girl. Even if your neck's dirty.'

Head. High. Chin. Up. Cold, completely cold.

A cup with steaming coffee, the milk foam frothing. Florin places his hand on hers, a dark strand of hair falls forwards onto his forehead, uniting with the arc of his brow. 'Beatrice.'

'Yes.' She says. She thinks. Has he heard her?

Jakob flings his arms around her neck. 'Frau Sieber gave me a gold star.'

That's true, Beatrice can see it shining. *Twinkle, twinkle.*

Now something falls. So loud.

Evelyn is singing Spandau Ballet's 'Gold'. She has such a beautiful voice.

'Bea. Look at me.'

David is here too. What does he want? He's pulling and tugging at her, it hurts. If she could speak, she would say she doesn't want to see him any more. That she can't.

He pulls at her, and she can fly.

'We've got her!'

'Bea!'

Don't disturb me, not now.

'We have to wake her up. Bea!'

Shaking. Pressure on her face. Light.

'She's opened her eyes. Thank God. Everything's okay. Can you hear me, Bea?'

Yes. No. Slow.

Then things come back, the shapes, the names. Florin. The cold.

★

Beatrice felt firm ground beneath her feet. Headlights cut through the dark grey of an early morning. People were walking close to her, many people. 'Wha-w-w-' Her mouth wouldn't obey her.

Someone lifted her upper body and peeled off her shirt. 'Where are the blankets? Why is it taking so long? Stefan, give me your jacket.'

The scent of chewing gum.

Florin was kneeling next to her, dripping wet. Bechner handed him a woollen blanket, and he put it around her shoulders, wrapping it so tightly that she couldn't move her arms. Then he pulled off his own wet shirt.

'The ambulance is on its way. It shouldn't be too long now.' Florin pulled her close to him, holding her tight against his chest. 'We have to keep you awake, do you hear me? You're hypothermic.'

'H-h-how di—'

He held her tighter. 'Your text message sounded strange. I brooded over it for five minutes and then called you, but your phone was turned off. You didn't answer the landline, but I know that Achim—' He left the sentence unfinished. 'We had to look for Sigart, of course, and I had an uneasy feeling. Who could have kidnapped him from the hospital, completely undisturbed, without anyone noticing? So I spoke to his doctor on the phone and asked him what his condition was. 'Not bad at all,' the doctor said. He said he had recovered quickly, that the amputation wounds had been operated on, and that he could be released in two to three days if he didn't get any infections. I asked about the blood loss and he said it wasn't that bad. And the wound on his neck? He

423

said it wasn't that deep, and that no major arteries had been affected.' Beatrice could feel him shaking his head. 'Then things started to drop into place in my mind. I got in the car and drove round to Sigart's flat, but there was no one there. Then I went to your place. I'm not sure exactly why.'

Florin's chest rose and fell slowly and calmly. Beatrice tried to match the rhythm of her breathing with his. All around them, policemen were roaming around the meadow, and from snatches of their conversation she could tell they were looking for Sigart.

'I kept a lookout for your car, but I couldn't see it anywhere, even though there were plenty of parking spaces free in front of your building. So I rang your doorbell and tried to reach you on your mobile again. Then I drove back to Sigart's flat and scoured the surrounding streets. That's when I found your car.'

And you immediately worked out what had happened? Beatrice tried to get her question out clearly. It took a while, but she managed it.

'It was my first theory, yes. The cellar in the forest. A shot in the dark, to be honest, but when we found your mobile down there I knew I'd been right.'

'M-mine and . . . N-Nora's.'

'No. Just yours. But you weren't there. Then we found the sign on the slats of the shed, a six, and everything became clear.'

'Sigart,' whispered Beatrice. 'D-do you already know, w-where . . .'

'No. I'm not sure, but I thought I saw someone disappearing into the forest as we arrived. Maybe it was him, maybe it was just an animal.'

424

Had he waited? To find out how their bet would turn out? 'I w-w-won,' she whispered. 'Florin? My mobile. P-please.'

'Really?'

She nodded. Sigart had taken Nora Papenberg's mobile with him and left her own. *And I know why.*

'Stefan?' Florin didn't let her go. 'Beatrice wants her phone – could you bring it to her, please?' She felt him stroke her hair gently, and closed her eyes. Maybe she would sleep after all, just for a moment.

'What did you win?'

'Hmm?'

'You just said you'd won.'

'Oh. Something . . . like a bet.'

Florin didn't probe further. Every time Bea shuddered, he held her closer, as if he wanted to absorb the trembling with his own body. Now and then, a drop of water fell from his hair onto Beatrice's cheek, running down it like a tear.

Then Stefan came with the phone. He squatted down next to them. 'The ambulance will be here in a moment. I just called to check.' He smiled shyly at Bea. 'Are you feeling better?'

'Yes.'

'Glad to hear it. We were so shocked before when we found you in the well. Didn't you hear us shouting for you?' He didn't wait for an answer. 'Florin climbed down straight away, and he would probably have brought you up even without a rope if he had to.' Now his smile wasn't so shy any more.

'Thank you, Stefan. Could you give Bea her phone now, please?'

She tried to sit up straight, but even a hint of a movement hurt; every muscle in her body felt sore. Florin supported her as she reached for the phone, but her fingers were too clammy and stiff to be able to hold it. It fell next to her in the grass. She clasped her whole hand around it, but it was like trying to handle an instrument she had no experience with whatsoever. The mobile slipped out of her fingers again. 'Did you put the battery back in?'

'No, we found it like that,' said Stefan. Florin released one of his arms from her and reached for the phone.

Then it had been Sigart. In case the police turned up. And they had.

'Do it for me,' she asked Florin, once Stefan had gone back to the squad car on the street with his walkie-talkie. 'The pin is three seven nine nine.'

That familiar beeping sound as he pressed the buttons. The melody with which the device signalled it was ready for action.

But nothing else.

'No new messages?' she asked, to make sure.

'No. Lie back down, okay?' He pulled the blanket right up to her neck. 'Your circulation isn't stable again yet. Do you think you could manage to eat something? Bechner has some chocolate in his bag, and the emergency doctor said on the phone that the combination of sugar and fat helps to warm the body up.'

Shivers and laughter shook her body simultaneously. 'If I pinch Bechner's chocolate he'll like me even less than he already does.'

Florin pressed her against him, but differently this time,

as if he wanted to share more than just body heat. 'I think that's a risk you should take.'

'Okay,' she murmured. There was a small, curved scar on Florin's chest, just below his collar bone. She wanted to reach out and stroke it, but she couldn't move her fingers. 'Damn.'

'Hmm? What did you say?'

Had she spoken out loud? 'Nothing. Just that I'm tired—'

All of a sudden, Beatrice's mobile beeped, and she jumped as if she had been electrocuted. A new message. No question as to who it was from. She was suddenly overcome by the searing fear that Sigart hadn't kept to their agreement. What if he was sending photos of Mooserhof in flames? Why hadn't she got a hold of her wits quicker? A squad car could already have been on its way to make sure everything was okay with her family. To make sure they were all alive.

'Bea? Are you feeling worse?'

'No . . . I – open it, Florin.' She closed her eyes tightly, pressing her eyelids together. 'Is it a photo?'

For a second he didn't answer, and she felt as though something was about to tear apart inside her.

'No,' he said eventually. 'But I don't understand all of it.'

'Show me.'

Florin held the mobile in front of her face. At first, the words blurred before her eyes, but then the letters became clear and sharp.

Thanks for the hunt, Beatrice.
JAFT.
N47° 28.239 E013° 10.521

427

She should have been relieved, but the only relief she felt was for her children. He wouldn't do anything to them now. Or anyone. It was over. She said the word silently to herself again and again, but it didn't take away the emptiness that was spreading out inside her.

'He's sent us new coordinates.' Florin seemed to be hardly able to believe it. 'Hasn't he realised that we've initiated a major manhunt for him and that we won't play his games any more?'

'Yes. He has. No doubt about that.' She would have to explain to Florin exactly what Sigart had been thanking them for each time. Just Florin. But not today.

'JAFT. What does that mean?'

Beatrice remembered that particular abbreviation; it was one that had amused her. One that was easy to remember. 'Just another fucking tree,' she murmured as the ambulance pulled up on the road above. 'It's a tree cache with rope technique.'

Florin couldn't be talked out of going in the ambulance with Beatrice. The call came while they were still en route to the hospital. Using the coordinates in the text message, Stefan had found Sigart. Hanging from a tree.

So quick. He must have prepared it all in advance – after all, it was easier to tie a noose with ten fingers than with seven.

The doctor checked the drip administering Beatrice with warm saline solution. She closed her eyes. *A loser, with scars inside and out*. Had he had a chance to win something after all, in the end?

A bet, perhaps. Or a departure on his own terms.

The aeroplane circled around Beatrice's bed, carrying out daring manoeuvres and making worrying noises.

'I'm a Boeing 767, and I'm just about to land in Africa,' crowed the plane.

'Be quiet! Mama needs to rest.' Mina was sitting next to Beatrice, holding her hand carefully, as if she was made of spun sugar. 'He's always so loud. Watch out, he'll knock the drip over in a minute.'

Jakob really was dangerously close to the drip stand, sweeping the newspapers off the side table with his emergency turn.

'Jakob! Pick those up at once!' Mina's usual commanding tone, but by her standards it was almost loving.

'Whoooosh! I'm a deep-sea digger, and I'm pulling the sunken ship up–up–uuuup!' The pile of papers landed back on the table with a loud clap.

In two days, Beatrice would be able to go home. She longed so much for her release that it almost hurt.

'Shall we go for a special meal when I get out? What do you guys think? Or should I cook?'

'No, you're not so good at cooking,' said Jakob, planting a wet kiss on her forehead. 'I want to go to McDonald's.'

'And you?' Beatrice stroked the back of Mina's hand.

'I don't know. Maybe something at home. Or . . . we

could eat at Mooserhof, and Papa could come too.' She looked at Beatrice hesitantly. 'Do you think that would be okay?'

Well, he doesn't have to sit next to me, I guess. 'Of course. Let's do this – one evening we'll eat at Oma's, one at McDonald's, and I'll cook on the other.'

'And then we'll start back at the beginning and do it all again,' cried Jakob, falling sideways across her.

There was a knock at the door, and Richard came in. Yellow roses in his left hand, and a newspaper in his right. Since discovering that the man who had nearly killed his sister had used him as the main source of information on her past, he hadn't once turned up at the hospital empty-handed.

'There's something new about the case in the paper again,' he said, lifting Jakob down from Beatrice. 'An interview with your boss, Hoffmann.'

'Oh, God. What's he saying? That's he's proud of having solved the case despite the incompetence of his colleagues?'

'No. He's praising everyone actually. Including himself, of course.'

She would read it later. Or maybe never.

Richard asked an exasperated nurse for yet another vase and busied himself with putting the roses in water. Mina told new stories about Cinderella the cat and Jakob played at being a steam engine. Beatrice's thoughts, however, wandered back to Bernd Sigart. The analyses were coming thick and fast in the papers; forensic psychiatrists had given interviews, including Kossar, who had depicted Sigart as one of his post-traumatic stress cases with aggressive behavioural patterns.

Platitudes. Not wrong, not by any means. But not complete either.

If I had finished my studies, would I have realised sooner who the Owner really was? The thought had been on Beatrice's mind for days now. She had asked Richard to get her some information on courses she could do alongside her work, but her request had fallen on deaf ears. She was supposed to be resting.

Half an hour later, Richard decided she needed some peace and promised the children an ice cream, taking them off to Mooserhof.

My ex-husband drops them off, my brother picks them up, my mother cooks for them. Beatrice turned over and closed her eyes. Richard was right. Studying on top of her existing workload wasn't a good idea.

When she woke up again, Florin was sitting by her bed. She knew he was there even before she opened her eyes; she smelt his aftershave and smiled instinctively. Then she sniffed. There was a second scent in the room.

'The focaccia is still warm,' she heard him say. 'Goat's cheese, prosciutto and spinach. And antipasti with sun-dried tomatoes and chard *involtini*.'

'Delicious,' she murmured, still with her eyes closed. 'And the Prosecco?'

'Unfortunately not. We'll make up for that later. But I can offer you three kinds of freshly pressed juices. Orange and mango, pear and elderberry, or papaya and kiwi.'

He had pulled his chair close to her bed and was waiting patiently for her answer, his elbows propped on his knees, his chin in his hands. Beatrice pushed her hair out of her

431

face and sat up. He didn't want her to thank him for his daily visits with gourmet treats — he had already made that perfectly clear.

Each day, she resolved to ask him why he was making so much effort, but every time he was sitting next to her she couldn't get the words out. She didn't know what answer she wanted to hear.

'Carolin Dalamasso dropped the complaint,' said Florin, interrupting her thoughts. 'Hoffmann was a little crestfallen, but he's enjoying the limelight too much right now for it to have that big an impact.'

So she wouldn't be suspended. Beatrice took a deep breath. She had suppressed the thought so much that only the relief she was feeling right now told her how much it had bothered her.

She reached out for the small fork Florin had laid on a dark blue serviette and speared one of the sun-dried tomatoes. 'Are you eating too?'

He looked down at his hands briefly, then into her eyes. 'No. Anneke's here, we're going for dinner in half an hour.'

'Oh. Okay.' Guiding the tomato into her mouth in such a way that the oil didn't drip down onto the bedding was demanding all her concentration. That was good. The time it took to master the manoeuvre would allow her to regain her composure. 'Then hurry up, don't be late. You see each other so rarely, and you see me every day.'

He didn't answer, instead handing her a piece of focaccia, warm and aromatic. She took it, gesturing at the door with her head at the same time. 'Go on, don't leave her waiting.'

Florin nodded. 'Are you sure you've got everything you need?'

There was something in the tone of his voice that made Beatrice think he wasn't just talking about the food.

'Absolutely,' she said.

'Okay, then see you tomorrow.'

'Listen, you don't have to come, if Anneke—'

'I know I don't have to,' he interrupted her. 'See you tomorrow then.'

At the door, he turned around one more time. 'I left a little something there for you. I hope you like it.'

She looked around and couldn't see anything. But when she turned back to ask Florin, he was already gone. With a sigh, not knowing if it was one of contentment or longing, she leant back onto her pillow and ate until there was nothing left. Then she flicked through the TV channels, not finding anything that interested her, and reached over to the side table for the book that she had started the day before. *The Terrors of Ice and Darkness* had been lying around unread on her bookshelf for years, but after the night in the well she had asked her mother to bring it to the hospital for her. No one except Beatrice had been overly amused, but she liked the style of writing. She opened it, plunging with the helplessly lost *Admiral Tegetthoff* into the pack ice of the North Sea.

All of a sudden, she was interrupted by the warm tones of Frank Sinatra, singing the opening to 'Moon River', her favourite song. Looking around, she saw a mobile phone on the bedside table, but it wasn't hers. Confused, she picked it up and tapped to open the message blinking on the screen:

For Bea, it said. Florin's present. She waited for the song to finish before reading the rest of the message:

Sleep tight. Florin x.

She stared at the three words for a long time. Then she laid the book aside, gazed up at the ceiling and listened to the nocturnal sounds of the hospital.

After a long while, she turned out the light.

Afterword

Most geocachers are nice people. I know, because I'm one of them. They love nature, treat it with the utmost respect, and even tend to clear away other people's rubbish if they stumble across it. I just wanted to say that.

If you happen to own a GPS device, find yourself near the coordinates in the book, and feel the urge to seek out the places depicted in it, then I hope you have a great time – you'll get to see some of Salzburg's idyllic spots. I admit I had to tweak reality here and there for the sake of the story – like moving the odd rock face by a few hundred metres, for example. But in general you'll find the places look pretty much the same as they did to Beatrice and Florin, apart from the caches and their gruesome contents, that is. A word of warning: if you get to the final coordinates, watch out for the stinging nettles.

You'll find a wooden shed there too, by the way, but I'm afraid I can't tell you what's inside it (it's not my shed, after all); here, too, I adapted the facts to fit the story. While I'm on the topic, I'd like to apologise to the owners for what I did to their property in my imagination.

A thank you to:

Ruth Löbner, for driving the indecisiveness out of Beatrice and cracking a few really hard nuts with her. I initially used a good few superlatives here when writing about Ruth, before deleting them because she would probably be embarrassed. But that doesn't make them any less true;

Lieutenant Colonel Andreas Huber, who offered me important and fascinating insights into the work of the Salzburg criminal investigation department, an indispensable help during the writing process. But the 'poetic licence' which I employed for the novel and any possible mistakes that slipped past me are solely on my head;

My editor Katharina Naumann, who I overburdened not only with my Austrianisms, but also with number puzzles – the former are probably here to stay, but the latter won't be. That's a promise;

My agency, AVA International, who took my announcement at our first meeting ('I'd like to live from writing, and I'd like to start doing so quickly') more than literally;

Leon and Michael, who roamed all over Salzburg with me searching for good hiding places for body parts.

Ursula P. Archer was born in 1968, and worked as an editor at a publishing house. After the success of her first young adult novel, she now dedicates much of her time to writing fiction. She lives with her family in Vienna. *Five* is her first thriller for adults.

Jamie Lee Searle's recent and forthcoming translations include Andreas Maier's *Das Zimmer* and co-translations, with Shaun Whiteside, of Frank Schätzing's *Limit* and Floridh Ilies' *1913*, which was Radio 4 Book of the week. She co-founded the Emerging Translators Network in late 2010, and has been a member of the UK Translators Association Committee since late 2013.